SAD AT THE EDGES

Published in South Africa
by Stephan Phillips (Pty) Ltd 2003

STEPHAN PHILLIPS

Design and layout: Mega Digital, Cape Town

Printed by Mega Print, Cape Town
ISBN: 1-91994709-4

Stephan Phillips (Pty) Ltd
PO Box 1230, Somerset West
7129
South Africa

www.stephanphillips.com

To Jayne,
with love and thanks
for all you've done for
me.

sad at the edges

Jo-Anne Richards

She had always envied Francesca her time in jail.

A spell in detention would have made life so much easier. People like Francesca didn't need all the trappings that Megan spent her life accumulating. The worthy jobs that never paid, the clothing that was a bit severe. And of course the boys – the ascetic boys with iceberg cheeks and strict tongues. But let her not start thinking of Jake now, for God's sake.

Francesca could allow her Indian bracelets to chime her dissonance from all that. She had once been detained without trial. It had given her a muffled glow, as though there were a scrunched up halo about her, tucked inside a hat or crushed into a pocket somewhere.

In an hour and fifteen minutes she would see Francesca again. Megan wondered what she'd be like now. It was a new world after all, a new society. Would she have changed? Probably not. People like Francesca didn't need to. Her detention would always hang around her neck like a talisman, protecting her from the fear that she might not find a place for herself.

Other things changed. Other people scrabbled to belong. Nations struggled to come to terms with a new normalcy. But her cousin Francesca was one of the charmed ones.

That was probably one of the reasons Megan had left, now that she thought about it. Just as the gloom of their shameful past shattered into vibrant possibility, she had packed her bags and left the country. Megan had made for more settled worlds, where she had hoped to find the space to be commonplace. Francesca, on the other hand, would always be spared the disillusion of being simply ordinary.

Francesca didn't know whether to be excited or defensive about her cousin's homecoming. Oh for goodness sake, of course she was excited. They'd grown up together. She loved Megan to bits. She was thrilled she had finally come to her senses and decided to return.

It was just that Megan could be so bloody irritating. She had this way of idealising their past, as though Francesca had marched in glorious leftist formation through their worst years. As though her detention cell had left patches of nobility, like moss, upon her skin.

She could never enlighten her though. Megan was her little cousin. Megan loved her because of whom she believed Francesca to be. She couldn't bear to lose her exalted place in Megan's life – much as it might burden her with expectations.

This was real life, this life she led now. And, considering all that had happened and all she had done, she had no right to expect more. 'No-one promised it would be easy,' her mother used to say during the spells of sombre nodding that always followed suburban setbacks. How she had scoffed at the old-toppie – because of course, *she* would be different. She and her generation were unique. And, of course, her life would be uncommon. She was wild and free. All of life lay waiting for her to impress her image upon it.

At what point in the passage of years does it dawn on you that your life might not be screened in Technicolor? Francesca knew though. There was no need to ask. She knew precisely the point at which her own image had shivered before her and she had understood that life would not always present her best side. She would never permit herself to speak of it though, not to anyone.

She wondered if Megan could cope with this real life. For two years, while she had been gone, they had lived a dreamtime. Through change and chaos, they had lived to see what they had barely dared hope for. Euphoric days had followed frenzied nights, as though a religious fervour had seized them.

It was almost gone now. For two years they had been muffled, seeing the world through a blush-coloured haze. Now, as winter approached, Francesca felt it melting like a jellied mould left too long in the sun. Soon it would be gone, leaving them sticky with fears and sentiment.

Francesca negotiated the parking lot and locked her car. It would be a miracle if she and Megan ever found it again, in the confusion of airport upgrading. The funny thing was, she no longer wished for an extraordinary life. She no longer hoped to stand out from the crowd. She wanted so badly to be ordinary, and to be happy with that normality.

Francesca saw a safety in the banal, free from past lives that carried people too far – into times they were unfitted for, and places that demanded that they be exceptional too. Anyway, enough of that. She didn't want to be thinking of that now that Megan was nearly here.

She had to make this life work. This real life she had now. If she failed at this, what would it say about her? She had not managed what was out of the ordinary, lacking the strength, the bravery, or whatever it took. At least she should manage suburban life. Everybody did it. Oh, they had their ups and downs, as her mother would say. But they coped. She must deal with what she had. She didn't think she could survive another great upheaval.

Her friend Penny was inclined to say that the people in this country suffered from collective post-traumatic stress. They couldn't face up to the hurt and shame of their past, yet the anxiety of it affected them all in everything they did.

Perhaps that was what had happened to Paul. Perhaps he'd become overfilled with fears for their futures, while still trying to deal with the pain of his own present. More than anyone, she knew he'd not be able to express such things.

Francesca wondered what Megan would make of him now. He had been so good to the youngster she had once been. It was one of the things that had first warmed Francesca to him – his inarticulate, but robust inclusion of the prickly teenager.

She had felt that here at last was someone who could protect her. Someone who was solid enough for both of them.

Of course, their marriage was probably not what Paul had expected either when he'd been young and idealistic. Though, whose was? And God knows, she herself wasn't quite what she'd expected, when she'd been full of youth and the knowledge that life would be special and she extraordinary. When she had still believed that nothing could touch her.

She had been thinking that things would be different now that Megan was returning. Perhaps it was a sign. It might draw them all back to the people they had once been. Or remind them of what they might have become, before all that had passed since then. She knew it to be a whimsical little wish, but she did hope so.

THE MAN

The man sat on the rock, as usual at this time of evening, the air heavy with salt and the richness of sea. The south-easter flurried about him. It would bring in bluebottles. He fished, but not with any great compulsion. He liked to be here, slightly distant, not quite part of the crashing sea. Sometimes, if he sat here long enough, still and not quite human, the darkness would wash in with the tide and the otters would surf and slither to shore.

He had always liked that feeling. He had the patience, the skill to be silent – part of the landscape, and of the sky and sea. He was proud of it, and of his slight removal from the whirls and eddies of human involvement. It was the watching he enjoyed. The game. It had always been the game – watching himself, laughing at the poor fools caught up in it all, the ones who fought and fucked themselves in the process.

He liked the sense that he could dabble if he chose. He could dive in anytime, dangle a foot ... or watch, still as the rocks beneath him. All that choice, all that control. Five steps from where he sat and he'd be pulp – part of the maelstrom mashing itself towards the blow-hole. Five steps ... but he knew he never would. For fuck sake, he had survived. He was the great survivor. This was the life he had always wanted. It was how he had always pictured himself in his middle years.

Behind him on the beach, his five callus-footed boys churned the sand, ripping at flailing shirts as they pounded a rugby ball between the rocks. How often he had sat here without turning, picturing the sturdy sight of them. Somehow the sound of his sons made it all worthwhile. The tumble and grace of them gave him peace. Hell no, he was not about to fall into that trap. He didn't need peace. Look what he had here. How many people had a life as good as this? It had all been a huge game anyway. Everyone knew that. And he had survived. That was an achievement in itself.

It was this TRC thing about to start. That's what it was. Truth and reconciliation. God! Who were they kidding? And whose truth would they be trotting out for all the foreign voyeurs with an itch for human drama? The whole process was going to irritate him. It was like a horse-fly that hovered at his ankle, stinging itself back into his consciousness each time he forgot, or determined to ignore it.

He despised everyone involved in the whole wallowing debacle. The so-called perpetrators as much as the self-styled martyrs. Loss of control, that's what it stemmed from. Some arseholes always took things too far, especially when things were slipping away, minute by minute, death by death. But there it was –

that's what happened when you became embroiled in all the emotional kak that life threw at you.

But in any case, everyone had known the score. They couldn't tell him they hadn't known the consequences. They had all played the same game – they had been on different sides, that's all. It had been one helluva game. But it was over now. Over. It was time to pack up and go home. Why talk it through over and over? What good did that do anyone?

Darkness wisped past him, floating in with the wind, wafting up from the rocks and crevices about him. Behind him, boy-sounds flew with the seagulls, whipping against the wind, soaring over the sea. They had no sense of all that. That was the important thing. He had held them apart. Kept them safe. It was their world now.

MEGAN

Megan's plane taxied to a halt. It looked grey and windless through the distorting porthole. She wondered if Francesca would be waiting for her. How would it be between them, she wondered, now that she felt so much older?

Before she left, Fran had never discussed anything of importance with her. And certainly nothing to do with her earlier years of activism and detention. It had been so unfair, as though she were reproaching Megan for being too young to know of such things. Megan had always sensed in her silence the criticism that she was somehow clinging to the skirts of the Struggle as it rushed past.

Just like Jake. Oh God, Jake, sitting in England with his ever-present cigarette. She shouldn't think of him. Not now that she was home again. Tramping across a runway mesmerised by heat-shimmered fumes, she longed to catch the burnt wheat smell of the Highveld.

And there was Francesca waiting for her in Arrivals. If you could call that waiting. Fran never actually waited. She had that knack of finding someone fascinating and hypnotising them into telling her their deepest sorrow or guiltiest secret, all in the time it took for a robot to change or an aeroplane to land. But she surrendered her conquest easily enough.

'Meg-child ... Sorry, you hate that, don't you?'

'It's okay, I've been homesick, remember?'

'But you've got so thin. I hate you.'

Francesca wasn't actually the better looking of the two, in the way society judges these things. Strictly speaking, Megan felt herself to be the prettier. But alongside her childhood benchmark she always felt a trifle bloodless.

Fran had a simplicity that could appear plain if you gazed at her straight on. But it was in the obliqueness of her that you caught her quickness. Then her features seemed unimportant, a backdrop to all that she carried inside.

Fran unlocked the car with a beep of her remote and they packed the boot and much of the back seat.

'How's um, how are you managing with Daniel?' Megan asked, concentrating on her seatbelt. 'How's he doing?'

'Fine. Very well, in fact, far better than anyone expected. He's five now.'

Too emphatic, her tone warned Megan that now was not the time to expect confidences. It collided with her hopes of togetherness and for a moment she was hurt. Megan glanced at her cousin, rummaging the ashtray for coins with a troubled energy.

'Have you got change ... no of course you haven't. Jeez, I can't believe you've been away two whole years. You went just after the election, didn't you?'

'You think that's weird, don't you?'

'No, I knew you'd come back.'

'And it was an amazing time to travel. Seriously Fran, I mean not to be the pariah of the world anymore ...'

'And so? What's with you and that exile boy, what's-his-name? Will he come back?'

'It's finished, which is ... Ja well, London suddenly seemed very cold and grey.'

'So instead, you're going to skip summer and come home for winter.'

'I didn't mean ...'

'I know. Tell if you want. I won't tell the mothers.'

'He said we had nothing profound in common, because I hadn't been in the Struggle.'

Fran smiled and waited. Megan was squinting out at the Highveld thunderheads, stalking them from the east.

'But he wasn't serious?' Fran said at last, scrabbling for the cellphone that had begun to ring insistently somewhere on the floor.

'Aunt Marg. Yes, I have her ... It's your mother.' Megan took the phone with an exaggerated sigh, so that both women grinned.

'Yes ... yes, Ma. It was lovely to spend a couple of days with you ... No I couldn't have stayed ... I start work next week ... We're on our way to Fran and them. No, Ma, I won't rush to move out, but Fran doesn't want me in her guest cottage for the rest of time ... Ja, I will. No, I promise. Bye now.'

She found a space for the phone in the rubble on the passenger floor. Fran hadn't grown any neater with time.

'So now this boy ...' Francesca persisted. 'He wasn't serious, was he?'

'Well, what can I say? He broke up with me.'

Francesca threw her head back and laughed. 'I'm sorry, Megs, but ... you were too young to be in the Struggle.'

'I know.'

Megan had searched Jake's face for irony – anything that could dilute the pomposity. It had all been ... well of course it had hurt like hell. But after all she had thought and dreamed of him, it had been disheartening that he had turned out to be such a prat.

Fran laughed in great gurgles which, of course, she could do since she had been in the fucking Struggle.

It felt suddenly very ordinary to be back. She hadn't expected that. She had tasted this journey into Johannesburg, sharp with autumn's bite on her tongue. She had smelt it in the pungency of winter soil. She had felt it in the weeks after Jake had left her, when she had been light-headed with the nausea of wanting to be home again ...

She had hoped for totemic towers and the solidity of mine dumps, orange and symbolic in the setting sun. But Fran was driving through a suburban slew of rooftiles and Vibracrete. The razorwire was new. Only the odd one, but there it was, sedentary wall lashed down by the violence of blades. She turned from it, not wanting to watch the fall of another fantasy.

'I forgot to ask how Paul was,' she said.

'Oh fine. Very busy. But he likes it. Making lots of money.'

'How did he cope with ... you know, Daniel. With his diagnosis and everything.'

Francesca paused and Megan feared she had intruded beyond her allotment of confidence. But then she spoke.

'You know what South African men are like. They don't talk about stuff like that.'

'Well, it's not as if Daniel's so bad. When I left, you could hardly notice anything.'

'Ja it's fine. He's ... we're all fine. I'm sorry I'm bringing you the non-scenic route.'

'Well, there's certainly no mountain.' Megan had spent a year in Cape Town before leaving the country.

'But we have minedumps. What can a mountain do that minedumps can't?'

'Pragmatic stock, you Highveld types.'

'Sure. You want a mountain? We'll dig a big hole and make one for you. So why've you decided to settle in Joeys anyway?' Boundaries redefined by banter, they felt comfortable again.

'Oh ... I suppose to get as far as possible from my mother.' Megan swept her eyes upward.

'You did that quite successfully by moving continents.'

'But I wanted to come home.'

Megan had known suddenly that she should return. It had been after another unsuccessful attempt to talk to Jake, on the pretext of going through their CD collection. The CD collection, disparate in age and taste, about which she no longer cared.

There had to be more to it, didn't there? A girl, perhaps, who lived in Notting Hill and knew all the party places. Perhaps it didn't matter about the Struggle if she hadn't lived here. Perhaps she was exempt.

She never had found out. And now she never would. But she had known she had to come home. She had known it suddenly in the crush of people you could never escape. She had known it when she had begun to long, not even for mountain or sea, but for anything of home. Alone in the crowded tube, she had longed for the fragrance of Highveld grass, frosted to yellow. For the brave march of pylons across the veld.

An electric darkness overtook them suddenly from the east. Swallowing the light, it brought a mud-brown dusk before its time. The sky fractured, drenching the light-stilled scene. Raised on drought and drizzle far from the Highveld, Megan shivered at the ferocity that seemed about to bore at the metal and gouge them from within. But Fran was enjoying herself, laughing into the teeth of the gale.

'Wow!' She had to yell to be heard. 'Must be the last of the season. Isn't it great? What a welcome.'

Her face reflected none of Megan's unease. She relished this. She lapped at it with the tongue that protruded from parted teeth. This was an edge or an extreme, an expression of power.

Fran glanced sideways at her, seeming to demand that she enjoy it too. It was a Jo'burg thing.

MEGAN

The three of them were discussing the men across the way, and how long it would take them to strike up a conversation with the woman reading a book.

Francesca, the peal of laughter and bracelets about her, was citing precedents. She said it was all about sociology – a predisposition of over-confident old lefties. Her friend Penny declared it to have not a bloody thing to do with sociology. It was to do with a chemical imbalance triggered by the Y chromosome.

There was a moment of silent tension as the blonde man leant sideways. But his companion spoke and he shot back to the important business of man talk.

They were pavement sitting in the last of the sun. The place was packed – it was a Friday afternoon in Melville. They had all escaped duty except Megan. She was only to begin work the following week.

'Well, I just think ...' Megan said tentatively, new to the game and the group, '... they seem a little old for that kind of thing.'

The other two laughed, Penny with an alarming bay that ended in a slight snort. 'She's looking at the Emperor's clothing,' she murmured to Francesca. With the confidential air of one correcting a social lapse, she turned to Megan and added: 'Where old lefties are concerned, that's not old, dear. That's dashing.'

Megan decided she didn't really like Penny. Too loud and emphatic for her taste. She didn't look like someone Fran should be friends with. She had a reactionary ... well, at least a corporate look about her. Something to do with the jacket, she supposed, or the skilful auburn of her immaculate head. Okay, she was attractive, but without Francesca's soft, fluid qualities. A slight toughness at the mouth and corners of the eyes drew her out of pretty and into what might once have been called handsome.

It was hot under the umbrella and the ice cubes had melted in her wine. She had dressed wrongly, led astray by the chill of early morning. Pushing her sleeves up, she tried to appear unflushed and unfased and ... God, they'd been right about those old guys. She nudged her cousin.

'Yes!' Fran slammed her fist into her hand. 'That's one lunch from each of you, thank you very much.'

The two men were leaning over to hear the woman, who was holding her book up to her chest for them to see. Penny remarked that the woman had managed to thwart their intentions neatly by holding the book where she did. But by then they'd gone on to other things.

It was the previous night that Fran had invited Megan to meet her best chinas. Megan had been struggling to cook them dinner, out of gratitude for having her to stay. It wasn't her strong suit. Fran had been perched on a kitchen stool, her child – seeming younger than his five years – clutched to her chest. She had rocked him as she spoke.

Fran had a strange quietness about her at home, a stillness of eye and feature for which Megan couldn't quite account. Fran and Paul were really the only married people she knew, apart from proper grownups like their parents.

She had been chopping the vegetables on the counter top, wishing she'd bought ready-cut from Woollies.

'Hey!'

She had started violently at Paul's tone. 'Can't you get your bloody ditsy cousin to use a chopping board?'

She had twisted in shock, a 'sorry' ready on her lips. But he'd been smiling. 'Fool,' he'd said. Paul was charming in an unexpected sort of way. She was used to him now, but when she'd been younger and less sure of herself, she had found it difficult to work out when he was joking.

She noticed that Fran had started too, but then she was still again. Trapped in the window's gathering in of the day's last light, the child and she were like a frieze, unmoved as marble. Megan and Paul had stood a moment, watching that unassailable unit. But then he had moved, clattering at the fridge for a beer and filling the room with profit margins and stockholdings.

Paul was Fran's mother's darling, probably because of the respectable place he held in the world. But she had wondered sometimes, when she was younger, why Fran had chosen him. He seemed so very different from the Fran she knew. Or the Fran she had grown up with, she should say. After her detention she had been different.

She had been all dank moods, contracting even a mossy redolence to the chill sweat that plagued her despite the jerseys in which she entombed herself. That was when Fran had met Paul, and perhaps he had been good for her, clip-clopping in with, not exactly a white steed, but a workaday sort of horse. Fran was fine now, of course. Except for that weird blankness she showed sometimes. It was funny that.

Megan had spent a pleasant evening, where she had not particularly expected to. It had seemed the sort of evening she must bear in order to stay in their house – the dutiful evening bookends which must support those spent in the way this town expected. She wanted to jol here. She wanted to forget Jake and every speck of his ascetic scorn. This was a new country now, a new planet. She wanted to be out seeing the changes.

But when she had finally gone to bed, she found the evening had warmed her. And in some ways it had been a relief to see that stillness in Fran, her features silenced in their yammering. And Paul had been nice, like some long-lost older brother, advising on banks and places to stay, and questioning her closely on uncomplicated subjects like the weather and British television.

When it had been time for Daniel's bed, it had been Paul who had drawn attention to it, almost as though he had been watching the clock, waiting for a permissible time to break the spell and crack the frieze.

'Come to your father, boychik ...' He had spoken in the same tone of robust good humour he used with adults. She had wondered if, in some ineffectual way, he had thought to transfer a touch of his own vigour to the wraithlike boy.

'Come tell your father all the things you did today ...'

Pale as a pupa, the child had curled slightly away, leaning inward to the warmth of his mother. Fran had placed an urging finger in the small of his back.

'Go ...' she had whispered, and briefly, Megan thought she'd caught a trace of anxiety. But she couldn't have, because a minute later Fran had relented with a click of the tongue and small exasperated laugh.

'Oh Daniel ... what is the matter with you, silly child.'

She hadn't left the room until Paul shrugged, throwing his glib laugh like a lonely lifeline. 'They're not quite of this world, those two,' he said and shook his head.

He had rustled *The Star* from the floor in one unruffled movement and disappeared behind it.

'God, will you look at that? They're downscaling the Carlton. That hotel was like a symbol of Johannesburg. Of course you can't blame them. Town's a bloody mess. What do they expect?'

Waiting till Fran was out of earshot, she spoke at the newspaper shield.

'How've you coped with knowing he has cerebral palsy? It must've been a shock for you both.'

'Funny time you've chosen to come back,' he had said then, as though he hadn't heard her. 'If I was earning pounds I'd have stayed. The rand's fucking out entirely.'

'But now I get to convert my pounds. That's a nice feeling.'

'Mm. But it's a bad sign. The honeymoon's over now. It can only get worse.' The newspaper lowered slightly.

'Daniel's only minimally affected, you know. There's really very little to cope with beyond poor balance and muscle weakness. They've always got to put a label on things. In my day, the child would've been called clumsy.'

There'd been silence then. Megan had watched the barrier lift again slightly. She'd thought he was done with the topic, when suddenly he said: 'I wish people would ignore it. If he were treated as normal, he'd be normal. I wish people didn't have the compulsion to talk things to death.'

Fran had slipped back into the room as he spoke. Walking to the window, she had commented on the moon or something. Megan had watched her in the glass. In the strained, yellow light from the street, it was as though she and her reflection had traded something of themselves, the window accepting the fullness of her bright figure, her face flattening to the sheen of glass. It had been odd that.

But now, the Melville pavement was a congealed mass of tables, umbrellas and shifting groups. A tangle of noise reached out, stretched between tables and snarled in the great to-ing and fro-ing between them.

There was a theatrical feel to it, if only because she felt very aware of herself. And because she felt it, it seemed they did too. They were like a crowd of milling extras waiting for the director to arrive. But if they relished a certain image of themselves, she forgave it for being playful and perhaps even slightly ironic. Jake would never have approved. They were all having far too much fun. Well, fuck Jake. He wasn't here now.

Disputes jostled for attention, while sudden ideas and instant schemes spun webs of wine-filled purpose through the afternoon. For a girl from the Eastern Cape, where everything happened torpidly, like the buzzing of a lazy fly, Jo'burg seemed intense and ardent. And to have come here from London, where society was venerable, its manner settled in custom ... well, it was disorienting.

Here, all history seemed suddenly in the making, and everything seemed possible. Even for a girl who had been too young for the Struggle. Even for an older cousin who had something odd about her, but nothing you could ever put your finger on.

As the white clouds clotted over the street, it seemed ridiculous that she could have thought Francesca's vivacity of spirit quenched. Megan watched her laugh, she and her bangles competing in quicksilver brightness.

There was a strange urgency to the scene, as though a great natural disaster were to occur in an hour's time, with a lifetime's worth of mingling to fit in before then.

But she discovered a faint disappointment within her. It was two whole years since the election. Perhaps it was naïve, but she had pictured all races and creeds simply falling together once the barriers had been removed. Not this lightly raisined mixture.

She felt tired suddenly. She knew she wanted to find her home in this oddly compelling city. Yet now she must learn all its who-knows-whom rules and brash new customs. It might not be the country she expected, but neither was it the country she had left.

'Well, here I am at last, girlfriends.' She was beautiful, Megan thought, this woman pulling up a chair to join them.

'I knew you'd be needing me. Apparently I'm an accessory much in demand in the new South Africa. That's according to my directors anyway. I've spent the day being paraded around before some hot new investor.'

'And was he hot?' asked Penny.

'Not particularly. Which is why I've rushed right on over to improve your social cred.'

Nombulelo, Buli for short, launched straight into a discussion of shoes, of which she apparently had many. She had bought a good four pairs over lunch.

It was odd, but in a way she hadn't even considered, things were completely different. In the severity of Struggle culture, people like Buli hadn't seemed to exist. Megan wondered what Jake would have made of her. Of course he would probably have permitted Buli her flightiness, just as he accepted it in English girls. She suddenly envied Buli the exemption that permitted the ostentatious earrings chiming gently alongside her cheeks.

Buli had returned from exile to take up an executive position in one of the big corporations. God, they must love her, Megan thought. So smart and black and filled with American confidence. Yet she had a jittery quality. Not that she bit her nails or anything. But there was a quickness of shallow breath, a sharp tapping of piano scales on table. It was as though a deep furrow lay concealed just beneath the surface of her smooth forehead.

She had another peculiarity that was difficult to place. It was attractive, Megan thought, aspiring to cultivate it. Buli had an ethereal air of being not always quite with you, as though she hovered somewhere just above the table. It gave her an incongruous mix of earthiness and unworldliness.

'I must go soon.' Penny made no move to leave, but poured herself another half-glass. 'I've got the whole fucking shabat catastrophe tonight.'

'You're such a dutiful daughter, Angel-face,' Buli said in a soft voice. There was a moment of silence, during which Megan liked Penny the less for her virtue. But then the table exploded into laughter and Megan smiled, not knowing these people, or why the remark was so funny.

Buli and Fran withdrew into a secretive huddle. Megan strained to catch a few words, drawn to eavesdrop by the intimacy between them.

'... how long I can stick it ...' she heard Buli say. The skin had stretched across her cheekbones, puckering in the hollows under her eyes.

Fran said something she couldn't catch. And then she thought she heard her say: 'Look, you don't have to tell me. God, you know how it is with me ...'

Their closeness caused Megan a moment's grumpiness. Why could Francesca never be as intimate with her? Megan always seemed to be cast in the role of younger – cousin, girlfriend, friend, it didn't matter. It had been that way since they were children.

She envied Francesca her ability to draw people. Despite her animation of grin and gesture, Fran seemed to exude a softness that caused near-strangers to pour out their guts to her. Megan, on the other hand, knew she quite often affected an air of severity to counter her youth and prove that, despite what her mother termed her 'quite undeserved prettiness', she really was a serious person.

A cell shrilled and they all shuffled and clutched for bags. Around them, people patted pockets and scrabbled under tables.

'Okay, you can all relax,' yelled the blonde comedian they'd been watching earlier. Gesturing at his companion, he added: 'Quickest draw in town.'

While the dark guy conducted his sheepish conversation, every table joined in the gust of laughter. Weighed down by all the hopes that hung about her neck, Megan thrilled to a moment when the intensity of their togetherness seemed to transcend their fears and resentments. A Jo'burg moment, she thought, when intimacies formed over foibles and shared restaurant laughter seemed suddenly proof of anything.

'Howzit, you guys. Hey, Francesca.' The dark guy had completed his conversation and the two had apparently decided to amble over. The blonde one, now demanding Francesca's attention, was grinning and bearish. The other was lean and unwilling to let go of his serious self.

'I've been hoping to bump into you,' the blonde one said. 'I wanted to tell you how I enjoyed that documentary you did on sport and the psyche of the nation.'

'Thanks. But I'm surprised. I thought someone like you would consider it less than serious.' Fran's Indian bracelets shivered as her hands spoke for her. They had an exotic flow, a sharp-edged boldness that countered the gentleness of her eyes.

'Actually, I thought it was insightful, especially what you said about the World Cup and the Africa Nations. I think we did use them to prolong the post-election euphoria.'

'Ja. I actually thought we were almost aware of what we were doing, but we did it anyway because we needed to. I got hugely criticised for the documentary though ...'

The man shrugged in a what-did-you-expect gesture. He was not as austere as his companion, radiating warmth from his shambling body.

'I heard you went to work for government,' Francesca said.

'Long-term consultant. Not as exciting as what you do, of course, Ms Hotshot Documentary Maker.'

'No, I think that's brilliant. Are you enjoying it?'

'He's enjoying being EU funded,' the dark one interjected.

The blonde man grinned. Bringing his fist up in a long slow arc, he tapped his friend on the chin. But he addressed Francesca. 'No, you're right. I'm really lucky to be involved in the process.'

They were flirting. The idea took Megan by surprise. She had never really seen Fran as a sexual being beyond the confines of her mother's or her husband's house. Fran didn't flirt as others did. She fixed him with the straightest of gazes. Then her hands took over, pivoting like the dance of a Persian courtesan.

Drawing Buli into the conversation, he seemed impressed by the companies she had worked for in America. He had a mellowed, self-effacing air that made him hardly seem a leftie at all. But then, he really was quite old.

'And now I'm busy being unbundled,' Buli was saying, and he laughed. It seemed her corporation was unbundling its subsidiaries. For the big conglomerates, it was apparently the way to go.

'So, are you an accountant by trade?' he asked her.

'No, I studied social work. Eesh, but that was a million years ago. I did a Masters ...'

'God yes,' he said. 'Sorry, I should've recognized your name. You did that study on the post-traumatic effects of detention and imprisonment. I read it when I came out. My mother discovered it through the detainees' parents' group. It was their bible, you know ... So how on earth did you wind up being a boss?'

'It's a new world. There's things to be done ...'

'... Money to be made, shoes to be bought,' added Penny, cocking her chin at Buli's parcels. 'We're not all prepared to hang about earning nothing forever.'

'And don't get too happy about having discovered her either.' Francesca grinned up at him, one eye closed against the sunlight. 'She's my tame detention counsellor. Go find your own.'

'Well,' he said, rubbing a rueful hand across his chin. 'I have my eye on one.'

Pink from the sunlight, or from the interchange – Megan couldn't be sure – Francesca dropped her eyes and launched into a rather frenetic explanation of the documentary projects her small company was trying to sell, even into the great and mythical land of overseas.

Her next project, the one that really excited her, was about the start of the Truth and Reconciliation Commission hearings. You couldn't get more drama or pathos than that, she was saying. And so important ...

'You know,' Buli interrupted, 'I was just thinking how amazing this is. We're all so involved in such interesting things. I can't help thinking how lucky we are to be here.'

'I know,' Fran answered, voice brimming with enthusiasm. 'It's the energy, and all the new ideas ...'

'Well no, I actually meant that, with us being mothers and all, we couldn't do any of this if we didn't have maids.'

The laughter blustered around them, as darkness fell about their ears. Across the road, the little shops were all closed, except the café on the corner, where the owner had been shot in a robbery the previous week.

THE MAN

The spume showed luminous through the gloom. One white ship glowed blindly, clutched in the last, jealous grip of the sun.

The man turned from the light. Bending his head into the darkness, he walked towards the evening. Night came still and heavy in this part of the world, dropping suddenly from the sky to drape thick folds across the dunes.

As he let his towel fall above the tide-line, the air felt dense about his face. You could lick it. You could squat at the water's edge, the day behind you, and you could taste the plankton on your skin.

One swift otter's dive and he was part of it. He never allowed his sons to do that. It was too dangerous in the gulley. He had made damn sure they knew the currents of this sea. He had confidence in the lithe bodies that rode the waves past its rips and pulls. But this shoreline would never be the extent of their universe. They would never have need to know this rocky shelf quite as he did. Or to memorise each rock that jutted from the sand when the westerly blew too hard.

Any case, what reason had he to avoid this one nod towards recklessness. Should he miscalculate – should he veer a couple of centimetres left – he would probably break his spine against the rocks lying hidden by the tide. That was all.

Sometimes he felt the sensuous pleasure of it. The quick pain followed by the wash of himself and the sea. The sea and himself. Which was which ...

A sharp sting throbbed suddenly around his thigh. And of course, that was how life was. That was how it would draw to its end for people like him. Not in the ecstasy of sudden oblivion, but in all the stings and thorns that slowed the drag of years.

He left the water, taking his time to unwrap the bluebottle from his leg. It was almost dark now, impossible to see each tiny hook of its sting.

He started back, the sky over the dunes pastel light. It was peculiarly still, one of those windless evenings that swaddled the senses in moist warmth. Plucking a beach fig from the fat cluster beside the path, he paused to burst its juice over his smarting skin. If only all of life's barbs were so easily soothed.

And suddenly she was there – conjured by the ectoplasm of darkness and the haze of evening's last gasp. Against the last pink glow of the sky, her face shimmered at him. Coquettish, tempting – just as she had seemed the first time he had seen her. She'd had that ... for God's sake, she had just been a girl. She could have been any girl – of her time. Any girl of a certain age and class. But she'd had that rare mix: a lithe sensuality muddling for room beside a frank innocence.

Where did she come from now? Why could he never be free of her? There were many things in his past. No, he had no regrets. No guilt. But there were many things that might choose to sidle up to taunt him, if he allowed them to. Why her though? Why did she choose to slip silently into his consciousness, like the sand in his old fishing takkies, to chafe and rub at his view of himself and his life.

She had been nothing special. Nothing.

He just ... he wondered, that was all. He supposed it was the way they had always felt unfinished to him. The two of them, drawn together by the game they had played, and the time in which they had played it. The game was over now, goddammit. Why couldn't she leave him alone?

Unfinished business, that's what it was. Perhaps he would never be free of her. Or perhaps it was time they had done with it all, in one way or another. Perhaps he should deal with it, once and for all.

He wondered where she was. It wouldn't be hard to find out. He wondered what kind of adult world she inhabited, now that she was grown? Now that everything had changed?

MEGAN

Johannesburg had never seemed to Megan a community like other cities. Drawing from every part of the country, every township and suburb, it was a place where people seemed seldom to have rubbed smooth together in schools and teams and matric dances. They came from everywhere and formed communities in flux. They came for their jobs, or their loves, or the beat of the big city – a beat more African than the gentler pulse of the Cape. New people came and went, and yet those that stayed never entirely lost the urge to move one day to the mountains or the sea, back home, or to Perth.

Megan was losing the battle with minibus taxis and the angry swirl of rush-hour cars. There was little tolerance for dithering at half-past seven in the morning. They drove hard and fast, volatile in gesture and the blare of hooters.

Oh hell, which way? Left. No, that was wrong. And so she cut her way right, up the hill through the far end of Braamfontein, and down to Hillbrow. She remembered it from holidays, scattered with bookshops, Greek pavement cafés, prawns and Middle Eastern delicacies. It was a different country now, carrying the colours of the continent and a beat that was purely African.

She feared suddenly to be lost in this place she no longer knew, although surely it couldn't be because it had grown so much more black than white. She wasn't like that. She really wasn't. Forcing herself to stop, she asked directions of a black man with a French accent, selling handbags on the pavement. And suddenly the taxi-clogged streets were exciting again.

Such a strange city this, in the way it constantly redefined itself, shifting its communities and the character of its neighbourhoods. She knew how firmly it carried its stocks and credits, wheels and deals, the rush of suits and the ring of cellphones. And yet, large enough in its unpretentious heart, it seemed able to hold all of this life within it. It allowed the colours of Shangaan turbans, the bustled trade in saris and silk, the sizzle of street-fried boerewors and the pavement commerce in tomatoes, china dogs and junk.

Surreal, when brief exile had given you outsider's eyes, that all this clamour could lie just fifteen minutes' drive from arching malls, where fingers stretched for acrylic extensions, Earl Grey tea and carrot cake. Here the gritty swirl of chip packets danced where alleys and doorways still skulked from the early sun.

She knew exactly where she was now. She had been this way before with Fran. She hoped Fran was okay, come to think of it. But of course she would be. It was Megan who wasn't used to the dire screaming of children and conspiracies of maids and madams. That's what had made her late.

She had taken her breakfast outside, leaning against the kitchen doorway to absorb the early sun. Suddenly the screaming had begun. It was the abandoned shriek of a child shaken free of all sense of earth and its bounds. That's how it sounded anyway. Bolting into the kitchen she had found Beauty – a bowl of porridge in her hand – trying to shush the rigid child. Fran had rushed through half dressed.

'Daniel, please my boy. We're all going to be late.'

'Eesh.' Beauty was wiping at the mess on the table. 'He is bad this morning, I couldn't stop him.'

'He's hysterical about going to school again.'

The child had shivered in strained tension, hair slicked with perspiration.

'Paul'll be out of the bath soon. He won't cope with this. Daniel, please. This doesn't help. Stop it. For God's sake ... shut up now.'

She had given the child a shake, then struggled to hug him hard. It had seemed an attempt to press some warmth into him. Yet his arms had continued to rail against the unfairness of it all. Megan had watched in shock, lacking all experience to suggest what she should do. He had continued to scream, his face an ailing blue, his mouth outlined in white.

'I'll take him ...' Beauty had said, pushing Fran aside. Grabbing the fragile child by an arm, she had swung him on to her back. Pinioned by a towel, the child had begun to calm while Beauty jiggled her body as if to soothe a colicky baby.

'I'll take him to my room. You're going to be late. Go.' She had shooed Fran with a gesture.

'Here ... here, take the porridge. Perhaps he'll eat. Beauty ... thank you.'

Coming in later to find her keys, Megan had been halted by the sound of Paul's voice in the hall. Something in Paul's tone had held her back. Beneath all his brotherly charm, she sensed the potential for a gruff irritation at her presence, should she seem always underfoot.

'Have you booked Daniel for his school readiness assessment?' he had asked.

Beauty had come silently into the kitchen with Daniel. Pale and subdued, his damp hair had been marked by comb ridges.

'Paul ...' Odd that Francesca should sound so tentative. She had always been so definite in her opinions. 'Don't you think we should assess him at the Cerebral Palsy School? We shouldn't mainstream him if he can't cope.'

'Why shouldn't he cope? He's a bright child.'

'He's not coping that well with the pre-school ...'

'That's the school's fault. It's their job ... teachers are just too lazy to deal with anything that differs from the norm. I'm still convinced you should never have told them ...'

'About the diagnosis? Paul, I had to. They have to know ...'

'Sure, everybody needs a label, don't they? Makes it easier to deny their responsibility.'

As the door began to open, both Beauty and Megan had turned to busy themselves at the counter. Daniel had stood in the midst of it all, seeming not to have heard them argue over his future.

Striding through the kitchen, Paul's eye had strayed to the stiff child. He tossed a surprisingly gentle 'Bye bye boy'.

Her office lay over a railway line and under a highway – in a street desolate of people, ponderous with trucks. Why was it that she always felt compelled to find work in the most obscure of non-governmental organisations? But actually, she knew exactly why. It made her feel like a good person, clear about her place in the world. She loved the clarity of new potential created for people who had nothing and expected less.

A young black man followed her in, rubbing his hands from the shaded chill of the street. An inner door swung open with a crash. A man who looked to be in his late thirties stood, arms folded before him. This must be Tebogo, the new director.

'Nice of you to be with us at last,' he said to the young man. 'Do you wish to come into my office?'

'Eesh, it's not such a big deal,' the young man burst in. 'So I took the car. I needed to see my mother ... The Bochum project was in the next district.'

'You disappeared with a funded car for two weeks.'

'Hey chill, bru,' cut in a pale, pony-tailed boy. 'If one of us really needs a car, it's cool. Like, I mean no-one's going to take it for nothing.'

The older man appeared almost military in the languid gathering of his workers. 'Let me make something clear. There are no longer endless funds from places like Sweden.'

'Yeah, but you can't just suspend our democ ...'

'I am accountable. Surely you can see how important it is to run things according to rules.'

Oddly, mutinous behaviour was limited to mumblings. Perhaps they felt as she did – slightly relieved that every urgent detail might no longer be bogged down in weighty committee process. Tebogo was brave though. Hell, it was something to have initiated a new order around here. Tadpole-swift, the thought squirmed through her mind that it was fortunate he was black.

In his office later, she met him properly. He had a weary kindness to his smile, but she could sense an obduracy of manner which he applied as much to himself as to others. He suggested coffee, then grimaced at the taste of his sugarless cup.

'I find it hard,' he answered her gaze, 'to keep in shape, now that I sit in an office.' She smiled briefly, wondering why he didn't use a sweetener. But perhaps he'd consider it soft.

'Were you in exile?' she asked. He had an alien edge that she couldn't quite place. He didn't seem like a returned exile, in whom local custom was overlaid by the ease of America, or the sureness of England.

'No. In the camps. Up north. Besides when I was sent to study in Moscow.'

Instantly, she wished to ask him a hundred questions – what it was like and what he had done. But she didn't know whether she could, or if she had to earn the right.

'I left after '76. The student uprisings, you know?'

'Yes of course. I'm ... not that young.'

An Umkhonto we Sizwe soldier. Training in Moscow. It hardly seemed real. Before the elections, people would never have mentioned these things in casual conversation. She had the lunatic urge to say: 'Sh, don't say it aloud. Let's hide you.'

Her first week of work was bound up with her new life so that she gave very little attention to Fran or any oddities she might have developed. Perhaps this was what marriage did. Perhaps it plucked the brightness from people like Francesca and staunched it in porridge and school runs. What did she know about being married and settled? And anyway, she had her own life to deal with now.

Tebogo had a steadiness to him. She enjoyed bringing small contentions to lay at his feet so they could gnaw on them pleasurably during the workday. The others were pleasant, joshing over who was to cook lunch – the one truly egalitarian institution that remained. Probably for the sake of symbolism, Tebogo poured good faith into the process with zest and lashings of beetroot. Megan thought his Borscht very dreary. So much for symbolism.

It was also the week of Nicholas. And he could banish anything. With that strange energy of his, with all his schemes and brave new ideas, he seemed to represent the city for her.

She was always to wonder whether she would have considered him to be her soul love had they not met in Jo'burg. This city engendered intensity. It flouted convention in exchange for melodrama. But it was also true that a curtailed relationship leaves a clearer imprint of love than one that, in the familiarity of bathrooms, begins to curl at its worn edge and grow dim with age.

He swung in on her second or third morning, his words lost in his slipstream. Megan was sitting in the resource centre, the only room with decent light, her bare foot in her lap. She had picked up the splinter in the kitchen, where floorboards had eroded with time and damp. Oddly, Tebogo was the only one of them to carry a small sewing kit.

'Hey, an African Cinderella,' Nicholas said, pausing at the door. He was the sexiest man she'd ever seen. Just like that, as though he simply expunged from living memory all other contenders. He had the slightly scruffy air of someone who doesn't give a rat's arse that his freckles only just rescued his features from intimidating perfection. Or that his sandy curls gave him a scattered look.

'And are you the prince?' she asked, longing to smooth his hair and tuck his shirt in where it had tugged free of his Levis.

'Nooit,' he said. 'Of course I'm not the prince. I'm the revolutionary who gives power to the people.'

And that was it, of course. In that instant he represented everything she had longed to be part of, but been too young for.

'And what shall be the fate of Cinderella in your new social democracy?' she added, wanting nothing more than to make him laugh.

'No,' he said. 'Oh no. My socialist state.'

'But I thought all old socialists were now making money ...'

And then he did laugh, eyes running for cover among the smile lines that etched his cheeks. 'Everyone knows,' he said, 'that real socialism hasn't been tried yet. The real revolution is still to come.'

He was joking of course. But she sensed beneath his whimsy a gravity of purpose. He seemed an emblem of the very best of Johannesburg, of the idealism which had carried it through the dark years.

'And as for Cinderella,' he added, 'she should join a trade union and campaign for minimum wages for domestic workers.'

'So you've met Nicholas,' said Tebogo, wandering in with his soft smile. 'Don't mind him. He's a trade unionist. All trade unionists are partly insane.'

Nicholas couldn't prise the splinter from her foot. He tried – not very hard, but he did try. Eventually, he dropped the needle to write her telephone number on his hand. It was Tebogo who sat patiently beside her and dug the splinter out. He had quite the gentlest hands she'd ever encountered in a man.

Oh God, Penny and Buli were here. Buli was okay. But she couldn't cope with Penny right now.

Three whole days ... Perhaps he had washed the number from his hand without thinking.

Penny always seemed so tough. And she said things that were completely insupportable. Like the time she'd said Fran was 'good fun'. For God's sake, you couldn't say that about Fran.

'Penny was just suggesting that we all go to this new South African Thanksgiving party. It's at some place where everyone dances on the table ...'

Megan couldn't tell if Fran was playing straight, or whether she was hearing an invitation to a little sardonic solidarity. That morning, she had thought of asking Tebogo for Nicholas's number, but crossing to the urn, she had found his eyes on her. It had seemed then that she couldn't.

Later Tebogo had perched on her desk and inexplicably begun speaking of Nicholas. In his mild speech she had almost imagined she heard a warning. But surely not. With a slight smile, he had spoken of Nicholas's wildness of purpose, of his intemperate addiction to a cause.

'I miss that,' he'd said suddenly. There was such yearning in his voice that Megan was brought back from flying in the face of him in search of the other.

'I miss having heroes. When people were great and we believed in the cause above all things.'

'Did your parents support you?'

'No. They were conservative ... it was 1976. Times were wild.'

'Was it ... was it hard?'

'Of course. Eesh. But it was like a religion. In the camps, we would sit up all night reading, Marx, Lenin, Trotsky ... We argued like crazy men, but we all believed.'

'That's what I so wish I could've had.'

He had looked at her a moment and taken a breath as if to speak. But he had let the moment go. After a moment he had added: 'After my training, an old man came up to me in Soweto and asked: "Are you from Lusaka?" Then he got tears in his eyes and touched my hand. That's all he did – touched my hand.'

'It must seem like a miracle now.'

He had taken another breath, but released it on a small laugh. She felt very young suddenly. It wasn't fair.

'I suppose I miss the lives we lived. They've taken that from us – all that faith. Now they're just politicians and this is a system like any other.'

He had stood then and half reached out towards her. But his hand had dropped as though he had no right, as though his hands were weighted by a century of constraint against a black man reaching out for a white man's daughter.

'The Berlin wall coming down ... eesh,' he had said as he wandered off. 'It really fucked us up. Not that the feeling we had ... not that it would fit in a real society.'

He had stopped and sighed, turning again as he rubbed the flat of his hand over his eyes.

'Everything then was for the collective good. All I believe in now is people. But I feel the loss of what we had.'

Penny's snort of laughter drew the collective past aside to reveal the individualists of the present. Buli was saying something about why the corporation was holding the party. Megan hadn't been listening, but it didn't matter. It was April after all. Obviously expedient companies with too much in the PR budget and too little in the sense department would be holding election anniversary parties.

She began to wander off, thinking how desperate it was to be single, how none of them could possibly understand ...

'Wouldn't you like to come with us?' asked Penny in her efficient way. 'It's bound to be good fun.'

'Oh God no, thanks. I can think of nothing worse.'

Penny gave a little laugh and a shrug and then the phone rang.

'Megan.'

'Mm?' What could she wear? She hadn't wanted to ask him.

'Megan!'

'Ja?'

'How could you speak to Penny like that?'

'Oh shut up, Francesca.' She didn't have time for this. 'You can't tell me you like that girl so much. You can't tell me you want to go to some mindless party where they dance on tables.'

Fran stared at her a moment. Then she gave her head a shake and broke into one of her infuriating gurgles of laughter.

Buli, wandering in with her air of being not quite where you had thought her, gave an absent little smile. 'Actually,' she said, 'the party's my PR exercise. I had to arrange it for my company. Penny was just being sweet about gathering up the masses to support me.'

'Oh.'

'Gotcha, Miss Read-people-by-their-labels.' Francesca was still laughing. 'Jeez Megan, grow up, won't you?'

'Don't throw my age at me, Francesca, just because I happen to've kept my principles.'

'But ... oh Meg-child. Everything has changed. You can't see it because you haven't been here. What do you even know about this country anymore?'

'Oh don't get all full of cultural cringe, just because I've spent a couple of years in England ...'

Daniel limped into the kitchen. His hair had blown back from his face. He was giggling, although enjoyment for Daniel never seemed entirely wholehearted. Beauty followed him in, laughing and rapping at his legs with an old copy of *Fair Lady*.

'Been watching *Bold and Beautiful* with Beauty,' he said, but stopped when he saw them. 'Oh ...' he said, hands lifting to his face. 'Oh, please don't be angry. Please don't shout.'

Fran dropped to his level, her face a tangle of guilt and other unmentionable mother-stuff.

'Oh Daniel, we're not ...'

But Beauty was there, scooping the child up with a whoop and the sound of an aeroplane taking off.

'Nyeee-nyeee okay, boytjie, you said you'd come visit Betty with me. Let's get the plans for my house to show her ...'

'She must've got the plans today. She wanted me to look at them,' Fran said, frowning absently into the fridge.

Buli perched on the kitchen table, sipping ethereally at her wine and looking as though this whole mess of emotion were happening somewhere far beneath her.

'I hate it when you do that to me.' Megan felt unable to let it go. This was how Francesca always made her feel.

'Okay,' said Francesca. 'I'm sorry, okay? But it seemed like you were laying some outdated austerity trip on us. And these parties ... they're harmless. A way for people still to believe in the mixing and the rainbow and the happy ever after.'

'But Penny ... Come on, Fran, she's nothing like you. What've you got in common, for God's sake?'

Fran spun from the fridge, her bracelets dancing animatedly.

'Will you ever learn to see past a haircut or a political t-shirt? And for that matter, what do you actually know about me?'

'Well, at least you did stuff. You were an activist.'

'Leave it alone, Megan. Surely we've left all that stuff behind us ...' With the slightest edge of amusement, she added: 'And you never know who you could meet. The most surprising old lefties turn up.'

Francesca couldn't know about him already, could she? And surely he wouldn't be seen dead ... but things were so mixed up How could you know?

'But Penny's just so ... like corporate.'

'Listen here. Before you say one more word, let me tell you what Penny's really like. When Hannah was just a baby and she wasn't working, she started fostering the abandoned and abused babies that Bara couldn't handle. This was long before a black child was the accessory of choice.'

Placing a dish in the microwave, Francesca rinsed her hands and ran them agitatedly through her hair, leaving it damp and slightly spiked.

'Her own kids always had snotty noses and the school mothers thought twice about letting their kids come over, but she didn't care a stuff. Eventually, the whole thing grew too big and some NGO took it over. Turned it into a home – mainly for AIDS babies now, of course. I couldn't have done anything like that.'

'Oh for God's sake, Francesca, you were detained.'

'Jeez, Megan. Don't you get it yet? It was nothing like you think. There's stuff you can never ... oh hell, can't I ever just forget it?'

Well, of course, Megan thought later, Francesca might say she wanted to forget it while her cousin was around, but she clearly hadn't quite the same constraints around Buli. Returning to the kitchen, she had discovered the two of them hunched over the table, wine bottle empty beside them. She couldn't be sure what they'd been talking about, but she caught the word 'interrogation'. Just that. Obviously it didn't exactly prove that Francesca couldn't trust her younger cousin with anything important ...

Nicholas fetched her – not because she was a girl of course – but because she was likely to get lost. He scoffed at the idea of eating in Melville. He wanted to show her Jo'burg. Melville was too trendoid to be the real Jo'burg. She didn't tell him how much she'd enjoyed it last Friday.

He took her to Yeoville, where dark doorways beckoned into darker clubs where people moved to some rhythm she had never learnt. Nicholas seemed quite at home.

'Hey ma bra,' he greeted at least a dozen people. 'Sharp,' he'd say, offering his three-phased handshake and easy grin.

Perhaps it was the profusion of drugs – although she wasn't really anti. She did take the odd toke now and again. But here, every room seemed submerged in torpidity.

Nicholas had a long conversation with a group of Ethiopians, who were so stoned they could hardly move their mouths. They carried a bag of little sticks, which they chewed on and spat to the floor.

Looping his arm about her neck he strode with her out into the street, where little shops huddled together, selling records and second-hand clothing or offering to do the dry-cleaning.

'Excellent,' he said. She wished that perhaps he had asked before marching her out. It all seemed so full of the youth and vigour of a new society. She wanted to learn its rhythms. She wanted to be part of its people – a new class, a new breed – for whom youth was an advantage rather than a drawback.

'I wanted to get a line on their thoughts,' he said. 'It's shit, but our guys are turning against illegal aliens in a big way. But I think we should ...'

She lost him somewhere in the run of his words. His arm was looped tightly about her neck. It was slightly painful in its intensity, but she would never have said so. She enjoyed the tightness of him, the coal-smoky scent of his sweat-shirt.

'... the job market can carry.'

He could never let go. But she loved him for that – for his urgency about everything she hadn't been a part of. She let him come home with her, and she let him make love to her, there in her bed at her cousin's house. In the rush and the struggle and the clutching at clothing, she whispered something about a condom, but he muttered that she shouldn't worry. And so she let him, but she worried just a little.

Megan hoped that Beauty couldn't hear, in the room alongside them. And then she forgot, absorbed in her own power to quiet him. She listened to him breathe as he lay boneless and still, entangled in her limbs and her hair. Just before dawn, he opened his eyes and grinned at her.

'Hey you,' he whispered, 'I must go.'

'Why?' she asked.

He laughed quietly, rubbing his hands over her face with a sureness that was comforting. She held her breath, but couldn't help asking again: 'Why do you have to go now?'

'My wife doesn't like me to stay out all night.'

Later, when she was alone and the light crept through the cottage panes, she thought it was funny that with all his tentative words of warning, Tebogo hadn't thought to mention his wife. She supposed that even he, with his braveness of new orders, would think himself bourgeouis to utter 'but he's married'.

MEGAN

Megan felt a little like Daniel. She felt like crawling through to Fran to say she couldn't sleep. It was the dark. The blackness of gnarled shape against a sky yellowed by smog and streetlights. Somehow, the city at night always pressed down upon her, rubbing her nose in the eternity still to be filled, and the life to be created.

She was still in that disinvested space between youth and maturity where her life could not be just any old life. It still, particularly at night, had to become a life of great meaning and purpose.

She lay and thought, and tried not to think, listening instead to the sounds of the streets. High revs, hi-fi – she wondered where they were coming from, and where they were going.

There was a sound at the back gate – someone trying to be silent, shifting a load through the narrow opening. It was probably the mealie lady. Beauty allowed the Mealie Lady to store her load of corncobs behind the outbuildings after each day's hawking.

The German Shepherds across the road rattled their gate and began to howl in unison. If they kept that up, she'd strangle them through the bars with her bare hands.

Was that a knock? A tentative little knock at the gate, which tried not to reach beyond the ears it was meant for. Which of Beauty's friends could this be?

'Megan? Wake up. Can you hear me?'

Her feet were icy on the autumn-chilled paving. And it was he, of course it was he. And (as she fumbled with keys and locks and a dressing gown that kept opening) surely nothing else mattered?

Clutching and grappling and reaching for ears and hands and cheeks, they giggled quietly like bundled rabbits in children's theatre.

High above them, the jacaranda floated, lightly nested with hadedas. The air tossed them the scent of chilled raw soil. Soon it would be winter, with all its dry despondency and chapped spirits. For the rest of Megan's life, the loam of autumn would be a gift, the rich smell of him and of this city – of renewal and intensity.

They didn't sleep. There wasn't time for such things. She must feel him, know all of him. She had to stroke the darker places of him, ease her fingers over his smoothness, press them into the recesses between his toes ...

He taught her sensations she didn't know she had, urging her further into herself. He praised her each time she came, gentling her when it seemed too strong for her

She felt the loss of him, as he withdrew from her sometime in the early hours. When they should have been one. When she could have drawn him into her being.

He whispered to her as she crushed her face under his arm, taking his essence to keep when he was gone. He whispered of love, and the scent of her, and of his need for the quietness of her hands. So tired. He grew so very tired sometimes.

At last, as the hadedas scrabbled and squawked in the early light, Nicholas fidgeted away from her. He seemed impatient with his own vulnerability, even as he longed for her still to nurture him. She forced herself to be still, knowing enough not to clutch at him and demand it back.

'What about ...' She didn't want to mention the word 'wife'?

'It's fine,' he said, showing a quick glint of his grin. 'We don't have that kind of relationship.'

That was worse, in a way. Worse than love faded, outlasted by time. They had probably been student activists together, or young trade unionists. There were so many couples like them. Scorning jealousy as some diminishing device of suburban control, they would have slept with comrades, parading their honesty with hurtful intent.

'I'll make coffee,' he said, untangling impatient limbs from the last grasp of her feet.

But she, that wife Megan had never seen, would have lived through those times with him. She would be tied to him by some unshakeable bond that Megan would never know. Because she ... she was young, and ... oh God, how she hated her.

'Adele thinks ...'

She didn't want to know. She hated his ease in speaking of the other woman as though she were there with them. As though she would always be, this immutable force whose opinions and thoughts were engraved on his life.

'... it's a betrayal of everything, but I reckon it's a good move, and you?'

'Uh, about?'

'About my new position in COGWU.'

'Just explain it again.'

'I'm in charge of their investment portfolio.'

'You mean like stocks and shares? I didn't know unions did stuff like that.'

'Well ... we've always invested our pension funds ...'

'Ja, I did read that somewhere. And that union pensions were only invested in socially responsible companies. So, what's wrong with that?'

'Well, it's more like ... see, things have changed. It's not just pension funds. It's surplus subs. And ... we borrow from the big financial institutions.'

'So, why doesn't your ...'

'We're involved in massive investments, right in the mainstream of the economy. Full-on into all the unbundling corporations.'

'Why doesn't ... your wife like it?'

He handed her the coffee, sitting on the side of the bed with his cup curled between his hands. Gulping at hers, she scalded the roof of her mouth. She set it down and watched him.

'She says I'm a glorified bond trader. But it's not for me ... except I do get the commission ... But like I said, it's clearly a way of empowering the workers. I mean it's so obviously a pragmatic way of moving into the next phase of the revolution.'

He seemed to have no self-consciousness about his naked body. Had she been sitting there, she would have lifted her torso to keep her breasts pert and her stomach flat. Megan bet his wife would never bother with such vanities. How she hated her.

'... redistributing wealth from the middle class. But she reckons ...'

'I don't fucking want to know what she says.'

'Sweetheart ... what's the matter? I'm just ...'

'Oh I know. It's okay. I didn't mean that. It's just that, Nicholas, I ...'

'What's it?'

'... I just don't know if I ... No, it's nothing. Never mind.'

'Well, I was just saying that she reckons things will get muddled and lines crossed. She thinks we'll get confused about who we are.'

'Yes, I see. But Nicholas, will ... will I see you again?'

His light face, so lacking in artfulness, turned to hers, blank with lack of understanding.

'But of course. My Sweet ... that's what I've been trying to tell you. You understand me. I could ... you know, I think I'm in love with you.'

She couldn't say anything. She was frightened to reach for him, so she sat in her bed, hair shielding the tears that threatened to fall.

He left soon after, crushing her to him as though he hadn't learnt his own strength. He left her door swinging, and the morning air rushed in, grey and rank with the sulphurous approach of winter. It would settle on despondent lungs, the smog and the terrible dryness of it.

Francesca juggled the firelight from feature to feature, dancing with a vivacity that burnt through her limbs. And then Megan lost sight of her – staunched by some smothering group.

They had driven miles to this restaurant out in the sticks, all thatched roof and rustic wooden poles. The tables were knotted pine, varnished to a gleam in the light from the great fire. A little early in the year for such a fire. Already, she could feel the heat building from the skirmish of dancers.

She had come to the party after all. It had been for Fran she supposed, to make amends for her rudeness to Penny. And she had thought ... she had hoped that perhaps he might be here. It wasn't likely, being a big corporate function. But then it was Buli's company, and they were unbundling. Perhaps his investment portfolio might just include one of its unbundled parts.

So here she was, but she had not yet given in altogether and decided to be part of it. Feeling gangly and adolescent, she slouched in the doorway to the covered verandah. On one side she could smell the heat and thatch and bodies and, on the other, the chilled Highveld grass. There was a delicate wildness to that grass, an enticement to wander out and gawk across at the bulked Magaliesberg, or back toward the yellowed profile of the city.

'Are you okay?' Odd that it should be Penny who came to find her, rather than Fran. She thought she caught a waver of concern in her eyes, but it disappeared when Megan nodded and compelled a smile to her mouth. She watched as Penny shrugged and disappeared back into the crush.

There was Francesca again, dancing with some black guy who was flinging her away and curling her back to him, bending their knees in some ancient phata phata from the '50s. It was as though the strange glassiness that encased her at home had shattered, releasing this wild creature into the night.

It bore some resemblance to the Francesca she had known in another time. In another world, really. In the cramped enclosure of their small-town childhood, Francesca's touch of wildness had been legendary. She had flown from unruly fancy to rebellious mayhem, but always with a tease in the tilt of her head and a warmth in the lilt of her voice.

Those who had prepared to admonish had been reminded instead of their own wild imaginings. And those who had thought to disapprove would find their mouths quirking toward laughter.

For a younger cousin with a secret crush, there had been a romance surrounding her. Returning from England now, homesick and miserable, Megan had expected to find that flashing girl again, safe in the castle of her capable knight. He and his plodding workhorse must surely have rescued her from any last dank thoughts of imprisonment, and allowed her to enjoy the freedom it had won her.

Instead, she had found these two Francescas, and this one a distracted doppelganger of the Francesca she had known before.

But Francesca had always known exactly what she wanted. She could surely take care of herself. Megan had no need to be her cousin's keeper. She had other things to worry over. Grappling with the probability that he would not be at the party, Megan searched anyway, glancing at profiles and weighing the set of shoulders.

All the revellers in ethnic garb were white. Well, that wasn't quite true. But most of them were, wearing their hearts embroidered on their Madiba shirtsleeves, and their woven skullcaps from Ghana.

Francesca was being frenetic, twirling between groups of dancers. There was an urgency to their mixing, an intense concentration on the merging of dance and cultural styles. Of course, this was just old African jazz. They'd be lost with some new kwaito sound, like they played in Yeoville now, and in the townships.

A squirming sense of superiority made them all seem terribly old. Did these white people think they were being part of the new South Africa, dancing to some old stuff which harked back to Sophiatown in the '50s? They all found the Sophiatown legend terribly quixotic and attractive – Jo'burg's Atlantis, sunk in the tides of her repressive history.

It was easy on them, she granted. Who couldn't relate to those old tales of mixing and music, of gangsters and poetry, thrown into romantic resistance by the rattle of government trucks and the roar of bulldozers set on forced removal?

She, on the other hand, was set on clubbing where the real new South Africa moved and shook. She intended to be hanging where mixing was freer and more genuine, where youth of all colours danced and drugged and slept together – because they had been born to it. Fuck them all, she thought. She may have been too young, but now they were too old.

They were cheering two of the more energetic dancers, embracing in the earnest way South Africans had, as if to celebrate their tactility as a shared cultural trait. As if to congratulate each other on a job well done – a miracle they claimed as their own.

Oh now she really was being petty. At least they were trying. They just hadn't grown up to it, that was all.

She found herself alongside the two old lefties they had met in Melville. She was briefly astonished, then reassured. If they were hanging out with all these business types, there was no reason other lefties might not be. It was odd though, as though there were no difference anymore, as though all that previously defined them was gone.

Suddenly she felt warmed by the reassuringly South African sight of them. Drinking Castle from the bottle, they stood bulkily to one side, legs astride in that companionable boy way that reminded her of brothers.

The dark one seemed to have permitted some of his intensity to evaporate in the heat, laughing over some point of laddish lore. She hung about on the edge of their discussion, unacknowledged as they weighed women, the Labour Relations Act, and local versus imported beer.

'Good oke?'

'Ja, he's a good guy. Subscribes to the affirmative thesis, but with the proviso – let's not jettison all the honkies just yet.'

'Hey howzit, you're Francesca's cousin, aren't you?' The blonde one loomed in the way very warm men had. 'Where is she by the way, oh yes ... predictable.' They both laughed and Megan turned to see Buli pulling an only slightly reluctant Fran on to a table.

'How do you guys know Fran?' she asked.

They hesitated, seeming unwilling to bring the past here to the present. It was the dark one, Henry, who spoke at last.

'We all met at university. We were academics when she was a student. But she and Martin ...'

'I only really got to know her after we were released,' Martin added. 'We were detained at the same time.'

'Also in East London?' Megan asked. Martin hesitated so long that Henry answered for him.

'Clearly it was the place to be in the '80s.'

'I know nothing about that time. Francesca never talks about it.'

'Ag, not worth talking about really.' Martin lumbered his weight from foot to foot. 'So I must tell you guys my new theory on the causes of crime.'

'In any case,' Henry cut in. 'Most people don't want to know about that time anymore.'

'So,' said Martin. 'My theory. I've come to the conclusion that crime can all be blamed on tourists. They come and parade themselves before muggers. Bloody temptation, that's all they are.'

'Quite right too,' said Henry. 'A drain on law and order.'

'They should be locked in their hotel rooms for the duration of their stay.'

She drank steadily as they bantered desultorily, with the deadpan lack of acknowledgment of old friends.

The room flared with small bursts of light, catching on the dancers. She had been drinking fast while she stood alongside them. And suddenly it seemed that everyone in this town breathed slightly faster or their hearts beat more quickly, or something.

Francesca and Buli danced sinuously above their heads, breath quick and illicit. She could feel the heat of the old lefties on either side of her. The whole place seemed to have caught and blazed with the excitement that spread across the dance floor, leaping between eyes and sparking off sweating bodies.

Perhaps that was why she ached. Perhaps that was why, unused to the way this town seemed to snatch at intimacy, to dash itself into this dervish whirl, it seemed suddenly too intense to bear.

Around them, figures collided and swooped, dark muscles flexing and lifting and flipping. And then suddenly ... suddenly Buli was hysterical.

Megan could never remember quite how it happened, or what had led so quickly to that fever of weeping. Someone must have said something, she supposed. But Buli never enlightened them.

It was Martin who moved first, ducking and weaving through the crowd like the rugby player he might once have been. He plucked Buli from where she had fallen against Francesca and carried her to the tiny room beside the manager's office.

He laid her on the small couch, as Megan, Francesca and Penny trailed in softly behind him.

'It's okay,' he said, his bulk awkward alongside her sudden frailty.

'It's okay,' he said again as Buli sobbed. 'Sometimes everyone should allow themselves to let go. I bet you don't even know how many people you helped with the stuff you wrote. You made a lot of people feel not so alone.'

He spoke quietly to Buli, a large hand patting her shoulder. She continued to sob unrelentingly.

'And who've you allowed to help you, I wonder? Who've you allowed to make you feel not so alone?'

Suddenly aware of the three women hovering behind him, Martin again became the emotionally maladroit boy he showed to the world. 'So, like I'm in the way here. I'm going to leave you to your friends now, okay? Women are much better at this kind of thing.'

Taking his place on the couch, Francesca shushed Buli as she would a child. But it was Penny – strange that it should be Penny with her bustled efficiency – who got her talking.

Somehow she managed to slice through the viscosity of all that emotion, urging Buli to speak, or they couldn't help. It seemed so obvious when she said it.

'It's ... it's just that I don't know how I can ever fit in. I've never fitted anywhere ... since I left here.'

Penny held her by the shoulders, more to steady her, Megan thought, than as a gesture of affection. Fran gave a soft little 'no-oo' that wandered into the air like a lament, rather than a denial.

'You fit with us,' Fran murmured, and Megan knew that she wanted it to be so.

'Not all the time ... Well, maybe. But ...'

Penny interrupted: 'You fitted in America. They doted on you. You had this incredibly important position ...'

'Title! You should have said I had this incredible title. I was their toy.'

'Oh nonsense, Buli. You're just putting yourself down.'

'No I'm not. They gave me this title, and trotted me out as their tame South African exile. I helped them look good – their emblem of social responsibility. But they never taught me anything. To do ... to be anything.'

'But Buli, that's nonsense,' snapped Penny. 'TIH snapped you up, you're ...'

'They took me because of America. And because of ... this.' She pinched contemptuously at her flesh.

There was silence, as they all watched her. She had begun to shiver, her nose running untended. Her face was suddenly lined, entangled in all her tears.

'I'm sure that's not true,' Fran murmured, but Buli let it drop unanswered. A knock sounded and a head appeared, tense and unwilling – the corporation host.

'Uh, you guys okay in here?'

Buli turned away, holding her grief out of sight. Hardly waiting for the expected affirmative, he disappeared again, relief patent in the decisive closing of the door.

'I hate South African men,' said Buli at last, her voice wavering. 'All races. They're equally horrible.'

'But Buli,' said Francesca. 'Vusi's great.'

'Oh in public he is. He knows how to do that. You should've seen him in America. All American, never mind that he'd never been anywhere before he left here. But now ...'

'Difficulty fitting?'

'No, it's me that has difficulty fitting. He's fitted, more than well. There he knew all about women's rights. He would never have shown himself so unworldly ...'

Penny held Buli firmly. Her body appeared to waver and dissolve, head teetering on her neck like a hand puppet without a hand. The spaciness she had shown in Melville was returning now, blanking out her features.

'Now he's an African man again. Can't bear his family to see that he doesn't control me. Demanding his food on the table, his tea in his bed. Yelling at Thembeka when he's drunk – she's frightened of this new daddy.'

'And the family? Can't they help?' Penny, ever practical, ever reaching for the firm solutions.

'They don't understand. And they're jealous, of course. I'm not like them anymore. And, the thing is, I don't want to be.'

'Can't you ...'

'No! Stop saying that. It's useless. And he bullies me into being the kind of wife his family expects.'

'I think,' said Penny calmly, Buli's body boneless in her hands, 'I think you need to persuade him to go for therapy.'

'Oh you just don't understand, do you? Your lives ... you're just different. You could never understand.'

THE MAN

The gale had blown all day, smashing waves against rocks in a petulant display of force. But as the sun prepared to set, the wind dropped. Just like that, as though it were drained of all energy. If it wasn't for the sea, the evening would be utterly still. The waves, having been provoked into a turmoil of their own, continued battering at the shoreline that imprisoned them.

The man sat on his stoep, relishing the passion he felt so much a part of, and yet could not share. He didn't know how. Somewhere in the odd life he had so far survived he had lost that passion. He had become a man without fervour, without the enthusiasms that directed the pursuits of more ordinary people.

It was strange how life worked. He had not intended to become this sidelined person. This onlooker and vicarious participant in other forces. It was as though just one or two choices, taken with a laugh and a shrug when he thought himself immortal and immune, had drawn him into a life he would never have considered for himself. Once upon a time, he had been a different person. He had thought grand thoughts, and imagined wild imaginings. Hard to conjure that boy now, even to himself.

In the fullness of the dark, that person would have seen himself as a participant – wife and children about him in the warmth of winter lamplight. Instead, here he sat as the spray needled him, mocking the pillar of salt he had become.

He was cold. Inside it would be overheated, a cauldron of boys and chatter and the television Rolene was addicted to. It suffocated him, that constant intrusion from loud places and hearty men. The ersatz intensity of weeping anorexics.

He wondered what they were watching. It was unusually quiet. He had heard no bickering, no yelps of pain from cuffed younger brothers. His youngest was in bed now. They had said their gruff good nights an hour or so ago. Soon he would slip inside and spend his ritual few minutes staring at the sleeping boy. That's what made everything worthwhile.

The darkness on the shore had the texture of flesh. Impenetrable and unthinkable that it might be ruptured – until the precise moment it was pierced by a ship rounding the bay. Sit here long enough and the dark flesh would close again, healing itself of the bright rip that bled over the water. As the ship passed beyond the bay on the other side, it would seem as though it had never been.

Blackened to the shade of oblivion, an East Cape night was far from dead, if you knew how to sit quietly within it and be patient. If you could avoid the dread of the void, you could just detect the murmurs of movement of all that existed parasitically on its living body. You could smell the feral cats in the rustle of sudden escapes. The anemones in their salt. And probably, if you sat long enough, the whales in their pheromonal romancing beyond the breakers.

He had no fear of the void. Oblivion held an attraction that he might just surrender to if ... if it weren't for the boys of course.

He rose and stretched, breathing in salt and ozone. He would sit a few minutes and watch his youngest son sleep. Rolene would still be intent upon the images that replaced the life she had tossed out to be with him. He wondered if she also thought of the person she once had been, and the life she might have lived if she had not been so reckless in her choosing.

They seldom went to bed at the same time, lacking the language that might still draw them into the togetherness of a marital bed. And often as not, Rolene would crawl to the spare bed in their middle son's room. He snored, she claimed – not that he had actually requested the explanation ...

Passing the lounge door, he noticed two of his sons intent on a Gameboy. His eldest was snipping his toenails on to the carpet while Rolene stretched forward as though she longed to join the TV announcer in some nebulous earnest land. The man paused, considering a rebuke over the toenails, as the credits scuttled over the screen. Some solemn documentary, no doubt, over some matter of what passed for life and death in this new society. As if the 12-year-old documentary-maker knew anything ...

It passed so quickly he was not sure he had seen it. The documentary-maker could not be a 12-year-old. Not if he had known her when he had. Could it be the same person? Unlikely, he supposed. That wasn't how he imagined her. He had pictured her growing into a stately middle age in a settled place like Cape Town, arranging flowers for her professional husband and ferrying her children to and fro.

It was a shock, seeing her name like that. Not that he cared. He had his life now and she obviously had hers. They had passed in a doorway of history, that was all. There was just this tiny niggle of something unfinished. As if there were something ... But there was nothing special about her. She had been no different from the scores of others. He was curious, that was all.

He wondered what would happen if he should phone the television station and inquire? But even as he thought it, he knew he probably never would. He was the onlooker, not the doer. He sat and he waited. That was his way. Whatever life thought to toss in his direction he would field. But he would never seek it out.

MEGAN

Megan wished she could slip out of herself as though she were a ruined suit. Curled over her bed like cats, Francesca and Penny groomed and licked, self-indulgently filling her small bedroom with smoke. She would reek. Lucky it didn't matter anymore.

Megan felt she creaked and grated like a broken thing. It was as though the pain had transferred into the nerves under her skin, smarting with the smallest touch.

Penny was filing her acrylic nails. Megan assumed they were acrylic. No-one had real nails so perfect, did they? Actually Penny wasn't so bad. She had been really nice last night.

'Drink some champagne before the two of us finish it,' said Penny suddenly. 'It's you I brought it for, really. Nothing fixes a hangover quite like it.'

'It's not ... oh never mind.'

'No, I know.' Funny, Penny sounded almost gentle. 'But I think we should talk about it. I mean, how bad do you really think it is in the scale of things?'

Well, that was a stupid question. And she couldn't talk about it. She had spent the morning tinkering with her hurt and her humiliation and she knew that it was just too ghastly.

It had all happened after the party. How about coffee in Melville, the old lefties had suggested, and they had innocently agreed. After all, who would have expected still more drama?

Greying gently through his tousled curls, Martin had flirted in the back seat with Fran while Henry drove. They hadn't touched – Megan would check periodically, turning suddenly to remark or inquire. But between them there had been that viscous eroticism that caught at their eyes and bound their fingers almost to connect.

In Melville ... oh God ... they had found Nicholas, just when she had finally given up on searching for him. In the Bassline, where Pops Mahommed was winding up his last set.

'So,' Martin had said as Nicholas joined them, 'I see you and Cyril are making serious inroads into grasping capitalism.'

It wasn't the kind of news story she would normally have spent time on. But her need to have something intelligent to discuss with Nicholas had drawn her to study it feverishly. Cyril Ramaphosa, former big deal unionist, had just turned down a cabinet post to head up a black business conglomerate. And one that had its sights set on unbundled bits of Anglo. Dear God, could one assail any more symbolic a face of South African capitalism than Anglo American?

'Wouldn't have believed it ten years ago. You?' Henry had asked, wickedly tossing his question in Nicholas's direction. 'Change the face of business and labour relations, I should think. Warm little bed for you guys, all together.'

Nicholas had laughed with them, tilting his chair back on two legs while running his hands through his already disordered hair.

'Well, I wouldn't expect you okes to understand this new, subtle phase of the Struggle. Lost your principles somewhere on the gravy train, didn't you?'

'New subtle phase?' Henry had muttered. 'Where are we? I could've sworn this was 1996.'

'As a government worker,' Martin had added, 'I'd just like to point out that, unlike myself, you guys seem to have taken to the second phase of the revolution with indecent haste and alacrity. That new cabriolet, Henry. Very subtle. Very, very subtle.'

'Fuck you, china.' They were all laughing now. 'I can be subtle. I'm a subtle guy.'

Of course it was a boy thing, that ritual banter. She had always considered it a substitute for intimacy. But deep down, she was sure Nicholas must regard them as old and tired, their fervour dissipated in more comfortable concerns.

'Surely I couldn't have heard you correctly, Mart?' Nicholas had scoffed, plucking the last Camel from his pack. 'Government worker? Busy worker bureaucrat for the new democracy, are we? For fuck's sake. You're EU-funded – just another of the plague of consultants running the country.'

'And in contrast,' Martin had said, 'you haven't entered into the spirit of money-making at all. Notwithstanding your little skill for investment.'

Nicholas had held his grin, rocking back confidently on his chair. Megan wondered though, if only she had been able to see that Martin's remark had stung.

'I might have made money,' he had said, 'but at least I'm not as conspicuous as you guys.'

'Oh is that what it is?' said Martin. 'It's okay to make money as long as you don't spend it?' Turning to Henry, he had added: 'Nicholas thinks conspicuous consumption means a bulge under his mattress.'

'Well ...' Henry had sighed. 'It's a noble cause – making money for the revolution. I wish him joy of his mattress.'

A woman had entered. Greying and tired at the edges, her hair had been snagged in a careless bundle.

'At least ...' Nicholas had been saying, '... Cyril has the cred to use his position ...'

'He means this new captain of industry might actually spearhead some real transformation.' The woman had allowed smoke to flow derisively through her nostrils.

Megan had been struck by the way he mislaid his words and even his faith in his argument when she appeared. It was as though she had guardianship of something that should be his.

Fran had been saying something about the danger of Cyril's being 'co-opted by the existing order of things'. Flirting with Martin, her hands had been those of a courtesan, opening in unclad invitation and closing again in coquettish enticement.

Speaking fast, Nicholas had launched into an earnest exposition on opportunities for social transformation. Projects that would bring lower returns, but still be good for society, like housing. His coherence had deserted him though, in the presence of this woman who tied him so steadfastly to the person he still thought he was.

'I think ...' she had said, so tranquil that she silenced the clamour, 'that real unionists must wonder whether Cyril really was one of them, or whether he just used them to join the gravy-train ... What is your name?'

Megan had dropped her eyes, unmasked by the youth she displayed so openly on her face. The two of them had felt suddenly beached on a small reef of their own, the others' talk lapping at the edges of them.

'So you're the latest one,' she had said. 'They get more and more like you as time goes on.' Megan hadn't asked what she was like, but she could've guessed. Oh God, she could've guessed.

'Leave it, Adele,' he had said. 'Why're you doing this? Leave her alone.'

Nicholas had been struggling to light another cigarette. She had thought she'd heard Penny trying to change the subject.

'It doesn't matter, you know,' the woman had continued. 'I just want you to know. There've been others, and there'll be more. Don't think you're any different.'

'Well, why're you making a scene then ... if you have such an open relationship?' She should have kept quiet. She was in the wrong, if there was a wrong in this. She didn't even know anymore.

'Adele,' Nicholas had tried again, 'just los it now. Give it a break. It's not her ...'

'That's the point.' The woman had been bright with the embers of her fury. 'You'll come and go like all the others.'

Megan had turned her hands palm upward, like a dog exposing its belly. Perhaps the woman had misunderstood the shrug. But she had lifted a glass of wine and flung it in Megan's face, while the whole of Melville – the whole of Jo'burg – bore witness to her hurt and her shame.

They had left soon after, and she remembered thinking that Melville smelt of petrol. No richness of soil and sweetness of Highveld grass. Petrol, from the cars aimed by senseless, barely twenty-somethings. It had smelt of smoke from doorways – dark and jazzy, or lank and metallic, where long girls in short skirts had been grunged to their eyebrows.

'... everyone knows she's a complete lunatic,' Penny was saying, but it didn't help.

'It happens every time,' said Fran, 'even though they have this agreement.'

Megan didn't want to know about 'every time'. It was just too bloody painful. And what made it worse was that she had done this to herself. She had walked straight into this most stereotypical of situations. Well, never again. She would never, ever see him again. Not ever. Sitting up, she flung her tear-matted hair behind her and swigged the champagne straight from the bottle.

'You shouldn't take it so hard,' said Penny.

'Why not? It's my own fault. He *is* married.'

'That's his problem, not yours. Your problem is taking it that way. You should see it like a facial, or a nice massage.'

'And of course you do take your own advice, don't you?' Francesca asked her archly. 'You've been seeing the same man for years – who adores you, by the way – and of course you feel nothing.'

'I didn't say I feel nothing. But you've got to protect yourself in these situations. Men ... they're not like us.'

'So where is he today? Isn't Allan away?'

'Ja, and so is he, the bastard. And not even a phone call. That's what I mean about men. It just doesn't occur to them to pick up the phone.'

Megan said nothing. She was conscious of the power of this incantation of secrets to admit her to the covenly group. Huddling into the circle, she felt her straggled hair brush against Francesca's. Given life by the crackle of Highveld air, it stretched itself and reached out for her.

Megan's sadness still lay leaden in her gut, but her head began to lift into light-headedness. The alchemic mix of too much emotion and girl-bonding fizzed with the champagne in her mouth.

'How's Buli?' Penny asked suddenly. So buried in her own misery, Megan had forgotten to ask.

'She's ... she's sort of okay,' said Fran, opening a new bottle of wine.

'That girl is seriously on drugs,' said Penny severely, schoolmarm leaping suddenly from her lips.

'She is not,' said Fran. 'You heard what she said about her husband.'

'Well, I don't know. I still think she's seriously on drugs. Not that we don't all take the odd splif now and again.' She snorted at the absurdity of her objection. 'But we don't do drugs like that, Sweetie. Sure, she's our friend, but I just think you should be a little careful of getting too emotionally entangled.'

'She's helped me a lot, you know,' said Fran. 'I just think we should help her. It's hard for someone to come back. And I really want us to be friends with her.'

'Of course you do, dear.' Penny patted Francesca's dishevelled head.

'Bitch!' Francesca intoned, pink with indignant laughter. 'It's not because of that.'

'Of course not,' Penny replied.

Megan laughed, enjoying Penny making fun of her cousin. She remembered the excruciating gatherings of earnest students Fran had organised while still at university. She had envied them, at the time. But now it seemed their lives had been too impossibly divergent to talk of anything real. The white kids had allowed their wine to be ploughed and their food to be plundered, too humiliated by privilege to complain. And the black kids – slightly belligerent, just a little defiant – had allowed themselves to be used as accessories of the Struggle, their friendship worn like a badge of belonging.

Even now, there was an earnestness to the mixing she saw. Of course it was different in the hangouts of those her own age. But this lot wanted so badly to believe they could merge their cultures, just a bit. There was a solemnity to the chats at the school gate, a gravity to their invitations to perch on each other's couches, admiring the furniture they would never dream of owning. They could talk, they could even discuss – but they could never hunker.

Buli could hunker. She could curl up and talk girl-stuff. She could belong – almost, almost ... and yet not quite.

It was a time of omens, that year which stumbled briefly over autumn's dry heat before toppling into rigid winter. It was a time for oracles and a searching for signs. Oh please tell us what will be? What will become of us?

Actually, Megan believed in nothing of the kind, although she suspected that Fran did, with her superstitious touching of head and toes and wood. Megan believed in nothing so spiritually unwieldy. It was emotionally disordered, all that watching for signs. All that waiting.

And yet, what cosmic cruelty had declared the winter of that year should be so very hard. Or that a sudden despondency would dry up their hope, just as the air grew parched and the mornings frail and frigid? Who could have foreseen this sorry sense of themselves that settled, with the flu, over their nostrils and lungs?

The office was chill and clammy. Megan felt like hell. Every surface froze the fingers and a small spectre of winter twisted from beneath the floor, coiling about the ankles.

They were mole people, squeezed beneath highways and behind railway tracks. And why? Why, when her head ached and her sinuses pounded, could she not be in some spacious office block where sunlight sparkled and plants could grow? Coffee scalded her rasping throat, but it felt good anyway.

'Megan, you look like hell. Come with me.' She didn't have the strength to protest as Tebogo drew her into the resource centre. He waited while she took a sip, shuffling his shoulders as though unused to involving himself in emotional skirmishes.

'I don't think they still love each other,' he said with a great gentleness. 'But he'll never leave her.'

'Who?' she asked.

'Look, in many ways, Jo'burg's just too small.'

She gazed into her coffee. She wished Tebogo hadn't heard, with all his dignity and soft calm.

'It's his tragedy. All that passion for revolution with all that skill for making money. He can't come to terms with coining it. And he can't let go of what he was.'

'So I'm just ...'

'No, don't do that. This is his issue, not yours.'

Without volition, she found herself curling against him on the faded couch. She didn't mean ... she didn't know what she meant, except that it wasn't sexual. She wanted a father or a brother, someone to dandle her. But she felt his sinewed arms close about her and she heard his breath deepen. Oh shit, she thought, and then she didn't care.

They sat like that as the thin morning sun crawled through the meshed grating high on the wall. She thought of nothing. She just didn't want to consider things right now. As if he knew, he told her a little of himself. Of military camps up north and, passingly, of Moscow.

'Tell more,' she said. And accepting her need and his role in it, he yarned gently of people and colours and the small details he must have known she loved.

'I had never imagined such cold. -35 degrees sometimes ...'

'I can't even think what that must be like.'

These were probably the stories he always told. He had a way of colourising his past beyond the grey of mere telling. With splashes of lustrous detail, he gave clarity to the dark hats and pale skins of men who spoke strangely. And to replace her faint sketches of triumphant warriors converging on Moscow, he showed her dark, silent men from Africa whose alien affinity to warmth held them always apart.

'But, it did teach me that life didn't have to be all uprising and revolution. And that all people, even white European people, were just people. Now,' said Tebogo, bleaching the words of colour, 'people are just concerned with making money. And in some ways, we've all lost the faith. Like you, nê?'

She never forgot that, through all the trysted turmoil they brought upon themselves later. He was the most politically worthy man she had known, and yet he had given his blessing to her small and human pain.

He lifted her face and gently kissed her chapped lips, and she understood that it was set. Whatever had just come about between them was now set in some mould of jellied history still to come. But what did it matter? What else was there? And perhaps it was good.

'Tell me quickly, you guys. Remind me why we shouldn't emigrate.'

They all laughed. Penny was camping up their secret fear – that one of them, one of their special ones, might leave. But in that Sunday's sunlight, the threat of winter seemed to recede, with their dread of despair.

'Who've you been talking to, Pen?' asked Francesca. 'You mustn't mix with those people. I've told you before.'

'My God, do they actually think it's any better elsewhere?' Buli, a little drawn, had come without her husband. 'They never fit. Not really.'

'I couldn't help it,' added Penny. 'It was the school sports day. I must've been asked twenty times if we're also going to Melbourne.'

'Oh for God's sake,' said Buli. 'All that blathering about everything that's wrong here. It's just racism. A black President! How standards have fallen. Tell them all to fuck off.'

'I did, you don't understand. But it made me all worried again. Counsel me quickly before I join the PTA mothers in Perth.'

They all erupted into laughter. But Fran looked anxious, as though she took this banter seriously. Could that be all it was though? Megan had only recently begun to notice that there were things about Francesca that held her back from the tranquillity of the suburban life she had chosen. Things that wouldn't grant her the resignation to forget her child's slight flaw.

'Always fancied your possie,' Penny's husband was murmuring to Paul by the fire. 'You have really good tree coverage.'

'Ja, it's in a good position. The garden's what sold us on the place. We were helluva lucky to get it so reasonably. Property prices were really low.'

'They'll drop again now the rand's collapsed. We're probably crazy to be holding onto property. We should be schlepping everything offshore.'

Allan had the lumbering presence of a rugby player, deceptive of his sharp brain and, Megan had heard, his wily negotiating style. Odd that both Penny and Fran had married such obdurate boys – shambling in awkward conversation as they twisted caps off dumpies and stared at the fire.

'Oh, I almost forgot,' Francesca said. 'Morris phoned from London. Remember him? From the Wits left?'

'That appalling Stalinist,' said Penny.

'This friend of his is coming over. I couldn't get him off the phone. He went on and on about the guy's credentials in the left ...'

'Didn't you tell him no-one does that stuff anymore?'

They were all laughing, unbridled and uncurbed. Megan was more restrained. Five years ago, cred had been currency. And perhaps because she had been away, the change still made her uncomfortable.

A family of hadedas launched suddenly from the jacaranda, forsaken Aaahs growing fainter as they headed for Zoo Lake. In the pause that followed their flight, Megan could have sworn she saw something approaching exaltation smouldering on the faces around her. And in that moment she knew beyond doubt that not one of them would be anywhere else.

As they began to eat, Francesca – way over time, in Megan's opinion – gently shoved the child from her lap. His dark eyes overflowed and Fran looked shattered, as though she had caused him grievous psychological harm.

'Come Danny, sit with the others,' said Penny in her straightforward way. 'They're dying for you to talk to them.'

Allan's two boys, with him for the weekend, had settled their plates beside Penny's and Buli's girls. Even Megan could see they were not dying to talk to Daniel. Sturdy feet toughened and soiled, they were earthed in the tangible world while Daniel appeared not quite corporeal, as though he still had one leg in another world.

Penny shot a look at her daughter that to Megan said 'Death'. The child didn't sigh too audibly as she shifted and patted the grass alongside her. But despite his fragility, Daniel had a will that could halt a train in its tracks. Fran's food began to congeal before she had whispered and prised him from her.

'I just want you to know this is all just to mislead you,' muttered Paul. 'The child's actually been offered captain of the Under-6 fifteen.'

Perhaps it was the way he said it, but it was hard not to laugh. Francesca didn't look up, but she must know that was just Paul. Whoever stood in the way of his jokes became briefly their brunt. They were all stepping stones to his wisecracks. Even, she supposed, his son.

Megan had noticed that Francesca sometimes stood between them, as though she mistrusted his strength and suspected him of a Spartan desire to shove the runt into the street. Well, in a way it had been done to Paul, being sent to boarding school at nine.

'You know,' said Penny in her pragmatic way, 'when you see Daniel with the other kids you can hardly tell.'

'But he feels different,' said Francesca, looking up at last. 'And he's treated differently. Other kids are so cruel.'

'Look,' said Buli, 'maybe I can relate to that feeling of being separate ... But even so, maybe he's a little too attached. Perhaps he does spend too much time on your lap.'

'Please don't start to make this my fault. You don't know – not one of you – what it feels like to have a baby that screams.'

'Well, I did have a colicky ...'

'I'm not talking now and again. I'm talking all day, all night. No sleep. No time to bath. No time even to cry from tiredness. No time for anything but that constant madness.'

'I know that, Sweetie,' said Penny. 'Who was it saw you through that mad time? But he's five now. And he's still on your lap ...'

'He spent every bloody moment of his first two years on my lap. It was the only way he'd shut up. How do you expect me to cut that kind of attachment ...'

'I think the main problem is that, for some obscure reason, you feel guilty about him,' added Buli. 'It means you can never be tough.'

'Of course I feel guilty. Life's harder for him than for other kids. And I brought him into it. And besides, there's ... there's also stuff no-one can ...'

'Don't start with that bullshit about somehow being responsible for his condition,' cut in Penny. 'There's stuff no-one knows about every single one of our pasts, and it doesn't cause birth defects.'

'No, of course not,' murmured Francesca. 'That wouldn't be rational. And we don't speak of what's not rational in this house ... do we? She glanced at Paul, still staring into the fire. 'But maybe one day someone will allow me just one chance to feel what I actually feel over this.'

Silence. Megan was absolutely not going to get into this. She picked olives from the salad as the other women foraged for some way to make amends. Paul and Allan had simply removed themselves, toying with the last fragments that were still on the braai.

'You know,' said Penny at last, obviously feeling really bad. 'I think he'll be fine. All he needs is a bit of confidence.'

'Oh sure.' Fran was still defensive. 'How do you suppose I do that – especially when the whole world conspires to take it away?'

'I don't know. I suppose you just have to tell him ... or something.'

In the uncomfortable silence that followed, Francesca pushed her plate away and steadfastly watched the fall of jacaranda leaves around them. She looked very alone.

'Come on, you guys.' Paul spoke gruffly and quite unexpectedly from the fire. 'Leave her be. She knows more about this stuff than anyone. If there's something to be done for Daniel, she'll be doing it.'

Lumbering around the table, he deposited a charred morsel on Francesca's plate, as proud as a cat displaying a dead locust.

'Hey babe, look what I kept for you. The last piece of boerie.'

Francesca brought her eyes around to meet his. They held a warmth that Megan remembered from a much younger Fran. Megan suddenly saw the two of them as they might have been, toting each other's troubles, carrying each other's fables without contradiction, as if there really were some family folklore in this house, instead of experiences which hung always discrete like his and hers towels.

MEGAN

'Fran, are you busy? Could you come in here a minute?'

'I'm just ... Hold on, I'm coming.' Fran was standing at the garden gate. It was a quiet street, especially on a Sunday afternoon, muffled by jacarandas and the heavy green of mulberry trees. Only later would you see the dog-walkers emerge. As the evening sun flitted above breeze-jostled leaves, joggers would greet each other, while walkers padded briskly toward the golf course, sticks swinging. At any other time, automatic gates gaped silently open, disgorging cars like lapping tongues. Except for the house next door, where hordes of men hung about in cars, whatever the time of day. How the neighbours came to be so very popular she'd often wondered.

'D'you know, I think next door is a brothel. Actually, I think it's a gay brothel.' Fran appeared suddenly at her door.

'Serious? In this neighbourhood? Surely not. Listen now, Frannie, I need your advice on what to wear.'

'Where are you going?'

'Jazz club in Soweto.'

'It'll probably be more my age-group then. Don't be too casual.'

'So why d'you think it's a brothel?'

'No, Megan. That ethnic stuff was okay straight after the election. Take it off. You're making me cringe.'

'Yes, but I also don't want to seem all dressed up and out-of-place ...'

'Well, the other day I saw these young guys hanging about. Rather gorgeous they were too.'

'Coloured guys? I've seen them.'

'So I thought maybe they were new neighbours and I didn't want them to think we were unfriendly in the white suburbs ... Meg-child, for God's sake file that ANC t-shirt in your archive drawer.'

Megan was grateful that Paul was ensconced in front of the rugby. How he would jeer to see her trying so hard. He thought it hypocritical to adapt his way of life to suit other people's cultural cues. He didn't think he had to do that for anyone.

'So I asked what they did. They giggled and said 'Shall we tell her' kind of thing. Then they said they were escorts.'

Stretching her mouth to apply lipstick, Megan allowed a small bubble of laughter to splash from between her lips.

'I didn't know what to say.'

'Ja, like: "You must meet such interesting people." '

Daniel came in, for once lively. The drag and shuffle of his feet was hardly perceptible. Megan leant to catch him in a hug. She liked kids more or less generally, but she had never really been able to relate to Daniel.

He submitted to her hug before dematerialising from her grasp. Melting as though he had no substance at all, he launched himself at his accustomed place on Fran's lap. She shifted slightly and let him, like a kangaroo making room for the cub which was growing too large for her pouch.

Tebogo would come no further than the gate. He was frightened of Fran's dog – an ancient labrador, more than a touch overweight, which Megan had ceased to regard. He had never done more than sleep and give the odd indolent woof at random passers-by.

'Nearly ready,' called Megan. 'Come in. He's fine. Don't jump or he'll know you're scared.'

'I can't,' he said.

She turned and gazed at him. That, more than anything, separated them suddenly. She had grown up with bounding, lollopping dogs, and those of her friends, while he had probably only known those that snarled behind suburban gates. It didn't help though – that sudden feeling of alienation. Their other differences, of upbringing, of experience, made him interesting. It was just this, suddenly.

She had once gone out with an English boy. In a country detached from the outside world, his accent had given him currency. But at the beach one day, he had been unable to scramble the sandstone cliffs in bare feet. Knowing it to be irrational, she had nonetheless despised him for it. She had known it to emerge from the buried part of her that was still the unreconstructed daughter of rugby players, large men who could fend off threats to lifestyle or women. She had never subscribed to that. She was different. And yet she, who could run across rocks barefoot, who could approach any Rottweiler with hands outstretched, struggled with this.

'Walk, just walk,' she said, words glossed with impatience. The dog lowered and bristled, gums slightly raised.

'Stay then, I won't be long,' she said, brittle with irritation – at his jumpiness, at herself, at the old dog who had decided all at once to fulfil every stereotype.

They drove to Soweto almost in silence. Perhaps he felt the same difference with her, now that he was home, passing commentary for the sightseer that she was.

'Orlando West,' he declared. 'The oldest part of Soweto.' They swept past a smoking skip and passed into the narrow streets. She had been in many townships since she was grown and could do as she pleased. She felt a familiarity in the chickens that scattered, fine-dusted before them, in the children kicking soccer balls and the young people leaning against walls.

She felt home again, as though this scene could be nowhere else on earth. Yet she felt alien too. She remembered it as a place forbidden – even by law, and certainly by her parents.

'Lots of building-on being done,' she said, to show that she was noticing. And saucily, with a sideways glance: 'Garden walls creeping up, aren't they? Almost as high as the honkies' walls.'

Tebogo exploded into his surprisingly childlike chortle. 'Oh yes. This here was a stronghold of the ANC. Street committees were strong. To this day, there are hardly any criminals here. But there are hit-and-run crimes from other areas. People are starting to get shit-scared.'

They drove past the desolate block rows of the Diepkloof hostel, and into Meadowlands. On the next corner a man lay on the verge, welding an exhaust to a great winged American car. His customer kicked idly at stones, waiting for him to be done.

Tebogo turned into a rain-rutted street, leaning from his window to greet a child tinkering with a go-kart. The kart had ancient pram wheels. She'd had a similar one herself as a child. Squeezing his Toyota between two Mercs, Tebs waved to the starched church ladies chattering past in red uniforms.

Kitchen chairs had been set up in the carport outside the back door. A small breeze just stirred the heat, distilled by the corrugated blue plastic over their heads. The breeze brought with it a dusting of grit from the mine-dump which imposed its chalky sides upon their lives and their gathering.

There was a red bottle-brush to the side of the house. Searing its blooms across the white wall, it gave almost no shade at all. Of course she had dressed all wrong. Mostly men, mostly in chinos, they mopped foreheads and sipped sun-warmed beer. The women were in suits, even jackets. Or they wore dresses with matching handbags. And there she was, disrespectful, in her jeans.

Her host was jovial, squeezing past the rose bushes with peanuts and sausage. He served her first, to her mortification. They seemed delighted to have her. Embarrassingly so. She wished they were able just to take her for granted. Wouldn't that be something.

Of course they discussed themselves and each other. When did South Africans not speak of politics, picking away at their lives and the way they lived now?

'I've been away,' she said. 'But I do think there's more mixing ...'

Almost to her surprise, they all agreed. She sometimes wondered if it weren't just her own private fantasy. She glanced at Tebogo. He was silent, his crooked arm angled proprietorially above her shoulder.

'There is a desire to mix,' proclaimed Phetole, standing declaratively astride.

His bottle cracked open with a hiss of spurting beer. 'Even among whites. I think they do want to come together.'

'Not like America. I hope we never get like them, the way they just want to be separate.' Linda had just been there, to study. Like Buli she thought.

She wondered where the hell Buli was. Fran had phoned her at work during the week and been told, right out of the blue, that she had left the company. But no doubt she would turn up.

She felt heartened by the discussion, and yet she wished they didn't have to speak of it. She wished they could discuss clothes or music ... anything. The jazz poured helter-skelter through massive speakers, their wires fed through the lounge window.

'It doesn't matter.' Phetole was proclaiming still. 'The desire's what's important. We'll never get it right now, I mean in this generation. But I think perhaps the next ...'

Megan excused herself quietly. She wandered into the kitchen to help carry plates, and perhaps to chat about furnishings, or even kids. But the women fell silent as she entered. And – 'No, no, no' – they wouldn't hear of her carrying.

Later that night, she lay in the dark hollow of Tebogo's arms, against his satin chest. She marvelled at how pale she appeared beside his dark limbs. Pushing the duvet aside, she demanded that he wonder at the beauty of their entwined flanks, till he broke into laughter and told her to stop. Reaching for the unaccustomed cushion of his hair, she felt a strange pleasure, as though this had always been intended – this coming together, this merging of differences.

The sex was fine. Good really. Just not astounding. She was tired, grimy from the heat and the grit, and he felt good inside her. What did it matter if he didn't raise the hairs on the back of her neck? So what if her nipples didn't reach for him as though they had life of their own?

'In Moscow ...' She had waited for them both to be still before asking for stories. That was when he led her into the charmed circle of those who hadn't been too young.

'I was a communist. It was like a religion, so fervent. Everything was for the cause. For the collective good ...'

She drowsed in his warmth. He didn't mind that her eyes were closed. He knew she was listening.

'And then, one day we were taken to the Bolshoi. I had never seen anything like it. It was like ... it was a revelation to me, that people could do such things. 'It was that, more than anything else, which started me questioning. Before that I just believed. After that, I began to see that if people could produce such beauty, they were the most important things. An individual – that was what was special.

'Since then ... that's what I believe in. I'm a humanist, I suppose. I've lost the rest. I believe in people – that's all.'

'They're all Mercs and 4x4s, you know. Have you noticed that about your brothel creepers?' Penny had popped in for exactly one minute to bring Fran a book.

'Ja,' said Fran, mixing something for Daniel's supper. 'But it's the ones with darkened windows that give me the creeps. Quick glass of wine, Pen? Megs, you want one?'

'Okay, but I must be out of here in ten minutes.' Penny perched on the kitchen table. 'I wandered up the road a bit and one of them actually had babyseats in his car.'

'You know, I don't mind at all that we're no longer madly prosecuting sex workers,' muttered Fran. 'But why they have to set up a brothel right here, I don't know.'

'Interestingly, this oke came out while I was wandering back so I asked him exactly that.'

'What did he say?' Paul came in, loosening his tie.

'He said: "This is the new South Africa. We have a constitutional right." '

'What – to run a brothel?' Francesca exclaimed, a flair of animation searing the papery calm that had suddenly overwhelmed her when Paul entered. 'Since when's that become a human right?'

'It's the bloody mentality in this country now,' said Paul. He was so vehement about things that he always seemed to be shouting. 'People think they can do what they like. And no-one's got any standards anymore. Look at the road – the municipality came and dug this great hole ...'

'I saw,' Penny said. 'They've left this great pothole. Paul, do you really think standards are dropping? I mean, do you think those things – you know, I mean the basic infrastructure ...'

'Oh Penny, for God's sake,' Francesca broke in. 'Don't be so paranoid. You sound just like one of the school mothers'.

'I am a school mother,' Penny laughed, a touch sheepish.

'You know,' said Paul, 'two years on I find this country really inspiring. It inspires me to consult the New Zealand embassy about the points you get for being an engineer.'

'Oh, don't tell me I've dropped in on yet another bloody how-standards-are-dropping discussion. I'll just have to leave again.' Buli stood in the kitchen doorway. Beauty must have let her in.

'Buli.' Francesca allowed her irritation to show – unusual for her. 'Where the hell have you been? I haven't been able to reach you.'

'In a minute, girl ... Paul, be a doll and pass that wine ... and shut the fuck up about potholes. We've always had potholes. Why didn't you lot go on bleating about how shit the standards were then?'

'Ah, but then we knew the government was shit.' Rolling up his sleeves, Paul was all rough charm now. He clearly liked Francesca's friends, maintaining a robust camaraderie with Penny and a chivalrous flirtation with Buli. Megan he treated gingerly, as though her English sojourn had given her the quality of a rare artefact that he hadn't quite got the hang of yet.

'So where've you been?' Megan's curiosity had got the better of her. Francesca appeared to be maintaining a hurt silence next to the microwave. 'And what's with this stuff we've been hearing about you leaving your job?'

Standing by the window, Buli appeared ethereal enough to slip through the cracks into the dark.

'It's not a big deal. I'll get another job easily. I've already got a couple of interviews lined up.' With a frail attempt at heartiness she added: 'Don't worry, girlfriends. I'm fine.'

'I just wanted to know you were okay,' Francesca added. She had always been quick to forgive, even as a child. 'I'm going away in a couple of days.'

'That's why I popped in. You said you were going to the first Truth and Reconciliation hearings and I saw they were due to start. I wish I could come with you.'

'Christ, I don't know why,' said Paul, filling their glasses.

'Paul!' uttered Penny on a scandalised gasp. Penny often hid her serious intent protectively beneath a derisive tone. Megan was growing wise to her now.

'Bloody hell, Penny. Don't be so fucking PC. Look, I knew what was going on. I never denied it. I just don't feel like wallowing in it anymore. I've had enough of bloody constant guilt. Can't we let it go now?'

'Poor lambkin,' said Buli. Paul shot an arm out, grabbed her around the waist and held fast against her feeble struggle. Laughing and manhandling, he tickled her until she shrieked in unpractised animation.

Placing Daniel's supper on the table, Francesca turned and smiled.

'Put my friend down, Paul ... and by the way, I never made it to the ATM. Have you got any money?'

'Ja, that's all I'm good for these days, isn't it?'

'Absolutely.' Francesca's voice rumbled with amusement, but she retained her stillness. Surely this unaccustomed Paul must remind Fran of the young Paul who had courted her. Megan remembered his gruff courtliness in drawing Francesca through her difficult times. That old Paul popped out so seldom now. Pity, thought Megan. But, she supposed that happened in real-life relationships. Not to her, though. She would never let it happen to her.

'What d'you need it for?' Paul was searching pockets.

'Don't be silly, Paul,' said Penny. 'You know she never leaves home without money. What if she came upon an emergency – like a beggar at a robot.'

'Ja, that I know about my wife. Even the blind beggars see her coming.'

THE MAN

The morning's heat had slowly siphoned off as the day moved through its motions. Seagulls wailed into the wind, which had picked up since morning.

Rolene was trying, you had to say that for her. Brow tangled by tension, she was intent upon struggling through this picnic. The man could see her tautness in the jerk of the hand that slopped the tea just slightly upon the sand. But then, it was she who had insisted on it. His wife did things like that sometimes. Meek to the point of pathology, she could at times be obdurate about the strangest things.

He was fishing, of course. Sitting some way from them towards the blow-hole, he liked to watch it all quietly in his unmoved and unmoving way. His clutter of boys milled about her, churning the beach and raising a sandy mist that dusted across her basket. Unused to these more conventional family rites, uncomfortable in the inactivity and in their adolescent selves, they were impatient to be gone. Held only by the last threads of umbilical duty, they grasped and gulped and squabbled among themselves.

Never quite part of them, he knew nonetheless that he was there to protect them. His life had run its strange course. It was his boys' world now, and he remained in it only to stand sentinel over their long scramble to manhood.

They were so very like the turtles he and his brother had lain awake to see hatch one summer's night in Maputaland. He had watched their over-confident rush to leave their shells and reach the sea. As the thick night air did its best to swaddle and disarm, they had watched the gulls pick them off one by one. He had felt that if only he could stand before them, if only he could flap great primeval wings at all the predators of sky and sea, he could perhaps have saved more of them. They hadn't contemplated all the dangers. Tumbling boldly across the sand, they never considered their shells might not be as tough as they believed them to be.

How very young they had been, he and his brother. That was when their world had been a different place, and possibilities had hung about them in thick bunches, ripe for the picking. But he wouldn't draw those two boys into the present, not just now.

He watched his boys stuff last mouthfuls of cake into already full mouths and they were gone, shirts flapping in the wind. Their legs flashed through the haze of sunlight that still glazed the spray. And then there was silence – a full silence fattened by the cries of gulls and the breathing of sea.

Glancing back, he saw Rolene scrape rigid fingers through her hair before slowly beginning to retrieve the cups strewn across the sand. She did this picnic planning occasionally and each time he felt her disappointment. It was as though she had the need to assert at least the appearance of a normal family. But would she never realise? What on earth constituted normal in this Godforsaken country?

He blamed this latest bout of picnicking on the TRC. Why people could never leave well alone ... Why could they not adopt a stillness, at least now with all that was past. Life hadn't turned out the way he had once thought it could, but he flowed with its tides anyway. Somehow he managed to bypass its rips and drift quietly in its shallows. And he was content there.

Why did people feel it necessary to swim so purposefully into the current and then kick against it? Only exhaustion came from splashing desperately back towards the past.

His youngest had come home this week with the news that they were to produce an assignment on the first hearings of the TRC in East London. Rolene had flustered about the kitchen, stuttering about not knowing of such things. He had felt himself grow cold as she glanced towards him, but she had thought better of asking.

'Do you know anything about them, Dad?' the boy had asked him anyway, catching the direction of her gaze. 'It's amazing it's all starting here in the Eastern Cape, hey? Sir says that ...'

'I thought we were in the "New" South Africa now,' he had said. 'Why don't you tell your teacher to rather set you an assignment that concerns the future. We've problems enough there, for God's sake.'

He had walked out then and headed for his rocky shelf, where he escaped every late afternoon of his life.

He could hardly see his sons now through the shimmer of sun against sea. Rolene had begun to labour her basket heavily back toward the house. She never seemed to enjoy the beach much, treading almost distastefully through the sand.

He enjoyed being left alone. He didn't have long before the dog-walkers and strollers would be out. He sometimes thought that if he listened intently enough, if he drew himself beyond the great sighs of the sea, he should be able to hear the tiny gulps of sea anemones, or the bubbling breaths of crabs.

Perhaps he might just take a turn past East London when these so-called human rights hearings began. Why not? It would be interesting to see if all this wallowing could possibly be as appalling as he imagined.

MEGAN

Megan allowed the harried city to carry her through the week Fran was away. Constantly shifting, the city sifted over the days with the swiftness of dunes powdering over the bones of the city that had come before.

Each day she would look in at Tebogo's office and feel ... she honestly wasn't sure. He was a good man. Wiry and smaller than the white men she knew, he was a product of the city's hind-tit. Yet even as she felt the predictable wash of guilt and compassion, she was unable to consider exactly what it was they had together. But why should she? Why should she have to, just yet? And besides, there was always so much to be done.

Not that much was required of her at home. Beauty calmly packed Daniel off to school each day and filled his afternoons with friends – or rather, the children of his mother's friends. It was Megan's furtive thought that perhaps Francesca should go away more often.

Francesca had always struggled with the guilt of leaving Daniel. But this time she'd been distinctly odd about going to East London. Even odder than she'd seemed in the past weeks. She had snapped at Megan for asking a simple question about how it felt returning to the city that had detained her.

Francesca phoned on Wednesday, before Paul got home. Megan heard her struggling through a monosyllabic conversation with Daniel, who hated the telephone. She grabbed the receiver before he could drop it and run.

'So how's the TRC?'

'Oh God, Megan ... but first tell me, how's everything there?'

'Absolutely calm and perfect. You should go away more often. But tell me now. I want to know everything about the TRC.'

'I hardly know if I can ... It feels so strange to speak of it, as though no-one who isn't here could possibly understand.'

'Francesca, if you start with that now ...'

'No, no, Meg-child, it's not you. It's this place. It's the intensity, I suppose. The emotions. It makes you feel odd ... altered in some way.'

'Ja, but I ...'

'No, I know you're interested. It just makes it hard to relate to people normally – people who aren't here. Like a dislocation, as though this is the only reality and all those people out there, mouthing and gesticulating, aren't even aware of it.'

'You okay?'

'Yes, yes. Sorry. It's just so incredible, I think, for anyone to take in. Even the journalists are weeping.'

'And the stories? Are they really awful? I've followed the coverage, but ...'

'No, it couldn't give you a fraction of the atmosphere. It makes you wonder how people can speak of this stuff – and how we can hear it – and still stay sane.'

'You must have tons of material then.'

'You know there was this woman ... oh God, there're so many. How do these women bear the burden of their tragedies?'

'Francesca, are you sure you're okay?'

'Yes, of course. This isn't about me. This is about them. This one woman particularly ...'

Megan heard her name called from outside. There it was again, with a rattling at the small gate.

'Fran? I think I'm going to have to ...'

'No, it's fine,' said Francesca. 'I can't tell her story over the phone anyway. I'll tell you when I'm home.'

It was Nicholas, who could vaporise from your life as though he had never been and then materialise just as easily. Oh God, the smell of him, the roughness of his shirt, the way he dimpled and crinkled when he grinned. They stood, he with his hands laced behind her head, and laughed gently at the shake of their fingers. Nothing else. No moralising self leapt to her shoulder to upbraid her. Nothing.

In her tiny room, he unbuttoned her and pulled her to him as though he belonged. He entered her and enclosed her as though there were no way he could ever press himself close enough. At the end she cried.

'Did I hurt you?' he whispered. 'I was ... it was a bit savage.'

'No. No, but you'll leave me now.'

'No,' he said, his eyes urgent. 'I came for the evening. We'll be together.'

He had a new car. It took her by surprise but then, why not? He was making money. Why should he not spend it?

'Oh,' he said, flapping a hand at her. 'My old car was fucked.'

'What is this? A Volvo?'

'Hey,' he said and shrugged a sheepish shoulder. 'I couldn't buy a Merc or BM or something. This ... well, it seemed more acceptable.' He laughed as he opened the door for her, camping up courtly. His laugh held the smallest lilt of self-mockery.

He took her to Yeoville. There was something worrying him, or he wouldn't have come. He parked carefully in the jumble of double-parked black okes who hung about the street, mid-conversation or mid-negotiation.

Not much remained of the Yeoville she remembered from her youth – blasé and mixed and so proud of itself for being anti-apartheid. It had been so cool, with its slouch of sophisticates, its mellow blues and African jazz.

It had seemed wicked enough for all of them, but never really dangerous.

Now it had a risky air, a dark silent periphery of figures on the edges of vision, of blatant transactions and the primal beat of a third-world town.

'Some Swazi, ma bra?' The man had slipped from the welling shadows of a pool hall.

'No thanks, bru.' Nicholas flashed a grin as he led her through the drug merts, past the pool halls and bars.

She liked it. She enjoyed the newness of it. The other Yeoville had been from the old world that Fran's lefties still tried so hard to inhabit. Nicholas said this was the real city. It was what Jo'burg was really all about.

The clubs were slick and shiny with bright young things. Dozens of women seemed to know Nicholas. They were all young and exotic – audaciously sensuous, or brazen in bisexual chic. She felt young and vogueish and African. Nicholas fought his way through the crush of drinks before squatting beside a table of Nigerians.

'Howzit, bru ...' and he was off on a discussion of attitudes and unions and how the locals viewed them. She gazed out over the street, patrolled by jollers and gangsters, thieves and whores. Men strolled by selling leather belts and watches. And, outside the squat shops, the ubiquitous trade in wire sculptures hustled passers-by.

This had all been Jewish once. Men in sidecurls and hats had strolled up here to the draper's shop and the dry-cleaners, or further up to Feigel's, the kosher delicatessen. Feigel's had moved now, along with the shtetl it served, to the slightly safer north.

'Baby, if you were my woman I'd give you a big squeeze,' some guy in a baseball cap muttered into her ear. She thanked him with an amicable hug. He mimed a drink, and she shook her head, looking around for Nicholas. Slipping his hand from his pocket, he proffered a small packet of white powder and a credit card. Megan dithered. She didn't want to seem uncool.

Nicholas was there, very cool and mellow, slipping her from the situation with a 'Sharp sharp, ma bra'.

'I don't think you should get into that coke scene,' he said, a touch severely.

'It's decadent. And I reckon that guy's a Nigerian. Of course it's a stereotype, but these ous can't get work here. What do you think most of them do?'

Nicholas left her with a friend while he struggled through the crush to order their drinks. She was amused and slightly flattered by his protectiveness.

'Joseph,' said some guy in Rasta crochet. 'From Ethiopia. You smoke ganga?'

'Sometimes.'

'Here is a little present.' He said, pressing a joint into her hand. She was touched.

'Got a little present, did you?' asked Nicholas's friend. 'I'd sidle up to him too, but ...' he sighed, 'I don't think I'm Joseph's type.'

'But it was sweet of him,' she said, laughing at his expression.

'I think,' he said gravely, 'that Joseph is new in town. And keen to develop a grateful clientele.'

Nicholas wanted to leave. He paid off the guy that had hung about pretending to watch his car.

'Thanks, bru,' he muttered, but rubbed at the spot where the guy had been leaning.

He stopped outside her house. It was icy with the engine off and the heat dissipating through the windows. A breeze slithered through the dark, slicing at the jacarandas, which scattered their leaves in surrender.

She was a little afraid to ask if he would come in. But it didn't seem likely now.

'I'm caught in a different game, Megan. It's MVAWU, see? They've declared a wage dispute. You see, the problem is that we have a chunk of shares in SA Investment Holdings.'

'But that's not your union, is it? And I don't see the problem with owning shares in SA Investment. You're making money for your union. That's your job.'

'Exactly. I mean, it's not even just the money. It's empowering. It's giving some control in business to those who've never had it.'

'Absolutely.' She would take a different line from that cow if it killed her. 'I definitely think the unionists can make business more moral.'

He lit a Camel and with one hand, pulled her against him. His jacket smelt of old smokes and musty meetings. He took a couple of drags and allowed a hand to drift through her hair.

'Except that now we own a piece of SA Investment. And they own Tirelli Tyres, down Eastern Cape way. And now the guys down there, MVAWU, are in dispute with Tirelli.'

'So what? It's not your union.'

'Yes but ...' His hand tightened involuntarily on her hair. 'they're expecting solidarity. They kind of expect it, with their buddies on the board.'

He flicked his stompie into the street where it glowed briefly before catherine-wheeling across the road in the stiff little breeze. She wished he would roll the window up again. Nicholas paid no heed to the stories of hijackings and holdups. There seemed to be a million cars outside tonight. A black Merc hunched furtively on their pavement, its windows darkened. Creepy.

'But you'll support them, won't you? Isn't that part of the moral reason?'

'No, bugger it. They're pushing it too far. You can't think that now your chinas are on the board, you can push far enough to kill the cash cow.'

'So, what ...'

'I don't know. But I reckon it's my responsibility to protect our investment. I can't just support something that's going to destroy that.'

'Oh.' What else was there to say? He was in a different league now.

His loyalties had never been tested like this. All she could do now was kiss him, perhaps taste the disillusion as he did.

'Oh Jesus.' He pulled back, looking suddenly tired. 'Sometimes it wears you down. All this.' He swept his hand across the street, where the dog across the road had begun howling at the gate.

Megan lowered her head to her fieldworker's report as Tebogo approached. She just couldn't see him tonight. Not after Nicholas.

'I have everything for tonight,' he said above her head. 'It is tonight, nê?' Oh shit, she had totally forgotten – *umnqushu* and spicy mutton at his place. He had insisted on cooking her childhood favourite, despite the fact that she had never once cooked for him.

His head cocked and his smile almost coquettish, he appeared more light-hearted than she had ever seen him. Why did she have to feel responsible for this now too?

She drove there straight from work. Tebogo lived in Berea – a no-man's flatland, eaten away by the decay of urban poverty. He could afford to live in a suburb, or at least a house. He spoke with such longing of his mud-caked Diepkloof days – kicking balls on land scattered with the litter of impoverishment. Yet he wouldn't live in Soweto. And he snorted at the picture of himself in a white suburb. So it was here – neither white nor black. Flat after flat of crowded survival, loud with the smell of curry and pap, redolent with the blare of ghetto blasters.

She ran up the front stairs quickly, glancing about her. There was a crowd of kids hanging about her car. But what was she going to do? Ask them? Excuse me, could you possibly inform me of your intentions towards my car?

Tebogo opened after one knock. He had a dishcloth over one shoulder and she could smell the mutton. He stood aside for her to pass, all mock-subservient. She hated when he did that. She walked to the window to check on the kids. They were still hanging about, but her car hadn't moved.

Tebogo appeared at her elbow. 'Shows how little has changed, doesn't it?'

It irritated her suddenly. What did he expect, two years down the line? 'I thought you told me we should be thrilled to live with the making of so much history?'

'I never said enough had changed.'

She stared out of the window, seething. She knew this. She agreed with him. So why should she feel so defensive? He gave a little snort, hunching his shoulders and pressing his hands deep into his jeans pocket. 'We don't know each other very well, do we?'

She glanced up quickly.

'What do you mean?'

'We don't talk enough, perhaps.'

'We talk all the time.'

'That's not talking. That's stories. Ah no, it's okay, I do like to tell you stories. It's been my life. But I also know it's what keeps you interested.'

She reached out a hand, but no longer knew how to touch him. She'd had a kind of careless control – the callous power of the girl who knew she was wanted more than she wanted back. But now she knew that she needed Tebogo. She couldn't be left alone with this city, and with Nicholas.

They gulped their food in silence. What a waste. It had been intended as such an act of love. Taking her hand, he led her to the bedroom. He seemed different, less tentative in his touching. Their love-making was slow, but more emphatic than it had been. Maybe it would be okay, she thought. Maybe it would still be fine.

'You know,' he said, turning away from her to reach for his drink. 'I am grateful to have been part of something great. But now, instead of a cause, we have a bond and payments on the car.'

'Isn't that real life? I mean, it's not such a terrible place. Even if things aren't right yet?'

'You want me to say that things have changed. You want a happy ending.'

'But things have changed.'

'Of course they have. When I came back I was amazed that I could go to a white man's toilet. And I can be with you, go anywhere. That is astonishing, after the way we grew up.'

'I know it's not enough ...'

'But I look at squatter shacks and I feel bitter. Is this what I was fighting for? So people could still suffer?'

'But you can't expect ...'

'I know. I must learn to look intellectually, not with my emotions, because these things take time. But you know what worries me? Even in the old dispensation there were white people who didn't make it. Now there's a black elite developing, with fancy cars and cells and maids of their own. And in the end, they will look after their own. And the same thing will happen all over again.'

She didn't like to think these things. They had once been a nation scattered – heroes, pariahs and victims. Since her return, she had seen the divisions fall away. They greeted each other in lifts, smiling because they knew it would all be well, at last. She wondered why it couldn't stay like that. Why did old resentments have to rise again, and imperfections stand out to be picked at again and again?

'Were you with Nicholas?'

It shocked her, the suddenness of it. She felt the slight panic rise to prickle at her forehead.

'Yes.'

He didn't say anything, but nodded.

She made herself coffee, and some for Tebogo. Slipping tentatively into his office, she left his coffee on the desk while he spoke on the phone.

It was a fragile thing. Yet it still existed. It saddened her that she might never again see that light-hearted side of him. She wished she could be all that he wanted her to be. She wanted to make up to him for everything in the world that had made light-heartedness hard for him. She would never, ever see Nicholas again.

Her phone rang, startling her. It was Paul.

'Megan?'

Megan was instantly wary. Paul did not phone. He wasn't the type to phone his china for a chat.

'Megan. D'you think you could get away from work? I can't ... I've got this board meeting. I can't just walk out ...'

'What's the matter?'

'It's Francesca. She only got back last night, but I don't know what's wrong with her. I had to go and fetch her this morning. I had to walk out of my presentation.'

'What happened?'

'Apparently she collapsed in the supermarket. The paramedics said she hyperventilated or something. Anyway, she fainted. But look, Megan, I really can't afford to take more time today.'

'Is she at home?'

'She's on her bed. But I just ... I don't know what to do about this kind of thing.'

FRANCESCA

'Lizalise idinga lakho ... Lizalise idinga lakho ...' Palm trees stalked the city hall, slightly ridiculous in its colonial pomp. In many ways, East London was such a little town.

'Lizalise idinga lakho ... Lizalise idinga lakho ...' The singing grew louder as Francesca reached the steps, where she paused to look around her again.

Francesca didn't feel up to sifting her muddled feelings about the place – not their home town, but close enough. The heat and hibiscus blossoms, the humidity that buzzed in clouds of bougainvillea. Small, stocky streets, fragrant with a barefoot childhood, yet malevolent with a brutality of frontier purpose.

It was a place of warmth, where it was good to be a daughter. It was a place of inherited memories, of ancestors dumped in this forsaken, this achingly beautiful no-man's land. Meagre in imagination, rich in legend, they had been the Empire's shield against the Xhosa-speaking people.

It was inevitable that, in another dangerous age, the Eastern Cape should form the passionate nucleus of another uprising. And perhaps also inevitable that the region's reprisals should be so cruel. It was a place of blood, dust, warmth and love. But it was also the place she had been detained.

It was dark inside the hall, after the bright street. High above her, dust squirmed to escape the tongues of light that lapped over their heads.

'Lizalise idinga lakho ... Lizalise idinga lakho ...' The forgiveness of sins makes a person whole.

The people filing into the hall. The crowds, mainly black. The smells – heat and sweat, urban Omo and rural woodsmoke.

Her cameraman and soundman were off getting cutaways somewhere. The actual footage they would buy later from the SABC, the official feed.

The victims filed in while the hymn was being sung. Francesca noticed the woman while the commissioners were greeting those who were to give testimony. Other women in doeks or hats bent awed faces to the ground and sketched small curtseys of greeting. But that woman glared out at the Archbishop until it was he who turned from her.

'I want to put my appreciation to this Commission,' the woman said. 'I am Noxolo Sedumile, a daughter from the Piko family at Inymakwe.'

She smouldered in the darkened hall. But as the morning progressed, her story melted from her like heated wax until, by lunchtime, the flame within her was almost quenched.

'As time went on,' the woman told them, 'I met an activist there called Pabala Sedumile. My husband was fighting for human rights. We had children. The first one was Tumelo, the second born was Thembisile.'

'Now let's have a look at Thembisile,' said the commissioner appointed to be her questioner. 'He is the one you are representing today. He went into exile after passing his matric. Did he come and say to you, "Mum I'm fighting for the freedom of this land"? And then he went to Angola, then East Germany?'

'Yes, it's so. Then he was back in the country, and in and out of jail.'

'It became clear at the time something was going to happen to him, is that so?'

'Yes, it is so. Shortly thereafter, Thembisile was released. Then, one Thursday my daughter called and told my husband Thembisile has been injured by bullets. I had a premonition of this. I dreamt that this child of mine was looking into death's eyes. I dreamt this on the Tuesday.'

The woman paused to sip at her water. Her tale had struck flashpoints of emotion through the hall, yet she seemed unmoved by it. Her face was pressed smooth by the pressure of all she held inside.

'When I saw him I knew it.'

She was silent so long the commissioner intervened with a quiet: 'Knew what, Mama?'

The woman showed no sign, yet Francesca could feel the weight of those words in her throat. The heaviness of lifting them through her mouth. She sensed the tears Mrs Sedumile should have been weeping for herself. She felt no release, but she wept for the woman standing before her. Perhaps somewhere, sometime, someone would do the same for her. For all the tears she was unable to weep. For all that she could never forgive.

'The doctor, he said the bullet only touched Thembisile's head. I was so happy for that ... until I see his eyes. His eyes are trapped. I see at once how my child suffered inside that body.'

'He was still alive, but he was no longer the same, is that it, Mama?'

'I took him home. The doctors tell me Thembisile is still inside that body. But the body has become a cage. Deep inside his eyes, I can see all the things he can once do ...'

'He couldn't do them anymore?'

'He can do nothing. He is like a child. His hands they shake and flap when he tries to eat. I see him cry with the hardness of trying.'

Francesca felt the tears hot on her face, but strangely cold where they fell upon her hands. They were still the other woman's tears. Not her own. Certainly not her own. This was not Daniel's story – and Daniel so scantly affected that she had not earned the right to grieve.

She could do nothing for this woman – give her no comfort, lessen none of her pain. And yet perhaps there was just one thing she could do for her in the isolation of that loss. One small human thing. She could listen. She could listen to her story and grant her all she had to give in these circumstances –

a mother's empathy for her grief.

'We went on in this way for two, three months.' The woman counted off the months on her fingers. 'And then one day when I come in the house, I can feel there is a cold wind and I go into the kitchen and I close the door. From there I am walking down the passage.'

'Thembisile's room – it was opposite yours?'

'Yes, it's opposite mine. Well, I can see his door is open and right from there I can see everything is full of bullet holes.'

'And Thembisile?'

'He was dead.'

There was silence while the commissioner waited, to be sure she had finished. She said nothing more.

'During your testimony,' he said at last, 'you have the right to make any appeal to the Commissioner.'

'I will ask only two things,' she said quietly. 'Firstly I'd like to find out who is the person who removed his brain and filled the skull with plastic and papers. And secondly that person should state how he could do that horrible thing.'

'Lizalise idinga lakho ...' The forgiveness of sins makes a person whole. She was sick of the way that song stuck in her head. She was sick of the heavy-handed symbolism of it.

Francesca was doing a documentary on women and forgiveness. The woman had been a good subject. Her story had been profoundly moving on a personal level, and yet there had been others. Tales as harrowing, sorrow as entrenched. Why did this particular story have to follow Francesca back and stalk her through the supermarket?

If that woman could forgive then perhaps ... But perhaps forgiveness would always come too hard and too late for those who needed it as much as they needed to grant it.

She pushed her trolley through the supermarket aisles, yet even that most prosaic of duties lacked the ordinariness to drag her back to earth. The woman and her story had shaken her, dragging her beyond privacy to witness another's anguish.

Considering the comparative aptitude of crackle pops and dino hoops to tempt Daniel out of bed in the morning, Francesca felt herself hyperventilating. Contesting the possibilities of sausages or chops for supper, she felt the heat rise to her face and the nausea to her throat.

As the dark ambushed her from the periphery of her being, Francesca understood that it was about herself too. In that hot Eastern Cape town, the woman's story had seemed stitched to her own in a patchwork of light and dark, of guilt and sorrow. It was part of the same great tale.

Francesca could smell her own warmth on her pillow – a straw-coloured, East Cape morning smell. Shifting slightly, she could still catch the pink-tongued smell that little boys have while they are still kin to puppies. Daniel had his spot, his hermit shell of pillows and mother's body into which he curled each morning in a last-ditch bid to escape – from school and all the hard things life threw at him.

Francesca preferred not to venture beyond her own circle of childhood pillows. Surely, when she had first met him, her husband had not held so very definite a smell about him. He seemed to exude something foreign – metal and machinery perhaps, or the working smell of tasks and industry.

When she had met him, he had seemed to have a no-nonsense smell about him, the practical odour of day and doing. She had been attracted to that at a time when the very scent of her seemed in danger of disappearing. It was only after Daniel that Paul's essence had grown stronger, becoming slightly more alien with each year that passed.

He had stood alongside her earlier, suited and stilted, his embarrassment feeding hers. She wished the supermarket hadn't phoned him. The way he had thanked the supermarket manager with excruciating masculine solidarity. It was as though they had bonded over this shame they had, if not shared, at least understood in some manly way.

The thing was, she felt the shame too. It was such an idiotic thing to have happened. The worst was that she suspected there was a piece of her that had wished to collapse.

She resented the way it could all still affect her and yet ... perhaps she had somehow longed for someone to understand, or perhaps just to listen. Paul never had. Penny and Buli, with their tangled best-friend smell, almost, almost did.

The sins of the mothers ... they were buried with the past she herself could never unearth. She didn't want or expect them to understand the atavistic guilt she felt over Daniel. It was her grief that needed expression now. It was all the unshed tears over the hard world into which she had brought this fragile little boy. No-one seemed able to allow her that moment of mourning over her loss of the perfect child.

Oh, she knew they were only trying to make her feel better. But she felt her teeth grit each time she was told 'you could hardly tell', and that it really didn't matter. Anyone could see that it did.

It had been mounting for some time. But of course it had taken the Eastern Cape to dig it all up again. That and the truth commission, with its aura of stories being told. Where it seemed one's greatest pain, and possibly one's greatest shame, could be ritually laid down.

It was right that the hearings should begin there. It had always been there, somehow, that the centre of things lay. Her country's past turmoil had grown from its infancy there. But it was also where she had conceived her own bitter unrest, in a prison cell.

'You okay?' Megan stood in the doorway, gawky and uncertain.

'No, I'm fine. Really.'

'What happened, Frannie?'

'Oh, it was pathetic really. I don't know. I forgot to breathe or something. Don't make a big thing of it.'

Francesca breathed, concentrating on it, hearing it ripple through her limbs. How could she have been so stupid as to let this affect her again? She had watched her husband walling it away over the years, and she had known she had to be strong.

'Well, I think I'll go back to work now,' he had said the afternoon Daniel was diagnosed, and she had known she was not permitted to dwell. She had to be strong.

'Well ... okay.' Megan was clearly uncomfortable – not knowing what the hell to do with this excruciating level of emotion. 'Can I make you some Rooibos?'

'No, for God's sake. I'm not an invalid. I'd like strong coffee.'

Francesca spent the week trailing about, not sick and yet not feeling entirely well. Eventually Penny insisted that Francesca attend some book launch with her. The author was a friend of hers. And what the hell, she said. They needed to get out and jol a bit.

Penny knew her so well. Francesca loved her son. She loved him with a depth of guilt and hope and fear that was far too complex for simple pleasure. But sometimes she needed to forget him. And Paul she would forget tonight too, with his seeming coping, his daily ability to make her feel inept and inadequate.

Discovering her cameraman and soundman she paused, awash with friends and connections and people she hardly knew. She felt the flight of her hands, quickened by freedom. She was enjoying this. She felt a different person when released from having to protect, to defend, and to hide.

Who had declared her grown-up enough to cope with a child like Daniel? Sometimes she needed to forget that she was wife to a man who couldn't speak about his son. She needed to behave in a way that was unmotherly, as though she had never given birth to the anxiety and guilt that had burst, bloody and blue and too quiet, from her body those five years ago.

And perhaps they all needed to forget that they feared for their futures. Trapped in her role as optimist, she could never speak of it. Yet sometimes she also felt the fear.

She found Penny among the fawning boys she always kept about her.

Francesca held close to her. She felt her friend enjoying their joint power to draw and hold people.

'You are okay, aren't you?' Penny muttered at one point. 'Hey, of course you are.'

The sound system crackled. Francesca half-turned and found herself colliding softly against someone's belly. It was Martin.

Martin had a way of dimpling, without breaking into a full smile. But he also had a poignant little tic that played beside his mouth. It made him seem reassuringly flawed, like a comfortably worn toy.

On the podium, someone was introducing the journalist and the political analyst who had written yet another book about what was to become of them all. This was one of those launches that everyone attended. They stood and sipped as the authors set out all the scenarios, all the possibilities that might befall them.

'Do you like him?' Penny whispered into her ear.

'Yes ... I don't know.'

'Of course you do.' Penny gave a curt nod.

'But I'm not going to do anything about it.'

Penny shrugged luxuriantly.

'And that,' said the political analyst from the podium, 'is the way we could go in this country ... unless we take heed now. And unless the government takes heed.'

In that moment of relieved applause, Francesca felt that everyone in the room tasted the tiny hope, and swallowed the fear that they might not in fact take heed. Then they were hustling for drinks, frenetic groups forming and re-forming. And no-one discussed the oracle anymore.

She and Martin flirted with strangers, with friends and with each other. There was a charge between them that sparked through her fingers and made her legs restless. She had lost Penny to a group of company executives. Thobela and Fuzile, her crew, she had lost to a crowd of black guys, all sharp creases and haircuts.

When mingling melted to intimacy, they still separated out like this. For comfort's sake, she supposed. For the reassurance of shared language, of upbringing and expectations. It was hardly a surprise, when you considered how it had been just five years before. If they still mixed with resolve and some difficulty, surely they were permitted to be learning still.

There was a party afterwards. She heard it passed through the groups like a broken telephone. Somewhere in Bertrams ... The crowd spilt outward like grains of rice from an overturned caddy. The mall echoed with their footsteps, and was silent.

High over the hollowed south of the city, people cluttered the balcony. Far beneath them, homes scattered the green maw of the valley, wide and wild and toothed by distant mine-dumps.

To the right of them the city thrust its brash profile into the teeth of the dark. Rough and ready towers shouldered the skyscrapers behind Ponte – Coca Cola branded across its belly.

Martin pushed through the crowd to lean against the railing alongside her. It felt good. Almost too good ... But perhaps she didn't have to think that through tonight.

He spoke about his work as a long-term consultant to the Department of Labour. It felt good to be confided in. It warmed her that this man, with his heavy mantle of political credibility, should speak as though he really cared what she thought.

'But why aren't you joining the throngs of short-term consultants making heaps of money?' she teased.

'Probably because I'm stupid,' he said and laughed.

'I don't think you're stupid.'

Thobela grabbed her hand through the haze of cigarettes and the reek of splifs. 'Dance,' he said.

'Breyani in the kitchen,' someone shouted as Penny and a couple of young black women joined them. Jiving to an old Merry Nightingales song, they became chaffingly competitive until they fell about laughing.

It was chilly at the balcony rail, where she returned like a homing pigeon. You could smell winter in the musty wool of the boys' jerseys and jackets.

'Oh God, isn't this just exquisite?'

She turned at the sound of Megan's voice. She and Tebogo were standing viewstruck, further along the balcony. Only Jo'burg people ever said things like that. How fast Megan had assimilated their quirky idea of beauty.

'Makes you pleased you didn't emigrate, doesn't it?' Martin muttered and she warmed to him, lightened by his peculiarly Jo'burg sentimentality. It was an acquired taste, this city. There was nothing gentle about its aspects. It was rough and brusque, assaulted by contrasts, battered by ironies.

Megan had an almost contented light to her, shivering and cuddling up to Tebs. He was good for her. She really hoped they would last.

Francesca wandered off in search of wine, leaving Martin and Henry to hatch brave new ideas. In this society made small by division, she found herself entangled in the almost tactile delight they all took in incessant discussion of each other.

She returned to find Buli had rocked up, late as usual. She was working for one of the new cellphone companies, she told Francesca triumphantly – 'I told you I'd have a job before you knew it.'

Buli seemed scattered, leaping between topics and people as though they were stepping stones over a treacherous void. With much girlish giggling, she flashed and flirted with Martin before dragging Tebogo around to face her.

'Come here,' she uttered imperiously. 'Come and flirt with me for a while.'

Francesca knew this mood, when Buli's unhappiness reeled into frenzy. There was no way to calm her. Like a toy wound too tight, Buli would spin until eventually she ran down of her own accord.

Turning to Buli, Tebogo first reached out a reassuring hand to Megan who smiled uncertainly, caught on the sidelines.

'Nombulelo,' Tebogo said as Buli stumbled against him. 'Uzevakahle?' – 'You don't seem well.'

Catching and steadying her, gentle as a girl with a bird in the palm of her hand, Tebogo bent to listen. But Buli was in no mood to confide.

'Let me go,' she said. 'You don't even like black girls anymore. We aren't good enough for you these days.'

Tebogo gave a rueful laugh, rubbing at his chin. 'It's not her colour that attracts me,' he said. 'Please don't think I am not still a great connoisseur of beauty, whatever package it comes in.'

He nodded a small acknowledgement in Buli's direction and she preened. One thing about Buli – she loved to be affirmed, lapping at it like a parched cat at a saucer.

'My girlfriend,' said Tebogo with a smile in Megan's direction, 'is more than your average white girl.' He was drawing her back from where she stood marooned on the edge of the circle.

'My girlfriend ...' It was all for Megan's benefit now. He really was the sweetest of men. '... has a freshness – unjaded and unharmed by the things that damaged us. She might resent it but, for me, she is all about the new ... perhaps she still needs to discover that for herself.'

Martin steered Francesca away then, out along the balcony rail where they hung suspended over the dizzying drop.

'Your friend ...' he began.

'I know,' she said. 'She's unhappy. She's not really like that. She's an amazing person, with such an intuitive ability to listen. She's the only person I've been able to talk to about my detention. To some extent anyway.'

'That's rare,' Martin said. 'Most people can't understand things they haven't experienced. It's like grief. Most people haven't the ability to empathise and it makes them impatient. It leaves one very isolated.'

'Exactly,' Francesca said. She felt something swelling within her. Something she couldn't place. But she felt suddenly that it might burst and shatter her.

'Sometimes ...' she said, 'I feel like the last time I really spoke about detention at any length was to my interrogator.'

Martin laughed, lighting them both smokes. He leant forward and her skin erupted at the damp breath in her ear.

'Come with me,' he whispered. 'Let's get out of here. Come to my office and we'll talk.'

She couldn't of course. It was too late. Too dangerous. His hands were cupped over his smoke. When he drew them away, she watched for the tic that tugged the side of his mouth.

'Just to talk?'

'Just to talk. Did you see where I parked?'

'No.'

One of his eyes fluttered slightly outward. Daniel's eye did that sometimes, like a butterfly battering against the body that trapped him.

'Down the road a bit. First left. I'll meet you there.'

Slipping from the balcony she saw Nicholas enter. Oh God ... well, it was nothing to do with her. Tebogo was with Megan. And ... oh shit, she couldn't leave her now.

Nicholas always looked as though he really wanted people to notice that he really, really didn't want to be noticed. But then she had never liked him much. Of course, he was utterly charming, but in the way of feckless, untrustworthy boys. There was no doubt he was devastating. But it was all about Nicholas, somehow. Everything always revolved around him. He was beginning to develop a slight dissipation around his rakish edges, she noted with satisfaction. But it only made him sexier, more's the pity.

He paused, open beer in hand, all unassumingly obtrusive. Seeing Megan, he made his way to the balcony rail. He stood, seemingly mesmerised by the view, just inches from Megan's back. Megan still stood slightly to one side, as Tebogo good-naturedly fended off Buli's attentions. She should go, Francesca thought. Nicholas lifted a finger and, as if the action came so naturally that he hardly noticed it, ran a finger down Megan's spine. Megan shivered and turned. Turn back Megan, she urged silently. Don't do this tonight, for God's sake. Tebogo had laid himself open. He had exposed his damaged vulnerability for all to see.

Megan seemed trapped, as though she really wanted to turn from Nicholas, but sticky threads adhered to her.

Suddenly everyone was still. It occurred to Francesca that, inexplicably, they had been waiting for this. It was a bizarre sense that all their frenetic discussion, their frenzied drinking and flirting, had been a mask to hide this tendency towards violence – from the world and from themselves.

Tebogo hadn't moved. And yet suddenly Francesca feared him. He didn't frown. He didn't glare or anything. Yet, if he had still been a soldier, she would have hoped against hope that he was on her side.

'Touch her,' he said to Nicholas. 'Touch her again, and I will kill you.'

Francesca knew in that second that he meant it. And she knew that everyone there knew it too.

Nicholas must have understood because he turned and left, pausing only once. Just before re-entering the house he smashed his half-full bottle into the side of the empties bin. He did it with such savagery that the sound exploded across the balcony, ricocheting out of the valley to pound back at them once, twice, and then there was silence again.

Francesca thought she saw blood. And she thought Megan saw it too for she gave a little sound.

Silence followed Nicholas for only a second or two. Then the noise returned – all the noise and laughter, even the drinking and flirting. The curtain had briefly been drawn aside to reveal what lay inside. But finding it unbearable, they had drawn it back.

The cold clutched at Francesca's hands as she negotiated the steep road. She turned the corner and saw his car. She was fairly sure it was his, but they all looked the same, those square generic things.

Perhaps he'd gone back to look for her. But if she returned, he'd probably be on his way out again.

She wasn't even sure why she was here. She hadn't thought it through. She had been seduced by his warmth – and the promise that he would listen. When last had anyone really done that?

He wasn't coming. He must have waited too long and gone back to the party. Stupid, she thought. Stupid fool.

Her cheeks stung as she bent into the mean little breeze. What was the matter with her? She was mother to a lovely, if fragile, child and wife to a successful husband. What had been happening to her these past weeks? Why should this loneliness suddenly well up and leak across her face?

'What's wrong?' Penny asked, the instant she saw her. 'Oh God, you two! He's been looking for you.'

'Did he ...?'

'He looked bereft. But we all thought you'd gone ... He left again. I'm sorry, Sweetheart. I swear I thought you'd gone.'

'It doesn't matter, Pen. It's probably just as well.'

'But you must phone him. Tell him what happened.'

'Oh no, I don't think I could. It's too ... I don't know. I just couldn't. But it really doesn't matter. It obviously wasn't meant to be.'

THE MAN

The man had gone to East London. He couldn't really explain why – not to Rolene, and not even to himself.

She had asked him once, and then she had let it be, tugged back into the world that only she existed in, she and her boys. Slightly irritable, always busy, always tremulous with the weight of her trivia. This one needed new school shoes, that one forgot his homework book again, and why on earth couldn't the eldest ever be prevailed upon to drag his scrumpled blazer from his schoolbag and hang it up?

It wasn't a world he inhabited. He loved them – of course he did – though it was not a word he had ever learnt to use. He liked to sit apart, on his stoep where he could see the sea; and where, in a storm, he could feel the tang of icy spray on his closed eyes. From there he could hear the warmth in the kitchen. He could feel the boys at the table, squabbling over homework or rugby sides. They were everything he wanted them to be. Everything he had hoped for. And yet he no longer knew how to enter their world.

He could ruffle small heads. He knew how to do that. He could even mend kites and patch bicycle tubes. All that he could do. Gruffly. He knew he was gruff. Yet he could no longer be any other way. If he had ever known another way.

He couldn't feel his love for them, that was all. At night, when he could no longer sleep, when he slipped silently from the house to fish from the rocks, he tried to feel it. He imagined them lying dead. He pictured them falling from the rocks into the blow-hole.

He knew without the slightest hesitation that he would leap in and, futile as it might be, try to drag the small battered body to the surface. He had never suffered much from physical fear. He knew he would do that for any one of them without thought. And yet he still couldn't summon the feeling. He didn't know how it would feel to have one less.

One of his brood – Rolene considered him one of the brood, and he had learnt to speak of him this way – had been still-born. Years ago, it was now. He had watched as Rolene suffered. He had tried to help her, to bring her soup, and videos she never watched, while she refused to leave her bed. But he hadn't known the child. How could he be expected to suffer over its cramped, blue body?

Perhaps it was his punishment – this inability to experience what he knew he must feel. But that was plain stupidity. It had been his strength. That was what had enabled him to live, and to do what was necessary. And it had been necessary to cultivate that ability not to feel things, if he were to pretend to be what he was not. If he were to befriend people. Make them trust him. It had never been a straightforward war. The sides had never been ranged neatly along trenches for all to see. Sometimes it had been necessary.

He had learnt never to say 'I love you'. Girls had said it, so many girls seemingly fascinated by his slight detachment. And each time they had, he had said thank you. Just thank you. Once he had said: 'Don't ask for more. Never ask for more. The cause must always come first.' And he had meant it, though she had never known which cause he spoke of.

Perhaps he hadn't either. Not completely anyway. Things had become snarled in his head by that stage. It was not easy to play so many lines for so long and still keep the strands from tangling. That was part of the game. It was what he did so well – like handling a kite in each hand, manipulating their swoops and dives without ever allowing the two to collide, or their strings to snag. It was only towards the end that it became more difficult. Perhaps he had become a little too confident. Or perhaps he grew a little too close to the other side. Whatever. It didn't matter anymore. He had survived, and that was the important thing.

It had become ingrained in him though, never to say 'I love you'. It was too dangerous. It could have destroyed him. And the important thing had always been to survive. That was what people forgot now, with their maudlin goings-on. With their playing on how hard it had all been. They had all been part of the game, and those that survived should be ... well, proud at least. In the end, they were all the same type of people. They had, every one of them, learnt to be something else in order to survive.

Rolene had known. He had told her before his cover had been blown out of the water. And she had stuck around. That was why he had married her, he supposed. He had been grateful for that. Now, of course, with all this wallowing in what had been, and what had been done, she was growing funny about it all. She didn't want to talk, and that was fine. He had no desire to sit around weeping into her lap. He had never been the kind to talk it all through and say how he felt.

She didn't read any of the truth commission guff. He watched her in the morning, irritable frown in place, snatching at the newspaper – covering, covering the pages where it was all laid out. And so far, thank the lord, they had left him alone in his small town. He wasn't hiding. This was where he had always pictured himself, close to nature, close to the sea. It was the journalists he meant, of course, with that type of 'What's happened to so-and-so now' kind of story. Not the truth commission. There were surely far more important fish to fry than he.

And she, the one he inexplicably could not forget ... certainly couldn't complain. In any case, he couldn't see her making a fuss about it now.

He had thought of her again, in East London. He had sat, quietly and anonymously, watching that parade of emotions; that uncontrolled sloshing of tears and sentiment.

But stupid as it might sound, in the middle of all this gushing, he had experienced a strange sense of her, or of her tears. He had sensed that she was weeping. He had got up then, just as the woman came to the end of her grisly story. He had left as her final words echoed so dramatically through the hall – an attempt, of course, to shock them with the inhumanity of everyone who had fought against her.

He had found a bar, an old-fashioned men's bar that reeked of beer and cigarettes and abrupt East Cape ways. That's what he wanted – just a drink. They had asked him bluntly what it would be and then let him alone. He didn't usually drink much. Never smoked either. But he drank that day, brandy and coke. Not uncontrollably. Never out of control. But he had spent the afternoon there, never gulping, but sipping, sipping.

Just once, it must have been towards the end of the day but it was hard to tell in that beer-sodden hole, he had tried to picture himself in that woman's shoes. He had tried to test himself again, to picture his gawky eldest there on the bed, with plastic bags and rubbish in his skull.

He couldn't do it though. Just couldn't.

FRANCESCA

Francesca always popped from sleep at six, like a cork through water. In the pearly dark of these autumn mornings, she liked to wash gently on the swell of her morning languor. She lay still and separate, so as not to alert her husband to her waking.

When he awoke it was with a vigorous splash of agitated duvet and broken silence, an interwoven litany of things to be done and television news.

Daniel made the slightest whisper of sound, one foot lagging on the wooden floor. Slipping his wild-wheat body alongside her, he lay as still and silent as she did.

The TV flickered on, jarring from channel to channel with a clash of colours across the ceiling.

'... up early this morning. You know that board meeting ...'

'... *Freedom Day address on Saturday, President Mandela spoke at the Union Buildings in Pretoria, to mark the second anniversary of the first democratic elections* ...'

'... anyway, he's got his head up his arse half the time. There's people in the company with ten times his experience ...'

Daniel turned rigid in her arms. Too silent, too still, this child of hers – either too compliant or too lacking in all control. Quietly, my child, she told Daniel in her head, softening, bending his taut limbs. How could he be other than he was? He was different. The extent of his difference had no relevance. He felt different, and that was all that mattered.

He was a child whose mewling sickliness had caused him to spend the first years of his life on her lap. Not even Beauty's back would quiet him. Claustrophobia and sleeplessness had driven her to the distracted edge of madness, so that only she knew how close she had come to battering him. But she never had. In that split of a mother's personality, rage had warred against tenderness, and tenderness had won.

Yet only she understood that she had to make it up to him – because he knew. Through the umbilical cord of their closeness, he had absorbed the sense that, if he didn't hold and nag at her, his mother might want to hurt him.

Daniel began to cry. 'I don't ... I don't want to go to school,' he murmured. Oh God, not today. Please, Francesca begged silently. She had an edit suite booked and there was no way she could be late.

'Daniel, out of bed. Now.' Keep it down, she silently urged herself and the sobbing child. Please don't set your father off.

'Danny?' she murmured. 'Daniel, please?'

'Oh for fuck sake.' Paul yelled it. 'I can't stand this. Deal with it, Francesca.

It's not so very hard.'

'Okay,' she said. 'Okay, okay.'

Thank God, she could hear Beauty. He'd be out of range of Paul's fury in the kitchen. Beauty would love with no issues, cuddle with no conflicts and chivvy him through breakfast. She returned to the bedroom to find Paul still raging.

'Can't you ever do anything without it turning into a soap opera? Are you so useless at anything to do with normal, everyday life ...'

It was as though a layer of rage seethed always beneath Paul's urbane shirtfront, in constant risk of erupting. When had this happened? He hadn't used to be like this. His strength had seemed a bolster, a protection against all that might still threaten her. What pain or turmoil had caused his life-force to turn inward, against Daniel and her?

'For God's sake, how does everyone else seem to manage motherhood and jobs without all this bloody drama?'

'Okay. I said, okay.'

He stood facing her, still holding the TV remote as though he were contemplating switching her off. She had packed herself away in her jar on the shelf, from where she could safely watch his face redden and contort.

'And don't look like that, for fuck sake. I'm just getting on with the business of life. God knows, someone has to.'

Somewhere deep inside her, a small child crouched with hands over ears, chanting: 'Don't shout. Please don't shout.' And then it darted through her head before she could snag it. She wished he would die. For doing this to Daniel. For doing this to her. For turning her into the kind of person who watched her words and waited her moments. The silent holder of secrets shaped from any simple thing that might once more set him off.

Oh God, she thought. Oh God, I didn't mean it. Please don't let anything happen to Daniel because I wished Paul dead.

'Martin?' Her hands were shaking.

'What happened to you?'

'I was held up at the party and then I missed you. I went back but you'd already gone.'

'I thought you were running out on me. Should we try again, d'you think?'

'I'd like that. Perhaps we could meet for drinks.'

'Not this week though. I can't.'

'Next week? Wednesday? Thursday?'

'Wednesday it is.'

She returned to the lounge where Daniel sat alongside her, arms stretched across her belly.

'It would be nice if the Pedrania people had dragons, don't you think, Mommy?'

'Well, I don't see why they couldn't find a clutch of old dragon eggs. Perhaps the eggs were preserved in a cave at just the right temperature ...'

She had no conflicts tonight. With Paul working late, she was released from her watch; almost light-hearted without the need to listen for his car, to tiptoe over the eggshells that formed the issues of their days. She could relax her vigil over herself and her boy – watching, listening for each incendiary word that might once more fan that mysterious fury, wherever it had come from.

'Dragons are useful for all sorts of things, aren't they, Mom? Just think how they'd help the Pedranians.'

He was so beautiful, this miraculous child of hers – his delicate face showing every hurt and every happiness. When he had first been diagnosed, she had felt only relief. At least it was not she who was slowly killing him with the residue of sin imprinted on him in the womb. She knew it to be irrational. Of course she did. But when you have lived with the fear of a secret's ability to destroy you – when it has necritised your gut with guilt – it's hard to give up your belief in divine punishment.

But after his diagnosis, she had found that she looked at him differently. His inability to kick a ball was no longer an endearing inheritance from Granddad. It was a symptom. He was damaged. She'd had to learn to lose that. Like learning to walk again, she had taken step after step until she could now almost see him as imperfectly perfect as anyone else in the world. All that remained was her need to protect him from those still unable to see him that way.

'Jolandy could find them, and he could warm them by putting them in his bed.'

Jolandy was the boy who saved his planet periodically from some new and dreadful scourge. He had fought against worse odds than Daniel. An earth-child, he had been in a wheelchair since birth. Stung by his nobility of purpose, the wicked witch Careena had whisked him high into the air, hoping he'd fall to his death. But Jolandy had kicked his poor legs, and fluttered his brave arms, until he had battered his way into space. It was then that the powerful ruler of Pedrania, recognising the courage of the boy, had lifted him to safety.

Megan had slipped quietly into the room with Tebs. Francesca didn't alert Daniel to their presence. She wanted them to see Daniel before he closed up again. Everyone always saw the frustrated tantrums, the clinging and whining. But she would so love Megan to see this preternaturally angelic little being.

'So Jolandy trains this big bunch of dragons ...'

'A whole flock,' she agreed, nodding gravely.

'... and when the wicked snowman piled the land with snow so everything would die, then Jolandy flies them back and forth, melting the snow.'

'What story is that?' asked Tebs. 'It's a very good story.'

'It's his own,' Francesca replied and gulped at her wine. Such homely approbation. Such common or garden praise. It was too ridiculous that it should suddenly bring the sting of tears to her sinuses.

'That *is* a thing.' Tebs was smiling at Daniel. 'That really is a thing. What a wonderful gift!'

'Well yes,' Fran mumbled, stroking the hair from those great eyes, 'yes, I also think he has a talent.'

'I mean ... of course that goes without saying. But what I mean is that this makes it all worthwhile. These are the children of peace. They don't grow up dreaming of tanks or AK47s. And making heroes of rag-tag armies. They have this gift, this freedom to speak of dragons.'

Perched on the arm of Tebogo's chair, Megan allowed her legs to flow across his lap, all long and indolent. She leant against his arm while her hand plucked at the little pills that gathered on his sleeve.

'But this can't be the first time you've seen that?'

They could be so calm as a couple, exuding a pacific mist that muffled the glare of real-life. Nicholas wasn't real-life either, though she worried that Megan thought he was. But sometimes she feared this lack of reality more. She feared what it might do to this gentle man with his buried furies. And to her wild-edged cousin who had never been bound, or been content to be bound, by this foggy calm.

'Well, I don't socialise much with children,' Tebs answered at last. 'It's like in Moscow. It was the first time I realised families could ... I suppose, do simple things together.'

'Oh come on, Tebs, you must've done things with your family?' Megan's hand continued to groom.

'In Diepkloof, I suppose there were just too many of us. And my parents worked hard, and long. My Mama ... if she wasn't at work she was cooking, or shouting at me for losing something.'

'But in Moscow?' Megan never seemed to get enough of his Moscow stories.

Tebs glanced at her. He really loved her – you couldn't help seeing that. But now he gave her a weighing, speculative look. He wasn't blind to her, that was for sure. Then he smiled and reached up to tangle fingers in willow-hair. He gazed at the finger-spun strands almost in perplexity, as though he suddenly lacked all memory of how he came to hold such red-gold treasure.

'I saw families having picnics. Skating on ponds and never thinking of politics or troubles. I had never known that. There had always been too many important things to be done. But suddenly I longed for that. For a normal time, when I could picnic with my family ...'

'And have you?' Francesca asked softly, feeling again the sting of tears.

'Oh ...' and he gave a soft laugh. 'Not my family. No. But I would like to, perhaps with another family.'

He glanced at Megan and then away, ashamed perhaps at the weakness that had permitted it. Megan pretended not to see, but her colour seemed a little more vivid.

Francesca dialled Buli's number for the umpteenth time. She and Penny had been trying to reach her all week. After the way she'd carried on at the party they'd wanted at least to check she was okay.

It was strange that no-one had answered Buli's home number, but stranger still that no-one seemed to know her at either of the cell companies. In frustration, Penny had phoned Buli's old company again. Human Resources had been rather short with her, saying she had left suddenly and they'd had no further contact.

Of course, Buli could have called them ... unless something awful had happened. She tried Buli's home again, allowing the phone to ring fourteen, fifteen times. And then quite suddenly, Vusi answered.

Oh yes, he said, Buli was fine. Doing well at a new job at the Independent Broadcasting Authority. Phone her there, he said, in a hurry to be gone.

She dialled again.

'Nombulelo. Good morning.'

'Jeez, have I struggled to find you. Are you okay? What's happened?'

'Oh ... did you struggle?' Buli's tone, breathy and not quite of this world, sent a spurt of irritation to the tips of Francesca's fingers. Of course, she was fine.

'Buli, what's going on with you? We've been worried.'

'No need. I'm fine. The cellphone company never came through. But what the hell. This is a great job, you know. I have a company car and...'

'Why the hell couldn't you ...'

'Oh, and I've finally taken the step. I've moved out from Vusi.'

'Oh Buli. I knew there was a crisis. I just knew ...'

'No crisis. It's the best thing I could've done.'

'So where are you and Thembeka living?'

'Not Thembeka. Just me.'

Just that, and then silence. Francesca's irritation ebbed, leaving her fingers limp with pity.

'Oh Buli.'

'It's fine, really. It's probably better this way. I get to see her on weekends, and Vusi's mother's mostly at home ...'

'But you hate Vusi's mother. Couldn't you fight them?'

Buli gave a small croak of laughter.

'I'm back here now. Back where his family rules. Anyway ... how are you guys doing?'

'Fine, Buli. All fine. Oh Buli, I'm really, really sorry.'

'Oh ...' and she clicked her tongue. 'It's not such a big deal.'

'Look, we can't talk about this properly over the phone. How about coffee or lunch over the weekend? You can tell me everything.'

'Sure, girlfriend, why not.'

How was it that someone as punctual as Francesca should have collected so many habitually late friends? She had been known to wait three-quarters of an hour for Buli. On one famous occasion, she had waited an hour and a quarter for Penny. But then Penny spent so much of her time juggling too many things and too many selves, it was no wonder.

Half an hour. Well, she owed Buli time. Rosebank sashayed past – midriffs brazening belly-studs. Young women doubled over in the solidarity of laughter, long legs and flat stomachs. All that terrible sureness of the young and stunning seemed to her poignant. Where had they come from, in this concoction of colours, just in the past five years or so? All these variegated girls with braids and bubble-gum?

The odd pram-wielding mother dawdled in the sunshine. Two blind men stood sentinal at the zebra crossing, where they always did, sticks and begging cups to attention.

Francesca felt chilled, with the sun not yet creeping past the Mall across the road. Later it would cut and run, bounding over the steps and tables. By lunchtime, bodies would scurry lizard-like from crevices to bask the ice from their limbs.

'So my china, is this where you spend your Saturdays, while the rest of us sweat and slog?'

Watching for Buli, Francesca started, and then laughed.

'Ollie, my china. Must you scare the shit out of me?'

Grabbing Francesca in a paralysing hug, he impressed a kiss upon her. Ollie was one of the girl-gang's oldest Jo'burg friends. Funny-looking in the best sense, he acknowledged with great humour his gnomish face and awkward body. Turning to his companion, he interpreted: 'Adam, this is Francesca, one of my biggest mates. I dig her *stukkend*.'

'I've heard about you and your crew. Join us.'

'I'm waiting for someone, but maybe till she comes.'

They ordered while Adam trotted down into the tumult of bartering on the pavement, where hawkers sold art from Zaire, or artefacts from Soweto and Ivory Coast, or wherever.

'Not the wire sculptures,' Ollie yelled. 'They'll squash in your suitcase. And the giraffes don't fit.'

Adam turned and grinned, one eye closed against the sunlight, looking so scrubbed and stocky that she laughed. He was the freckled face of her youth, of boys' schools and sports fields.

Adam was Ollie's best friend from nursery school, here only briefly to see his parents. 'Emigrated to Canada two years ago. Largely because of his wife. Dog of a wife. Absolute dog.'

Adam returned laden with carved games and tin-can insects, carvings and hangings. His cellphone rang and one large finger assaulted the off-button.

'Has to be my wife,' he said glancing up.

'So, why aren't you divorced?' Fran asked.

He gave a quick laugh. 'Why aren't you?'

'Why should you think ...'

'Maybe it takes one to see one.'

Francesca shrugged and they all laughed. Hurriedly, she scanned the clustered groups for Buli. She loved the patterns of their companionship – the side-long sight of a head's piquant flip, the gurgle of laughter. And Buli had always been there for her, understanding the details of post-detention disquiet as no-one else had quite been able to. Not that she had ever told her everything. There were things she would probably never be able to tell a soul. But what she had been able to speak of, Buli had understood. Now she was anxious for her, certain there was something terribly wrong in her life.

'You've gone quiet,' said Adam. 'I'm sorry I said that, by the way – about getting divorced.'

'It's fine.' And she found that it was, although she had never asked the question of herself, perhaps afraid to hear the answer spelt starkly in her head.

'But could you guys?' Ollie asked them both. 'I mean, could you be alone?'

Adam shrugged, glancing at his hands. Francesca thought she would also shrug enigmatically, but instead found herself blurting: 'In many ways I'm alone already.'

It was probably Ollie's warmth – that and Adam's raw vulnerability – that encouraged this straight-talking latitude. But once formed in rare moments, these instant intimacies had a life of their own. There was an intensity to them that she found addictive. Ollie ordered more capuccinos without asking, perhaps to hold the mystic circle together. As the sun stepped closer, they spoke of Adam's marriage and the misery of constant conflict.

'So what's with your marriage?' Adam asked at last.

Staggering on new emotional feet, she found herself telling Adam things she hadn't spoken of before. She spoke of Daniel and the conduit his diagnosis had been for her – the lonely channel that had opened out to a new self.

'So your husband failed you,' Adam said.

'No ... I'm not sure. Isn't that just a man thing? That inability to deal with things like that?'

'Well ... I'm not sure I'm really qualified to say. Coming from the other camp and all.' Adam had a delightful laugh – a great neigh that caused all the other tables to turn and smile.

'But on his own he's a good oke,' added Ollie suddenly.

'He is, yes,' said Fran. 'That's true. And maybe he's always been able to sense, you know, that I'm not entirely there myself. I've always had my own baggage to deal with.'

Ollie frowned. 'What is this baggage shit all of a sudden ...' But Adam motioned him to silence.

Fran shook her head, as if to negate what she had said. 'No,' she said, 'no, it's just my own issues. Stuff I haven't faced, I suppose. The only thing is that I'm not sure I ever will.'

'You will,' said Adam, encircling her hands and squeezing till she winced, as though he willed his physical strength into her psyche. 'When you're ready. God, but I wish I could wave a magic wand.'

'Thanks, Adam,' she said. 'What a lovely thing ... oh jeez, why don't you just come home?'

Adam's mouth sagged. Without a word, he brought his head down to arms that he crossed on the table. He made no sound so that he might have seemed to be laughing. Francesca draped an arm over his one shaking shoulder and held, just held.

When at last he raised his head, there were no tears. His eyes were red, and his neck taut with muscle, but he had held his tears at bay.

'They don't ...' He stopped and cleared his throat. 'They don't do this.'

'What, in Canada?' Ollie gave his arm a biff of boy-solidarity.

'Ja, like, people wouldn't just meet and talk like this.'

'So why do you stay?'

'I ... Jesus, I miss everything. I miss the colours. I miss the way we hug. I miss the blacks. I miss talking to people in the street.'

When they were gone Fran sat on, still waiting for Buli. But the longer she waited, the less likely it seemed that she would show. Perhaps Buli no longer wished to be her friend. Perhaps after all, their differences made it impossible for their friendship to withstand the hard times. How could she know?

'You're a friend for life now,' Adam had said as he kissed her goodbye. She had removed one of her bangles. From it dangled a fish that shivered in the sunlight.

'Fishes bring luck,' she said into his neck. 'Give it back when you come home to live.'

THE MAN

There was the muttering again. The man was aware of it, even with his back to the charge office, as he took the key for the unmarked car. There was always muttering. Fuck them. They were utterly inconsequential to him or to his life, despite his being forced to exist alongside them. They were nothing, these grubs and crawlers, scurrying about their business, grey with uniformed drudgery.

He was disaffected and he took a pride in that – indifferent to the grubby world he had been wedged into. A little nebulously granted. He knew they wondered about him, what he actually did, how connected he really was. They couldn't be quite sure. And he intended to keep it that way. The uniformed drones had always existed on a different level of the force, distinct from the educated few, like himself. And then, the guys from the old Security Police still retained a cetain aura. It was a mystique, with some glinting element of fear to it. And that was the way he liked it.

He edged the car from the yard. These days the fence was electrified. Funny that – it never had been in all the years that civil war battered at their gates. He enjoyed his little ironies.

There were never enough cars, but this tattered Corolla had become tacitly his. And for the meantime anyway, the mutters were unlikely to graduate to full-scale plaint. He was a captain after all, a plain-clothes captain with a line of command that bypassed their small-town police station.

It was his exposure as a spy that had done this to him, the cover that had blown him out of his high-flying world and robbed him of the game. All he had now, basically, was an office – a cubbyhole beside that of the station commander in which to keep his head down.

Originally, he had been drawn into it inadvertantly. He had never intended that it should last, and certainly not that it should define him, or mould the shape of his life. But there it was. What the hell. He had survived. At first it had been the money he supposed ... or perhaps never entirely. He had always been drawn to the game, to the spy vs spy world of shaded meanings and hidden motives. But even so, he had never had the advantages of some of those rich kids, pacing out their BAs with plodding essays and political protest. The money had been important. It had allowed him to go post-graduate, which he would never otherwise have managed.

He stopped the car. The scumbag was late. He was always late. And with less and less useful information to squeeze from him. He settled to wait, absolutely still. He was good at this, as practised at sitting out people as he was watchful for otters on the darkest of nights.

On the whole, he had despised the lot of them, those middle-class children who fancied themselves communists. He had fooled them all, rising in the ranks of student politics and beating them at their own game.

He had fooled them with truthfulness. That was the mistake of some of those baby-spies on campus. Pretending too hard. It always showed. He had been an anomoly – the Nusas boy who was a liberal rather than a Marxist. It had made him different, and that had made him interesting, but only because he had carried it with confidence. It was his 'fuck you' approach that had made it possible.

And had he fucked them – the charisma of his position, the romance of student protest drawing them like flies. He had fucked them and despised them and reported on one or two, few being important enough to warrant more than a mention. How they would hate to admit that now, over Country Club dinners, married to their doctors and lawyers. They probably still lived off their unwavering belief in some heady time when there had been a file on them somewhere. The odd one he had cared for perhaps, but he had remained ceaselessly the outsider, scornful of naïve preoccupations and activist pretensions. 'Don't ask me to choose. The cause will always come first.'

The nobility of it all had seemed to erase, in their pounding little hearts, the bastard element. He had despised them for the ease with which they had accepted it. He had despised them for believing him, for not seeing through him.

Watchful, always watchful, he caught the scumbag on the outer edge of his peripheral vision. Without moving his head, he brought his eyes around slightly to watch his slouched approach. He wouldn't come straight to the car. He never did. He would first scuff his feet a bit there, and exchange greetings or insults, or whatever it was they did, with the crowd outside the bottle store. Then he would disappear into the café for ten Luckies on tick. Still and silent, he waited.

After university, of course, he had come into his own. It was the game he had loved and, yes truthfully, he had hated communism. But through it all, it had always been the game which had become increasingly addictive. He had grown cynical about both sides by then, or perhaps he always had been, but that's what had made him the master he had been.

He had played them off, one against the other. He had sniggered at spy-masters, run revolutionary groups better than revolutionaries, reporting on whomever it suited him to report on. He had lived high – to Sweden for funding, to here or there or wherever he'd had some chick or workers' co-operative. He had been cleverer than all of them, schmoozing the funders and schlentering the funds. In the end, who had known what had originated with fascists and what with communists? In the end, who knew from whom he had siphoned his tidy little secret stash? And in the end, it wasn't even for the money. It was for the joy of it, the playing of the game.

Perhaps that was why they had sacrificed his cover. He had been told to cool it, warned that he was too convincing to be trusted. But he had believed himself smarter.

And then one day he had been called as a witness. That's what had done it, and he hadn't seen it coming. And not even for the trial of some grand and angry bomber. An academic, just a paltry researcher. Hell, he had quite liked the guy. He had only reported on him in a desultory way, as an excuse for a couple of trips. He had lost his touch, you see. He had got his strings tangled. He had ceased to see anything dangerous about some junior academic, even in the eyes of his bosses. Little scraps of information sent off, all cloak and dagger, to dead letter boxes. Little scraps of research he had been collecting for someone else's PhD. Little scraps that the ANC could have read for themselves, two years later, in some exiled academic's thesis.

So completely fucking futile. That was the first time the game had lost its glitter, when he had watched that innocent idiot disappear for five years. When it had been up to him to send him down.

They had muttered darkly that it was just as well, that he had been getting too close, and just a little too entangled. And when he collapsed in the witness box, unable to continue, unable to breathe, they had concluded that he'd lost it entirely.

It was all bullshit, of course. He couldn't deny it had been stressful. But it hadn't been anything like that. He had been coming down with a cold, that's all, his chest all congested, his breath coming short.

But what was the use of considering it now. They had sent him off to a farm, where all their old loose cannons were safe from themselves, or from assassination – probably, in his case, by disgruntled women who wondered suddenly which cause it was that had allowed him to fuck their best friends and their best friends' sisters.

He had enjoyed the farm. That was what he savoured most in life. It was the only other thing he was good at. He had whiled away the days ringing birds and getting his strings untangled.

And then they had sent him to East London. Just as his muscles unknotted, they had posted him off to Fort Glamorgan, in East London.

The scumbag zigzagged across the road. Christ, and this was his informant – bottle of Klippies already under his belt. He opened the car door and nodded, without a word. The man watched him quizzically, and waited.

'Ja? What?' The scumbag fidgeted, scrabbling for a match which he used to scrape at yellowed teeth.

'What've you got?'

'What you paying?'

'Depends what you've got.'

There was silence. The man waited, still as a python considering his prey. The scumbag scratched and fiddled with his match.

'It's fucking big, man. C'mon, what you paying?'

The man shrugged, while the silence expanded.

'If it's big, you pay big, ja?'

The man lifted a hand from the wheel in shrugged assent.

'Okay, okay. Car parts. Workshop. Spray-painting parts from hijackings up in Jozi.'

Such were the things with which he now filled his days. His nights he kept as his own.

FRANCESCA

Francesca had spent the week trying to find Buli. From editing suites, scurrying from brain-storming sessions, she would grab for her cellphone and try just one more time. Vusi never answered their phone again. The IBA said that Buli had left them. She was a great loss. Personal issues, they said. And no, they had no forwarding number for her. But if Buli still wanted to be her friend, surely she would make the effort.

She closed it all off now. Paul, Daniel, Buli, all of them. She wasn't sure what she was doing here. Meeting Martin at his office for drinks could surely only mean one thing. And yet here she was, her decision not yet made. She had simply come.

She hadn't meant to phone Martin. It had just happened. After the latest of Paul's rages, her hand had reached out of its own accord. But even then, she had tinkered with the idea of phoning to cancel, or perhaps not pitching at all. Oddly, it was meeting Adam that had resolved the issue. Those piercing moments of instant intimacy had cracked the shell of her longed-for normalcy and shown her the terrible vulnerability of the loneliness beneath. Just to talk, as she had with Adam. Just to talk. That's all she wanted.

Francesca spent a long time locking Daniel's books and scattered jerseys in the boot. What if her car were broken into? How would she explain its presence in this street at this time, when she should have been editing?

'Come in,' he told her through the intercom. 'I'm on the phone, but come straight to my office. It's at the end.'

She wandered slowly through, touching silent desks and thieving a snippet of him from an abandoned memo, a hint of his essence in the framed photographs of his days in student politics.

He motioned her to sit, intent upon the telephone. His austere voice enumerated something about training techniques that she couldn't follow, while her mind flitted about, considering flight.

Replacing the receiver, he was Martin again, blond hair gravely cut as though to retract all the rampant curls of youthful photographs. He came around the desk to her.

'Are you going to run away from me again?' he asked, embracing her with so little pressure she wondered if he thought she might break.

She looked up and watched the little tic begin to tug at his mouth.

'No,' she murmured.

He offered her wine and they drank it on the visitors' couch, each laughing hesitantly at the other's unsureness. Each self-consciously distinct from the other.

They sat that way until she felt she couldn't bear it. She wondered why, suddenly. This was how she lived. She passed her days and her duties in a parallel universe, she and her husband passing each other in the passage of their lives. And it was fine. Anyone could do it. Only now, suddenly now, it seemed unbearable.

Reaching a hand to her hair, he drew her closer and kissed her gently. She could feel his cheek contracting against hers. They sat like that, he caressing her hair, she straining for that one touch of tenderness.

Paul ... oh God, she was so confused. He was not a bad man, she knew that. And she thought perhaps he raged at the closeness between her child and herself because he grew frightened to approach it. Unschooled in touch, he had never learnt how to reach out to them.

And it had been fine. She had built a separate space, for her and for Daniel. From it they had watched Paul mouthing from his own bubble, avoiding the openings they left in theirs, for fear of the emotional contamination. And in time, they had left fewer and fewer for him.

Only now she grappled a need she hadn't known she had. Martin had said they would talk and that he would listen. That was all she wanted, wasn't it? And yet she wanted more. From Martin she wanted the impossible. He had also been detained – and also in the Eastern Cape. And beyond all conscious thought slid the shadow of a hope that he might just be able to understand the person she had become and the things her detention had caused her to do.

'It's so good to just sit here,' he murmured. 'Sometimes I get so blimming tired.'

'Does it still affect you, d'you think? The detention, I mean.'

'Oh that. No, God it's so long ago. I was talking about work, I suppose.'

Lifting her head she said: 'You're lucky.'

'To be working with Government? Ja, I must say it's great to be part of the loop. I keep this office but I've had to mothball my consultancy. The contract's worth it, though. For the opportunity, I mean ...' he gave a hiccup of laughter, '... if not for the money.'

He bent his head to kiss her. She could taste his passion, feel it in the fingers that strayed to the hollows of her throat. But as she felt his advance, so she felt hers recede. She had lost the impetus.

What the hell was she doing here? He wasn't like her. He was nothing like her at all. He had handled his past and he was part of the future.

'Martin.' He held her away from him. She was very aware of the sad little tic that dragged at his smile.

'You're running away from me again, aren't you?'

'Oh God, I'm sorry, Martin. I just can't do this.'

'I think I knew that,' he said. 'I suppose I just hoped.'

She felt tears hovering like seagulls for scraps, but she shooed them away fiercely. So, she was still on her own. So what? She could handle it. She always had.

'Hi Sweetie. I'm going to bookclub with you tonight.' It was Penny, abrupt as always.

'Oh ... yes, but you're not going in real life, are you?'

'Yes, that's right. I'll pick you up.'

'Allan in the room?'

'Yes, they're all fine. But we'll catch up later.'

'Well, keep your cell on, just in case.'

'Okay, seven it is. Ciao for now.'

Half an hour later, the phone rang again.

'Okay, we can talk properly now,' Penny said. 'And by the way thanks ... you know ...'

'Oh shut up. You're my best buddy. What else could I do but be your alibi and promote the cause of adultery?'

Penny gave her gentle snort of laughter. 'I just wish I could do the same for you.'

'Ja, well I put paid to that, didn't I?'

'Seriously, Francesca. You desperately need an affair. It'll rejuvenate you, like a good facial.'

Francesca gurgled with enjoyment at her outrageous friend. 'Jeez, where've you been getting your facials? I want to go there too. Listen, I can't talk too long now. I'll be late for the bookclub.'

'Don't tell me you're still going there. In real life, Sweetie, the only use for that bookclub of yours is as an alibi.'

'I quite like going to bookclub. I find it comforting.'

'Oh please. You find it comforting to hang with a bunch of tight perms and track suits? They're from another world.'

'Maybe it's us that're from another world. Anyway, don't forget its real function. Who can afford to buy books since the rand's dropped through the floor?'

'But their choices ... and they hardly talk about the books. I've never come across a group of women who can find fodder in their children's PTAs for an entire evening of conversation. My God, where do they bury those Stepford tits between bookclubs?'

Penny had Francesca laughing out loud now. 'But don't you ever think that that's how normal suburban people live?'

'But why d'you want to be part of that?'

'Perhaps it's my last foothold in normality. Sometimes I wish I was a bit more like them ...'

'Oh for God's sake, Francesca.'

'No really. I wish I could be happy with that. It seems so comforting and so simple. I bet they don't fall about in the supermarket.'

'I'm not listening to this anymore.'

'Their lives don't have nasty surprises ...'

'Okay, that's it. I'm off to commit adultery. You can go join the tuck shop moms.'

A touch late for bookclub, she was drawn to the cosy group about the fire. More logs were brought in by the good-natured husband who greeted them in his tracksuit before disappearing to the bedroom TV.

'Oh, we thought you weren't coming.' That was Jude. 'How could we have coped without our little bird of paradise?'

Was that irony? She had always considered bookclub irony to be an oxymoron of sorts. And she rather liked Jude. So perhaps she had meant it. The thought warmed her to these plump women whose perms always seemed to be growing out.

Perhaps they could sense the wildness that still swelled within her. And perhaps it reached down into their own embryonic wild selves, stunted by girls' schools and duties. Perhaps, under the clucking of knitting needles, those rounded tummies also felt the kick of what they might have been, as she did.

One of them was impressing the others with what they'd seen at the game reserve, and how her eight-year-old had identified a shrike in flight. The fire crackled. It was only May, they really had no need of it. But it helped, throwing an animation over the gathering.

Actually she agreed with Penny. Such unbridled normality bored her. It bored and dismayed her. Yet, and this dismayed her even more, there was a part of her that wished to have been born to this. They seemed to have no longing for what was other. She would bet that not one of them wished never to have married or given birth – not to have done that to themselves.

Daniel was special. Some days you could see a light within him that other, less different children would never kindle. But there were days when he struggled with life, growing white-tinged with fury, brawling with the person who loved him most. There were times when motherhood seemed nothing but drudgery.

Ladling chicken a la king from the hot tray, they swopped stories of husbandly sighs over being left to their own supper devices. They had all – other than Francesca, of course – left Hubby with a cottage pie or wholesome bobotie to pop in the microwave.

Suddenly she felt glad not to be truly part of this lumbering group. She felt a savage joy for her own gang and their little rebellions. Backs against the wall, arms about each other's shoulders. Always, always. Never like this.

What was it with her anyway? All these years she had held it together, pressing firmly down on all that she had tossed inside herself to rot and ignore.

Now was drawing back to then. Threads she had thought severed were jerking her back. Drawing them together again – she and the man she had vowed never to think of, never to picture in the dying night, when the grey birth of morning brought back to her the ache of other births and other deaths.

It was like the drip-castles they had made as children. Just as each peak grew, it collapsed upon itself or became hollowed out by the tide.

They were brainstorming – she, Thobela, Fuzile and an English woman from the BBC with whom they were co-producing. 'Two years on' was the working title, a state of the nation piece on the mind and heart of the country.

It was a year now since she had completed her World Cup piece, when it had seemed the whole country had willingly suspended its disbelief and allowed a few rugby games to prolong their miracle time.

A year could be a terribly long time. And perhaps South Africa was just that type of place. Nothing was ever quite as you longed for it to be. But just as you were about to surrender entirely to disillusion, it would throw up some anomalous marvel that would defy all loss of hope.

They'd spent the afternoon at it, watching their castles grow and topple again in soggy heaps. Just as they invoked all those parts and places where goodwill flourished and people mixed, so they would conjure resentments past and present, and too many hurts ever to heal.

Just as it seemed they reeled on the verge of perdition, some sturdy hand of sentiment would point to the rainbow they might still muster – with or without the pot of gold. She still hoped most of them would do without the pot of gold, if they were offered a good solid rainbow.

Those who prized the pot above the rest were busy counting their points for Perth – escaping their fear of disunity in homogenous havens, or perhaps it was the unity they feared, who knew.

To make matters worse, they were going to Penny tonight – a send-off for some friend leaving for New Zealand. It always made her insecure. Even a pantechnicon parked in her street summoned a visceral fury at the self-fulfilling prophecy each seemed to confirm.

Claire, the English woman, had the strained look of someone consciously holding her tongue in the company of savages. Francesca knew she was being unjust, but there were suddenly so many of them – earnest Americans and helpful English rushing over to assist in the transformation. And it was unfortunate that they so often seemed of a type, and the impression of each adhered to the last and somehow attached itself to the next.

'I think,' said Fuzile very precisely, gazing longingly out at the twilight, 'that we are all very tired now. Perhaps we should resume tomorrow morning. uFranile, hamba uyo landa ibeer. We are dry.'

'Fetch it yourself, you sexist pee-eeg. You know where they are.' Pulling her cell into her lap, Fran surreptitiously checked for messages. She felt foolish for running out on Martin once more. She knew he wouldn't phone again. And who could blame him?

Penny, of course, said that boys never phoned – it was a genetic thing. And that old lefty boys were dogs. Dogs of dogs. But that was just Penny. Why exactly she still checked for messages Francesca wasn't sure. The whole idea had been foolish. And yet ... What else was there? The shaky stepping stones over Paul's torrential rages? Her desperate tip-toeing around the depths of their emotional silence? Was that all there was ever to be?

'Waiting for someone to call, Franile?' asked Thobs, with his Reynardine grin.

'Oh ...'

'Hm hm. You'd better remember that when you admit your error and leave your husband, you are promised to me.'

'I am absolutely aware of our impending engagement,' she said, a little absently.

'Although you are a bit thin for my taste. Too bony in the rear end. But then I could always fatten you up.' Thobela's eyes filled with tears when he laughed. It was one of his most endearing qualities.

'Oh what a wonderful prospect to look forward to.'

Perhaps feeling the discourteousness of their horseplay, Thobs twisted in his seat.

'So, Claire, how do you like South Africa so far?'

Oh God, thought Francesca. We can never resist.

'Well, it's interesting ... I can't wait to go to Cape Town though.'

They all shook their heads disapprovingly.

'No no,' said Fuzile, 'this is much more interesting as a city ...'

'But tell me, why are South Africans so very sensitive to criticism?'

Unable to bear hearing them all grow defensive and petulant, she threw open the door to let in the sounds of Beauty's interaction with the neighbourhood. There was a melodic tranquillity to it that Francesca usually enjoyed, but it was not conducive to brainstorming.

'Mea-lies. Mea-lies.'

The high-pitched cry trilled from the street. Francesca opened the gate as the Mealie Lady approached. She had taken to parking her shopping cart full of mealies behind Megan's room, and seemed to be spending most nights here too. The women of the house had remained tacitly silent over this.

'The Mealie Lady and me, we have some business to talk,' said Beauty, appearing behind her. Beauty called her the Mealie Lady, as everyone in the neighbourhood did. It was as though her job as suburban colour had expunged the person beneath.

'We will tell you of it later, Siesie. But the Mealie Lady's cousin has a place in Brixton. We think maybe we can run a shebeen and jazz club from there.'

'But d'you think you can ...'

'We'd have to watch for the tsotsis. But we have the Mealie Lady's cousin and his friends to protect us. It's a good business, Ousie. You'll see.'

The Mealie Lady seldom spoke in Francesca's presence. She and Beauty made an incongruous couple. The Mealie Lady dressed rurally, with a blanket at her waist and beads at her throat – Beauty with permed hair and city clothes. Beauty interpreted for her while the Mealie Lady stood by, the eternal, impassive woman. But late at night, when Francesca put the old dog out, she could hear the soft murmur of conversation in the darkness of Beauty's room.

Claire appeared in the study doorway. Francesca was glad. She felt suddenly terribly proud of these two women who had only a handful of primary school standards to rub together – proud of their entrepreneurial schemes and their streetsmarts.

'Can I ask you ...?' Claire said as they turned back inside. 'I'm interested. How can you still have a ... um cleaning woman? In the new South Africa I mean.'

'I ...' Thobela cleared his throat. 'I also have a domestic worker.'

'Me too,' said Fuzile. Feeling vaguely besieged, Francesca was warmed by their support. But was that all Claire had seen in the exchange? Had it not touched her at all?

'Perhaps,' Francesca said a touch drily, 'when Beauty is a successful Shebeen Queen, she'll leave me.'

'But there'll always be someone there in her place, begging for work at your gate,' said Fuzile. 'In our generation anyway.'

The dinner had begun badly. Daniel hadn't wanted to come, shrilly protesting that he wanted to be home with his dog. And no, he would not pack his pyjamas.

Paul had thrown the full weight of his logic behind an attempt to persuade the child. Stupid thing to do. Of course the child had wanted to be left with only the dog to look after him.

Predictably, the rand's disconsolate slump these past weeks accounted for the evening's dose of dejection. It was out of their hands, someone was saying. It was the fault of global currency speculators. But why was it, added some broker of discontent, that anything that happened anywhere in the world caused the rand to drop? They were a mess – what else could it possibly indicate?

Two of the men began discussing the Dennis Neer testimony. The Truth Commission had moved to Port Elizabeth, where the torture had always seemed more brutal and the cruelty more intense. Paul wandered off with someone's husband to inspect Allan's new CD player.

'I am so sick of hearing this stuff,' commented the school friend, who was leaving. 'Can't they just get over it?'

Francesca shook her head. Her experience at the Truth Commission still felt so raw that she felt she inhabited a different planet from people like this.

'Get over it?' enunciated Megan, catching Francesca's glance and flinging her eyes extravagantly heavenward.

'Yes actually,' the woman continued. 'Some people want to wallow in that stuff forever. I can't wait to step on to the plane. Everything's so shit here.'

'Oh come on, Gill,' someone broke in with gentle dissent. 'You have a lovely house, a nice job – not to mention someone to clean your house.'

'I don't even want that. I'm sick of being responsible for Anna's issues. I'm always having to worry about her daughter getting pregnant and her son's schoolbooks. I'm sick of worrying about crime and what the education will be like. The country I loved is dead.'

Oh that was it. That was just absolutely too much.

'How dare you say that?' Francesca spoke quietly, feeling all the irritations of her day coalesce in one thin stream of bile. 'How dare you speak like that to those of us who're staying? And which beloved country is dead? The country of PW? Or perhaps Verwoerd was more your style.'

'Don't be pathetic. That's not what I meant. But anyway, that's how I feel.'

'You lived off this country. You profited ...'

'Oh bullshit, I didn't vote the last government in.'

'No but you stayed. You got the best education it could grant you. And you did nothing.'

'Well, what the fuck did you do?'

'Never mind ...'

'She was detained,' muttered Megan. Penny was imperturbably setting out plates of olives and hummus.

'Well, you know what? Not everyone is suited for that kind of thing. So don't come all high and mighty with me. I did whatever I could.'

'Actually ...' Penny lifted her head, 'I think she did what she could, but for individual people.'

'And anyway, the country's failing me now. It's going completely down the drain – look what's happened to the rand. My responsibility's to my family now.'

'You have a responsibility to the country that gave you all you have. You have a responsibility to put something back.'

'No-one can be expected to live with this level of crime.'

'Funny you didn't kick and scream when people were being killed for political reasons.'

'They weren't my people,' the stupid woman spat.

'No, they were black people.'

'And you know what? I'm so thrilled that I will never be forced to have one more argument like this, as long as I live.'

Francesca stood without a word and went to sit in Penny's bathroom, where she tried to calm the shaking of her hands. Megan and Penny found her there. They sat either side of her on the bath.

'I'm sorry,' choked Francesca. 'I'm really sorry, Pen. Your supper.'

'Ag what! So, I should worry if my friends argue. I don't have that kind of house.'

The dinner was subdued. Gillian and her husband left before Penny gathered the energy to wander off and make coffee. The other couples left soon after, without Francesca having addressed a word to them.

'You know,' said Paul, just before they too left, 'I think you're stupid to argue that kind of case. You paint yourself into a corner. What happens if we leave?'

'I won't ...'

'Well, I can tell you, things are still okay as far as I'm concerned. But much worse and I'm not going down the drain with it. If it comes to that, we'll leave.'

A granite block scraped its way through her gullet, landing with a great thud in her stomach. They would leave, that's what he had said. They. As if it was his decision. As if she could conceive of a life uprooted from soil that, with the first drops of rain, could smell so richly of birth.

Outside it was still, the night-time chill bringing the wheatened scent of winter grass.

'You're not leaving,' she said to Allan and, as he didn't answer immediately, to Penny: 'Are you?'

'I do get scared,' said Penny. 'I must admit – every time I go to a school function and people ask where we're going. I think you must just keep counselling me.'

'Certainly for the moment,' said Allan, 'we aren't considering leaving.'

Francesca opened the fridge and stared blankly through the left-over pizza and Woolies yoghurts. What had she come here for?

If Penny left, could she survive? Could she live without her brisk affection? She seemed already to have lost Buli – another casualty of the times. What if Penny packed up and left, and she lost all the most important people in her life?

She was angry at being landed with the custody of their faith in the country. Penny must receive incessant reports of optimistic things if she were not to flag.

They must constantly be monitored. 'Not for the moment.' What did that mean? Which moment? When might the moment change?

We must, she thought, be the only sad people in the world who sit around tensely waiting for our country to disappoint us.

She wandered over to the kettle. That's what she had wanted. The milk for her tea. Far away, filtered through her thoughts, she heard Daniel shout. She glanced through the window, but couldn't see the pool through the trees. He and Beauty had been reclining on plastic pool chairs, squealing when their feet touched the icy water. 'You two are bananas', she had told them, and they had laughed – Daniel in his UV-protected sunsuit and Beauty large in her white panties and corset-bra.

What would she do if Paul announced that they were leaving? She imagined a flat in London with no-one but Daniel, Paul, and a city full of strangers. She thought of Adam in a cold place where no stranger would ever hug him in a coffee bar. She couldn't. She just couldn't do it.

She heard Daniel yell again, more urgently this time. Something about Beauty. Walking to the door, she suddenly made it out.

'Beauty's drowning, Mommy. Beauty's drowning.'

Panic scalded more painfully than the tea which splashed across her legs as her mug exploded on the steps. Beauty couldn't speak, but at least she was clinging to the side. Prising her fingers from the concrete, Francesca was nearly toppled herself. With a great surge of adrenalin, she hauled Beauty's dead weight sideways through the water, landing her on the steps.

'Beauty, are you okay?' She turned to run for the panic button, but tripped over Daniel, huge-eyed behind her.

'No,' croaked Beauty. 'No. Okay.' And, as if the effort had been too great, she began to vomit.

Francesca felt sick. Dear God, she might have been out. She could actually see Beauty's poor, drowned body floating in the pool, with no-one to save her but one bereft boy.

Francesca took the shocked child inside, placing him on the kitchen counter while she made hot, sugary Rooibos for Beauty. Of course, Beauty couldn't swim. But she had always seemed confident to splash about in the shallows. Daniel could keep himself afloat and, in any case, never attempted anything that might challenge his doggy-paddle skills.

By the time she returned with tea, towel and Daniel, Beauty was sitting up. 'Daniel,' she said, still out of breath. 'Daniel. You saved your Beauty.'

'Yes, it's lucky he called me.'

'No, it was Danny-boy. He saved my life. I would be dead now.'

'Daniel?' The child looked frightened, as if he wasn't quite sure what he had done. 'What happened?'

'Beauty slipped off her chair in the deep end ...'

'So what did you do? You didn't try ...'

'No, I swam to the side and pulled the creepy-crawlie to her. When I get tired, I often hang on the creepy ... Then I saw the chlorine bottle. Mom? Remember how my swimming teacher made us hold them when we kicked? So I threw it ...'

'He shout at me ...' Beauty broke into a laugh that was filled with the shredded remnants of adrenalin. ' "Beauty kick, Beauty kick. Kick." '

'Daniel,' said Francesa, 'I'm so proud of you.' She was filled with a great wonder. Daniel was so often the difficult baby that she couldn't quite believe what he'd done. 'My boytjie, you saved Beauty. But I ... how did you think to do that?'

'You told me never to touch a drowning person.'

Francesca had no memory of having done so. But she must have, she supposed. Again, she was filled with wonder that this quiet, pale child had stored her throw-away remark for an eventuality she had never imagined would come to pass.

The three of them sat by the side of the pool, Beauty with an arm fiercely about the boy. They didn't speak – Beauty was concentrating on her breathing, tasting the sweetness of it in the last of the sunlight. As the sun tipped over the wall, the hadedas howled and the chill of evening swooped across the garden. She could hear the distant rush-hour, bellowing down from Jan Smuts Avenue.

'Danny-boy?' said Beauty. The child looked up into her face.

'Danny-boy, we are now tied together. I must watch for you as you watched out for me. So you will always be safe.'

Daniel gazed solemnly into her eyes. At last, he said simply: 'I know.'

THE MAN

'Your sister called.' Rolene looked harassed, clattering pots from stove to sink, her hair fastened from her face with those little corrugated clips his mother used to wear.

'Hon, did you hear? Your sister called from Jo'burg. She wants to know if they can come down with the kids. For Christmas.'

The man watched his two elder boys fashioning something at the table. He might ask what they were doing, but in a minute. He didn't want to break the tableau of boys, faces gilded by the lamp, tussling with something as they grinned and cuffed each other.

'Hon?' His wife seemed always to look harassed these days, a small frown nestled comfortably between her brows, as if it had found its natural habitat. He looked at her properly suddenly, something he seldom did.

'I don't like the house so full. The boys need space.'

'Well, please will you tell her? Why must I always be the one to disappoint your family?'

Had he done this to her? With his demand for seclusion and his need for boys? But hell, he hadn't predetermined it, through wanting it to be so. All those pregnancies, and not one girl. Sometimes he thought she blamed him, as though, through his will, he had invoked some evil capacity to spite her in this way.

But he had never had patience with fancies, nor with psychic wounds; his own or those of others. She had known the truth – one of the few people who had. And she had chosen him anyway, knowing the consequences. He was never going to be drawn into pitying her now for her misfortune in staying with him.

If there was only one thing he had learnt, it was that great hopes, like great ideals, never lasted the distance. And if your choices returned to mock you, well, at least you had survived. To prevail – perhaps that was all there was to it. People rushed frenetically from new job to tarot reader, or these days from psychic healer to colonic irrigation – or perhaps, like his wife, to church. It didn't matter which. It was much the same thing. Searching for meaning, they all were, expecting happiness, as though this was their right.

There was none. There was none and they had no claim on either. They had no more right to meaning or happiness than the sea anemones that floated pink fingers in the tide pools, living out their allotted time, procreating, and dying when the time came.

She clattered more stridently now. He twitched slightly as the small scene of sons at the table shook in the clamour, and then shattered. He wished that she could grow more peaceful with the flow of tides and times. This wasn't such a bad place to live out your allotted years watching your sons grow, and the anemones live and die.

She had never been demanding. That was what had drawn him to her. In the midst of the girls he had bedded, all those girls who scrabbled after scraps of assurance, she had accepted just what she had of him. He supposed she had loved him, and for this he was grateful. But between them lay still that thing, that constraint. 'Don't ask me to choose.' There was no longer any pretence at a cause, but still it remained. He had built his life around that shell, that vacuum, and he no longer knew how to live it another way. And she, he supposed, had never learnt to ask.

He was comfortable with this. He had grown accustomed to watching the ebbs and the flows. He thought he had grown to a point where he expected very little else, for himself or even his sons. All he really wanted now was the chance to smell the sea each day of his life, to sit beside the waves and hold vigil for otters, and to watch quietly as his sons grew strong and sturdy.

And sometimes, just sometimes in the watching, he could see in his boys a looking-glass glimpse of another life, another way of living. When they battled for balls on the beach or grappled, as they had earlier, with some project of their own, he could sometimes pass through the frosted glass of his adulthood, just for an instant, to another boyhood.

Down through the cascade of nasturtiums, two boys had once careered into the Baakens Valley. Two boys, two brothers, drunk on bird-ringing and butterfly collections, intoxicated by every kind of grass and fern and fynbos.

Other boys had smoked dope or taken up surfing and smoking and girls, but he and his brother had subsisted on the valley, which bled through the body of their small town. Its Eastern Cape smells of *khakibos* and *bokdrolle*, the tangle of bush which absorbed and deadened the distant streets – this was what they breathed and fed off. And more than enough it was. More than abundant in the life it gave, with each shy glimpse of a Knysna lourie, the flash of a bloubokkie, the arrogant screeching dive of the plover, and his shoulders side-by-side with another pair of shoulders.

Unexpectedly sometimes, when his boys cannoned home on the last day of school, he remembered the smell of school holidays. He remembered the rough, virile smell of the bush – and he remembered the hot, sweet scent of sweat, his brother's and his own. Sitting shoulder-to-shoulder with their fishing rods, measuring time by the blasts through the blow-hole, it had been impossible to separate the baked clay smell of their flesh. Sometimes, late in the afternoon, when the sun staggered sideways to throw the last of its weight against the flank of each wave, they would sit, too lazy to move or unwilling to lose it, and they would peel the sunburnt skin, in long indolent strips, from each other's backs. And – without words, always without need of words – they would lick flat the salt-shocked hairs on their whitened arms.

Game rangers, they were to be. Ringers of birds and guardians of otters. Every olive strand of rough-edged grass seemed precious then, in those years when they could safeguard the world, preserve life itself.

Except that they couldn't.

He was to go to the army, as they were required to in those days. He was to go alone, marking time. *Vasbyt, min dae* – all that stuff. It meant nothing. He didn't hate it. He didn't love it. None of that troepie tjomminess touched him. He battered his body through the days, while his brother finished up his school time, waiting to join him. Except that his brother hadn't waited.

He was called from barracks because of the letter – that letter he had never forgiven his mother for. Bewildered, angry, he didn't know what-all. All he knew was that this simply wasn't possible. It could not happen. They were the guardians, the saviours of life itself. And anyway, it couldn't be serious. It couldn't be as serious as it sounded, if his mother had waited this long to write.

His brother died of a brain tumour a week later. Only once had he held the still conscious boy in his arms before he fell into the coma that imprisoned him until his death. The dying boy had whispered hoarsely that he should keep his butterfly collection; uttering, more urgently as he felt the life lift from him, that it wasn't complete, that he had never quite managed ...

And what did it matter that it wasn't complete? He already knew that. He knew every single thing about him. Except where he was now.

The very last time he could ever remember crying was when he smashed the butterfly collection, splintered the glass and hammered at the exquisitely fragile wings that bloomed beneath. In those days there had been such an abundance of butterflies, it had been an act of the greatest love to collect just two of each species, to display their petalled bodies for others to see their beauty, tenderly searching them out, waiting with the utmost patience for exactly the right one, at exactly the right time, just after their eggs should have been laid.

But what did any of it matter? There was nothing one could do anyway. If he couldn't save his own brother ... the fucking futility of everything. He remembered how he had pressed his healthy skin against his brother's chest, willing his own strength to heal him, wishing the illness would pass to him, because he couldn't bear it. He couldn't bear the thought of all they had planned.

But of course, none of that mattered anymore. He hardly thought of his brother these days. He had his boys, after all.

If he were a weaker man, if he believed in all that new-age crap ... but he had no patience with those who used past pain to justify their present, or who spoke of damage as though no-one else had ever experienced hurt. You got on with it, that was all. You made your choices and you lived with them.

FRANCESCA

Francesca felt tangled, with all her wires crossed by the day. Taxis shattered their way past her, only to stop with no warning but the flash of hazard lights. And then there were the Mercs, convinced of their inalienable right to cruise straight through every red robot.

She threw her car around the last corner, rows of jacarandas forming a sharp tracery against the sky. It was just about dark. When had winter come upon them so completely?

When she had come to Jo'burg as a child, it had held a wintry smell. The chilled soil had mingled with the sweet miasma of Sasol that spewed from every unbaffled Chevvie with its barrage of ducktails. The smell had seemed foreign to her – a child of the Eastern Cape who believed the evening air should smell of sea and stars and khakibos. Now that she was grown, the smell had gone. But the city was still like that, its crudity carried with a swagger and a gun-slinging sophistication all of its own.

Her street was filled with the bustle of cars, all somehow ending up on her pavement. Clearly it was better for one's car to be seen outside her house than the brothel. Soon, she would have armies of angry partners battering at her door.

Struggling to manoeuvre her car between a yellow Golf and a black BM with darkened windows, she felt a fury swelling within her. The darkened windows invoked a primal unease, like swimming in darkened sea beyond your depth. Especially in this city, this urban wilderness.

Without opening her gates, she wound down her window. 'Please move from my gate,' she yelled. 'Sit outside the brothel, can't you?'

The man in the Golf had a ponytail that tugged sparse strands back from a greasy forehead. Indolently he wound down his window.

'Don't hassle me, bitch. I've got a gun in my cubby-hole.'

Slowly the darkened window began to move. A small man in a suit, that's all. A balding man with nothing to distinguish him from a million others.

'You must have a very unsatisfying life,' he said, 'to be so bothered with this.'

'You're the one paying for it, arsehole,' she yelled, before opening the electronic gates and revving savagely into her driveway. She stabbed at her remote, but too slowly. The pony-tailed man was through the gate and beside her, tapping a gun on the glass.

'Touch my car, fucking bitch, just touch my car ...'

She began to panic slightly. Touch my car and I'll fuckin' kill you: that was the South African way.

'I'm calling the police. Get out of my grounds.' And, laughing at her, he did.

Beauty wanted to chat but she held her off with a hand while she phoned the police. They said they would be there as soon as they could, whatever that meant.

'I want to tell you what happened in the swimming pool,' Beauty said, pouring them both some tea. Daniel was showing her the drawings he had done at school – his self-portrait an odd waif-like alien.

'That's lovely, my sweetheart. Put it on the mantelpiece. You don't need to explain, Beauty. You must've slipped.'

'No, Ousie. There was more. It was magic that did it. Bad magic.'

'Daniel, don't you want to watch some TV, my angel?'

'I'm not allowed.'

'Well, you are today.' That's all she needed, Daniel up all night with the night terrors.

'You remember when I joined the church choir? Then I had to leave because Doris was jealous of my voice? I was scared she would kill me.'

Beauty had a piercing voice of such ghastly pitch she caused people for miles around to glance warily at the glassware.

'Now I didn't see Doris for a long time. But last week I had a dream. In my dream this voice says: "Watch out. Doris is back." Then, in the swimming pool, I see Doris again. And she is struggling with me on the chair. I fight her and next thing I know, I am in the water and drowning.'

'Oh God, Beauty.'

Francesca glanced across the table. The flesh of Beauty's cheeks had tugged tight so it seemed, in that instant, to have fallen away from her skull.

'Now Doris will kill me in the weeks that are coming.'

It was her calm, more than the words, that brought the chill to Francesca's arms. She didn't have time for this. But there was no way she could leave Beauty to wither away at Doris's bewitching behest.

'Let's make some more tea and I'll think,' said Francesca. She was worried. She had no doubt whatever that Beauty would begin to decline if she did nothing. Her hand straying upward, Francesca felt the crystal that hung at her throat – a present from Buli.

'Beauty,' she said.

'Siesie?'

'Look here. I know what to do. See this crystal? This has such powerful magic that people use them all over the world. This is the most powerful protection magic you can get.'

'Is that so?'

They could fix this, the three of them. They would have ritual. A magic circle, the moon. A ceremonial cleansing.

Daniel joined them as they ritually cleansed the crystal of Francesca's essence by soaking it in salt water. She had read that somewhere. It wasn't a full moon, but it was nearly full and that would have to do. The three of them stood hand-in-hand on the lawn, while Beauty held the crystal in her hand and invoked the potency and purity of the moon.

Francesca could only be deeply thankful that Paul arrived home after they were safely back in the kitchen, Beauty humming as she made herself tea.

'I can feel it,' Beauty whispered to Fran as she moved towards the door. 'I can feel this magic is stronger than Doris's.'

'More stumbling blocks to the constitution,' Paul said, tucking the paper under his arm as he reached for a beer. 'Only here can we not even decide on the basics of what a civilised country should have in its constitution. No wonder the rand is on this perpetual slide.'

So much anger Paul carried these days, bubbling just beneath the surface of him. Each evening his ritual declaiming over *The Star* seemed to bring him to the point of eruption.

The police arrived just as they settled to supper, the two offending cars having long disappeared from their gate.

'Good evening,' they said, ducking their heads. It must be difficult for young black men in stiff new uniforms to deal with the disputes of white people. They had already been next door, where they had clearly been subdued by the forceful air of those who had once been the master race.

'There is nothing we can do.' The more vocal of the two perched on a chair, his cap twirled apologetically between his hands.

'What do you mean, "nothing"?' Paul's tone was robust, as it always was when dealing with issues he thought to be cut and dried. The young policeman shrugged his hands regretfully. 'There is no law against homosexuality.'

'It's not the homosexuality,' said Paul. 'It's the brothel. There is still a law against prostitution.'

'It is about to be repealed,' the young man said, shifting in his seat. 'We have been told not to make an issue ...'

'Well, one thing it is, is a business. And this is a residential neighbourhood.' Paul was used to command, slightly perplexed by this ingratiating helplessness.

'That you must take up, Sir,' he said, 'with your metropolitan sub-structure.' The young policeman seemed barely a gesture from forelock-tugging.

'You see,' Francesca said to the policeman, almost confidentially, 'I don't care about brothels. But it should be in a business area. Suddenly everyone thinks they can do anything they like, just anywhere ...'

She was stumbling over her words. In the new laissez faire that followed their authoritarian past, she wasn't sure she was still entitled to a not-in-my-backyard attitude. It was hard to justify on logical grounds.

'Look, the issue's plain,' said Paul, but she motioned him to be quiet.

'... but the thing is, I don't feel safe, for myself or my little boy. There's all these people outside my gate. And some with dark windows. And constable, you see, these are not nice men. One of them threatened me with a gun.'

He nodded and sighed, taking his deferential leave. 'I will report this to the Child Protection Unit. If any of them are too young, then it will be easy to close it down.'

'Great,' said Paul, tossing his eyes upward. 'So now we have to hope these are all abused children before we can get anything done at all. What a fucking country.'

Megan burst through the kitchen door, positively glowing. Her relationship with Tebogo must ... Oh. Of course, it wasn't Tebs who followed her. It was Nicholas.

No wonder Tebs went crazy when he saw them together. They were laughing, breathless with the charge they got from seeing each other.

'Nicholas just popped ... he was just passing ...' She seemed embarrassed, which was natural, she supposed, after the scene at the party.

'Howzit Fran.' Nicholas's charm always managed to irritate her. He had a wastrel air that made his good looks seem somehow squandered. And she wished he would leave Megan alone. She'd be fine if he would just bloody disappear.

'Nicholas. Well, hi.'

'Nicholas thought he'd pop in because, well, we were talking on the phone and I thought perhaps he should come round and tell you himself. What're you doing tonight by the way? Can I hang with you guys?'

Nicholas was opening the fridge.

'Beers on the top shelf,' said Francesca. And to Megan: 'Sure you can.' Megan looked bereft, as though she was already aching with the anticipated loss of him. She wouldn't want to be alone after he left her.

'So, Megan says you know Nombulelo.' Nicholas perched on the table, dumpy in hand.

'Buli? Yes, she's one ... well, I thought she was one of my best friends. But where is she? Do you know?'

'I was just telling Megs. She's one of the real tragedies of the returnees.'

'Do you know where she is, though?'

'No. But I've got a mate at the IBA. They were really pissed off. At first they were amazed to get her. She had this amazing CV ...'

'Ja, ja. I know all that. Just tell me what happened.'

'Well anyway, my buddy says she was so spaced out most of the time, you needed a shuttle to reach her. Eventually they pulled her in and *tjuned* her she needed some rehab.'

'Oh God, so Penny was right. Is she ...?'

'No, she vaporised. Next day, her desk was empty and she'd gone.'

'Someone must know where she's gone, Nicholas. There must be ...'

'My buddy says she often spoke of going back where she came from.'

'The Eastern Cape? Well, that's where she was born, anyway.'

'I reckon. But who knows, hey? She could be anywhere.'

So she had lost Buli, just like that. She ached for her suddenly – for the wicked waste of her. And for Megan, her little cousin grown suddenly old, the hollows of her face holding dark secrets. Oddly, she had never seen her so poignantly beautiful.

Paul had refused to come to Tebogo's birthday party. It was odd because they had spent a fairly good week together.

When it was calm she felt she could understand him better – sensing an unease in him that sniffed the air like a high-strung dog, ready to growl and savage. You circled it, never making too sudden a move or too hostile a gesture. You were wary, always that little bit guarded, but what did that matter? At least it was calm.

She stood on the threshold, a little shy of these sparkly young black people, with their braids and designer shirts. She slid in and sat alongside Mohale, who said he was an aspiring millionaire. So much for socialism.

Tebs, by the look of the room, had one or two old lions of the left scattered about, nodding slightly unsteadily into their brandies. But the room was brimming with the fresh and the new, young laughter unsettling old gravity wherever it tiredly came to land.

The room was sprinkled with whites, like milky chips in chocolate. She and Mohale wandered across to a group of young men raving on about investments, portfolios and fixed something.

Megan whirled through, distractedly emptying ashtrays and unnecessarily clearing glasses. Tebs had ordered in pizzas and was calmly handing them around. On each circuit, Megan would make a point of passing him, with much ostentatious embracing and Sweetheart-ing.

'Where did they all come from?' Francesca whispered as Megan passed with a plate of scraps. 'Just ten years ago, you wouldn't have seen this kind of party.'

'Well,' Megan said, a touch patronisingly, 'of course, you hang in the suburbs. You don't go to the clubs.' She paused and added: 'In any case, they'd still've been at school. You forget that you're getting on a bit.'

Wandering into the kitchen, Francesca found a guy with a hat pulled down to his eyes, morosely swirling the dregs in a polystyrene cup. His name was Lebo and he was a law student, he told her in his privately schooled accent. And, with his next enunciated breath, the cousin of a cabinet minister.

'Oh yes,' he said when he heard her name. 'I've seen your shit. Of course, your white perspective has absolutely no relevance at all now.'

She cleared her throat of the hurt gathering there. 'But if I tried to work from your perspective, you'd say I was appropriating your experience.'

'I'm fuckin' sick,' he muttered, pouring a hefty tot of Tebs's whisky, 'of white madams being accepted as the voice of South Africa.'

A thread of fury spun itself across her chest. 'I think that's about as racist as talking of sculpture being done by garden-boys.'

'Perhaps it is.' He gave a short laugh. 'But I have to get rid of my bitterness somehow.'

'But you must be one of the most privileged people here.'

'I'm still black. It might have affected me less than some, but it still did.'

'I suppose it did,' she said, turning to the door. What more could she say?

Struggling back through the crowd, she felt the urge to make for the balcony. It was tiny and cramped, but it was cold enough that she hoped she would be alone.

Tugging at her jacket, she curled on to the icy metal chair. The street way below was busy, music seeping from cars and houses, people milling in that Saturday-night way. The door behind her opened. Perhaps, if she sat very still and didn't look up, they would go away.

Hearing the scrape of the second chair, she looked up, irritated.

'Don't you remember me?' He was smiling.

'Oh my God, I don't believe it. What do you mean, do I remember you? You were my Politics lecturer. You taught me to be a Marxist.'

He laughed, fervent eyes now somehow tamed. 'Oh my God, did I? How embarrassing.'

'No, no, you were so romantic. Everyone falls in love with the first person who teaches them to be a Marxist.'

He had been a hero to her, a ruler on which to lay other men and measure their shortcomings. She had loved him from afar at university, and had since held him penned in her imagination, just as he had been then.

During her detention, she had taken him out to play with, a Ken doll of the struggle, dressed in his ragged stovies and white T-shirt. They had rolled on beaches, making love on too-hot dunes. They had drunk red wine in Italian villages. They had made perfect babies and loved them together, wandering the parks with cooing child and still-ardent kisses.

The months in solitary had intensified her daydreams until, when she came out, she had felt herself blinking in the blinding light of reality, unable to make out what was real, and what evoked by prison fantasy.

Forever now, her memories of him would be tangled with the sense of joy and sensual comfort she had summoned to her cell.

'I thought you were living in England now.'

'I am. I'm out here for three months on contract, designing a restructuring proposal for the new SABC. Feels helluva funny to be working for the SABC, I must say ... Feels helluva funny to be back at all. But tell me what you've been doing?'

'Anthony, stop it. Why didn't you look at me that way when I was a first year.'

He laughed again, running both hands through his hair in his newly chagrinned way. Physically he had hardly changed, dark hair still there, if greying at the temples, beads still at his throat and wrists.

'Smoke?' he asked.

'Yours are a bit strong. I'll have one of mine.' He bent very close to light it.

She found she could tell him about her documentaries. The old Anthony would probably have been snide. He would have down-played her work's importance to the revolutionary movement, and revealed her topics to be trivial.

Now he flew with her every enthusiasm, laughing so that she believed herself witty and therefore became so. She spoke of her life. And he listened to her. Her sorrows and insecurities she turned to anecdote and the dullest of her duties to adventure. He sat enthralled, really listening as she had not been attended to in years.

'I can't believe how well you've done,' he said, lighting another cigarette from the butt of the last. And his saying it made it so. 'It's made you more beautiful than you ever were. You've gone through pain and its given you substance.'

He brought a hand almost to her cheek before dropping it again as though he hadn't the right to touch her.

'What have you been doing? I heard you were at the BBC.'

'Never mind me. I've got a comfortable job, nothing too grand. I just ... I don't want excitement anymore. I'm not like you.'

'What do you mean? You were a hero. You were only the most dashing leftie on campus.'

She vaguely remembered what she'd heard of him over the years. From university, he had joined the foreign press – snapped up for his dashing charm, she supposed, as much as his talent. Just a couple of years later, she had heard of his arriving in London a broken wreck. She knew none of the details, but there had been rumours that he'd been active in the ANC. In any case, the TV hacks had been right in the firing line.

'I wasn't really a hero,' he said at last. 'When it came down to it, I was a coward. You haven't even spoken of your detention.'

'Oh ...'

'I heard through the grapevine.'

'I don't really want to talk about that. I wasn't doing anything brave or anything. After you left things became really ridiculous. I joined the "End Conscription Campaign". All I was doing was talking to schoolkids about alternatives to the army.'

'It took courage to face detention.'

'Oh Jesus, Anthony. That's not brave. I didn't volunteer.'

They were silent. Again he raised his hand and this time brought it to her cheek, the barest glance of fingers against flesh. She wondered how he would react to the vulnerable secrets she guarded so closely. Would he despise her? Strangely, she felt he might not. His unrelenting rectitude was no longer in its judgmental armchair. He seemed unsure of his own worth, humble in the face of other lives and other frailties.

'You should come back, you know,' Francesca said. 'Everything's different. No-one worries about who was the bravest of them all.'

He gave a short laugh. 'I wonder if I even have the energy.'

'But you have so much talent. We need you here.'

'I don't care, Francesca.'

'Oh, you don't ...'

'I suppose, coming back like this, I do feel a certain yearning. But I decided a long time ago that I'd made such a cock-up of my own life, it wasn't worth salvaging. And if my life has any meaning at all anymore, it's my kids. They're my reason for being.'

'Anthony ...'

'Francesca, please will you see me again? I need to talk to you again. Please.'

'Oh God, I'm not sure.'

'Hell, I don't want to make complications for you. I ... I really just have to see you.'

'He said he couldn't phone last week because he was in Durban.' Penny stopped to retie her takkies. It was the only way she allowed herself to take a break from running.

'Oh,' Francesca nodded sagely. 'That's okay then.'

Penny whipped a sceptical glance sideways as Francesca ran past.

Francesca shrugged. 'Everyone knows that Durban doesn't have telephone exchanges. No-one could be expected to phone from Durban.'

Laughing too hard to run, they collapsed limply against each other and continued at a walking pace. On each round of Zoo Lake they came upon their children. Perched like an ancient couple on a bench, they were desultorily throwing bread to the ducks as the last of the sun glowed green through the willows.

The rowboats were all tied up now, and the lake belonged to the dog and baby walkers. The air began to chill, settling dankly upon their skins as they passed between the trees at the top end.

Young couples in warm pullovers strolled round with baby backpacks, while middle-aged women in sturdy skirts strode past between bounding packs of labradors and border collies. A few serious runners pushed by with a slight impatience to their arm gestures, but they smiled and said 'good evening' anyway.

'Well, I still don't understand what your problem is with Martin.' Penny rolled her eyes and tutted her way round one whole circuit of the lake. But she perked up when Francesca told her about Anthony. She'd been dying to tell her, saving it up till they could go over it together, examining all its implications.

'Anthony. Anthony from the left? You do mean gorgeous, brooding Anthony from our Nusas days?'

'Yes. What do you think?'

'I think you shouldn't fuck it up this time. God, you'd have to be crazy ...'

'It's funny, hey? The charisma of the left obviously still works for us old chicks.'

'Hey, be honest. He always had a good dose of his own, too ... D'you think we should fetch the children? It's nearly dark.'

'Let's make our way there slowly while we talk.'

'There's just one other thing,' Penny said, stripped suddenly of all audacity and mischief. 'I ... well, I'm not sure, but I'm wondering if Allan isn't seeing someone.'

'Why?'

'He's just been missing from the office at odd times. I don't know. Maybe it's nothing.'

'Do you care?' Francesca asked it gently. She lifted her arm, but dropped it again. In playfulness they could embrace and rough-house. But in fear and sadness, Penny snapped her carapace close about her.

'I know it sounds weird, considering my situation. But I do. You know, when I met Allan, I was so crazy about him that it scared me. I've always had this fear that he's so clever, and so desirable, I might lose him. And there's always been something a little withdrawn about him. Something you couldn't quite reach.'

'You've never told me that.'

'No and I don't show it much. It's never a good strategy.' She gave a mocking little snort. 'My oke is not a patch on Allan. Nowhere near as exciting. Sometimes I wonder if I don't keep him because he's so hard to lose. In a way, he's protection.'

Then Francesca did squeeze Penny's rigid shoulders. But Penny gave a quick laugh and shrugged Francesca's arm away. Perhaps she feared it was pity. She would never countenance pity.

THE MAN

The cold front punched at the sea, thumping waves against bitter-grey rocks and thrashing spray across the beach. The man walked, his legs bandy with bracing against the stark wind.

Tugging reflexively at the zip of his windbreaker, he bent forward, tasting the bite of the salt flung across the desolate stretch of sand. He was angry.

Brawling with the wind, he pushed defiantly through the sand that rose in spatters to attack his eyes and his nose. He was seldom angry, rarely summoning the passion organic to rage. Very little moved him to that extent. And lacking the experience himself, he found too much emotion in others unendurable.

He lacked the language, both of love and of fury, knowing that if he spoke at all, it would not be in the trifling flurries of dissension that others engaged in. Watching their futile conflicts, he experienced always the supremacy of the ninja looking on at a street fight. Generally, he responded to the rage of others with the cold blade of his lethal silence. If he spoke at all, he knew it would be to administer the sudden garotte, the compression of one fatal nerve. It would be over, coldly and mortally over.

Instead, he was walking, battling the spray and feeling himself at one with the waves that battered and burst to shore. He had not been ready to deliver the final blow, not to his wife and not before an audience of boys. He held it always warily, as one would a lethal weapon, never using it easily, and never impetuously.

This morning, the cold front had meant the lights and heater were on in the kitchen, where the boys had gathered for their rambunctious breakfast. His wife, dressing-gowned at the sink, had been washing distractedly as the boys yelled and jostled, the youngest snivelling at the combined ill-treatment of many elder brothers.

She hadn't been hearing them, her hands motionless in the water as she had gazed out at the sea. Slowly drawing her eyes back to the sink, she had finished with the cup and deposited it on the draining board.

Having completed the present round of washing up, she had slouched over on one hip, folding the morning newspaper against the draining board to read. He wondered if it were the boys she was avoiding, or the effort of standing again when the next round began. Or perhaps it was he.

Abruptly she had turned, as though she had planned it, psyched herself for the move before it came. Small frown nestled in place, her face was shiny with sleep and moisturiser.

'There's all these reports here,' she had said, her voice higher than its habitual pitch. 'About ... perhaps you should read them.'

He had raised his head slowly and gazed at her. Small corrugated clips had held her hair from her face. It was no longer ever quite straight, as it had been when she had straightened it for their early dates, whirling it about her head like a turban. But lacking the will and exuberance to curl, it quavered about her face, twitching this way and that.

'I mean these,' she had said, holding up the folded paper. She had a way of scrumpling it in an anxious fist so that it had to be smoothed and straightened before it could be read by anyone else. 'The TRC's in Kimberley now. Did you see?'

'I do read newspapers,' he had said, and dropped his eyes to his muesli.

'Well, I was wondering,' she had said and again, very deliberately, he had raised his eyes to her face, puckered now with the anxiety that hung always about her. 'You see, I mean they have finished with the Eastern Cape, but I don't know if that's the end.'

'Don't worry about it. It's fine, Seal. Stop worrying.' It was the name he had used when they were young, when she had been sleek and brown, wet hair slicked back from her face. He had been in his ascendancy then, ruler of all he surveyed. The name tasted strange in his mouth now, as though he had bitten into an alien dish, from another time and place.

He had used it designedly though, as he did everything. He had thought to remind her of how they had been, to draw her out of her small resentments and petty anxieties. He had used it to shut her up.

'No but ...' she had said and he had frowned, feeling the ice rise from his belly. His boys had quietened, rousing from their submersion in squabbled laughter, '... there's just all this stuff from the victims of detention.'

'The "victims", my dear – interesting to hear you use the word. Don't you find it amusing that the victors always get to name the victims? Of course, they would have created a nice cache of "victims" of their own, with quite as much facility, had the other side come out on top.'

The chill of his tone should have told her. He had not relished this discussion, particularly not in front of his sons. They never spoke of the past, had never found it necessary to rail on about what his role had once been. It was gone, finished. He had played his part and, while it might appear futile on superficial examination, he believed he had probably countered something that had required his opposition. Much of the pathetic student Marxism he had never taken seriously. But global communism had been a force to be reckoned with.

'Here, there's this story about this young guy who went into detention and he just died. They said to him when they got him: "Go say goodbye to your people because you won't be seeing them again." And they took him. And this other guy ...'

She had faltered. Allowing her eyes to escape his, she had loosed them to wander aimlessly about the walls that were always slightly grubby from the damp salt air. He had said nothing, but had kept his eyes on her.

'This other guy,' she had added, rushing her words to get them out before his stare could guillotine them, 'well, he said he was tortured – wet bags and electric wires and beatings and things ...'

That was the way it went, in life and in war. The choices one made conquered or were conquered. Only one side could win, after all. He had played the game and lost, but he had relished the game in the playing.

'He told them he'd had his hands cuffed to his feet over this wooden bar and ...'

'That's enough,' he had said. Aware of his sons who, like small tender beasts, sniffed the air for strangeness or conflict, he had added: 'We're eating breakfast. Must we have this litany of horror?'

'It's just,' she had said, 'that you never speak of it. I've just never known. And sometimes I worry ... I mean, when those hearings were down here, and you went off like that to East London ...'

He had risen then, abruptly, feeling the unaccustomed rage in his chest and his fists. Leaving the room, he had looked back – at his sons, his reason for being on earth at all. His two eldest had looked surprised, halted in the midst of a passionate discussion of Oasis. But the eyes of his youngest had caught at him in some long unused place.

Before him stretched the beach without end, the endless meander of perfect sand, bounded by dunes still topped with coastal bush. They had walked this beach, his brother and he, endlessly wandering the shoreline for days and sometimes weeks, tenting it in the holidays. His brother's eyes had held that look, the same vulnerable anxiety that was always at war with the defiant need to prove himself strong and adult.

She had also had that look – the young girl he had thought to have forgotten. Caged and fearful, she had struggled to appear unconcerned, stronger than they. It had strangely touched him, unused to the feeling there among that brash collection of senseless students and commies and terrorists. For an instant, as she had faced him for the first time, he had almost seen his brother staring mutinously across the cell. But that was absurd.

Sometimes he wondered where she was now, or whether she ever gave it a thought.

FRANCESCA

She took Megan to bookclub with her – a Megan whose beauty had altered, becoming older and somehow sorrowed. When had that happened? When had her baby cousin become a woman, with hollows and lines that rippled around her eyes?

They were a little late, held up by Paul, who wanted the brothel issue settled once and for all before the long weekend.

'We have to phone the council, apparently,' he was saying. 'But it's not as simple as that. It turns out we've been paying to the wrong substructure – we're on the border of Eastern and Northern. So we need to find out which of these newfangled substructure inventions we're supposed to belong to. Because now both are denying responsibility for us. Can you believe the fucking mess this city's in?'

They were silent for much of the drive. Parking her car, Francesca sighed. 'I've forgotten which substructure is which. I hope the car's all right here. There're so many trees.'

'Ask him tomorrow. The substructure, I mean. Let's hope not about your missing car.'

'He'll shout. About the substructure *and* the car.'

They began to giggle, struggling to recover themselves before the door was answered. Strangely, no comments were made about lateness. In fact one of the other women was later than they.

'Are you okay, Juliette? Is he home yet?' Their hostess stepped forward to greet the newcomer.

'Well, if you can call it being home.'

Francesca's attention was seized more by Juliette's tone than her words. That font of all good sense and PTA wisdom sounded unsteady.

'What happened?' she asked.

They glanced at each other, all those in the loop of this lore. Juliette took a breath.

'My husband had a nervous breakdown.' It sounded so incongruous from this capable woman in tartan pleats. 'He's out of hospital now, but he says that if he'd had anywhere else to go, he'd never've come home.' She took a gulp of wine. Juliette never drank wine.

Jude reached across and squeezed Juliette's plump hand. Francesca had always liked Jude, her dimples in waggish contrast to the lumpen frocks she chose to wear.

'I don't know how to go on with him like this. It's not like he's ever hurt me or anything. But it's the ignoring ...'

'My husband hit me once,' another of them broke in. 'Only once though. It was in the '80s when everyone's business was going under.'

Madelaine was a quiet hamster of a woman with a nervous quiver to her nose. As empathy rose from her belly, Francesca tasted shame. She had never truly seen these women. Not as individuals. They had been tokens of the kind of life she both wished she could want, and yet longed to be free of. Despite their respectable trappings and school-bound lives, she now felt a burgeoning sense of sisterhood with them.

'I was so angry,' added Madelaine with her crimped laugh, 'I grabbed him by the hair and I yelled: "Don't you ever touch me like that again." '

Francesca flooded with admiration for the strength in this twitching woman. She, who had thought herself more interesting than the lot of them, did nothing but bend and buckle for the sake of a quiet, and sometimes not so quiet, peace.

'Well, my husband never hit me,' said Fern, stacking plates for their lasagne. Behind her, their hostess and her plain children smiled down from the photo portrait above the hottray. 'But sometimes I almost wished he had.'

'Why?' asked Francesca, acknowledging a tentative response of her own.

'Just for the contact. He said he couldn't stand pregnant women so he never spoke a word to me from the time he learnt I was pregnant. Not one word.'

It seemed he had moved into the spare room, eating there by himself. If she approached, he would lock himself in, or leave the house. Not one word.

Francesca gazed at the stern woman by the sideboard, greying hair cut inflexibly across her forehead. She had always known that Fern didn't like her much. She hadn't cared, contemptuous of Fern's reverence for the institutions that ruled their lives. She should have been able to see some of this. Surely she should have recognised the signs.

As if by consent, all discussion of abusive husbands and troubled marriages closed as their hostess brought the coffee through. They discussed the books and chose in strict order, regulated by the ever-efficient Juliette, her cheeks just slightly redder than usual. At exactly half past ten, they all stood to leave.

'And you said they were boring,' said Megan as they reached the car. 'You said their lives were suburban convention personified.' She directed an odd gaze at Francesca, as though she were appraising a total stranger. 'My God, but this is a weird town. You think you know the way things are – you take them for granted – and nothing ever turns out quite like you'd thought.'

Francesca and Anthony met in the dim bar of his hotel.

'Sorry,' he said and shrugged. Strapping laughter echoed off the faux wooden panelling from the huddles of boys in coloured shirts, ties tugged askew.

She shook her head. It didn't matter at all. They hid in the corner, on the other side of the cigarette machine. She didn't have coins. Neither did he.

'Never mind,' he said. 'Smoke mine.'

They were too strong for her, but they'd have to do. His hands shook as he lit one for her.

'So, what have ...'

He held out a hand briskly, like a traffic-cop. 'No,' he said. 'Don't say anything.'

He reached out his curled hand and laid the fingers against her cheek. Slowly he closed his eyes and she watched all his fears and frailties scuttle across the lines of his face. He opened his eyes and they were gone.

Compulsively, they spoke of the years that lay between them. She matched him smoke for smoke and drink for drink, the intensity of the moment outmanoeuvring the alcohol.

He was dark and lithe as he'd always been, yet, somewhere in the intervening years, he'd lost the unattainable lines of youth. Of course they were all older, but he seemed altered – smudged at the edges by a softening of belly and a gentling of attitudes. Less glamour of the barricades, more humanity.

'Would you ... won't you come to my room?'

But she couldn't, she said. It was complicated. She told him something of her marriage, and about Daniel too. He seemed to understand. She explained about Martin and how she had not been able to follow it through.

'I don't want to make your life more difficult,' he said.

Obsessively, they sipped and smoked and spoke of themselves, their lives and their children. He didn't touch her at all except to stretch his curled hand across the space between them and lay it against her cheek.

The rumours had been true he told her, lighting two more Camels. He had been active in that dangerous '80s time. His task had been to gather government information. Not so much the ministers and MPs, ever-cautious with the *donderse* foreign press. It had been the clerks and secretaries he had charmed and taken for drinks and sometimes even slept with. Attitudes and state of mind had been his brief – squirming his way into the heart and mind of the enemy.

Lowering her glass to the scarred table, she lifted it again almost immediately. She didn't know what else to do with herself. Sting was singing, for the second time, about fields of barley. Perhaps it was their only CD. Her hands dithered about the table, gathering cardboard coasters.

She wasn't going to sleep with him. She knew she couldn't do it. But she couldn't bear for this to end. It was more intimate than sex. The sharing of secrets, the laying open of wounds and psyches, was more passionate than anything she had ever done with Paul. He stretched fingers, chilled from fresh drinks, to her face. And this time she bent her head to meet his hand.

'I don't think I was very good at it,' he said. 'Trying to pass on information.'

'I don't see why you beat yourself up over that. Being a hack, particularly then, was hard enough.'

Their voices had raised slightly, but there was no-one about them. The boys in their rolled shirtsleeves had gathered their boisterous laughter around the bar. Anthony lit two more Camels. She thought perhaps they were making her a little light-headed, but it seemed so confiding to share them with him.

'I knew I was failing,' he said, with a deep slug of whisky. He drank it neat, but it appeared to have no effect on him. 'I was getting shitty messages from London about missing this story or that. But it was more often that I got the story, but missed getting any useful information at all.'

His fingers were long, reaching for his drink in a delicate, almost painterly way. 'And all the while I was getting more and more paranoid.'

She lifted a hand to smooth his wild eyebrows. There was such clarity to them. She could see each hair in its forested scramble for existence.

'I couldn't sleep. I couldn't eat. I thought I was being followed and, as I became more paranoid, I became worse at everything. I was totally ineffectual, yet I was paralysed by the fear of being caught. I thought my phones were tapped, that I was being followed. I thought ...'

'And were you?'

'I ... who knows? It just seemed like it.'

He lifted both elegant hands so that the beads fell back against the sleeves he had rolled from his wrists. Laying them, open-fingered against his cheeks, he rubbed his face. Sting was singing, for the second time, about the shape of his heart.

'So is that when you skipped?' She wished she could hold his head to her breast as she did with Daniel when he wept.

'Now you see how cowardly I really am. I couldn't face the faintest possibility of being arrested.'

'At least you avoided the possibility of interrogation. This way, you couldn't give them any answers.'

'But I would have. Don't you see? I saw myself for the first time, and I knew I would've given them whatever they wanted if it would keep me out of jail. I couldn't ... there was nothing to do but leave.'

She felt very close to him, not so much for the past charisma she had kindled in her cell, although that still clung to him. She warmed now to his flaws. As one who had also failed, who had foundered at a game that grew too large for her, she felt she understood him. They were the same, she and he.

'I think that's brave,' she said.

He released a bitter salvo of laughter. 'That's very charitable of you ...'

Leaning forward, she was startled at the way his face slipped suddenly away from her, sliding sickeningly from her grasp.

'Are you okay?' he asked.

'It's nothing. I'm fine. I think I'll just find the loo.'

She made it there, thank God, before being sicker than she could remember since university, when she'd had the excuse of being young and stupid. But two minutes ago she had been fine, absolutely fine. How had she not felt this coming?

'You're not okay,' he said, when she returned. 'I'm sorry. It's my fault.'

Stupid, stupid. She felt about twenty years younger than she should be. Somehow he had time-warped them back to the time they had first known each other. And again, she was the novice to be tutored in the ways of the world.

'It's my fault,' he said again. 'I've got you all emotionally tangled. And that's just what I meant not to do. You've enough to deal with.'

'I should go.'

'Don't be crazy. You can't drive home like this. Come to my room. I'll make you coffee.'

'I'm sorry. I don't know how ...'

'It's all the emotion. It's affecting me too. Don't feel bad. It's nothing to be ashamed of.'

Sting restarted his cycle of love and whatever else he was wittering on about, just as she thankfully caved against his side. He was so tender, laying her upon the bed while he made her tea because she couldn't face coffee. Paul would just have been angry.

'Sleep now,' he whispered, settling into a chair by the bed. 'I'll wake you.'

Her body still felt the imprint of his support of her, and suddenly she missed it. With the poignancy of having experienced something for the first time, she felt the lack of a bolstering force in her emotional life.

'Please won't you sit beside me?' she asked him.

Anthony knelt beside her, holding a facecloth to her temple. She was never sure he intended it and, afterwards, he denied it. But moving across to her other side, his knee nudged her inner thigh. It was so blatantly sexual a gesture that every thought transmuted instantly to desire. She could almost taste her heartbeat, hold it in her mouth, dandle it on her tongue.

'Perhaps we shouldn't ...' he said.

His skin was dark and silken smooth. She would never have conjured it quite so soft. He entered her fiercely. He needed this too. Not just the sex, with its banality of modern implications, but the intensity of some terrible intimacy. A lost boy, he pressed himself into the womb of her, as though he could cease to exist and be reborn through her.

Flipping them over so that he lay upon his back, he reached both hands to her face. 'I don't want you to be frightened,' he said. 'I want you to feel in control.'

She loved him for that, a feral love born in the depths of her. Taking him inside her, she absorbed him, feeling their annihilation. And there in her belly she conceived them both anew.

He had no need to say anything. It was there. It was all there, but he said it anyway. Lighting a Camel and moving slightly so as to gaze on her, he murmured something.

'What did you say?'

'I said I think I have loved you my whole life.'

'There's the sea, Daniel. Look, the first glimpse of sea is always lucky.'

She felt ambivalent. She had been looking forward to this long weekend for weeks. But now she almost wished she hadn't come. They were all to spend these few days in a cottage Penny had cadged off a friend who couldn't get away from the city.

They arrived within half-an-hour of each other, setting off the alarm and battling to silence it again.

'Well, I'd say the neighbours know we're here,' muttered Allan, wrestling luggage. Penny was chivvying children – her own Hannah and Allan's two boys.

The children had begun to screech with delighted dismay. All except Daniel who crouched, hands cupped to ears, beneath the lala palms. He stayed there while they unpacked, curled beside the spiked leaves until Allan dropped a bundle of braai equipment and lifted him roughly away.

'Yussis, check this,' he said, pointing to the boomslang draped in perfect camouflage.

The children were shrilly sent for shoes as Megan, the last to arrive, gingerly trod the winding drive in her venerable Volksie.

'Doesn't this remind you of our childhood, Meg-child?' she yelled as her cousin emerged. But Megan was doing her morose thing. She had always had that dubious ability to sink into a sulk over some imagined insult and refuse to talk about it. No doubt she'd be able to coax her out of it sooner or later.

Francesca had always found something claustrophobic in the denseness of Kwazulu-Natal's green. It was as if there were too much air. It weighed upon the lungs after the spare Highveld bite, where the grass was brisk and bleached by winter frosts.

Here everything was overblown, a harbinger of fantastical childhood holidays in Durban, of trips to the Indian market – she and Megan choosing snakes on sticks, and tiny baskets for their arms between mountains of red and yellow spice.

They braaied of course, after a sundown wander on the beach. Francesca could tell they were all tired. Megan wouldn't speak and Penny and Allan bickered all the way back to the cottage.

'You can't possibly go for a run tomorrow.'

'Why the hell can't I?'

'Because you'll be boring and go to bed straight after supper. And we'll stay up late and you'll wake us in the morning.'

It was academic anyway. Francesca thought most of them would collapse shortly after supper. From where she sat, she could make out only a tiny blue triangle of sea. Mahoganies tangled with the darkening sky while, beneath them, a matted blanket of green draped itself over the ancient sanddunes.

Hannah, no doubt prompted by her mother, had joined Daniel in the garden where he had discovered a patch of *toktokkie* holes. They were doing what generations of children had, using twigs to imitate the movement of tiny legs, or dropping ants into holes, to be sucked slowly under the sand and devoured.

'Hannah,' called Penny, ever the practical one. 'It's time for your bath.'

Hannah, the dream child, scrambled to her feet. Daniel appeared at the steps of the stoep.

'I don't want to bath,' he said.

'You don't have to,' said Francesca. 'We're on holiday.'

'But I don't want Hannah to either.'

'They're all going,' said Allan. 'My boys too. Why don't you go with them?'

But Daniel wanted to go on catching *toktokkies*.

'Well, don't bath then,' Francesca said, worrying that, from the comfort of their easy children, they were picturing critically how this should be handled. Penny was logical with him, which was a mistake. He began to scream. Intensely aware of the others, their holiday, of their drinks time, for God's sake, she shushed him too urgently. Any minute now, he'd set Paul off. Please, please, she begged them both silently, let's keep the peace.

She dragged Daniel to his room but he was frightened to be left there, all alone in a strange house. She was so tired. All she wanted was to sit with the others, drink her wine and listen to the lush zing of insects. She couldn't leave the child there, if he was fearful, but she had to keep him away from the others.

'Oh Daniel shoosh. Please.' She could hear the gathering desperation in her voice. 'You know this drives me mad ...'

The child screamed, sweat beading his blue-tinged mouth.

'Daniel.' It was a screech, but she could do nothing about it. 'Shut up. Just shut up. I can't cope with this anymore. Just shut up.'

Daniel knew exactly where her emotional buttons were. Sometimes she thought he did this on purpose, pushing her to examine her own propensity for madness, which seemed to hover so near at times like these.

He calmed suddenly, as he did when he had pushed her too far. Daniel always followed the same pattern, gradually transforming over weeks from choirboy to devil incarnate. Then he would prod her forward till she was forced to gaze down into the open shaft of her own urge to hurt him. And then, quite suddenly, he would switch again.

The next day was perfect. They wandered barefoot through the bush and palms and wild bananas to the beach, weighed down with picnic baskets and little nets. The soil of the path was cool and loamy beneath Francesca's toes.

Megan went off on her own to the great, fat rocks where she sat with knees drawn up to her chin. She and Penny lay with towels touching, giggling and skinnering about that colleague of Penny's who, ice-maiden or not, was said to be having an affair with a labour consultant. Labour consultants thought themselves very dashing.

It was low tide and the children were roaming the rocks, Daniel peering into rock pools and poking gently with his net. He never caught gobies like Allan's boys. He hated to see them gasp.

Paul and Allan both read for a while, Allan busy with some management practice tome. But they grew restless as very boyish boys did. Shifting and stretching, they strode off to swim before pacing the beach, back and forth. Francesca could hear scraps of their conversation at each turn.

'It's the delivery that's a train smash. I mean, the policy's okay ...'

'They over-promised. That's the bugger. Certainly on houses and health.'

'But it's two fucking years now, and all they've done is fine-tune the policy ...'

Francesca lay and felt Anthony's skin in the silken touch of the sun; smelt the sweetgrass of his underarms in the sea-laden breeze. They would lie here and talk, if he were here, and she would make him laugh. He had become so fixed on her life, so fascinated by her every detail that his laughter came easily. Each school lift had become an adventure, saved up to tell him, and every shopping trip an anecdote, laden with wit and insight into human nature.

The kids flowed over for lunch – first Allan's always-hungry boys, then Hannah, and finally Daniel. The men opened beers.

'... if the Labour Bill goes through in that form, it'll make us the most pro-union country in the world.'

'That's my point. Here we are trying to be globally competitive and the whole slant is to tie business's hands. I just think it's an idiotic time to be doing this.'

'As well. And now this bloody deadlock over lock-out rights ...'

'I hear government's going to compromise eventually. The word is that if business gets lock-out rights in the Act, they won't be included in the Constitution.'

'Ja, great, isn't it? They get the constitutional right to strike, but we get no corresponding right if procedures aren't followed. Just brilliant!'

It grew chilly during the afternoon and they walked along the beach, bundled in jerseys. Where Francesca had grown up, the cold came in with fury, flinging wind and spray and sand across the beach. Here it didn't fight. Weighted by dark clouds, it lay heavily upon them.

As they turned for home, the rain began – sluggishly, in great, ponderous drops. Shrieking and laughing, they dashed for the cottage. She lifted Daniel, who laughed into the spatters of rain. Paul stopped to look back at them, but he turned again without speaking. Daniel could never have kept up, had he been forced to try.

They built a fire inside and dispatched the men to braai on the stoep. The rain was solid, screening them from the world outside. Just as the children prepared for bed, the electricity died.

Francesca sat up late, huddled under a crocheted blanket in the dark with Penny. They had moved outside to watch the rain and speak of the kind of things that sent Paul and Allan scuttling for their beds.

'Have you ever noticed,' she murmured to Penny, 'how couples with dodgy marriages always make these involved, sort of tacit plans to go to bed at different times?'

Her friend nodded. 'And they do it even before they notice it themselves.'

They awoke to rain, a constant drumming on the wooden stoep. They had grown listless with it by now, depressed by a cottage that was designed for sunlight and sandy towels. An expedition, they decided, was what was required.

The two couples settled into Allan's 4x4. They would get petrol and a few provisions, while Megan would follow with the kids when the adult duties were done. They left them playing Monopoly.

Francesca's cell rang in the Superette, where they were buying candles and eggs. Megan's car, it seemed, had lodged itself firmly and irrevocably into the sinking earth of the sodden drive.

'But the lights are back on,' she said. 'We're quite happy playing Monopoly. Go enjoy yourselves. We'll drag the car out later.'

'Well!' said Penny and they all laughed, lightened by the let-off-school atmosphere. 'Where should we go?'

They should have dope, they decided with much bravado and talk of past scores. Even Allan harked back to bankies in Hillbrow, and entered into the spirit of the thing. They stopped at every garage they saw, but it was too early in the day. However, if they were prepared to go with 'my brother to my village' ... Francesca and Penny were all for the experience, vying with each other to be young and adventurous, but the men were uneasy about being led off into the bundu.

'Oh well, that's that then,' said Paul, and Francesca felt a spurt of compassion at the relief in his voice, and at the small boy's heart that had not permitted its articulation. The rain still steady, they headed for the restaurant at the Old Pont, through the plantations where rain streamed from the blue packets covering the bananas.

It should have been romantic, although restaurants that should be, seldom were. But if you half-closed your eyes, it almost was, with its higgledy verandah and hibiscus plants. And as they ate, a spear of sunlight pierced the rain and bled emerald light over the dark bush.

They thought they might drive down to the river after lunch, to peer across the swollen water at the Transkei. But there was a boom across the road now – they would have to pay to reach the river. Somehow, in this immutable rain, it lost its appeal.

They drove on, reluctant to let go of their freedom. Somewhere near Port Edward they came upon what would once have been called a Native Trading Store, with a butchery next door.

'Look, this isn't the place to find great cuts,' said Paul, but the others pooh-poohed him. They all wanted to stop and stretch, buy smokes, perhaps just to feel less jailed by the rain which still fell in rods of metallic grey.

Taxis swarmed the muddy ground, and people scuttled for cover under the overhang of the store. Giggling girls in bras and shiny cardigans whispered and eyed strutting young men, cocky with bombast.

The older women had settled on flattened cardboard boxes, unpinning towels and nuzzling babies to breasts. An old man held court on a lone wooden chair around the corner, surrounded by a coterie of squatting men, rich with the smell of BB tobacco. The old man looked up as they passed, acknowledging their greeting with stately inclination of the head. Crumbs had gathered in his beard and spindled wrists poked from frayed sleeves, yet his yellowed eyes held a nobility of custom and his pipe-clenched mouth a distinction of musical speech.

The store was resonant of smoky bodies and new blankets. Francesca breathed in the elusive emanation of early, hardly conscious memory – the smell of paraffin from the pump outside, the tart scent of African print, the dark odour of deep shelves and mysterious commodities.

The counter ran the length of the room in deep shadow, almost concealing the middle-aged Indian who grouched and chided his customers. Packets of white sugar jammed against cans of curry, bottles of meths and tinny pots and kettles. On the counter, dusty sweets lay beside government bread, and an enamel bowl of hard-boiled eggs. At the far end, thin floral frocks crowded their colours into the drab room.

Hustling for attention, the locals showed an exceptional lack of curiosity about them or the planet they had dropped from. Their group was simply alien, of no pertinence at all to the lives lived here.

Having touched and bought and explored, they turned to the butchery off to the side. Ducking to enter the low door, Francesca felt the blow of its abattoir stench. Fly-specked haunches ornamented a room already embellished by pliant piles of offal, chicken legs and mournful sheep's heads baring yellowed teeth.

'Perhaps we should ...' Francesca, never the staunchest meat-eater, was fighting nausea.

'Ja, no, perhaps the meat can last another day,' said Paul.

'Well,' said Allan as they tramped the mud and dodged taxis to reach the car, 'that dealt with any illusion that we hadn't yet become a third world country.'

'Didn't it just,' said Paul. Francesca could hear the anger building in his voice again. 'All standards and regulations have gone to shit. It's like that brothel just popping up next door.'

'Those people are all buying that meat and feeding it to their children ... and we're expecting to raise a healthy generation ...'

'Oh, that is so not true.' Francesca knew she sounded defensive, but she felt somehow responsible for putting it all in perspective. 'Places like this have been here forever. It's because of poverty, not because we've got a new government. It takes time ...'

'She's right,' said Penny the fair. 'I can remember places like this from when we were kids. It hasn't just suddenly sprung up to annoy you.'

She was thankful for Penny's support. But it tired her to be always the compulsive optimist while Penny could simply weigh up and pronounce. Somehow they had all taken for themselves the roles of cynic, of questioner and commentator, while she must carry the burden of holding them here.

'Why must everything be some kind of symbol of how the country's become?'

'And I suppose,' said Penny a little uncertainly, 'if we were in some other country we'd think this was all kind-of picturesque.'

Francesca watched Penny oppressively, her best friend in the world, relaxing only when she saw her nod and grin.

'Except for the sheep's heads,' Francesca said.

'Ja,' said Penny, pulling a mournful decapitated sheep's face.

Megan had been crying. It made the men edgy. They didn't know what to do with her. Paul offered her a drink a trifle too jocularly and Allan just avoided her altogether. At one point Paul flopped beside her and nudged her with his shoulder. But it only took a 'Beer, china?' for him to lose his sheepish concern and leap up in search of firelighters.

Francesca drafted Megan into salad making, while Penny went off to drag granny-fingered children from the bath.

'Hey you guys,' Allan was sodden, dripping all over the parquet floor. 'My car's been broken into.'

The men were stoic and sensible. It was decided that Allan would go off in search of a town. He and Paul unstuck Megan's car first, bodily lifting the little Beetle when planks and suggestions failed. Mud to their elbows, hair spattered across thinning scalps, they trooped in to wash. Still phlegmatic, Paul began the fire as Allan left.

'Well, if it's like this again tomorrow, I think we'll leave,' Paul said as the children bickered over whose pyjamas sported the coolest super-hero. It made Daniel anxious, drawing him to stand beside Francesca in the tiny sentinel position that always irritated Paul.

'Well, we can't,' said Megan. 'I meant to tell you, but we've had so much other drama. I was listening to the radio and, well, we're trapped here. It's been snowing on the Drakensberg and all roads between here and Gauteng are cut off.'

'Serious?' said Penny. 'How exciting.'

'There must be a way out,' said Paul. 'I've got a helluva schedule next week.' He strode to the table and flipped the radio on.

> *'... so far been responsible for nine reported injuries and one death. Klaas Eiman from Calvinia froze to death on the roadside between his hometown and Loeriesfontein on Friday.*
>
> *'More than a thousand motorists who were unable to leave Harrismith have been housed in schools, churches and the town hall.*
>
> *'More snow is forecast for tonight and all roads from KwaZulu-Natal remain closed.'*

'At least we're here,' said Megan brightly, 'and not in a soup kitchen.'

'Soup kitchens are definitely not my thing,' said Penny, raising her wine glass. 'We'll just stay here and read and play games. It'll be delicious.'

They were all giggling now, except Paul. They were trapped in a world of childhood – of braais and lounge floor picnics, of Monopoly until 3am, drinking wine and sharing secrets. The rain seemed now a boon, rather than a prison. It all just depended on the way you looked at it.

'We can build a fire inside.'

'And I saw a whole shelf of murder mysteries.'

Paul's braai tongs clattered to the parquet. 'You people just don't seem to realise that some of us have serious work to do.'

'Yes, but Paul,' said Penny the practical, 'you can't go if we're trapped. And no-one can blame ...'

'It's not a matter of blame, for fuck sake. It's a matter of losing deals worth hundreds of grand.'

Paul strode to the telephone. 'I'll get the AA. I bet there's a way out.'

Daniel crawled on to Francesca's lap, rubbing his nose on her jersey. Raised voices upset him, which in turn seemed to agitate Paul still further. Penny lifted her eyebrows at Francesca, who tugged her mouth ruefully and shrugged. When Paul was like this, it was better to remain silent. Anything she said would provoke him. Yet she felt that Penny expected her to do something.

'Paul,' she said quietly. He ignored her.

'Yes?' he said into the receiver. 'Shit. But tomorrow? How about later tomorrow? Well, if Van Reenen's Pass is the worst-hit, maybe we could get back through Swaziland. Ja, I know it's a shit road. Okay, thanks anyway.'

'It *is* still closed,' he said. 'But the long route through Pongola and Standerton isn't so badly hit. I think we'll just wait till lunchtime tomorrow, then we'll leave.'

'Paul, won't you consider ...?'

'We should be packed by morning. Daniel, get off your mother. You're a big boy. Go sort out your clothes.'

Francesca held Daniel in place. Tugging a fistful of jersey with a clammy hand, he was rubbing it back and forth across his nose.

'Paul, please could you just think for a minute ...?'

'What?' His face had turned the ugly colour of his rage. 'For fuck's sake, what?'

'Paul, listen. I don't want to go if it's dangerous.'

'You want to stay and play house with your friends.'

'Paul, you're not being sensible,' said Penny. She shouldn't. She really shouldn't. 'You don't want to drive your family when it's dangerous.'

'Shut up.' He bellowed, causing even Penny to start. Daniel began to hum quietly and tunelessly. She could feel the tiny thrum of his chest against her stomach. Paul picked up the braai tongs and turned back to the fire.

'Paul, please.' She felt uncomfortable facing him down like this. She found herself glancing backward, positioning the doors in her head. She always faced Paul's anger in doorways. It was just that his rage left her battered. His loudness flattened her resolve and broke the spirit of retaliation. She needed the space behind her to duck and weave, to roll with the punches.

'Paul? Please don't be like this. We're just trying to be ...'

What? Sensible? She couldn't lay claim to sense, when he was angry. He was the sensible one. She was supposed to know that.

'Shut up.' A fine spray burst from his lips. 'Just shut the fuck up. Shut your fucking mouth.' There had always been something fearful about a male shriek, something torn from the depths of a shredded, terror-filled manhood.

'What do you know? What the fuck do you know about what's safe and what's not?'

Francesca glanced behind her, checking for doors. She and Daniel were silent, quiet as little mice, humming their tuneless tunes in their chests.

'Listen, Francesca.' His voice was quieter now, but his tone still harsh. 'You're completely bloody useless at anything practical. Just leave these decisions to me. You think I would do something dangerous? Are you mad?' He grimaced as he jabbed a finger at his temple.

Quiet, quiet as mice, gently rocking each other. Silent, silent as the grave, where she wished he was.

'I don't feel like any supper. I need an early night if we're leaving tomorrow.' He flung the tongs to the floor.

Banish it, she thought. Don't even think it. It was bad karma. But sometimes Francesca just wondered, could karma be that cruel?

She crept silently to her bed, slipping flat as a limp tissue beneath the blankets. Quiet, quiet, don't wake him.

She felt him shift behind her and tensed, not moving a finger. Don't let him ... oh please don't let him wake. Not tonight.

He slid across, pressing his body at her back. Oh no, she couldn't face it. Not now, with his rage still slick on her skin. She lay stony and still and, perhaps he felt it, for he turned without a word and slept.

It didn't matter. None of this mattered. Soon Anthony would come back permanently. Perhaps the wife would let him bring his kids. At least for the holidays. But it was inescapable.

Anthony felt it too, confirming it tacitly whenever they spoke. Not directly. Nothing practical. Just: 'Where would you rather live, Parkview or Melville?' or 'Are you happy with one child?' Little remarks, little reveries of another life, another time.

'Fran? Frannie, are you awake?' Megan had opened the door a crack.

'Yes. Shh. Go to the lounge. I'll come.'

'Sorry,' she said when Francesca joined her. 'We haven't had a chance to talk.'

And so she sat with her cousin, way into the early hours, watching the rain close them off from the world. Knees drawn up under the crocheted blanket, they crouched together on the verandah *bankie*.

'I'm pregnant.' Megan whispered it, although there was no-one to hear, no sound but the shattering of rain on the bush.

'Tebs?'

'I don't know. I just don't know.'

'Oh.'

'I'm not sure if I should have an abortion.'

'Do you want to?'

'Not really.'

'Okay.'

'But I don't want to ... I don't think I want to lose Tebogo. And what if the baby's white?'

Francesca had nothing to say. There was no answer to such sadness.

'And then what if the baby's black? I don't think my mother ... I don't think she could love it. And I'm not sure if I'm strong enough to do it alone. I want to be, but what if I'm not? What if I'm on my own and I'm not strong enough?'

'You would be, you know. And the mothers ... at first it would seem like their lives had collapsed. But they'd come round in the end.'

'D'you really think so?'

'Yes I do. But any case, you're strong. You'd manage – with or without Tebs, with or without our mothers.'

They got up to go inside only when the sky lightened, the bush beneath them still impenetrably dark. Two dry patches marked where they had sat, too near the eaves. But before they reached the door, the patches had disappeared.

THE MAN

'Dad, Dad, how's that for a cast?'

'Good. Far enough. But ... look, can you see you're about to get tangled there, in the gully? Try to cast that way rather, where the water is deeper.'

The child nodded, reeled in, checked his bait and recast. Then he settled beside the man, windbreaker crackling against windbreaker. His youngest was not a chatterer. This was the only one of his boys who lacked the boisterous puppy clamour of his wild litter.

He closed his eyes and felt the pale sun warm his face. The wind was cold. Beside him, a small body nestled into the hollow of his torso, sheltering from the lash of the spray. His two arms he rested on his knees, the rod comfortably between them.

Between gusts, the sun's warmth spread and settled, and he could smell the golden, salt tang of the child's head, resting on his shoulder. Of all his sons, this was the special one. This was the child conceived and born because of the baby that had died. And sometimes, very late at night, he lay listening to the roar of the waves and, had he believed in a god beyond the strange sea-borne deity he acknowledged, he might have given thanks for the death that had brought him this life.

Had his wife known this, had she even sensed it in him, it would have been the end of everything. Having accepted so much by marrying him, she had pushed the limits of what she would acquiesce in, and then she had pushed them still further. She had remained with him through the exposure that had named him publicly as a spy. She had even accepted this reclusive and ascetic life. But that was where her line was drawn.

She remained now because of the boys, and perhaps because she no longer knew of another life. He did not embellish his view of himself with the thought that it might be out of a passion for him. But strangely, with all those living, boisterous boys for her to love, it was the still-born corpse that held her most firmly. It was the one she had never known that was loved most protectively, mourned most obsessively, and sanctified as the perfect child.

He did not believe in God. He could not remember if he ever had, but after his brother's death he certainly had not. He believed in nature, that was all. He believed in the balance of cruelty and kindness that ordered the universe. It was epitomised for him in the sea, in its strength and gentleness, in the life it gave and the many lives it took. It had no reason. It granted no explanation.

His brother had been taken. And then, when the man had grown tired and ceased to look for the brother in the faces of his sons, when still another life had been taken, he had been given this boy.

The child was not Gavin. He knew that. He was different in subtle ways. He was shaped differently by a troop of older brothers, who cuffed and teased him and made him tough. And that was good. He would never know the gentleness of a twin-like closeness. But he would also never be unmanned by it, never torn in two by the gentleness it bred and the terrible harshness of its loss.

Sometimes though, when the sun warmed his eyelids and the rounded rocks pressed against his back, a body at his side, it could almost feel as though Gavin had been returned to him.

'Dad?'

He opened his eyes and looked down into those of his son, impossibly large and forested by eyelashes. Apart from his eyes, the boy's face was snub, a South African face, freckled and cow-licked. It was the eyes that gave him more. It was the eyes that welled, that darkened and hollowed when he was reprimanded. Gavin's also used to do that.

'Dad? The boys at school ... they were talking about their dads' army days. Kyle even brought an army helmet to school. And one boy, Thabo, he said his dad was in the other army. You know? MK? So we played armies at break. Everyone wanted to be in MK. But that's really because everyone likes Thabo.'

'Who won?'

'Oh they did. But they had the best team ... But Dad? I was wondering. I mean, you never talk about it. Were you in the army?'

'For a while, but then I finished up my national service in the police.'

'The police? But Dad, in those days, weren't the police bad? Thabo says ...'

'Thabo is spouting what he's heard, and from someone who was on the other side. You saw exactly what it was like at break. It's the same as real life. People chose sides and picked teams and, very often, it was because of people they liked or wanted to be like. And in the end, only one side can win.'

'But Dad? Didn't they kill ...'

'If you asked any one of those boys, you would probably find that their fathers killed people. Even Thabo. Perhaps especially Thabo. It was a war. That's what happens in a war.'

'But you, Dad? Did you?'

'While I was in the police at that time, I patrolled this wild part of Johannesburg called Hillbrow. I protected people. I kept people safe. I managed to get through national service without killing a soul.'

'Oh. Okay.'

The child was silent again, mulling. The man did not feel awkward in answering the boy's questions. He was a straightforward child who requested simple answers. He had never had a problem with that.

There might come a time, after a few more years of new moralities and new elites, when the tone of his questions might change.

Perhaps then he might retain just some of Gavin's objectivity. Perhaps he would comprehend how it had been, how different the world had seemed. There was also the chance that he might not.

But he could not worry about that now. It was as unfathomable and immutable as the lives and deaths of the sea anemones that waved so grandiosely and so futilely to the heavens in the rockpools around them.

FRANCESCA

'Penny, counsel me quickly. I'm sure I've forgotten something drastic.'

'You haven't forgotten anything. You're fine.'

'How's Daniel?'

'Daniel's having a wonderful time. Hannah's playing school with him. Appeals to her bossy instincts. So now, where are you again today?'

'You mean really?'

'No, arsehole.'

'I'm teaching a crowd of TV interns some documentary techniques. At the institute.'

'Fine. Keep your phone on, just in case. Now forget everything else and enjoy yourself. A whole Saturday. What bliss!'

Penny had been back only a day or two, having waited for the main road to open before they and Megan drove back in convoy. Francesca and Paul had suffered a tortuous journey during which it had rained constantly. They had never been in any real danger – a detail of some exultation to Paul – unless you counted the driving rain on secondary roads. But of course, Francesca hadn't mentioned this.

Anthony opened the door without a word, took her hand and led her into the room. It had not yet been cleaned, and the bed yawned before them. He leant to kiss her chastely, his skin smell fighting for space beneath the soap and toothpaste and lingering tobacco. They moved diffidently to the bed – there was nowhere else to go – and perched side-by-side.

Anthony took a hesitant breath and stretched out his fingers for her to see. His hands shook slightly. She laced them in hers and they laughed, abashed by their own intensity.

'I've missed you,' he said.

Her hands rose to blunder at his buttons, unable to bear the separation of fabric.

'No,' he said, finding her hands and holding them. 'No, not yet. Last time ... it shouldn't have been like that. This time is for you. This time will be slow.'

But it wasn't slow. He brought his mouth to her belly. His tongue reached for the gentle hollows at the top of each thigh, and it wasn't slow anymore. It was needy and consuming, each of them gorging on the feel and smell of the other.

'I'm sorry,' he said, gasping it into her neck. 'I'm so sorry. I meant it to be slow.'

'It can be slow next time,' she murmured. They put the 'Do not disturb' sign on the door and lay very close, playing and whispering, exploring and giggling.

If they were quiet, they could just detect the sounds of traffic, distant sirens and children's voices in the gardens of the hotel. But from the bed, she could see nothing but the trees tattooed on the sky.

The morning was almost over, hustling to be gone. She felt his perspiration, grass-cool beneath her cheek. And this time it was slow.

Rising to make them tea, she sang softly, half to herself and partly for him, feeling her chest unfold to the sounds of her song and the clink of cups. But when she turned, she found him coiled into himself and the impersonal bed. Glass in one hand, Camel in the other, he was swaddled in a dressing gown.

'What is it?' she whispered. 'What's the matter? Tell me.'

'I can't,' he said without turning. 'I don't want to soil you with all my disillusions. I'm old and tainted. Don't you see, Francesca? I've failed at everything I've touched.

'Anthony, no ...'

'No. You make me believe I can still have a life. But it's wrong. I don't deserve it. How could I ever have you? I'd ruin you.'

'No, Anthony. You're not a failure. You've lived with absolute integrity. You just demanded too much of yourself.'

She could taste the urgency of her need to dissuade him. Why was this always her role? Couldn't she ever have the luxury of faltering while someone else expended the effort to reassure her? This was not a desperate battle, though. His protest was desultory. He needed the comfort, as a child might call for his mother – not because of the darkness so much as to reassure himself that she was there.

'You ... Anthony, you need to forgive yourself. We both do, actually. We've both ... done stuff we need to forgive.'

'I don't know how to forgive myself. I had given up on all that.'

He hadn't heard her timorous plea that he listen and perhaps understand her own failures. But that was okay. She wasn't yet ready to speak of it, and there was time enough for that.

'It seems like you could give me back my life ... it's just that I don't want to drag you down with me.'

'But you don't know how I've also messed up ...'

'Oh please,' he said, touching a finger to her nose and laughing gently. He unfurled then, lighting two Camels from the stompie of his last. They lay, Francesca in the crook of his arm, smoking tenderly and sharing sips of tea.

'It is very different here now, isn't it?' he asked, almost tentatively. 'I mean, kind of relaxed, more forgiving than it used to be.'

'There's an austerity that's gone, I think. You no longer have to be a leftie with a capital L. Like it's okay now to live a normal life. Or perhaps we should translate that – to drive a fancy car and make money.'

'You sound disapproving.'

'No, I'm not really. It's just that it only touches the middle-class. But then at least it's not racially bound anymore. Suddenly there's this great, vibrant black middle-class ...'

'God, and how I would have disapproved of that once.'

'When you were a fine young communist? Wouldn't you just.'

They laughed at the rigour of the person he had once been.

'I was idiotic, wasn't I?'

'No, you weren't. You were awesome. But I like you better now, not so sure of everything. I just wish you wouldn't be so harsh with yourself.'

'How can I not be? Francesca, tell me honestly. How can we not be when each day brings more horrors from the Truth Commission? And now there's these Amnesty Hearings. They make me sicker than the stories of the victims.'

'But Anthony, must we carry the can for the Eugene de Kocks? I mean, we do bear some responsibility, but surely ...'

'Of course we do. Jesus, Francesca, of course. They're our countrymen, our colour ...'

'But there's another sort of mood here now. It's not like that. Really, Anthony. It's accepting of people like us.'

'Maybe it is, my sweetheart. And I hope, for all the people like us, that it remains after the euphoria is gone.'

'The euphoria *is* gone. This has been the cold year. Don't you see? It's been the year of disillusion. And yet still that feeling is here.'

Anthony took her stompie from her and placed his glass on the table. Turning, he pressed his warm, slightly damp body against hers.

'Okay, enough,' he said. 'You're very persuasive to a tired person like me. But I just think we ain't seen nothin' yet.'

The light had changed. From the blaze and chirrup of birds that had earlier spilt across the room, a darker, more poignant light now trickled over the window-sill and fell to the floor. As he kissed her, a single hadeda cried and yearned, and then was gone.

'What's the time?' she asked.

'It's okay. We still have a bit left. So ... do you think if I came back, that I'd be better again?'

'Yes, I do believe that.'

'Maybe I would. But it's not that easy to reclaim a life you've just left at lost property.'

'Worth it though. Don't you think?'

'Maybe it would be.'

Penny had seemed a little strange when Francesca picked up Daniel.

'What are you doing tomorrow?' she had asked suddenly, as Francesca started her car.

'Don't know. Why? Do you want to do something?'

'No ... I just need to tell you something.'

Francesca had taken the car out of gear and looked up at Penny's strained face, forehead resting on her arms as she leant in the window. 'Something serious?'

'It can wait till tomorrow. Go now, you don't want to be late. It'll just raise questions.'

Paul had been fine, showing a lack of curiosity about her day that would once have wounded her, but that she was now grateful for.

'I don't think I told you,' he'd said, 'but I had a few moments yesterday, so I got hold of the legal adviser for the northern metropolitan substructure. It turns out he's quite a good oke.'

'So we are in the northern then? Not the eastern?'

'Apparently. So this guy says he knows there's a brothel there. He's done an inspection.'

'So what's he doing about it? Have you got any supper preferences, Paul?'

'Not really. So this Mr Hlongwane says they're investigating a civil case to get the court to order them out. But he understands our position; says he'll put a rocket under the application.'

'So that's that then?'

'Ja, maybe. This seems to be the way to get things done now. You have to find someone to put the pressure on.'

'Well,' Francesca had said, opening the freezer, 'nothing's changed then.'

To Francesca though, everything had changed. The world had lurched in its orbit and the moon broken free from duty to tap-dance across the sky. How strange that, in the deceptive normality of supper and bedtime, only she could see it.

In the morning the sun was shining. In the shade, the chill could cut you to the bone. But in the sheltered yard, the dryness scaled the lips and the warmth was like a blessing.

She waited for Penny in the garden, watching Daniel play quietly with his figurines. He might not race up and down like other small boys, but he made the same sound-effects. 'Whirrr-ump, nyoing, twew-twew-twew.'

'Let me organise the kids,' Penny said when she arrived, late as usual. 'Pour me some wine in the meantime. Lots of ice.'

It took them a while to settle the kids before they could talk. In the end, Allan's boys were sent off with a pair of space guns, while Hannah and Daniel sat down to sand art.

'Okay.' Penny paced a couple of steps this way and that before stopping behind her chair to lean on its back. 'Okay. You know I told you I was worried about Allan?'

'Get out of here, boys,' yelled Francesca. 'This is adult-time. Go play space. Ja?'

'I ... well, I didn't know what to do. So I popped in at the office at lunchtime when I was pretty sure he wouldn't be there.'

'Oh my God,' murmured Francesca. 'Don't tell me you bribed the secretary. That would be just like you.'

'No, I acted all disappointed that I couldn't take Allan for lunch and ended up being taken out by his mate. Then I put major pressure on him, poor oke. I said I knew what was going on and, if he didn't give me the details, I'd tell his wife he was also up to no good.'

'The poor guy,' said Francesca. 'I bet he never realised what he was up against till it was too late.'

'Ja well, specially as it turns out he was also guilty as hell. He started blubbering about how it'd all started as a joke and I must please not tell anyone.' Penny paused to gulp at her wine.

'Apparently the boys at the office have been paying little visits to all those brothels that've popped up around town. It started with lunchtime strip joints, apparently. But then escalated.'

Francesca was startled to silence. This she had not expected. Oh, she had expected something. In the frenzied extravagance with which life seemed to be lived in this town, she had been certain of finding something hidden. But not this.

'So I forced him to take me to one of them, down Sandton way,' Penny continued.

'Oh my God, Penny,' Francesca exclaimed. 'Why on earth did you want to?'

'I wanted to see why. I wanted to see what kind of woman he would choose.'

'And did you?'

It seemed wrong, this talk of other, darker worlds. The sun was so warm, burning away the chill of the breeze. Francesca could hear her two grey loeries whooping in the leafless jacaranda they had chosen as their home since she had come to this house.

'She was so very nice,' said Penny with a rueful laugh. 'Such a terribly nice person.'

'Really? That's more than can be said for some of the clientele, if next door's anything to go by.'

'Yes. Like, she tried to make me feel better. The first thing she said was: "Men are such bastards. What business has your husband got coming here, when he's married to you?" '

'Did she say ...' Francesca paused. 'Um, did they use a condom, did she say?'

'She says you wouldn't believe the men coming to brothels now. All from the northern suburbs, with gold cards and *alles*. I don't know if it's because they're semi-legal ...'

'Or,' added Francesca, 'maybe now they're in nicer parts of town, they no longer have to put their cars in danger. Un-fucking-believable, isn't it?'

'Oh and ja,' said Penny, 'she did say she's very strict about condoms, thank God.'

So much harder, something like this, for someone like Penny. People were so used to her coping for all of them that it was sometimes difficult to remember the soft mollusc body that squirmed and shrank beneath the shell of her.

'Did you confront him?' Francesca asked at last.

'Yesterday.'

'And did he admit it?'

'Well, not much else he could do in the circumstances. He caved instantly. So I said: "What is this? Dogmeat?" ' Penny gestured to her body.

'And what did he say?'

'He said it wasn't me. Then he got tearful ...'

'I can't imagine Allan crying.' Francesca was thinking about Paul.

'Well, he didn't exactly sob. But he got a bit damp about the eyes.. He said everything's been so tense. He's been tense at work, and he feels such a responsibility. He says he hears of people leaving and he wonders if he should just make the decision and have done.'

'Oh for God's sake,' said Francesca. 'So now it's the country's fault he must fuck prostitutes.'

Penny allowed a small giggle to break through her sadness.

'You know Pen ...' Francesca hesitated, fearful of being insensitive. 'In some ways, maybe this is better than an affair. At least there was no possibility of emotional entanglement.'

Penny nodded and Francesca wondered if she would ever learn to see it that way. There was just something seedy and ramshackle about the whole thing that could never quite be dusted from Allan's imported suit.

It was an awful week, a tired week filled with despondent decisions and sad steps that had to be taken. Megan cornered her in the kitchen on Monday just as she was waiting for Penny.

'Frannie? I've made a decision.'

Her voice was steady and her words very precise. Her hair was a mess though. And her eyes ... Francesca thought her eyes as tangled as her hair.

'I ... Frannie, I'm not ready, you know. I'm going to have an abortion.'

'Oh Meg-child. Are you sure? I mean, it's such a ... there's just something about it you never lose.'

'You've never, have you? Had an abortion? No, of course you haven't. I would've known.'

'I've ... well, I've known people who have. I just know how traumatic it can be. You don't really know how much ...'

'I haven't taken the decision lightly, Francesca. I am a grown-up.'

'I know, Meg-child, I'm just ...'

'Don't call me that! Look, I know what you're doing. Just don't lecture me, for God's sake. Especially you – you've always done everything fucking right.'

She turned and bolted. Sometimes, Megan still had an adolescent springbok look to her legs and flying arms and hair. Perhaps she always would. Francesca hoped so.

Penny arrived then – not that she had relished going after Megan anyway. She would be easier to approach once she had calmed down.

'Are you nervous?' She asked Penny, as she climbed in beside her. 'Of course you are. Stupid question.'

'Ah hell, you know what? I'm not even thinking about it.' Penny lifted a hand from the wheel and wiped it on the cloth of her seat.

The sun was hot on the car and they did two circuits of the parking lot before someone finished loading their Woolies packets and deigned to drive away. Penny wiped both hands on the seat again.

'Come in with me?'

'Obviously. That's why I'm here.'

'Well, just wait till I go in, then you can come back and wait in the car. I mean, if that's okay. I'll go out through another door.'

It seemed a great distance to the lift, while all about them other women, with other lives, clattered trolleys and lifted toddlers. She thought they must be invisible to these women, as though they trudged this way along some parallel plane, in a different and alien existence.

'They said they're down one passage and there's a bunch of happy-clappies down another. If we hit the happy-clappies we've gone the wrong way.'

As they stepped from the lift, a burst of young people pushed past them, brandishing their laughter and the snatch of hymn they carried into the lift with them.

'Well,' said Penny with a little laugh. 'Take one guess where they've come from. Certainly not from our end of the corridor.'

When they called her, Penny turned to Francesca as though she wouldn't be going in after all – as a child might desperately tell her mother that no, she had changed her mind and wouldn't be seeing the dentist this morning.

Francesca squeezed her, feeling her heart through the perfectly structured jacket. 'It'll be fine. It really will.'

'I know.' She took another great breath. 'I'm fine.'

Francesca wandered Woolies for nearly an hour, staring absently at shelves of broccoli and pre-packaged meals. She was back in the car when Penny returned, still pale but perhaps a little more robust.

'Well, I'm to come back tomorrow. For the results. We had to have this whole talk about what I would do if it came back positive. I'm just ... shees, but I'm angry now. I can't even begin to tell you how furious I am that he's put me through this kak.'

She got back to find Megan and Tebs sitting quietly in the garden where the sun was warm but the breeze chilled the bones. Did nobody go to work today?

'Frannie,' Megan waved and she approached a little gingerly.

'Are you ...?'

'No, sit, sit. Have a cup. Oh, and sorry I snapped at you, by the way. It's Rooibos.'

'No thanks. I hate Rooibos. Howzit Tebs.'

She couldn't tell whether Megan had told him. He always had that quiet sadness about the mouth that quirked in sudden amusement.

'He and I were just telling stories. I was telling about when we were little and our families would go on holiday together.' Megan was being artificially bright.

'Oh my God. Is he ready for this?'

Tebs threw back his head and laughed. They were both being a little too buoyant. When he laughed, Tebogo sounded as whole-hearted as a boy. 'And I was telling her how it was for me, before I went to the camps.'

'Well, don't mind me. I only have an hour anyway. It's my liftclub day.'

'Maybe I'll come with you.'

Tebogo turned a level gaze upon her. 'Well,' he said. 'I suppose I should go back to work. I only came to see that you were okay.'

'Well, of course. I'm fine.' Her face glittered with a gaudy vivacity that was flagrantly out of place on features usually so still and calm. 'But please ... ple-ease don't go yet.'

She wheedled him, manipulative as a child. He knew he was being finessed. He must do. But, with a quick glance in Francesca's direction, he allowed himself to be beguiled. His tight mouth relaxed and he reached absently to smooth the tangles from her forehead.

'I'll stay just till you do the liftclub.'

'So you were saying ... about all the first-born sons having gone, and that's all you could think about.'

'Yes. And when we got to the camps, we would sit ...'

'Oh come on, Tebs,' said Francesca. 'Why don't you ever tell the bad parts?'

She was suddenly irritated by his fabling of the camps. That was why

Francesca had never been able to tell Megan what detention had really been like. People wanted these things to be heroic. No-one could countenance how people really behaved in such circumstances. And now Tebs... it annoyed her that he just perpetuated the myths so that Megan would go on loving him.

'Of course you're right,' he said seriously. Francesca had been smiling, but he had sensed her annoyance. 'There were times when we lay in our beds in a cold sweat. I'd lie with my gun beside me. We'd been told to kill informers. But sometimes that could be used for personal vendettas too. I've never felt fear like that.'

'But it sorted out, didn't it?' Megan wanted it to be so.

'The old man did. Tambo always sorted it. He had that ability. Not even Madiba had it in quite the same way – that ability to make everyone calm and listen. He used to say: "They're my boys. I must talk to them. And he'd sort us all out again." '

'People behave like shits in noble situations,' said Francesca.

'But there is also something unifying about it all. There were so many different viewpoints and we'd argue with such passion, and never agree. But now we talk with cynicism about the way we've become.'

'But,' interjected Megan, 'that's just ...'

'Yes, I know. I know what it is. But I had a religion before – a belief system aimed at making society a certain way. Now I have no gods, no belief systems at all.'

'But it's good that we've normalised,' Megan added. 'It has to be better, surely.'

'Well, I can say there is no personal satisfaction in killing. For any cause. For any belief system. I have done it and I know I never would again. I think it would kill me too.' He glanced at Megan, but she sat hunched in her chair, screened by the strands of hair she was playing with.

Megan lifted her head. 'I must get my shoes. Then we can go, Frannie, if you like.'

Tebogo and Francesca watched the stiff retreat of her defiant back, hair tossed back over her shoulders.

'I suppose you are wondering if I know or not,' said Tebs at last.

'The thought did cross my mind.'

'Yes, she has told me that she is to abort my child. And no, I am not happy about it. I would like something else to be fervent about now. I would like a family. But if she is not ready, then I suppose I must wait. But I just ... it's just that I do wonder ...'

'What?'

'No, it is nothing. I'm sure it is nothing.'

She hadn't wanted to take Megan for her abortion. It wasn't that she disapproved, or anything. The reality of it was just a bit much for her. But Megan hadn't yet made any close girlfriends. Between Tebogo and Nicholas, she hadn't had a great deal of time.

'Did Penny get her results?' Megan asked in the car. 'I forgot to ask with all my own stuff.'

'It was negative, thank God. She'll need to go for another test in a few months' time. But ... Anyway, I didn't ask how your first appointment at the clinic went.'

'Well, I nearly passed out when I phoned. They said they definitely don't do abortions.'

'Well, it is still illegal.'

'Yes, but everyone knows it won't be for long. And you'd think the police'd be turning a blind eye.'

'Well, I suppose they are, but that doesn't mean the clinic's going to invite you over for an abortion on the phone.'

'Anyway, it was fine when I got there. They counselled me and everything. It was all very ... you know. Caring.'

'Couldn't be more different, could it?'

'Say again?'

'I said so very different from the way it used to be for women.'

Lacking horror, the whole process seemed almost prosaic. Francesca sat in reception while Megan was ushered away by smiling sisters. The room was fluorescent bright, the daylight crowded out by the block buildings across the road. Even the rows of metal-legged chairs, the poverty of ornamentation, had a comfort to them. There was a control here, a quiet authority.

She had time for two cigarettes on the balcony. Across the road, the Jeppe post office, colonial to its pedimented frieze, stood its dignified ground against the encroachment of slabs and towers, and the vendors who sold fake designer goods and boerewors rolls. She didn't want to think about what was going on behind her.

'You can come through now.' A nurse who seemed almost too young to be here, led her through to recovery. Beds lined either side of a room made ordinary by its kettle and blankets. A ghetto blaster poured Highveld radio into the commonplace air.

'It was fine,' Megan said. 'It was quite sore, but not hard at all.'

Francesca stared down upon the cousin who had always been the baby of the family, who had always attracted people who could pick up after her, look after her and make her life easier.

Fuck her. How dare it have been fine. How dare it have been so very fine and not hard at all.

They were sitting in the kitchen when Nicholas arrived. Francesca's stomach filled with dread. It was irrational. But she had thought that, with the abortion and everything, Megan would come to her senses.

He was trouble. In some ways he was just a boy. A great disproportionate, slightly profligate boy.

She resented his encroachment on their family time. Megan sat with a teddy hot-water bottle she had borrowed from Daniel. Beauty wandered in and out from her ironing, making them tea whenever she made her own.

Francesca's anger hadn't lasted long. They were being gentle with each other, Megan slicing carrots for Daniel while Francesca tried to gather all the scattered ingredients for a Thai green curry that seemed suddenly too hard for any normal person to decipher.

They both looked up as Nicholas entered. 'How'd you get in?' asked Megan.

'Beauty was *kuiering* with someone on the pavement.'

Francesca waited for Megan to tell him this wasn't a good time. But he twirled a kitchen chair around, straddling it with his chin on his arms. He was a mess, his eyes bloodshot, ancient pullover pilled and unravelling at the cuff.

'God,' he said, rubbing two hands over his face. 'I am in so much shit. I need to talk to you, Meg.'

'Megan isn't all that well, actually Nicholas. I wouldn't exhaust her if I were you.' To her own ears and irritation, Francesca sounded just like her mother.

'No, it's okay, Frannie.' How pathetic women could be. Look at her now, glancing up demurely from her bloody carrots.

'Oh Jesus, was it today, Meg? Was it okay?'

Francesca was briefly dismayed, and then irritated with herself for being surprised. Of course Megan would have told Nicholas.

'No, it was fine. Really. I'm fine.'

'Thank God. I couldn't have ... Meg, I'm really pleased you're okay. I ...'

'I'm fine. Tell me what's wrong.'

Francesca gave up on the Thai green curry. She couldn't struggle with it – not with Nicholas here galling her. What about Megan's week? Why was his week suddenly the pinnacle of bad weeks? She was being harsh, but Nicholas had this way of blundering in with his scrumpled smile and his dimples and Megan was lost. Why couldn't he just leave her alone?

'Listen, you guys, I'm going to leave you to it. We can have Woolies tonight.'

'No, Frannie, absolutely not. I said I'd help. Nicholas, take the recipe and try to work out what we need first.'

Perhaps she was afraid to be alone with him. Nicholas nodded. He seemed too caught up in his own issues to care if Francesca were there or not.

'Meg ... look, I'm really sorry. I know I said I wouldn't come ...'

'It's fine. Tell me.'

'Maybe ... maybe she was right all along.'

'Your wife?' Megan spoke softly. Francesca couldn't see the face she held hidden over the carrots. If she chopped them any smaller, they'd be pureéd.

'Where d'you keep the green curry paste?' Nicholas asked.

'It's in there.' Francesca answered a touch sharply. He clicked his tongue, blundering into the jars that littered her fridge. But when he turned, there was a stretched look about his eyes.

'It's my union now, Meg. My guys work in supermarkets.'

'And so?' Megan had abandoned her carrots. She perched on the table, close enough to touch him.

'Didn't you see that Pilko's supermarkets are on strike?'

'But that's not your responsibility anymore, is it?'

'No, but ... see, SA Investment Holdings own a big chunk of Pilko. And the investment arm of my union is on the board of SAIH. We own shares in it. So ...'

'So the union owns the company it's striking in.'

'Basically. So this morning there was a board meeting. The whole board's suddenly dumping on me about our "common concerns". They started off all easy, like okay, it's not a train smash, but we have to sort it out. They said the prospects for the company were good, which obviously will help our investments.'

Nicholas stood at the table, absently separating the chicken pieces Francesca had thrust into his hands.

'So then they started in on my responsibility. This coming together of labour and business was a partnership – stuff like that. And if we rocked the boat, we'd all drown.'

'So what were you saying, all this time.'

'I told them I can't influence my union not to strike. That's not ... well, it wouldn't be ethical. I ...'

'But it ...'

'No wait. So then they start laying on the pressure. Jeez, how did I end up among the bosses? They start giving me all this shit, all with big smiles. Like, how it's my responsibility as a member of the board to lean on the guys. "It's not that we want to put you under pressure," they say. "But it is our responsibility to point out some realities." '

'So, what are you going to do?'

'Christ Meg, I don't know. I don't know who I am, or where I belong anymore.'

'Okay,' she said. 'Okay. It's all right.'

He sniffed, pressing his hands malevolently into his eyes. Francesca slipped from the room as Megan hurled her arms at him, pressing her face into his chest.

An exile from her kitchen, she busied herself with nothing, with small tasks in her own room and, when she had finished there, with tidying Daniel's figurines. From his window, she could see Beauty at the back gate, laughing skittishly as if someone were chaffing her.

Bending to dump the piles of little people, she heard the gate bang and Beauty's voice approach, still chattering away in seSotho. She lifted her head to see which friend was causing so much coy abandon ... Oh God. It was Tebogo. The dread rose again, bitter as vomit in her throat.

'Stay in your room.' Perhaps frightened by her tone, Daniel nodded. She reached the kitchen door just as Tebogo did from the other side, laughter suffocating in his throat. In almost biblical tableau, Megan's arms cradled the shattered form of Nicholas, his head folded in upon her breast.

Tebogo took one step. He didn't say a word as Nicholas gently, heartbreakingly, put Megan aside and stood to face him.

'Go away, Megan.' Tebogo's voice held a savagery Francesca had never heard in him.

'No,' said Megan. 'No, I can't.' Francesca reached her and pulled her aside as Tebogo stepped forward and head-butted Nicholas, exploding his nose with a crack and a small spray of blood.

Nicholas grunted, hands to his face, and collapsed to his haunches. Tebogo turned, but appeared not to see them, the pain of a wounded animal in his bloodied eyes. Blood spilt from the cut that ran from hairline to halfway down his forehead.

He stumbled toward Nicholas, fists balled in front of him. Megan, frozen beside Francesca, brought her two hands to her mouth and gave a cry. It was the cry of defeat, of strangled hopes replaced by a hoarse, ugly reality.

Tebogo raised his chin as a blind man would, to sniff the air for her presence. He allowed his hands to drop but stood absolutely still, legs straddled over Nicholas. Hunched at Tebogo's feet, Nicholas rocked silently, hands cupped to his face.

As an old man would, or a sleepwalker, Tebogo turned from Nicholas. Stumbling through the blood that blinded him, he gave the broken wail of a creature that wants only to be put out of its misery. It was a cry that welcomed pain, any pain that could dull the suffering that was already there, and that was unbearable.

Slowly, Tebogo raised his fist and smashed it through the kitchen window. It crashed through the flashing glass, spraying glittering fragments of glass and a shower of blood that seemed redder than any blood she had ever seen.

THE MAN

Rolene had returned, silent and spiritless, from the reunion. The man had warned her. He had said it would be a mistake. One should never go back, never try to reawaken what life has mauled and then left for dead.

He had understood that after Gavin's death. He had known then that one could never look back. And he had known then that he could never return to his barrack. Though Gavin had never been there, he had in a sense been waiting for him. And it had been filled with him, with his letters of birds and butterfly collections, and the leguaan he had caught in the valley.

He could never have returned to the troepies who waited each day for the post, who compared letters and gathered to listen to Forces Favourites. Instead he had applied, as a compassionate case, to serve out his time in the police. What had it mattered that he must serve double time? He hadn't been going anywhere anymore.

But he had gone on eventually, without Gavin – to university, where fatuous students had played at Marxism. They had irritated him, their soft lives chafing his rough edges raw. How could you ever follow a doctrine elucidated by boys in expensive jeans who cultivated berets or idiosyncratic bare feet. Boys and strident girls who had never known loss or pain, and who had never learnt to understand the forces they were toying with.

He had found digs with two young student leaders. Army terms deferred, they had wandered, almost without pause, from private school to SRC. It was they who had left hand-written notices on the windows of their house, exhorting the comrade children not to burgle them. 'We are just like you. Come the revolution, there will be no need to steal.' And little homilies in Xhosa, things like: 'For all of us, life is a heavy burden.'

And from that parapet of moral superiority, they had dared to mock him about having been in the police. Despising them, he had played the part required of the leftist he appeared to be. Seemingly just slightly abashed but: 'at least I never had to go to the border. At least I never shot anyone.' He wondered if they realised now, with their business suits and Perth addresses, how much of their rent had been paid from Special Branch funds.

It was in his first year that he had met Rolene, a sparkling girl with a loud, vivacious laugh. They had laughed a lot, she enjoying his tart take on the student body. 'Life is a heavy burden,' they would tell each other between lectures, she flinging her long hair back and laughing her deep, throaty guffaw.

That was when those around him had still laughed, when he had still been able to create laughter in others – in Rolene. Rolene never said that anymore.

She never sighed as she used to, limp wrist to forehead, declaring that life was a heavy burden. Perhaps because it had become so.

And Rolene had never understood that this was the order of the universe – that one could never go back. She had never quite seen that, even with the shifting of alliances, despite the changing of the guard, these things are inalienable and unalterable.

She had insisted on going to the 25th anniversary reunion of their first university year. He hadn't quite understood her insistence on targeting herself for this humiliation. Perhaps she had hoped that, peeping from beneath their existential partition, she might find a life out there to be lived by someone like her. Perhaps she felt that, with all this talk of amnesty and forgiveness, she might now be able to creep from the bunker and rejoin the world.

She should have known better. Self-righteousness doesn't die with Mercs and green cards.

Someone had apparently asked whether she was still married to him. They had registered their surprise, she told him, bitterly reproducing their little 'oo-oh's and 'amazing's. He could just imagine. They had questioned her on whether he was to apply for amnesty.

'And I didn't know,' she said on her return. 'I just didn't know. I know so little about you, and ... I need to know. Tell me now. Please. Tell me what you did.'

'You know what I did. It was nothing. It was a game.' He spoke coldly. His eldest son had entered the kitchen, bounding to the fridge for the bottle of cold water. This time he did not reprimand the boy for drinking straight from the bottle.

'Not that.' She was weeping and shrill, clattering the dishes from table to sink. 'Not the spying stuff. I even coped with that. I want to know about after that. What did you do to people when you were at Fort Glamorgan. What about the detainees you interrogated? What did you do to them?'

His son remained, water bottle in hand, eyes volleying from one to the other. The man did not know what to say to her. His mind was rigid, iced over with rage that she could do this. How much anger she must harbour in order to draw the boy in this way. He held his silence, willing her with stone-hewed eyes to be silent, or at least to wait for the boy to leave.

'Answer me,' she said, her hair curling spasmodically about her head, tangling with the pots heaped in her arms. 'I don't care anymore. I'm not scared of you. I want to know what you did.'

The water bottle slammed to the table and she jumped, dropping a cup that exploded against the floor.

'Stop it, Ma. Just stop it now.' The boy yelled at her, his features harsh with fury and something else, possibly fear. Rolene started again, her eyes on her son, her face growing slack with the pain of this betrayal.

'Ma?' he said, and he was pleading, his voice dipping and breaking to a half-grown wheedle. 'Ma? Don't do this to us. He's our father. Leave it, can't you? Can't we just leave the past alone? It's gone now. It's finished. There's a new world ...'

'It has not finished,' she shrilled at him. 'It could still come back!'

'If you leave it alone, it won't,' the boy yelled and bolted, blundering against the kitchen table to avoid coming into contact with him – with the father he had, just a minute before, defended. The two of them were silent.

He could no longer feel the worm-like wriggle of pity at her abasement. He gazed at her back, daring her to continue now that they were alone. She busied herself at the sink, clanking and uselessly stacking, lifting her forearm to wipe at her eyes.

'Someone asked ...' she said at last. 'Someone asked if you had been someone's interrogator. He said she'd been detained there, in East London.'

When, he wondered, had she grown so very old, fussing over her nest like a shrivelled bird, breast bowed to the constant task of feeding her brood?

'He said ... he told me he used to go out with her. But she'd never been the same after she'd been detained. He said it ... changed her. He wanted to know what had happened to her there, as if I would know. So I'm asking you now. What did you do to her? Did you ... was she ...?'

'Why the fuck do you think I had anything to do with her at all? Why doesn't he ask her what happened to her?' His voice cracked as sharply as the cup that had smashed to the floor.

'I know you knew her,' she said, words shrilling across the kitchen. 'I know, you see. And I knew when he said it.'

'What do you know? You know nothing.'

'I know, because he said her name. He told me her name.'

'And so? What do you think you know ...'

'I know because I heard you. That night when you got back from East London. I couldn't sleep because you tossed. And you talked in your sleep. And I heard you. I heard you say "Francesca".'

FRANCESCA

Blind. Oh God, she couldn't see. So dark. So very dark. She lay still, reaching inside herself for calm. Where was she? A cell ... no, it wasn't. Yet still she knew this place.

She could feel torn plastic against her cheek, sharp edges goading her flesh. For what she was about to do. Oh God, for what she was about to lose. For the pain. For all the pain. For thine is the kingdom. And the pain. The pain and the sorrow, for ever and ever ...

She was awake now. Amen, she whispered, tears wet and stinging on cheeks chapped by the rub of restless hands. She lay still and distinct on her side of the bed. Better not to wake him.

She slipped from the bed and felt her way along the passage. Tea. Tea would calm her.

'What're you doing up?'

For an instant, terror swallowed her whole. But it was Megan. Only Megan. Calm down, for fuck's sake. It wasn't an intruder. 'Jesus Christ. What are you doing in the pitch dark. I nearly died.'

'Didn't want to wake you. I'm making tea.'

She sat at the table beside her cousin, Megan's sleep-smell still soft and befuddled about her skin. She breathed in concert with her, allowing the night air to trickle through her throat and pool in her chest.

'Meg-child?' She was whispering, more to hold the visceral intimacy, than for fear of waking others.

'I'm fine,' Megan said with the suggestion of a laugh. 'You needn't worry.' She reached for Francesca's hand.

'Worried? Me? I was just going to ask if you had any smokes.'

'Dope. I've got dope, that's all.'

They slipped wraithlike from the house, two pale and insubstantial beings against the bulk of the frigid jacarandas. Settled on Megan's bed, Francesca watched as she spread and cleaned, reaching to hand her cousin a pip as though it were the most precious of exotic fruits.

'I ...' she began, placing the splif between Francesca's lips. 'I don't know how to thank you ...'

'Oh don't.' Francesca choked slightly on the first suck. 'Don't, Megan. I know. Really I do.'

'I feel okay, you know? About the abortion, I mean. It's just ...'

'Nicholas.'

'Yes, of course. Nicholas. It'll always be Nicholas. It's as though there'll never be any real closure for us. Okay, I can perhaps accept the lack of a happy ending with him. No really, Frannie. I think I can. But it's the lack of any ending at all ...'

'What? Where's my baby cousin gone?'

'Ja, I know. I was such a little snot-face when I arrived. With so many notions about how everyone and everything should be.'

'It's okay, Sweet thing. Penny always says this place knocks a person into shape sooner or later.'

It had done that to all of them. Time and politics might change, but Johannesburg remained as it had been through the turbulent prospects of all its gold-rushes. Unburnished by mannerly convention, its rough edges scoured at pretension. It had a way of biding its time before reaching out unexpectedly to tear at superficiality, to gut every preconception held of it or its people.

In its bandit's heart it held a raucous disregard for life's rules that made all things possible, great successes and great failures, great goodness and great evil.

It might suffocate romantic hopes, as it had done with Megan. Yet it brought in its place an inexpressible elation, and of course sometimes an acute despair. There was nowhere on earth, she was sure, that could grant such a strident sense of being alive. She had always thought this a gift. And yet, at times it seemed they were cursed.

'He's still there, you know. I don't know that we'll ever really be free of each other.'

Francesca sighed, reaching out a finger to swing Megan's hair back from her secluded face. 'Careful of that joint near your hair ... And Tebs?'

'I love Tebs. I do. It's a great, warm love. It's ... just not the same.'

'Poor Tebs.'

'I know. God, but what can I do? I want to be with him. There's no future with Nicholas. I just wish ... why can't I love Tebs the same?'

'Is it really that bad?'

'I can't help it. I'll try not to see him. I'll try, that's all. But he'll always be my soul love.'

'And of course, Tebogo's forgiven you, hasn't he?'

'Yes.'

Francesca gave a little laugh and shook her head. 'You don't deserve it, you know that, don't you?'

'I know.'

She paused and passed the splif, brushing hair from a face that had fluent hollows and tiny speaking lines where, before, all had been smooth and mute. 'I couldn't have gone through this, you know ...'

'Oh shut up, will you? That's what we're supposed to do for each other. We keep each other's secrets, and we hold each other upright.'

'Yes ...' Megan took a breath and frowned, snatching the splif back almost angrily. 'Yes, but you don't. It's supposed to go both ways. I've only recently started to see how un-okay things are with you. There's stuff bothering you. But you never speak.'

'I haven't been in the habit of speaking to you. You were family, my baby cousin. And there're just some things I've never felt able to tell anyone.'

'You were all upset about my abortion. I could see you were. It can't all have been because of me. But I asked ...'

'I know what I said. It was a lie.'

'So you did ...'

'I had an abortion. Yes.'

'And was it awful? Worse than mine?'

'And yes, it was awful, Meg-child. Nothing, nothing like yours.'

It had been so different from every easeful detail of Megan's that it had angered her, in that spiteful way of sisters and friends who were too close. But now, after all that Megan had been through, she felt unable to fling its ugly details in her face.

No-one had known of it. Not a soul had known about her fraught call to the number she had been given by her curious domestic worker. They had asked for R5 000, an impossible amount. But she had been desperate. And too far gone for a safe abortion. Even if she could have made it overseas for a legal procedure, she feared they would have turned her away.

So she had sold the jewellery inherited from her grandmother. She had told her mother she'd been robbed, possibly by the police who had come to detain her. And in a way, she had been.

The voice on the telephone had told her to wait at the Norwood Hypermarket, beside the entrance. Eventually he had come for her, a man with greasy strands of hair that tumbled about a freckled pate, and the acrid smell of too many cigarettes about him.

'Susan Smith?' he had asked, his features blank even of scepticism. His hands had been yellowed by nicotine and ridged with grime.

'Yes,' she had whispered, following him to the car. He had taken her money without a word, removing from his floor a roll of wide plastic tape. Tearing it with his teeth, he had attached it forcefully to her head, in preparation for blindfolding her.

'No,' she had protested in panic. Not her eyes. Not the blind, silent panic of the cell, the blank, unseeing walls of solitary confinement.

'Suit yourself,' he had said, his voice rough, unused to speaking. He had made as if to give her a slight push, and turned to enter his car.

'Okay,' she had said quickly. 'Okay, okay.'

She had allowed herself to be blindfolded and pushed down upon the back seat of his Toyota, her fingers shrinking from the foam innards of the torn seat, her face recoiling from the smell of smoke and old vomit, her mind blanching from where they were going. Oh God, what was she doing, who were these people?

With the whistle of the wind, exhaust fumes had seeped through badly sealed windows. The car had rattled and shaken with each nauseous turn. Cars and trucks roared past, taxi hooters blared, while she had tried not to cry, not to vomit, not to think.

Eventually, they had stopped. Clutching a handful of her sleeve, the man had led her from the car, tugging impatiently as she stumbled, first on uneven paving, then on a step.

She had felt the chill of an interior as he walked her down a short passage, before turning her to the left. One swift tug and the tape was torn from her face. She'd been left alone in a tiny room, darkened by the wall that loomed over the window.

'*Ek kom nou*.' The figure of a woman had passed the door. 'Lie down.'

And she had. What else could she have done? She had lain upon the plastic sheets on the narrow bed. She had lain upon the blood stains of other desperate women, of other babies who had never been born.

The woman had never looked her in the eyes.

'Legs up,' she had said, padding in on flat feet to boil the kettle that stood on the wooden floor.

At least the knitting needle had been passed through the boiling water once or twice. She had cried out with the pain of its sharp collision with her cervix and she had thought she might vomit again as it pressed through into her womb. Wave upon wave of pain had clouded the room with the blood before her eyes. And the baby. Oh God, the baby.

She had seen her baby, tiny and perfect and ivory pale. She had seen him two days later when he had finally fought his way into her toilet bowl. When she had finally cried and cramped enough to let him go. And she had not been able to leave him there. Gagging on her sobs, with the horror of it, she had lifted him and wrapped him in a sheet. She had buried him in a shoebox in the garden, beneath a rose bush.

'You never told anyone, did you?' said Megan as the silence stretched on too long. 'About the abortion.'

'No. No I didn't. You see, I ... I did that to my first baby. And my second ...'

'You weren't to blame. It isn't your fault, about Daniel.'

'I know that. Of course not. That would be irrational.'

The sound was wrong. Something wasn't right. Francesca stopped, her hand on Daniel's shoulder. Everything looked the same. Everyone was where they often were at Penny's house, ranged around the old stoep.

But still, there was something about the clamour of them that was different. Stoep sounds were comforting, the murmur of indolent drinks in filtered sunlight. Not this insect whine of disconsonant voices, humming together like an angry hive.

Allan had buzzed her in. Funny that he should be home so early. And funny, come to think of it, that Penny's entire family should be here on a weekday evening.

She had reached the stoep, fear reaching long fingers across her spine. Penny sat slumped in a wicker armchair, hair pulled roughly from her face with an elastic band. Penny never did that to her hair.

A swift rollcall marked Penny, Allan, Hannah and both boys present. Thank God, she thought. Thank God they were all safe.

But as that anxiety passed, another leapt to take its place. Whatever this is, she thought, please don't let it stop me from seeing Anthony. Let it still be okay for Daniel to stay here.

'Oh Sweetie, there you are,' said Penny, her smile pale and indistinct. 'I ... I'm really sorry ...'

'Penny's been hijacked,' said Allan.

'Oh Jesus, Pen. Are you okay? Did they hurt you?'

'No. No I'm fine. Just scared.'

'Where were you?'

'I was coming off the highway on to Corlett. Please don't talk about it now, Sweetie. Really, I'm fine.'

'I'll stay, Sweetheart. Could I help, d'you think?'

'No, no. Really, I've ...' her voice fell into conspiratorial murmur. 'I've got enough people right now.' Her eyes made a brave attempt to fling themselves upward. 'My entire family wants to hear it all six-thousand times. I won't be able to talk to you properly now.'

Penny's mother had been weeping. Her uncles looked embarrassed, unsure what to do with her. Allan's sons sat listlessly to one side with a pile of Tin Tin books. Hannah, the perfect child, was handing around tea.

'Do you want me to take the kids?' She released her last faint hope of seeing Anthony, watching it float away like a gossamer bubble.

'Could you?' Penny asked. 'Oh hell, Sweetie. I'm so sorry about ruining everything.'

'It's fine.' At last she found that she really meant it.

As they drove, she chatted to Hannah who, though pale, seemed to be coping quite adequately in her emotionally efficient way. She turned to question Thomas, the elder of the two boys, digging a bit, burrowing for trauma.

'Ja fully,' he said. 'I know what happened. Penny was hijacked.'

'As well.' William sounded excited. 'And they even had guns.'

'Shut up, William. She's okay. Nothing wrong. Fran? You've got DSTV, haven't you?'

Beyond that, she found it difficult to connect with these boys, as straightforward as they were. She had never known enough about Ninja Turtles or Spiderman to maintain a conversation. And Daniel, whose inept hands crept to his ears at the burst of a laser-gun, was lost with them. They were kind in an absent kind-of way, because their stepmother had told them to be. But they couldn't much be bothered with him.

Her phone rang two streets from Penny's house. It was Megan.

'I see Paul's away. I just wondered if you wanted me to do anything ... Fucking hell,' she said when Francesca explained. 'But she needs you, surely. Go. I'll babysit if Beauty's not home.'

'I've got all the kids ...'

'Go. Bring the kids here. I'll have them.'

Anthony was waiting in the car park, pacing beneath the leafless jacarandas. 'You're so late. I thought you weren't coming.'

'I phoned and phoned you. But I couldn't get a reply.'

'I was here.'

They waited to embrace, while every nerve ending squirmed upward to the surface of her skin. When they reached his room, she gasped as he touched her.

'Cold?' he asked.

'No. It's ...'

'I know.'

They undressed where they stood, just inside the door. His hands shook, fumbling with buttons and struggling with zips. They smiled, too intense even to giggle.

'You are everything,' he whispered. Taking her roughly by the shoulders, he pressed her into the tangle of dressing gowns and towels hanging from the door. 'You have given me back my life.'

They lay together afterward, and he was tender, almost too tender, as though he was sad.

'Is Daniel at a private school?' he asked. Perhaps he was considering how it would be when they were together.

'Well, he will be,' she said. 'He's still at nursery school.'

'So are mine. Do you feel bad?'

'About what? Private school? No, why should I?'

'I've been wondering about that since I've been back. It's a big issue in the UK at the moment – about Labour MPs sending their kids to private schools. Haven't the papers got on to that here? I mean, which ANC MPs send their kids to private schools?'

'I'm sure most of them do.' Sometimes she forgot how long he had been away. 'Those things aren't issues anymore.'

He turned from her, sitting on the edge of the bed as he scrabbled on the side table for his smokes. Without asking, he lit two, passing one to her.

'There's a bureau chief's job going here,' he said, his back to her.

'Would it ... is it the sort of job you'd like?'

He didn't answer, but sat with his back to her, taking deep drags on his Camel. She reached for him, but he seemed impermeable.

'I have a job that suits me in London,' he said at last. 'I'm not good for much anymore, you know. It doesn't require much of me.'

'But if you could just ... You're already starting to believe again. And you can't be satisfied for the rest of your life with half of everything.'

She had lost her breath. Almost angrily, she stubbed out her cigarette. Somehow he transcended everything: all her pain and guilt over Daniel, even her misery with Paul. She had been unable to heal her own child, or even her own marriage. But Anthony was like her. He was flawed. And Anthony she could heal. He was her redemption.

'I think it's wonderful,' he said, turning slightly to show his twisted smile, 'that you think I'm capable of so much. And sometimes I get carried along by the fantasy, that I could become a whole person again.'

He stubbed out his Camel and turned to her, rolling her up in his body and the tangled bedcover. He had come back to her.

'It's not a fantasy,' she whispered.

'God,' he said, pressing his face into her hair. 'Oh God. I don't deserve you. Really I don't. I don't deserve another chance. I've fucked up everything. Why should I be happy now? Why do I deserve that?'

Penny and Hannah lit the candles. The room was hushed. They smiled to each other, mother and child, before covering their eyes to say the blessing.

'Baruch Ata Adonai Eloheinu Melech ha'olam asher kidishanu b'mitzvotav l'hadlik ner shel shabbat.'

Francesca half expected Penny to pull her wry mouth. But this was a different Penny, surrounded by family and expectations. This wasn't her tough-mouthed friend. This was the only daughter produced between three sisters. Daughter, mother, niece – this person didn't smoke, didn't mock, didn't swear, and drank hardly at all. Who the hell was this person anyway? And where was her raucous friend?

'This is a lovely cloth you're using, Penelope,' said Auntie Fee, as they settled into their seats.

'Yes, Auntie Fee?' she said. Gentle laughter burbled in her throat.

'I'm admiring your table-cloth. What else should I say?'

'I just know you, Auntie Fee.' Hannah began to giggle.

'And now? What makes the child laugh? I was admiring your cloth. Although, I'm surprised you never think to use one of the shabbes cloths you got from your Bobba.'

Penny's mother injected a look of pure reproach, straight into Penny's heart. Penny, sweetness itself, reached over and patted her aunt's hand.

'I know, Auntie Fee. But I'm scared those cloths will get ruined and threadbare if I use them all the time. Imagine the long way they came, and all these years they've been around. And don't you think this one's beautiful? I found it in ...'

'Those cloths came over on the boat. How many shabbes nights haven't they seen? And now? You think now they should grow threadbare? After all this time?'

Penny shrugged, floored by her aunt's logic. But her laughter she held in her throat, fizzing there gently through her silence.

'And is this your lovely challah?' Auntie Deidre peeked under the bread's covering and lifted a slow, arch face to Penny's. They all laughed. Everyone knew that Penny never, ever baked.

'Sure, Dede. I bought it with my own credit card.'

'Oh well, I've never had anything against a Feigel's kitka,' Auntie Deidre said as Auntie Fee said nothing, in the pointed way she had of holding her tongue.

Paul was back from his trip, and making a real effort to be charming. He was chaffing Auntie Fee, the guardian of all that was sacred, over her klabbejas prowess.

'I knew the instant you played a hand,' said Auntie Fee.

'But I ...'

"No, don't argue with me, boy. The instant you played your first hand, I said: "This boy's not Jewish." I don't play amateurs.'

Uncle Ben blessed the wine and the challah, and Francesca looked around the table, at all the faces tinted by candlelight and occasion. How sad it made her in that instant, though she could not have said why.

Penny stood to dish, handing the first plate to Hannah to carry to Auntie Fee. 'Auntie Fee? Don't complain. How many years have I known you? I know exactly how much you like.'

The sadness rushed in again, cold as the tide's turn in a mellowed lagoon. Penny seemed quite separate from her here. She was no longer hers, the friend of friends. Compadre of a thousand adventures, companion for all that was less ordinary. Tonight she had lost her.

She was no longer shoulder to shoulder with Francesca, kicking at tin cans.

She was lighting candles, the archetypical daughter, the matriarchal Jewish wife. And Francesca, much as they all loved and accepted her, was an outsider.

Francesca sometimes forgot the extent to which Penny was other things to other people. Penny might resent it. She might need to affirm, by her wickedness and her vivacity, her existence as a separate person. But she had a place in the world. She had a belonging that Francesca had never felt. Penny had a tradition that bound, and a family that held sacred the unremarkable.

'I'm very lucky,' Penny was saying. They were all clamouring to hear every gory detail of her ordeal for the umpteenth time. 'It was just the car they took and my handbag. Just possessions.'

'Listen to the way we talk,' said Auntie Deidre. 'We count ourselves lucky if we're not shot, and our children not yet orphans. It's terrible, you know.'

'Did you hear about Stanley's nephew?'

'Yes. That was too terrible. Is he permanently blind?'

Oh God, it was to be one of those evenings. Quick, into a telephone booth ... Is it a bird, is it a plane? No, it's Super-Polyanna.

'That's awful,' Francesca said. 'But we have to remember it's a transitional thing. And when you think about it, we've been so lucky ...'

'... well, they just don't know. But the bullet lodged somewhere in his skull.'

'You know, that very nearly happened to Magda's daughter. They tied her up, her and the maid, and they would have raped her, if Ron hadn't come home and pressed the panic button. But she's alive, *baruch Hashem*.'

'Sometimes I just don't know,' said Auntie Fee. 'Sometimes I wonder why you young people aren't all in Canada or Australia. You know my friend Elsie? She has grandchildren in America, Canada and Australia and who can blame them?'

'Who can blame them?' asked Penny's mother. 'There's not one of us hasn't been touched by violent crime.'

'Oh that's not true.' With a sweep of her cape Super-Polyanna swoops to the rescue. 'Penny's been touched by it. She can say that. But the rest of us – we haven't all been touched ...'

'We have actually, you know,' said Allan, and Francesca felt the fear rise in her throat, that she might lose these people to the great South African diaspora. 'Each incident that touches a family, a friend or a member of our community, does actually touch us as well.'

'Perhaps. But that's no reason ...'

'Do you mind if we change the subject?' Penny's voice swept across the table. The whole clattering, chattering table fell silent. 'Truly, I am sick to death of talking about crime.'

Later, Francesca sat on with her friend after the family had gone home. They were drinking melon schnapps and listening to remastered Santana compilations. Allan was showing Paul some new application on his computer.

'How are you and Allan now?' she asked and Penny shrugged. 'Ag what! We're going to counselling now and we'll see ...'

'Do you think you can hold it together?'

Penny shrugged again. Of course she could. Francesca couldn't bear things not to resolve, for better or worse. But Penny ... she could jog along, not happy, not unhappy. That was how she was expected to be, and she could never, not in a million years, disappoint them all.

She did make her own little scraps of happiness, far away in some parallel dimension. And she could live like that, with her two lives and two selves never touching.

'And now,' Francesca added, 'enough with the "I'm fine" shit. Tell me what happened.'

'Ja.' Penny cleared her throat and wiped her nose along her sleeve, like a small, barefoot girl. 'You know, I am so sick to death of hearing Uncle Bertie's nephew's cousin's hijack experience that tops mine.'

'I know. Mine'd be just the same.'

'No, my family's the worst. "Well, you're very lucky, my girl. Auntie Edna's girl was raped 64 times." It finishes me, I swear.'

'I know. So now tell me what you really feel.'

'It was ... fuck, Francesca, it was terrible. I felt that gun, I felt it against my head, and all I could think of was Hannah and how she wasn't big enough to do without me.'

'I suppose in that moment it's always your kids.'

'And you know how people tell you to behave when you're hijacked? Well, I did everything wrong. I screamed. I could see people slowing down and reaching for their phones. But no-one stopped.'

'Do you blame them?'

'No, I suppose I wouldn't either, if I saw the guns. They told me to shut up and they clunked me across the head. I'm lucky they didn't shoot me.'

'Enough with the luck.'

'Okay. Well, the thing was, I only noticed afterwards, I pissed myself. All down my jeans leg. Can you believe that? I hadn't even noticed. And I had to go sit in the police station with my jeans all ... all messed.'

Francesca felt the tears sting the back of her eyes. For her friend. For her fastidious friend who would die rather than be seen in public with piss down her leg.

'But the thing I hate them for, I think, is the fear. They've given me fear. I didn't have it before. Now I'm frightened to drive anywhere, terrified to stop at robots.'

'I know, Sweet Thing,' said Francesca. 'But you shouldn't be so law-abiding. You're going to have to make like everyone else in Joeys. Just drive through them.'

'Oh hell, I forgot again, didn't I? Why didn't you remind me?'

'You were very busy. I don't mind.'

She had been meaning to phone the low-cost developer over Beauty's house ... oh, for a month at least. But there had always been something else that had to done at that moment. Once she actually sat down to it, of course, it was easily accomplished. Just a quick phone call to discuss finishing touches to Beauty's core house.

'Thank you, *Siesie*.'

'It's a pleasure, Beaut. You should've nagged me weeks ago.' Beauty watched her as she made them both tea. She could be very still sometimes.

They didn't share. Not really. She knew all of Beauty's troubles. She knew about the son who had got some girl pregnant. She knew that Beauty still paid the girl a little something every month, though she doubted now that the child was even his. She knew that Beauty had sent her children to school in the Transkei to avoid the brutal gangland of Soweto's schools. But she knew also that Beauty still worried over drugs and AIDS.

Francesca never reciprocated. She never told Beauty how very much she had needed Paul's strength when they had met. Or how his normality had reached out to her, just when she had felt so unsteady. She would probably never tell her that, over the years, that strength had seemed to turn against her and all that was good in the world. Beauty would probably be horrified had she tried. It just wouldn't be right.

There were things that Beauty knew though, that no-one on earth did. They lived, intimate as sisters, recognising each other's illnesses, aware of each other's menstrual cycles. And yet, most often, they passed each other absently in the kitchen, muttering about tea or how much sugar was left in the cupboard. Most days, they shared little beyond the odd chuckle over Daniel's latest comment or some scurrilous story passed on by the Mealie Lady.

But Beauty and Daniel had a new bond these days, solemnly felt by both of them. Daniel had a new pride around her, hoisted up to be praised and touched for his bravery by all Beauty's friends. And Beauty, who had always been Daniel's greatest supporter, outdid herself to be his constant protector.

'When will your children see it?' Francesca asked suddenly, feeling moved and saddened by Beauty's separation from her own kids, and her gentle surrogacy of Daniel.

'My children. Eesh ...' She gave a click that seemed to reverberate in the air about them. 'My children say they won't come to the Free State, for holidays. Suddenly they think Soweto is so exciting.'

'Well, I did ask if you didn't want to buy something here.'

'Free State is quiet. No troubles. No skollies. My children must do what they want. They are big now.'

The phone began to ring. Beauty clattered about desultorily as Francesca reached to answer it.

'Francesca?'

'Uh-huh.' She felt the poignancy of all Beauty's plans, and how they never quite worked out. Her life had been so hard. Why couldn't things just fall into place for her, even now?

'Francesca? It's Jude here.'

'Oh hi.' Beauty would be stoical, of course, and pragmatic.

'From the bookclub. You know?'

'Yes of course, Jude, I know. Sorry, I was just a little preoccupied.'

'Francesca ... this is hard for me.'

'What, Jude? What is it? Has something happened?'

'No, no, nothing like that. I ... Francesca, this isn't something I initiated. It's just that the bookclub asked me to tell you. They took a vote, you see.'

'A vote? What about?'

'About you.'

'About me?' She was being really dense here, or was Jude being terribly obtuse?

'Francesca, they don't want you in the club anymore, that's the thing. They don't want you to come again.'

No, she thought. There must be some mistake. She had only just begun to see them as they really were.

'They say you're not really one of them.'

'Why? What do you have to be to fit in?' She felt the hit of sudden fury. Who were they, these women? Who did they think they were?

'It doesn't make any difference, Francesca. They just don't feel comfortable talking about stuff around you.'

'Oh.' She wondered suddenly why anyone would feel vulnerable in front of her. 'And you, Jude? What do you think?'

'Francesca, I like the bookclub. I don't think you're a bad person. I just don't think you fit in.'

'Okay.'

Beauty was humming as she wiped down surfaces. Please don't let her sing. She was just too piercing to bear right now.

She took a gulp of her tea. It was cold.

'Eesh,' said Beauty, with that exasperated click she used with Daniel. Snatching up Francesca's cup, she flourished it into the microwave.

The bookclub had seemed to be her last grip on the sort of suburban life she had been taught to desire. It was as though she had long since plunged from the life she should be leading, and the bookclub was the ledge to which she had clung. Now she was on the outside, even of the unhinged normality of the last bookclub.

Perhaps it was irrevocable. Nothing would ever be the same. They could sense it. They could smell Anthony about her, and all that she planned to do.

'Here.' Beauty slapped her cup down beside her. 'Now it is warm again.'

She stepped back and watched Francesca closely. Francesca glanced up at her, but couldn't speak. Beauty shook her head slightly and returned to her shelves.

Francesca heard the gate open and close again behind Paul's car. She wished he would not come in just yet. She wanted to sit here quietly until she could speak again.

'I think you should say: "Thank you Super-husband." I have succeeded where all others have failed. Mr Hlangwane came through, can you believe it? At least some things still work in this fucking country.'

Once it would have hurt that he seemed so unaware of her, beyond the audience she composed to his tales of the wide world. But now she was glad she had no need to speak of what would only make him impatient.

'... so the brothel will be served with a notice from the council telling them to cease operating a business in the area. They'll be served tomorrow. So that's one for the neighbourhood. Only thing is ... Francesca, have you noticed anything odd about the corner house? The corner you'd turn to get to the café.'

Francesca shook her head.

'Well, I'm buggered if they're not running some business there. This country's a losing battle I swear. Hit one and two others spring up. I think I'll just wander up the road and check it out.'

Beauty rinsed out her cup and placed it on the draining board. Francesca could hear her humming across the garden to her room. The next moment she was back.

'Here,' she said.

'What is it?' Francesca asked.

'The other day I was coming past the golf course. You know where that bridge is?'

'Yes?'

'As I crossed the bridge I felt the cold. It was a ghost from the river. But I held on to my crystal and the ghost kept away.'

'I'm glad it's helping you.'

'Yes, but that is what I am saying. I will find another one, but I think it is you that is needing this crystal now.'

THE MAN

The ball felt good in the man's hands – a fine, smooth leather stippled with rough grains of sand.

It was a long while since he had played with his sons. He wasn't the playful sort, perhaps having lived too long for that. His way was to sit, preferably unnoticed, and marvel at them as they tumbled together in a disorder of hair and freckled faces.

But it felt right, the tensing of muscles and the heaving for breath, the grunts and cries of his sons about him. He had been walking along the water, the afternoon sun soft on his face, when he had first seen the game of touch rugby in progress.

He had turned up the beach to watch them, and had seen his two eldest sons laughing and dodging each other, sand flailing about their legs. Sun and hair fell about their eyes as they ran. He had thought of Gavin then, of Gavin and himself tumbling and elbowing each other. And laughing. They had always been laughing.

He had joined them almost without thought – spontaneously, as he did few things – and they had absorbed him without comment.

They ran hard, he and his competitive boys, bare feet gouging sand. The man passed high to his eldest son and watched as the boy leapt and caught the ball perfectly, arms moulding about its shape, muscles sliding under flesh.

When the pale sun slipped without warning beneath the water, they ran back along the waterline, the younger boys raising gouts of water with thrashing feet. The man tasted salt on his upper lip. He smelt the sweat of his five sons about him, robust with life.

Rolene started as they erupted through the kitchen door.

'Sand. Watch the sand on my floor.' But she was smiling. She had a warm smile, when she showed it, filled with quirky amusement.

They collapsed into chairs, the youngest panting ostentatiously. The man smiled suddenly and Rolene, startled, smiled back. It was this kitchen full of vigour, and he a part of it, that had roused him from himself. He was one of them, aware of lungs and heart and all of his limbs.

Living was something he had learnt to do vicariously, an onlooker on the vitality of boys. He cared about little. Disparaging about the country, contemptuous of politics, distrustful of colleagues past and present, he had only these sons to show that he still stood upon the earth. He had survived. But he had survived by being not quite alive, by walking each day as the undead.

Perhaps it was possible, after all, to begin afresh. Perhaps one could pick up a new life; leave the old discarded one against the debris on the shore.

Perhaps. Just perhaps.

'Would you ...' He paused and cleared his throat. 'Would you like me to cook a fish masala?' Rolene was staring at him. It was not a warm gaze but it was flecked with amazement. That was the best thing about children. They accepted what was presented to them without comment, without great shows of astonishment.

'What's a fish masala?' asked one of the boys.

'It's my speciality,' the man said, and he smiled again. It felt all right, not bad.

'Like you used to,' said Rolene wonderingly. 'Like you used to do when you were a boy.'

He began to fry his onions, discovering where Rolene kept the spices. The boys chattered and chaffed each other, one of the elder boys reaching across to swipe the youngest robustly across the back of the head. The man glanced across at the boy, whose eyes darkened and bruised when he tried very hard not to cry.

Removing himself from them, the boy rose and switched on the radio Rolene kept in the kitchen. Hearing the talk, and the testimony of men, the child would have switched stations, but the eldest boy stopped him.

'No, it's okay, Rugrat. Nothing wrong. I find this Truth Commission stuff quite interesting, actually.'

It was his inarticulate boy's way, the man thought, of telling his father they were a normal family. He was saying that, to him, they were everyday people without secrets and fears, and without guilt.

Rolene dithered at the sink. He could hear her there and he could feel her gaze upon him, although he did not look up. He hummed as he fried. He knew that Rolene ached to switch it off, but he also knew that she could not. Though it sliced through them all, she could not touch the radio without admitting something about themselves.

So he cooked, but desultorily now, while his family listened to a special report on the Amnesty Hearings.

'When these statements were made, that these assaults and onslaughts had to be tackled very harshly, how did you understand that?'

'I believed that these statements also supported the kind of methods that I used.'

This guy had been sixteen when he had entered the police, the poor bastard. His background and his belief systems could not have been more different from his own. This was a kid who had been conditioned into believing the way he did. What did they expect? He was a robot. How did they expect him to act when handed a detainee or two?

He himself had been cynical of everyone and everything by the time he had been called upon to interrogate anyone. Aware that his masters were fighting a losing battle, he had nonetheless had nothing but contempt for the fearful students and young academics who had been his speciality. They had brought their situation upon themselves, always unaware, mostly unwitting.

Some had worked hard at it, desperate for the badge of the detainee. Others had been astonished that this could happen; that privileged children from good families could still be kept in Solitary with one grimy toilet.

Cleverer than many, he had taken a certain pleasure in his work. He had enjoyed facing down the arrogance of young men who believed all police to be stupid. He had outwitted them and enjoyed watching them blubber as they informed on their friends.

He had known society could not remain as it was. He had known that some change was inevitable. He had also known that, at that stage, all that was left was to control the process; to crush the revolutionaries and court those who were not blatant communists.

> *'Yes, that's right. We interrogated him when we got there. Ag, mag ek asseblief in Afrikaans praat?'*

The report continued in Afrikaans, which would save at least the youngest boy from picking up most of this wallowing shit. How he despised men like this, men who showed no restraint in their cowering for forgiveness, just as they had practised no control in the past.

> *'At Cleveland Bos, or at the minedump, Mr Van Rensburg fetched a rope and the apparatus from his car. He tied the deceased's feet together. At that stage, there was already a canvas sack over his head. The deceased was then hung by his feet from a tree. Mr Van Rensburg attached the apparatus to his finger and his private parts and he shocked him. I also handled the apparatus, as well as my colleagues – all of us who were present.*

> *'Mr Van Rensburg collected a pile of leaves and sticks under the deceased's head and set them alight so as to make smoke.'*

The silence hung between them as the radio poured more and more of his grovelling guilt into the room. He cooked while they sat or stood like pillars of salt, their desperation to be normal making it impossible to turn it off.

> *'... tell the Commission, what was the purpose of this, do you know?'*

> *'It was ... the reason for the smoke was to make him uncomfortable and it was also to see if he was prepared to give us the information we wanted.'*

'One fish masala coming up.' The man moved decisively across the kitchen and clicked the off-switch. Rolene was standing in her place before the sink, her toe tracing the cracks in the linoleum. She did not look up. The boys were quieter than they had been. There was something wary, almost shifty, in the way their eyes slunk sideways to escape his.

He cleared his throat. 'I think we can sit at the table to eat.'

'I thought ...' That was his eldest. 'I thought we were listening to that.'

'We don't need the radio. We can have conversation instead.'

'But we need to ...'

'Wow, conversation! What a novel concept. But that's what people do, you know, when they have passed adolescence. They turn televisions and radios off in order to eat.'

The meal began in silence. Rolene had lapsed back into her deadened fish-eyed state. The boys all gazed at the table or the walls about them. The youngest kicked his heel monotonously against his chair leg, but no brotherly reprimand resounded against the back of his head.

'Dad?'

The man glanced up. Perhaps it was too late for him after all. But these children, they were all that was left of him. Should anything happen to any one of them, no life – no form of life at all – was possible.

'Dad?' His middle boy looked frightened 'Did ... I mean, Mom was talking about you having interrogated, I mean, questioned detainees. What ...? Dad, what did you think of that oke on the radio? Of what he did?'

'I think he showed a total lack of control. It was only stupid interrogators, those with no self-control, who resorted to torture. It only created martyrs.'

'Did you never ...'

'I never had to. I'm too clever to need those kind of methods. I always got what I wanted.'

'I told you so,' said his youngest, pulling his eyes down and flattening his nose at his elder brothers.

He had, to an extent. He himself had almost never lost control. Almost never, and never in an orgy of violence. He had never soiled the soft hands that were used to writing project reports. But he knew there were others who had.

And he knew too, that without the fear, he could never have been as effective as he was. His methods were built on fear. Play on the fear, watch it grow – and then offer them respite. Offer them niceness and watch them blubber.

'Why then ...?' Rolene entered the conversation now for the first time and he watched her coldly, knowing she was about to pull the emergent life from within him, like the fragile child who had come too soon from her belly.

'I wonder why that guy I bumped into at the reunion should have said that. You know, about that girl.'

He shrugged. 'Some people like to dramatise.'

'Ja, but you can't go on dramatising things for so very long. Who was she, anyway? What was so special about her?'

'Nothing. Absolutely nothing. She was one of a long line of arrogant, pushy children who were privileged enough to think themselves something special, as leftists of great note. She ... if I think of her sometimes, it's probably only because she represents the epitome, the sum of them all for me.'

'But then why, I wonder, should she still be weird from it all?'

He wondered why she felt compelled to nag at it like this. 'Perhaps she couldn't take the niceness. Perhaps she felt bad to have been so nicely treated when for others, life was such a heavy burden.'

Rolene held her eyes upon his. She didn't smile. His sons erupted though, collapsing in uncomplicated laughter. He watched them laugh, but felt suddenly that everything within him had been doused in local anaesthetic.

That woman. Francesca. How he disliked her. How he wished he had never laid eyes on her. Every time he thought to amputate the past from his existence, he caught a glimpse of her, or she turned up in conversation. Was she to haunt him all his life?

It was too late. He should have known better. It was too late to learn to live again. Better, far better, to accept the twilight life he lived. It was a bitter thing to anticipate more, and then learn again the futility of it all.

FRANCESCA

'Did I wake you?'

'It doesn't matter. I love to be woken by you. Where are you?'

'I'm still in bed. Paul's gone running. Daniel's getting breakfast. I hope it's okay ...'

'Oh Sweetheart. If you only knew how I love to hear your voice first thing in the morning.'

'Well, I wish I could wake you more gently.'

'Give it time, my precious. I still have to come to terms with this, you know. I never even thought it was possible.'

'Must go. Can hear the door. Just wanted to say I love you.'

'Know, my Sweetheart, that I love you with all the sorry remains that I am.'

'Who'll be there? What sort of people, I mean?'

'Yeoville crowd mainly. And old Yeoville refugees who've escaped into suburbia.' Megan eyed her with, Francesca felt, a slight condescension. 'Mainly the Yeoville crowd who've mellowed a bit and had babies and stuff.'

Why had she allowed herself to be dragged to this? But Megan had felt the need for some support at this stork party. Francesca had caught the appeal in her tough girl tone, if not in her words.

The new Rockey Street crowd made her edgy. They seemed to displace her to a some long lost generation from the past. To her, cool would always be epitomised by the Rockey Street of the '80s – a brave new world of resistance, drugs and music.

They had been proud of it, of a music and a mood that appeared to be new. It seemed to have drawn within it a synthesis of all they were in the country, and all that they could make it, in defiance of the system.

They parked next to a bedraggled hedge topped by a couple of lines of razor wire. Francesca decided against leaving her bag in the boot. She'd hate to lose that if the car went.

Daniel had fallen asleep on the back seat. She lifted him and carried him up the steep path. She should force him to walk, she supposed. But his face had been babied by sleep, his hair slicked and spiked by the hot car. And somehow, his disability always seemed more pronounced when he had just wakened, his hands and feet wrestling with the world and its demands.

The house had a bedraggled look, its dapper front battered by changing fashions and demographics. From the covered stoep there lay, in every direction,

Johannesburg. It was the Jo'burg of legend, an outlook to conjure on homesick nights away from home.

To the left lay the city perched in its bowl, Ponte's Coca Cola sash a brash reminder that this was, after all, a city of trade. And far to the right stalked the cooling towers, fuming away in some arcane industrial fulmination of their own.

'I'd love to live here,' muttered Megan. 'This is where Tebs says he wouldn't mind ...'

'But surely this view must cost a fortune?'

'Too near Troyeville to be smart anymore.'

A great pot of dhal simmered on the stove at one end of the great, open-plan room. Children skittered across the floor, while the adults draped and perched over the sparse furniture and sat cross-legged on the wooden floor.

Their hostess, gorgeous and black, swept Megan away in a flurry of greetings. 'Howzit doll. Where's Tebs?' she heard someone ask, but she couldn't hear Megan's reply.

It was like a club, this. In the circumstances, she felt her own child to be indecently white. All these bright young couples, trendy to their slightly tinted children. Where did they all come from in just these few years?

She knew that Megan aggravated her mother with tales of Tebogo. She was fairly sure her mother considered him an aberrant rebellion. She wondered whether that was still a factor for this roomful, for this whole new generation of partners, or whether they even noticed at all.

She and her friends seemed to lug so much about with them – bundles of defensive guilt over the lives they had been born to, parcels of shame at not having been braver about just living here and being moral.

Of course their children, this generation's and hers, wouldn't notice any of this mixing and marrying. What a gift that was. How wonderful that she had been able to give that to her child. Francesca might still notice – probably always would. But it was a matter of pride that her son would grow up differently.

She was joined by a small group of baby-toting parents. Through mouthfuls of roti, a man began a worried enquiry about bed-wetting. Francesca knew all about that. Launching into animated discussion of emotional security and the physical immaturity of boys, she felt suddenly quite at home.

Daniel was playing with the littler ones near the door, she noted gratefully. He was a difficult child – difficult to like. He gave so little of himself unless he chose to. And this he did rarely.

'Who is that wonderful child being so gentle with the little kids?'

Francesca was startled to discover that Sylvie, whose child was too timid in playschool and whose partner didn't involve himself in babycare, was referring to Daniel.

'He's amazing,' said Thandeka, whose son had a problem with beating up on other kids. 'You hardly ever see a boy being that gentle.'

'That's my nephew,' said Megan, appearing suddenly beside her. 'Isn't he great?'

Francesca was touched by Megan's claiming of him. And proud of Daniel. It felt good, giving a warm glow she seldom felt. She was so used to being defensive, coercing people into seeing the specialness of him, that there never seemed to be room for simple pride.

She knew this facility with those younger and more fragile was part of his problem. His slight physical imperfection seemed to him immense, particularly alongside the robust boys who beat their barefoot paths through his life. He felt more at home with those as weak or weaker than himself. But still, it was a special quality, that ability to understand the gentler souls, and to bond with those that heartier children bullied.

'Fran?' Megan said. 'I'm really tired. And I'm meeting Tebs later.'

'You know,' she said as they reached the car, 'I'm not really sure or anything, but I was wondering if Tebs and I shouldn't maybe have a baby.'

Perhaps they should. Who was she to cast doubt upon her cousin's commitment? Who knew? Perhaps it was exactly what she needed.

'I mean, it seemed so sad in there. But I don't even know if I'm ready for that. I wish I could get away, I mean away from them all, Tebs, Nicholas, everyone, just to think about it and consider my life a little.'

Francesca felt blessed in Anthony. He had children and so did she. She was pretty sure they wouldn't be wanting more, once they were properly together.

'Message from hell' it said. Message from hell? Why on earth would Anthony give his mail such a heading? And he never e-mailed her. Why should he? He phoned her every day.

Perhaps something was wrong. Perhaps one of his kids ... But of course it was going to be a really difficult time for him. He was bound to be filled with all kinds of guilt. She would have to bolster him really hard.

Dear Francesca,

How can I write this? I never intended that this should happen. I never intended that we should grow so very close, or that I should manage to glimpse such happiness again, with you.

The trouble is, Francesca, that I can't do it. And deep down I'm sure you knew I couldn't. I have failed at everything I have attempted. Except for my children. They are the only perfect, shining things I have managed to produce. I can't just leave them.

At first it was a fantasy with us. I went along with it because I loved it. And because I loved you ... But Francesca, it is a fantasy. It's not real life. For me, the only reality remaining is to do my duty, to continue to do what I have begun with my children to the best of my ability.

Who said that life should promise happiness? Why should I believe that I deserve it, at the expense of my children's security and possibly their happiness? With you I saw a glimmer of something more. You made me believe that things had changed, and that perhaps I should forgive myself for all that I have managed to botch and all the values I have managed to betray.

But I am not the person you think I am. For a while, I saw myself through your eyes and I thought perhaps I could become the person you saw. But I'm not. I'm weak and I'm a failure. I drink too much and, quite frankly, I don't care. I don't care about anything except my children. And you, Francesca. And you. I know that I will go back and, for a while, I will ache. My brain will burn for you, for the slightest smell of you upon my skin. But I will have to cut it off from me.

Eventually I will forget. And with that will come acceptance of what I have chosen to do, and hopefully a certain contentment.

I know exactly what you will say. I know that you will say this is half a life. But perhaps half a life is all that I still have stomach for.

I am sorry, Francesca. And I am sorry that I do not have the courage to tell you this face to face. But perhaps it is just as well. Perhaps you will begin to see that I do not have the worth you invest me with. At least now I am disillusioning you. Now, and then it will be over. At least I will not have to watch the creeping realisation that I am not the hero you seem to think. Perhaps I was, as you say, damaged by all that we were forced to live through. But perhaps, also, I wasn't worthy of the role I attempted to play. Perhaps I could never have been man enough to play the simplest part.

What I do know is that I am not man enough to play the part you want of me. There is not enough of me left.

I wish you happiness, Francesca. Truly I do. I hope that you banish your own demons. From my half-life, hopefully with a measure of serenity, I hope to watch you live with that boundless intensity of yours. It will give me pleasure. I wish us both peace. I wish that for the country too. I can't come back here, you know. There are too many memories and there is just too much I can't forgive. It's too hard, Francesca.

I love you,

Anthony

The cold chewed through her jersey. She didn't care. She welcomed it. The night was beautiful, cruel in its bitter clarity. Her only reality, the only living thing about her, was time. And even that must be mortally wounded, crawling forward as it did on its hands and knees.

Paul had taken longer than usual to fall asleep in front of the television. She had watched him heave himself to his feet and carry his sleep-stooped body off to bed. Still she had waited. How long? How much time would it take a man to fall into deeper sleep, unconscious of the slight creak of the floorboards, the whisper of the front door as she slipped outside?

Her cellphone was slippery from the hands that crouched in her lap. She wiped it with the sleeve of her jersey. Clearing her throat, she tried out the voice that had lain unused inside her all evening.

She knew Anthony didn't mean it. He couldn't really be rejecting the life they had snatched by the scruff of its neck and wrung every drop of intensity from. It was one of those things that couples went through. It seemed hard to him, that's all. She understood that. But he only had a couple of weeks left until his contract expired, and she couldn't allow him to go back home feeling as he did. He needed her strength.

Wiping her hands again, she dialled.

'Anthony?'

'Francesca ...' He breathed out on the word, as though it exhausted him to form it.

'Anthony, listen. I just ... I mean, I need to talk ...'

'Francesca, why are you phoning me again? I was asleep.'

'I'm sorry. I didn't mean to wake you. But I had to wait ...'

'It doesn't matter, Francesca. But there's no sense in this. I told you this morning ...'

'You told me you couldn't deal with it at work.'

'Francesca, I can't deal with this anywhere. Don't you understand? Fuck it, it took all the strength I had to write you that message.'

'But I don't understand. We need to talk ...'

'We don't need to talk, Francesca. That is what we do not need.' She switched hands, stepping further into the garden each time their voices rose.

'But Anthony, I know you don't ... I mean, you can't mean this. Not with the way we were. Even yesterday ... What happened, Anthony?'

'Nothing. Nothing happened Francesca. Only my children phoned me yesterday and I spoke to them. I ... I just realised, Francesca. Oh for fuck sake, you're making this so hard.'

'Anthony, think of what we've had.'

'We had a fantasy, Francesca. It wasn't real.'

'It was for me, Anthony.' She felt the tears come to her throat and pour through her voice. She couldn't help it. She hadn't cried all day, waiting for this moment, so sure that she could mend what they had so carelessly torn. 'It was the most reality I've ever had in my life.'

'Now you're fucking crying. I can't deal with this. Really. I told you this morning I can't deal with it anymore. Leave it at that, can't you?'

She pressed the red button, moving back to the step where she had earlier waited. All that waiting seemed pathetic now. She didn't care about the humiliation of it. She was beyond that. All she knew was that she didn't exist without the weight of his hurt soul pressing upon hers. With nothing to hold her down she would drift off, drying and crumpling in the parched winter breeze, powdering at last to nothing.

'Daniel, get up now. Please don't fight me today.'

For once he was biddable. Not yet fully detached from her umbilical cord, Daniel sensed something that should not be messed with today. She moved him through the motions of dressing and preparing for the day.

She did the same for herself, cajoling her limbs to comply. Only her hair would have to remain as wild as she felt inside herself. She could not raise the arms that lay leaden against her sides. How was it possible to hold this rage of pain so hidden and silent?

She dropped Daniel at school and sat in her car, willing herself to drive home. But she had no resolve to spare. She allowed her car and her limbs to dictate the route to his hotel. Through the morning rush hour, she pressed on past the taxis and buses and the cars that pushed and shoved at each other, dicing at robots and bends.

She should not have come. It was everything she had been taught not to do in a youth that required that she sit and wait, but never take the initiative.

She looked about her at the car park, so full of him, of the view from his room, of his kisses. An injection of fury tingled through her. He had kissed her in the car park, aching for her, crying that he could not live without her. He had muffled her good sense in intensity, pushing her so hard she was ill.

'Oh God, Francesca.' He was half-dressed and seemed harassed to see her. How strange, she thought, that he should seem harassed. Of all the things he could seem, how significant that he should choose mere irritation at her presence.

'I needed to see you, Anthony. You need to look me in the eyes and tell me you don't love me.'

'Oh Francesca.' And he sighed. 'Francesca, I have to go to work. I can't be late. This is my last week.'

'You have another two weeks of your contract.'

'I cut it short. They can finish without me. It's an unnecessary waste of money to keep me here.'

'Oh I see.' She stepped past him into the room that was muggy with cigarettes and sleep, a whisky bottle empty beside the bed. Emboldened by pain and rage, she faced him. Still holding his eyes captive, she sat on the bed and crossed her legs very precisely. Peremptory with him, with the weakness and prevarication she now saw wavering within him, she patted the bed by her side. Jittering with frowns, he sat nonetheless.

'Tell me now, Anthony. Tell me I was a contract romance. Tell me you don't love me. Look into my eyes now and tell me that.'

She watched his face change. Whimsical suddenly – oh, the impossible binds life threw at one – he creased his brow and reached out his two hands.

'Francesca, you're beautiful and lively and talented.' He gave a pretty little shrug. 'Where I come from, boys fall in love with that. And I did. I do, Francesca. How could I help but love you?'

'Then what about me? Aren't you running away and failing at one more thing? If what you say is true?'

She watched as whimsy made way for defensive fury.

'You knew, Francesca. You knew I was married. For fucks sake, you're married yourself. You couldn't have just assumed we would wander off together into the sunset?'

'No Anthony, I didn't just assume it.' She stood then, and walked to the door. This she could not bear. She could not sit through the things he was likely to say now. 'I didn't just assume it.'

She didn't look back until she reached the lift. He didn't come after her. Didn't even open his door.

She would never know. She would always wonder whether he had truly felt all that he had communicated with every finger that brushed her brow, and every kiss he lavished on her neck and her eyes.

But in the end it didn't really matter a fuck.

'What the hell's the matter with you, Francesca?'

Francesca looked up at her furious cousin. She hadn't the energy to do the 'Oh nothing, absolutely nothing, just tired' routine. She felt drained, not just of pain, but of everything.

'I'm fucked.' How strange she sounded, like someone who still had emotions and feelings and hurt.

Megan looked her over and sat very suddenly. She reached across the kitchen table and grasped her hand very hard, as though she were a drowning person.

'Where's Paul?' she asked.

'Asleep.'

'What're you going to do?'

'I ... have no idea.'

'You need to get out of here.'

'I don't care.'

'No, Francesca, you do. You need to take care of yourself now. It's not all about you and Paul. You need to look at what's messed you up so badly.'

'I tried to fix it. I thought I'd found the answer.'

'You didn't go to the right places. We need to go back to the source.'

'I can't.'

'You have to. Francesca, you're dying here.'

'What about you? What about all your problems?'

'Ah, Frannie, mine aren't in the same league. I used to envy you, but now ... look, I could also do with some time away. I'll go with you.'

'Where will we go?'

'We'll work that out as we go along.'

'We'll have to take Daniel. Paul won't cope ...'

'If we must take Daniel, then we will. But we need to do something. We both do. This'll be for both of us.'

THE MAN

'Go to bed, Rolene. You're falling asleep in that chair.'

'I can't. I just can't. Not ... not this one. He's my baby.'

'I'll be here. Can't sleep much these days anyway.'

'You ...' Her voice held contempt. The man glanced at her and she backed down visibly, shoulders and head shrinking into the chair. Almost quailing. 'You're not his mother,' she said, and looked down at the hands that lay in her lap.

This shrinking away took him by surprise. It always had, that people should have a view of him that was so at odds with reality. All he could truly say about himself was that he was alive. He was a survivor, no doubt about that. But apart from that he was nothing. He had ceased to be, erased from consequence by the movement of time and politics.

He had never been that important in the great scheme of things and now ... now he had been absorbed into the fabric of their lives. Into the curtains that drooped at the windows, into the kitchen wallpaper and the sea sand that, no matter how hard they tried, drifted constantly across the kitchen floor.

'Rolene, listen man. I'm speaking straight here. If there's nothing you can rely on, you must know how I feel about my boys. Go to bed. He'll be fine.' He stared at her hard, willing her to feel it. That Rolene should fear him ... oh, he was fairly certain she thought him a failure. She probably despised him. But that she should fear him, was strange beyond words.

'But you will call me ... I mean if anything ...'

'He'll be fine. He's got a helluva temperature, but he will be fine. I will call you, though, if anything changes. And ... Rolene?'

'Yes?'

The man cleared his throat, unused to uttering any but the most basic expressions of need or want. 'I don't know ... I suppose it's because he's so sick. It gets you to thinking. But I was just wondering ... do you ever remember the way we used to be? Before everything?'

He had no clear idea of why he had spoken as he had, except that this was his youngest, his special one. Life's way of making up in some small way for Gavin. And Rolene's small flinch had got to him the way nothing much had for the past twenty years. It was just that lately, with the spirit of change in the air, with this orgy of truth and reconciliation, he had begun to think.

'I don't know,' she answered at last. She sounded tired, as though the words were a burden. 'I used to. But everything changed so very much. I began to think that early stuff must have seemed like child's play to you. I felt stupid for having been so naïve. And it seemed like you must have taken such amusement from how stupid I was, not to have realised what you were. So ... I'd have to say I remember less and less.'

'Rolene ... It's fair enough. What you feel. If that's how it is. But I never thought that way. I was ... grateful, I suppose…that you stuck around.'

'Oh come on now. Now ... now you come with this. Now you try and tell me ... oh, fuck it. It doesn't matter anymore. But I just think you had a really odd way of showing it. I mean, what ...'

'Okay, enough Rolene. It was a mistake to speak of it.'

'No, but I mean really, what did you think I would be thinking, all this time?'

'Enough. I said enough, Rolene. It doesn't matter. Not anymore.'

'But it does. It fucking does. All this time I've been closed off. You've closed me off from you, from the world. No-one I used to know even wants to know me, because of you.'

'Rolene, sit down. Please stop it now. Jesus fucking Christ, I didn't realise I was bringing on this ...'

'And you ... I don't know what's going on with you. I haven't even known if you're about to appear suddenly before the TRC or something. I haven't even known that. And it's not that I care for your sake. Please don't think that.'

'Rolene, you'll wake the child.'

'Oh shut the fuck up, for once. I haven't ... I haven't spoken for twenty years because ... I don't know ... I had nowhere to go. I had nothing I could do. You'd closed me off and it seemed like all that mattered was the boys. But now the boys are threatened too. Listen to me now. I know you think I'm weak, that I'm nothing. That's why you married me. I wasn't ever going to challenge you, was I? I was going to stick around and be your housekeeper and ...'

'Rolene, don't be irrational. Don't do this to yourself.'

'Don't you dare ...' Her voice shrilled and she paused to swallow. More quietly, with a glance at the boy asleep in the bed between them, she continued: 'Don't you dare say I've done this. Just don't try. You're ... you're like a dead person. And you ... it's you that's done this to me.'

He sat on the uncomfortable, upright chair he had dragged in from the kitchen, and smelt the boy smell of this room. Spiderman curtains drooped from the windows where the boys had tugged at them in boisterous play. They were faded now, their red climbing figures almost obliterated by the sun. But Rolene had made them. She had sat in a corner of the lounge, making the boys curtains and endless tracksuits to replace those they ripped and wore through at the knee.

He remembered how her sewing table had annoyed him, with its drifting debris of pins and scraps. Each evening he had sighed and irritably gathered piles of remnants between his hands, dumping them on her lap, swearing when he pricked his fingers. Eventually she had given up. She had given that up too, taking her place in the kitchen instead, from where she could gaze out to sea. She had packed away the sewing machine and given all her patterns to the organisers of the church bazaar.

'I know,' he said at last. 'Rolene, I do know.'

She looked up at him suddenly – a stranger from another planet, with quite inexplicable customs and codes of conduct. 'But then why ... Jesus Christ, couldn't you, just once or twice, have shown me ... Couldn't you have said something?'

'I don't know. Maybe I thought you should know ...'

'Oh fuck me gently.'

His mouth quirked and he felt an unexpected sensation in his belly, one he would have difficulty locating, let alone identifying. There was a sadness there, a long, aching sorrow for something lost and so much wasted. Yet, it made him long to laugh, the sight of this worn woman uttering the words of the young and lively girl she had once been.

'Rolene. You must have seen ... there's so little left of me, I couldn't do it. Besides the fact that I had no right. I had no right to ask you to stay. I couldn't allow myself ... I felt sure you would leave, sooner or later.'

'Well, why now? Why must you drag up all this old stuff now.'

'I don't know. I just don't know. But ...' How to explain the bitterness of seeing men, men he despised for their lack of control, men who had done far worse than he ever had, grovelling to the truth commission and being forgiven. And all the adjustments people had made and were making, to the way they acted or thought about people.

The floor of their society had shifted downward, like that fun-fair ride he and Gavin had ridden as children. They were spinning at a disorienting speed in a great, nauseating void. There were those he had known who had killed insdiscriminately, who had tortured and taken a pride in the pain they inflicted. There were those who had assassinated and waged war. And yet these were the men who walked with pride in the new society. As though they belonged. Old enmities were reframed, new enemies formed, histories rewritten ...

He sighed. He might have reached a hand across the bed, had he been another man, had they had another life between them. 'Rolene, what ... my role was very small. It's not necessary for me to fling myself before the truth commission. But in this atmosphere ... I mean, I just wonder ... I don't want to drag up all this old stuff. But wouldn't it be possible just to forget it?'

'How would that ever be possible? I don't understand you.'

'To just cut it off, all the past kak? Maybe start again?'

'People would never let us forget ...'

'But everything's shifting. With some people, yes. But fuck them. Most people don't know where they stand anymore and who did what. No-one knows anymore who the real enemy was – whether it was the architects of apartheid or the liberals who whinged and whined and lived under it.'

'But, never mind other people, you would never let us forget. Don't you see ... If you did appear before the TRC, I would have to leave. I'd have to take the boys away. But in some ways, I wish you did.'

'But what I did ...'

'It doesn't matter, objectively, what you did and didn't do. It's just that it's not possible to have a future until you, or until we, acknowledge the past.'

'I don't know what you want me to do.'

'It's not me. It's you who won't allow yourself to go on from here. You won't exist, you won't survive until you make amends in some way. You have to ... fuck, I don't know. But I know that you have to do something. You're a weird and complex man. Once upon a time I loved that about you. I don't know what I feel now, but I know that you have a very involved sense of karma.'

'Rolene, you're taking this kak too far. I don't believe ...'

'I don't care if you believe or not. Somewhere deep inside you do. And I do know that almost everything you've done in your life was sort-of one in the eye for God, for taking your brother away.'

He felt the shock of her words spattering their acid across his forehead. But he could not move. His legs were embedded in the pile of the children's carpet.

'I know that now there's an imbalance again. I know you have to heal something you hurt, or fix something you broke. Otherwise, you can think you're going on living, but you're dead. You might as well be dead ... and me too. I might as well be dead, because I have nowhere else to go.'

FRANCESCA

'Where are we going, by the way? Or am I not allowed to ask?'

'You can ask. But I'm not sure I'll be able to tell you.'

Francesca glanced across at her cousin and they laughed, a hysterical conspiracy of girls bunking out on a schoolnight. She felt so many things. And yet, above all, she felt a lightening within herself. They had set out, they were on the road, and she might possibly still be granted another chance to deal with all that was undealt with. If she was lucky. If the car made all the right turns. If she was even able to, after all this time.

'Thank you,' she said, eyes on the long highway before them.

'Oh bullshit. What was I going to do? Let you have this adventure all by yourself?'

The late afternoon sun flashed its blinding eye at the diamond building and, beyond Doornfontein and Jeppe, stained the mine-dumps the dull red of old blood. They swung through Braamfontein and around the city, on to the Bloem highway, where Castle trucks boomed and taxis rattled. Clouds threw mottled patches over marching pylons.

Megan's skin was pinked and plumped by the evening sun. She seemed untroubled by misgivings, merely jubilant to be away. 'I was just thinking how weird it all is. How much has happened in the short time I've been in Joeys. And how we've both changed. Well, me really. What's changed is the way I see you, I suppose.'

' "Karma City", that's what Penny calls it. She says that if you come here with pretensions, it'll beat you about the head with them. It'll turn your preconceptions upside down. And every mistake you've ever made will come back to haunt you again and again. It's not the kind of city where you can escape stuff.'

'What did you say to Paul, by the way? About our trip? He can't have been too chuffed.'

'Not now.' She glanced quickly behind them, where Daniel sat in his carseat, his tray filled with books and disgusting yellow chips.

'Sorry. Forgot. Big ears.'

They drove in silence, Francesca enjoying the feel of the highway beneath them. She took a tactile pleasure in long-distance driving, the pulse of the engine a bit wild, a little controlled. It was a Friday evening, the roads weighed down by slack-backed taxis and transport men, tottering under towers of chairs, mattresses and cupboards.

The darkness hovered briefly and then dropped about them. Car beams felt their way through the yellowed murk of the highway, like the snails that trailed across the stoep after the rains, eyes stretched before them.

The air felt brittle and sharp as glass. Francesca turned the car heater on – not too high though. They had a long way to go, and she shouldn't grow sleepy.

They made it to Bloem in just over four hours, as darkness settled across the Free State's flat yellow plains. Francesca pulled into the Ultra-City and Megan began scrabbling for shoes.

'Daniel's asleep,' she said, with pathetic helplessness.

'Well, wake him,' Francesca said, a touch impatiently. 'He has to wee now or he'll wee all over my car.'

'Okay, okay. But he's disgusting. He's one great yellow chip mixed with tacky marshmallow.'

'Well, you're the one who wants to have a baby.'

Silence dropped between them like a lead curtain. She heard Megan give a small sniff as she lifted Daniel from the car. Oh God, why had she said that? She hadn't meant to. She followed Megan to the loo and found her washing her hands. Daniel was sitting on the wide counter, his hands clean but stained a nicotine yellow. Two women dressed in abayas were washing beside Megan. Francesca could smell the sickly pink of the soap dispenser. Behind her, a large, slip-slopped woman chided her child to wipe his bum nicely and hurry up about it.

'I'm sorry Meg-child.'

'It's okay.'

'I'm just ... it's no excuse, but I'm so wrought up.'

'I know. All sisters fight like that sometimes. It's no biggie.'

Francesca felt the warmth crackle and then flame between them. Because, you know what? They were. When had that happened? When had Megan become more than the irritating little cousin who had hero-worshipped her detention? Before this winter, she would never have considered a trip like this with Megan. Family were for hiding things from. And yet suddenly, nothing felt as right as this trip, and that they were on it together.

'Come on,' she said. 'Do you want something to eat? Toasted sarmie or anything? I have to feed Daniel.'

Neither of them could cope with the Wimpy. It seemed too much to bear that they should face psychic damage and pink sauce on the same trip. They bought a takeaway hotdog for Daniel and laughed a lot – that slightly drunken laughter of letting go.

They decided to head straight on into the Eastern Cape. With no clear idea of their destination, there seemed little point in hurtling headlong down the national highway. Arguing about where to turn off the N1, that straightest of all roads, they let go of everything. Let the car take them. What the hell. Whatever would be, would probably happen anyway.

They stopped at the Smithfield hotel, absolutely starving, at about half-past nine. The men's bar was off to one side and this being a Friday night, the bakkies had gathered in a tight bunch at the side entrance.

Moths battered themselves against the fly-pocked lights and 'Proud Mary' pounded from the bar. A lone woman in overall and matching apron sat in the lounge, minding the shop. All other evidence of life was to be found in the bar. Riveted to some seSotho soapie, she didn't look up as they entered. But she went off willingly enough to cook them mince, egg and chips.

Daniel lay fast asleep on the carpet, his legs covered by Megan's jacket. It felt warm and comforting to be here. Beside them, through the lace curtain, Francesca could see a large bull terrier, its nose pressed against the sash window. It was difficult for a bull terrier to gaze through a window. Her father had always said that being a bull terrier must be like flying a spitfire. You had to look down each side of your nose in turn.

'What are you smirking at now?'

'Absolutely nothing of any importance to the world. Megan? What'd you tell Tebs?'

'I said you and I had to get away. He didn't even ask.'

'No he wouldn't. He's such a cool boy.'

'Of course the other boy railed against fate. He asked how I could possibly go when his life was in such a state.'

'You are incorrigible. I might have known you couldn't resist telling Nicholas. Now, he's not a cool boy. He's charming and sexy but he's not the boy to invest your hopes and dreams in. You do know that deep down, don't you?'

'Speaking of which, what did you tell Paul?'

'Well ... Megan, pass that abysmal wine. Don't hog it.'

'You're driving.'

'We can always spend the night. I mean, we don't even know where we're going. I told him I was leaving him.'

Megan choked on her wine. It was so hackneyed a reaction that if she hadn't gagged unattractively, Francesca might have believed it to be a rather stagy gesture.

'Really? For good?'

'Yes, for good.'

It had been hard to tell him, knowing it would knock him sideways. She had always had difficulty disappointing people. But she had reached that point of desperation where it had almost burst through her flesh. She was taking her life back, just like that. She had traded it in for Paul's spurious strength, and for all the ephemeral normality of bookclubs and liftclubs. In the end she had sold it off wholesale to Anthony, in return for the distraction of mending him. But now it was hers again – to restore or destroy. Whatever would be, would be. But it was hers to decide.

Megan poured them more coffee from the heavy old pot. It tasted thick, like railway station coffee. Francesca had always loved railway coffee. It reminded her of childhood and journeys, of excitement and the thrill of the unknown. Oh God, this was all so hard.

Now what? Dear God, what were they doing here?

Francesca had awoken from barely an hour's sleep, fear thick as fog in her throat. What were they doing in East London? What on earth had possessed her to bring them here?

She knew, of course. It should have been obvious to anyone that her car would have set this inexorable course. It had all begun here. Everything that had caused her adulthood to take the track it had, stemmed from this small, overheated Eastern Cape town.

But now that they were here? All that talk of new beginnings – what did it all mean? It seemed so stupid, so utterly futile.

She hadn't come to see the structures that had held her. She had come for the people – to face them without fear, at least now after all this time. The spectre of her detention had always taken the form of those who had caged her. The chatty one who had fed her, the harsh-faced ones who had watched her sprint madly around the prison yard twice a day, the sad-looking one who had escorted her to interrogation, even those sniggering women who had forced her to strip and bend double before them. These were her phantoms. And they were all probably long gone.

'I want coco-pops. I said ...'

'I heard you, Daniel. And I told you there weren't any.'

'Why did you bring me here? I want coco-pops.' Daniel's small face was puce with fury, his mouth a great rent in the puffy flesh. How was it the child managed always to find that spot of guilt, like a pinched nerve, and bear down upon it?

'Don't take it out on me, Daniel. We only just got here. I can't help it that there aren't any coco-pops.'

'What can I eat then?' His eyes were two narrow rips, frayed at the edges by tear-clumped lashes.

'I can send for some toast. You can eat that.'

'I don't like toast. I want coco-pops.'

'Daniel, I'm losing patience. There are no coco-pops.'

'Tell me what I can eat then.'

I have offered you dried fruit. I've offered you toast. That's ...'

'I don't like dried fruit and I don't like toast.'

'No breakfast for you then.'

'But I'm hungry. I'm so hungry.'

'Well, choose something then.'

'I want coco-pops.'

How the hell did Megan manage to sleep through this racket? Francesca had driven all night and now here she was. It was eight in the morning and she longed only to lay her head upon a crisp pillow. And here she was with a child who had slept firmly through the darkness and whose eyes could not have been more firmly propped open had they been fixed with matchsticks.

Daniel grew so very angry. He became furious at himself for not managing things, and at the world for holding up a reflection of himself as different. And he always took it out on her. He raged against her for all that made life hard for him. How did he know how culpable she really felt? How could he sense what a mess she had made of everything?

Now she had left it all – all that had held her safely all these years. What had she been thinking of? She felt ill. Her limbs tingled with a feverish energy that had no goal, a panic that had no point. How could she have left Paul? How did she hope to manage? What if the insecurity of it all affected Daniel? Oh God, she was such a hopeless mother. She was so incredibly irresponsible.

She wished above all things that she could make him better. No miracle stuff. She had no vision of the lame rising from their beds. There would always be a hardness to Daniel's life that other children could not even see. It could never be dug for like a thorn, and plucked from within his soft little soul.

But surely Daniel could learn to sense his own normality. She would like to be able to give that to him. Like a gift, she needed to hand him a sense of himself as similar to other boys. He was only a little different, and much of that was what made him special. Why could he only see his difference? How could she show him his inner self, which had knees as scuffed as any other boy's? If she were able to do that, she might just be able to forgive herself.

'... and you will stay in that bathroom until you calm down. You either eat or don't eat. But you will do it ...' She felt her fury gathering its forces, '... you will do it quietly.'

Oh God, if she could only lie down. She sat in a hotel chair, laying her head back and closing her eyes. All she could hear were her child's heart-rending sobs. She opened her eyes and reached for the kettle. It was empty and she was barred from her own bathroom. Tiredness burrowed into her brain like a parasite, feeding off her nerves.

They had only left Smithfield at midnight. It had been madness, of course. They had considered spending the night, but she had felt a rebellious bravado grip her by the shoulders and shake her to wakefulness. They were on the road. They were doing it.

They had crossed the Orange and entered the Eastern Cape, the steel bridge frigid with the icy blue light of a full moon. Through Aliwal North they had crept, Francesca straining into the darkness that cut a long, straight path ahead of them. As hills multiplied about them, it had been too late to stop anyway. The moon had seemed to illuminate only the stubble of bushes and rocks and, on the horizon, the cragged mountains that rounded into unexpectedly soft peaks.

Megan had dozed for a while as they passed the sleeping silence of Lady Grey, crouched among its blackened hills, and pushed on through Barkly East, where she awoke again.

'So ...' she had said, trying valiantly not to spill the coffee she was pouring from the thermos. In the moon-blind car, she had looked like a small child, hair all bird's-nested on one side.

'So ... what?'

'Frannie, don't you think maybe it's possible to have a perfect kind of marriage?'

'Oh Meg-child, I don't know. I'm probably the last person you should ask right now.'

'I wonder what would happen if I married Nicholas.'

'Oh Jesus Christ.' They had laughed then, with the quiet hysteria that had crept out of a long night of no sleep and a surfeit of emotion.

The stars had burst from the sky in almost gauche display, after the sullen slinking of Jo'burg's city stars. They had hit Queenstown at speed. It had been deserted. Not a soul to be seen as they whisked around the hexagon. It was funny how instantly recognisable these little towns were. First came the garages where men and cars strutted their daytime stuff, then the ubiquitous High Street, cluttered with furniture shops, clothing chains and toy-town banks.

Life was fundamental. People did concrete things, like the large-armed man who, come morning, would probably rise early to saw up carcasses for the butcher shop. So close to the parched land, stalked by aloes and sturdy bush, towns like these had nothing spare, and little space for the esoteric.

Only the lone steeple, built from local sandstone, still soared and aspired to the unexplained, long after its church had crumbled away. And only the rainbow lights flitting across the hexagon fountain brought a whimsy to its frontier stolidity.

'Maybe ...' Francesca had taken a last gulp of coffee and handed her cup to Megan, 'what you had with Nicholas was a great love that would've lasted forever and ever. Who knows? But ...'

'Don't tell me this, Francesca. I don't want to hear.'

'... but maybe it's a great and perfect love because it isn't possible. You're lucky though. It will always remain suspended for you in its flawless form.'

The sky had begun to lighten, profiling the hills that cupped but could never contain the vast plains of *wag 'n bietjie* bush and wild bursts of aloe and euphorbia. Every farmhouse was marked by a long palm. Megan had pointed out the first and they had smiled, without need of speech. They both remembered the family trips, with stories of forts and frontiers and of the palms that had once drawn thirsty travellers to the next water source.

They had passed through Cathcart where the past was a keepsake held for them in the delicate tracery of stonework and sash windows, corrugated roofs and wood-edged stoeps. Past the starched dignity of the Royal Hotel and on to Fort Cunningham. The mist, so jealously guarded on the winding pass, had held them in eerie silence until Stutterheim, where the lightening sky had pinked bougainvillea streets, and somnolent little houses harked back to other wars in other Frontier times.

The forest of the Izele Cuttings had swallowed them back into twilight just as they passed the famous rock. For as long as they could remember, that rock had teetered precariously above the road. And for as long, people had known that one day it must fall upon whoever was driving beneath. But according to Eastern Cape wisdom, one day was another day that hadn't happened yet.

They had reached East London just as the sun was beginning to rise. It was warmer here. Palm trees scattered the hotel garden and the breeze held the sea in its breast. The air was plumper, fed on plankton and the living soul of the sea.

'Francesca? Let's just sit here in the garden a bit.'

'We'll have to, I think. I'm sure they won't be up yet. And if I lift Daniel now, he'll wake up.'

They had sat on a bench and felt the pale sun warming the night from their stiff limbs.

'Are you going to be happy, Francesca?'

'Too soon to tell. But since we've set ourselves free, I think it's probably worth having a bloody good bash at it.'

'What are you going to do?'

'I have absolutely no idea. But one thing I can say is that I've taken responsibility for my own life. I think that's a big thing to have done.'

'I wish I could do that. Then maybe I wouldn't expect so much from people like you and Tebs. And maybe I wouldn't be so drawn to the Nicholases of the world.'

'Anycase, most times people like me and Nicholas can't give you what you need. I don't believe we have it ourselves. But maybe you'll eventually stumble on that yourself.'

'You mean I still have to find out all your ghastly faults and weaknesses? You mean ... you mean you're really human? I'm not sure I really want to find that out.'

Francesca gave a small, cracked laugh. 'Well, I'm not sure I really do either.'

'D'you think we can do it?'

'Well, we're here.' Francesca shrugged. 'We've all got things to face, all three of us. But look how incredibly brave we're being.'

'I can't do this.'

'Yes, you can.'

'I don't know what I thought I could find here. But I don't think it's here. Not anymore anyway.'

'Pull yourself towards yourself, Francesca. It's you that you're facing. If you haven't realised that ...'

'Then what're we doing here? Why didn't we stay in Jo'burg or go somewhere nice and far away, like Switzerland?'

'Maybe this is where you need to face yourself. Anyway, this is where the car brought us, so it's as good a place as any.'

They were sitting outside Fort Glamorgan, where she had been detained so very long ago. When she was still young. When all of life had seemed to lie before her.

Megan had done this. She had awoken at some stage on Saturday morning and demanded a huge brunch, much to Daniel's delight. He had cheered up immensely after being fed. Then with that slightly officious efficiency that reminded Francesca of Penny, she had taken control, hauling Francesca's precious laptop from its bag and faxing the prison authorities for permission to visit the prison.

It had taken a couple of days for the reply to come – days in which they had wandered East London, bought ice-creams and eaten them on the sand. They had spent much of their time on the beach. It had been blustery but fine, too chilly for swimming, but perfect for walking along the shore, jeans' legs damp and coated in sand. It was a time removed, time between the time when living had to be done and decisions made. With nothing to think of, they had conjured their childhood, clambering the rocks and running from the tide. They had laughed into the wind and given little thought to all that had still to be done, and all that must be faced.

It had been there though. It was a curtain she had drawn and refused to look behind, knowing that on the other side lay blackened rooms lumped with shapes grown sinister with darkness. Each day, Francesca had removed Daniel's shoes and given him little shoves in the small of his back. Desperation and uncertainty had brought a slight impatience to her touch. Run. Run like the wind, she had implored him in her head. His gait was awkward, his run halting. But so what. There had been few to see him, and no-one they knew. There had been no-one to turn back impatiently and tell him to hurry it along. He could run at his own pace, enjoying the feel of the sand on his feet, the roughness of rounded rocks. Couldn't he? Couldn't he feel it? Couldn't he enjoy it without self-consciousness, as they had done as children.

He had held back, clinging to her legs when the wind fluttered about his cheeks, crying when the sand stung his bare legs. His nose had run miserably over his upper lip as grits of sand had embedded themselves in his ice-cream.

At last the reply had come from the prison service, spitting back through the hotel fax machine. Megan had telephoned to make the appointment. Francesca couldn't. What if she had recognised the voice? What if it was someone ... she had thought suddenly that she might vomit.

'What did they say?' She had been watching Megan in the mirror, sitting on the bed with the phone in her hand.

'They said: "Come and have a nice cup of tea with us." ' Megan had slowly raised her eyes to meet Francesca's in the mirror. Laughing raucously, Megan had flung herself face down upon the bed, battering at the pillows that lay strewn about from Daniel's cloud game. Francesca had thought she couldn't laugh. It was all too surreal and yet too sore. But the laughter had trickled out of her involuntarily, trailing from her mouth in bursts that left her winded and gasping for breath.

And now they were here. The prison looked strange. Smaller somehow, and also less menacing. There was something quaint about it, almost laughable – government brick, old public works style with a banner splayed across its entrance: 'Warders for Peace.' How terribly odd this country was. How ironic that this, of all buildings, should display a white dove on its peace banner – the symbol used by the Truth Commission.

And suddenly it was all too much. It wasn't funny, any of it. It was a delusion. This place was sinister. It should look sinister. Once before she had been ensnared into thinking perhaps they were not all bad. But they were. They had been. It should show. Evil should flap about these walls with webbed bat wings.

She had been so sure on the journey, living out some kind of road movie, that she could change the direction of destiny. Through sheer force of will, she had thought to change her and Daniel's lives. In the warm car that flew them through the frightening darkness, it had seemed she could make it happen merely because she so wanted it to be so.

How stupid she was. This place had defeated her before. It had taken her hopeful girl's heart and squeezed it from her. The people within these walls had held that plump, living organ within their hands and they had wrung it out until it was a limp, dry thing. Why on earth had she thought she could be different now?

'Go,' said Megan. 'Go on, get out. Daniel and I will come back for you in an hour or so.'

She stepped from the car. The wind blundered off the sea. But here it smelt of the dead – of lifeless fish and tug boats. The building before her was bleak, cracked from a lack of love. No love could flourish about this building.

'Go,' said Megan again. And suddenly she was walking towards it. Daniel gave a small shriek to see her leave, but she did not look back. She walked a step at a time, feeling herself shrinking into the young girl who had first walked this desolate concrete. Shivering in the wind that had blustered then too, she had been thrust from a security police car. Cold and terrified, but filled with a furious bravado that had made her struggle to hide both, she had been fingerprinted by dull-eyed men. Shuffled like an unwieldy bundle, she had been handed over to two women who had sniggered between them, at her or at their own private joke she had never discovered, as she had slowly undressed and bent over for them to inspect her most intimate orifices.

She was met at the door by the prison head. 'Piet Swanepoel,' he said, engulfing her icy hand in his burly embrace. 'This is the captain of the women's section, Ena Myburgh.'

'I remember you,' the woman said. 'I wondered if I would. I was a warder then.'

Fransesca didn't particularly remember her. She might have been there, and she might not. Hers were not the eyes that haunted her with their taunts, or their coldness, or their exhortations to give in ...

'Anyway,' the woman said. 'It doesn't matter. Come and have some tea.'

They moved through to the warders' lounge, Captain Swanepoel unable to contain his pride at the changes he was pointing out.

'It's different now,' he said, standing back to allow her to pass, in that courtly way East Cape men had with women. 'We try to care for people, to do something good here. Not like the old days when all prisons believed in "shout and shove". No ...' he shook his head, 'it's not like that now.'

Lines meshed about his eyes, white as a spider's web on his tanned face. Weekends, no doubt, spent in boats or on the shore with fishing rod in hand and sandwiches from the wife. He looked so sincere, so very simple and solid a man.

They served her rooibos, which she detested, and chocolate biscuits in the brownest of rooms. Brown sunfilter flapped and whickered at the windows, speckled browns leapt from the floor. She sat in a chair facing the other two, confrontational still. They smiled at her, heads framed by a floral that would once have been known as Autumn.

She said very little, sipping and nibbling at the brown tasteless thing she held in her hand. The woman watched her, dipping her biscuit before biting it with a slight suck.

'And so now that you're back?' she asked Francesca. 'Would you do it all again?'

What had she done? The irony was that she had not done very much. She had never been in the forefront of the leftist phalanx, always slightly intimidated by the seeming sureness of their tightly closed ranks.

It had been only in the latter years that the End Conscription Campaign, with its populist approach had opened its down-to-earth ranks to all the leftie failures and wimps, even to would-be Marxists who were closer to liberals. The ECC had represented a new world of the Struggle, opening itself to the huddled masses of the middle-class left, yearning to breathe free of the strictures of Stalinists.

She had always been pretty clear on who owned the means of production, but had never seemed able to keep straight which communist got the ice pick in the brain and which had figured gravity to be a bourgeois concept. But the ECC had given her a place.

It had dealt with issues around the army moving into the townships. Everyone could grasp that. Anyone could go into schools, feeling brave and part of the Struggle, to advise boys on their alternatives to conscription. The ECC had picked up on a new suburban mood. Almost every staunch liberal parent had accepted, in gruff approval, their sons going off to a border war against insurgents and terrorists. But this ... this was a new and ugly thing. Their sons driving tanks just kilometres from their own homes to mow down children with stones in their hands – this was not the liberal way.

It had been easy. But it had also posed a seeming threat to the shaky, but defensive establishment. So, would she have done it all again?

'Yes, I would,' she said at last, facing the woman down, though she had not been the worst of them. Perhaps, considering the way this woman was now, she had not even been the real enemy. 'I would. We had right on our side. We had ... we've kept the moral higher ground.'

The woman nodded, sucking at the last of her soggy biscuit, licking the sediment from her fingers.

'But,' Francesca continued, 'I would like to think that, if I did it all again, that perhaps I would've done it differently. Perhaps I would have been ... stronger.'

'Very few of them really were,' the woman said. 'At the time anyway. But come, let's take you to your cell. Do you remember where it was?'

She and the woman drove the couple of hundred metres to the women's section, the wind battering across the treeless grounds, layering the scalp with grit.

Her cell was nothing. It meant nothing to her. She stood in the middle of it, trying to picture herself lying on the bed reading the Bible, since that was all she had been given. 'In the beginning ...' That was where she had begun.

She had lain there, legs twitching their rebellion at the inactivity. She had read the Bible and thought about life, her most mundane thought elevated to profundity by the desire to draw something meaningful from all of this.

She had moved between the steel toilet and the bed, sometimes standing on the toilet to clutch at a stray whiff from the sea. On Sundays the wistful strains of the church choir had drawn the tears to the face she had forgotten the sight of. Her emotions had drawn to the surface of her skin. Even Adam and Eve had brought the tears to her throat and a chill to her flesh.

She had longed so for a touch, mesmerising herself with daydreams of a hand on her skin. Her fantasies had played on hands touching hers, enfolding her fingers, reaching out and stroking her face and her hair. Strong hands, gentle hands, she had become obsessed by the movement of fingers and the feel of another's touch.

'Do you want to see the interrogation rooms?' the woman asked her.

'Yes, but can I just have another minute?'

'Take as long as you want,' she said.

Francesca struggled to feel it, to gain something from coming here. This was why they had come. She should feel something. Surely it should grant her some meaning. They owed her that.

She had forgotten how very small the room was. It still had a 'listening box' on the wall. She remembered how she had read aloud in a fire-and-brimstone voice, or chattered to herself, in different voices and sometimes accents, for fear that she might forget the sound of her own voice. She had played out little scenes from her imagination, wondering if they thought she had been driven insane.

Eventually she had lost it all. She had grown tired. Too tired for knee bends and squats, too exhausted to read the Bible. She had lain, no longer able to fight the stream of time, unable to concentrate, hardly able to summon a coherent thought.

Impressions, rather than thoughts, had flowed through her, steady and unchecked as the time that had no end. Colours had flitted past the back of her eyes, bright primary colours. She had imagined fabrics – smoothing the reddest of silks and the bluest of satins.

And always there had been touch. She had no longer seen faces. Curled on her bunk, she had seen hands – soft hands and rough hands, those that caressed and those that held her gruffly. She had lain with her eyes closed, feeling the fingers that flowed through her hair.

'Okay,' she said. 'Okay, let's go.'

'What does it feel like – coming back?'

'I don't know. I ... I feel nothing. I thought I would, but it's ... it's all so banal.'

'I think most prisoners just want to forget that period of their lives. I don't suppose it gives them any special feeling or anything – to be back, I mean. They just want to avoid ending up back here.'

'But ...' she lifted her eyes to this woman's, 'I was a political prisoner. Can't you ... oh I don't know.' Couldn't she see the difference? Were they all just part of a great flow of bungled humanity that muddled through this woman's life?

'I know that,' replied the woman. 'But do you think imprisonment is any different, for anyone?'

'Well, perhaps there should be a scrap of something decent, some martyred nobility or something, that one could take from it.'

'Only from the outside.'

'What do you mean?'

'I mean you won't find that here. That's what I think anyway. There is no nobility to be found in Solitary. It leaves you none, if you had it before. So ...'

The woman led her from the cell into the corridor she remembered in precise detail. The walls were the same, to the same smudges and stains she had passed on her way to the interrogation room. But possibly they were different smudges and stains, ever-present in places like these.

'So?' Francesca asked.

'What?'

'You were going to say something.'

'No, I was just going to say ... Well, I wasn't sure it was my place to ...'

'Go on.'

'Well, I was just going to say that if that's what was worrying you ... whatever happened, it's okay. It should be okay now. We ... well, we were on different sides in a way. But you were all people to me. It's time to forget all that stuff. Maybe forgive, if you can ...'

'It's not really that.'

'You said you should've been stronger. Only, people shouldn't be held in Solitary, I think. It makes them strange. And whatever ... I saw lots of you come and go. And I can tell you that everyone gives into it in little ways. I'm sure everyone feels they should've done it better. Like the movies, you know? They think they should've been different. But maybe that wouldn't be human.'

The blast of a ship's horn brought her suddenly face to face with the girl she had been. She shuddered with the aloneness of her. She smelt her fear. It was strange how sound, far more than sight, could carry great burdens of past emotion, lugging sensations and moods into the future with them.

'I remember that noise,' she said.

'Yes. It's a train.'

Francesca suddenly hated her. How could it be a train? She had heard it always as a ship's horn. Was even that to be taken from her? It wasn't fair. She was free. And yes, it was easy for this woman to say she should just embrace it. But she had paid the price for that freedom with the mess that was her life. She had paid and paid. And this woman had been part of the place that'd had the power to alter the very DNA of her. She could never again be the girl she was before. Everything had changed after that. Everything had flowed from the moment she had been told to pack her things. All her choices, every decision, were linked back to that time.

'Perhaps ...' the woman said, turning back as she led the way. 'Perhaps you should just allow yourself to have been human.'

Perhaps she should. Fuck them all. She wasn't the baddie here. She wasn't the enemy. Why had she always considered herself to be? She had been the victim. They had done it to her. They had manipulated ...

They stepped into the interrogation room, and her righteousness was sucked from her with a force that left her weak. No, God, that was too easy. It couldn't just be cleared like that, with a little anger.

It was still the same. Leaders could rise and fall, power lost and taken, but government issue would always be government issue. The civil service desk, large and dark and marked by pens and pain and the people who had been here. The wooden office door, the barred window whose mesh blacked out the sky. The filing cabinet against the wall.

'Did that filing cabinet ever have anything inside it? I always wondered if it was there for show.'

'I think it's got the same in it now as it always did. Someone's junk that no-one knew what to do with ... I was just wondering, who interrogated you?'

'I ... I never knew their names. They knew mine, but they never told me theirs.'

'Two of them used to come in for the political ones. They used to come and order us about. Well, I thought you might be interested. One of them is dead now. Strange, isn't it?'

She felt the aversion crawling across her forehead, prickling at her hairline and under her arms. She was pleased. He should be dead. She had never, ever wanted to see either of them again. She would have vomited had she been in the same room with either of them.

They had come in here, like it was any other job. They had joked and quibbled between themselves. They had messed with her head until she hadn't known who she was or what was up or down. Or what was right or wrong. And then they had knocked off promptly at half-past four. It had always astounded her, the way they had glanced at their watches and nodded to each other before escorting her to her cell.

She had never known when they would call her. It had never been regular. But it had messed her up. She had dreaded it, feared the call. And yet ... and yet she had longed so for a human face, craving the sound of a human voice. And the one had been educated, English speaking ...

'Which one?' she asked.

'What?'

'Which one is dead?'

'The dark one. The Afrikaans one, with a moustache. You remember him?'

'Yes.'

'He went a bit *bossies*. People who knew him said it'd been coming on for a long time. But he took his police revolver and he shot his wife and two children. How anyone could ever do that, I don't know. But anyway, then he blew away his sister-in-law and his wife's old granny, who was watching *Bold and Beautiful*.

'So was he ...?'

'Then he put the gun in his mouth. Blew away half his face before he actually died. *Vrekked* in hospital. I'm sure the nurses must've seen to that. I would, anyway. How anyone can do that to their kids, I just don't know.'

'And the ... no, never mind. It doesn't matter.'

'The other one ... ja. He thought himself such a bigshot. Just because he was English and he'd been to university. But he was no better than us. No ways.'

'You didn't like him?'

'I thought he was sneaky. He thought himself clever. At least the other one was straightforward. He came from that background, you know what I mean? You always kind-of knew where he was coming from.'

'It was the English one who pretended to be nice ...'

'That's exactly what I mean. They were both after the same thing. But at least you knew where you stood with the Afrikaans one. I'm sure ... I mean, not that I've experienced anything like it. But I'm sure it's easier to deal with in a way.'

'I suppose that's true.'

'Anyway, like I was telling you. Someone told me the other day, he's in the police. Everyone hates him. He doesn't fit – still going around like he's better than everyone else. But apparently he lives ...'

'I don't really want to know. The further I stay ...'

'No, I know. But it's interesting. He lives like a hermit apparently. In this isolated little seaside village on the outskirts, but you wouldn't know it if you're not from here.'

'I come from the Eastern Cape.'

'Do you? I never knew that. Then you'd probably know it.'

The great door swung open. Outside it was light. There was air to breathe. She could see the car waiting for her. Two steps. Just two steps and she was free of this place forever.

'*O magtig man*, I clean forgot. There's someone here wants to see you.'

'Never mind now. I need to go. I ...'

'No, it's important.'

'... don't think I can see anyone else now. Honestly, I'm ...'

'*Just mos* quickly. It'll only take a minute. Oh, in fact ...'

'... too tired to see anyone.'

'... here she is now.'

Francesca turned slowly, hating to take her eyes from the sunlight to face whatever new horror this place could conjure to prevent her from leaving it forever.

For an instant she stared, her brain incapable of grasping the image before her. It was not a figure from the life of the young girl she had once been. Dreamlike, it brought together, without rhyme or reason, new worlds and old, a lifetime that was past with that of the present.

It was Buli. Standing there, head to one side as though she belonged in this nightmare place of past cruelty and cowardice, she allowed her beautiful mouth to curve into a smile.

A little tentative, she stepped forward and opened her arms.

'Oh dear God. Buli. But ... how ... I mean, I just don't understand.'

'Well, I work here now. I heard you were coming, so I ...'

'Buli ... Jesus Christ.' She felt a spurt of anger break through the disorientation of this dream sequence. 'How the hell did you end up here and ... why the hell didn't you tell me?'

'Come,' she said, as calm as if they were normal people meeting in the supermarket. She led her back to the brown room with its autumn curtains. Francesca allowed herself to sit again in the chair with the cool wooden arms.

'Oh, it's not so very odd, you know. This is my stomping ground – prisoners and prisons. Sooner or later I suppose we all return to where we come from.'

Her lips quirked into a smile, sad at the edges. Buli had new lines scored from nose to mouth, but she had a new serenity too. This wasn't the spacey calm that had once deceived them all. It came from somewhere deeper, and held her more firmly.

'Are you working as a social worker?'

'Yes. And now that I am free ... well, it somehow seemed appropriate that I should work with those who were not.'

She gave a little laugh and reached across for Francesca's icy hand.

'But where did you disappear to? Did you come straight here?'

'No, I ran away but ... I did know I needed to be in rehab. You didn't ...'

'I knew by the time you disappeared.'

'Okay, well, I think I needed to come full circle, and do whatever healing needed to be done here in the Eastern Cape.'

'It's where I come from too,' said Francesca.

'It's one of the things we had in common,' said Buli. 'Except ...' she gave a deprecating laugh, 'that my Eastern Cape was a different country – a different continent – from yours.'

'Messed us up just as properly though, didn't it?'

They were laughing as the tea was brought in, same little biscuits to dunk in the rooibos.

'So did you go to rehab down here?' Francesca asked when the tea lady left.

'Yes. I faced all my demons and I think I'm going to be fine now. I went back to Fort Hare, you know. Thought perhaps I might try to lecture or something. But one of my old lecturers persuaded me to come here. He thinks it's terribly symbolic – that someone like me should come here.'

'Do you like it?'

'Yes. Of course I've got my own ideas about changes and I still have a lot to accomplish before I'll be happy. But it's ... well, it's a challenge. But it's not too hard. I mean ...'

'It's a challenge in your field.'

'Yes, I know what I'm doing here, thank God. At last.'

'And Thembeka?'

Buli dropped her eyes to her teacup. 'That is my one heartbreaking regret.'

'You lost her then? Can't you do anything?'

'I'm trying. I've seen an attorney and we'll do what we can. There's upsides and downsides to my case. But I have hope. I'll keep you posted.'

'Will you, Buli? Will you really?'

'Yes, I promise. Now go. Go chase your own demons now. The Eastern Cape – great place for demons.'

'I think I've had enough of demons for a while.'

'Now you listen to me, little miss Francesca white girl. If I can face down my demons and say "fuck you", then so can you.'

Francesca embraced her friend, laughter giving a shake to her voice. 'Were your demons so much more fearsome than mine?'

'All demons are fearsome. But it's time, don't you think? If we don't bring the past and present together now, when will we ever?'

THE MAN

There was something so very familiar ... no, no it couldn't be. Bugger it. Was he never to be free of her?

She was just one of them – one of the fatuous children who had lived out their privileged dreams of glory on the back of the Struggle. She was just one of a long procession who had strutted and crept, tiptoed and flounced through his life.

For some inexplicable reason, his brain had chosen her as their envoy. It was always she who appeared in his dreams. It was always her wide, fearful eyes he thought he recognised in a crowd. It was her voice that caused him to turn in the street and fight against the stream to see her, just to see if it could be her. It never was though.

He would probably never see her again. More than anyone else, he was probably the one person she would avoid for the rest of her life. Even though he had never been cruel. In his way. Within the structures they had chosen. And yet, it seemed that she would always be there, taunting him with the direction his life had taken and with all that might have been.

The man shifted on the rock. He had seen a woman on the sand ... but it was impossible. She would never come here by choice. Prisoners had an aversion to meeting their former captors. And the thought that she might have come, unknowing and unaware, was to give too much credence to chance.

He squinted through the spray, a crystal shower in the sunlight, but she was gone now. Relax, he told himself. Calm down. You despise men for their lack of control, for their jitters and shakes, their grovelling to former enemies. And now, here you are, straining for a view of someone who might or might not have been a detainee.

Well, whoever it was, she was gone now, so it hardly mattered.

The afternoon sun skidded across the rounded rocks, falling into the sea with a splash of brilliance. The breeze was gentle, twitching at clothing and teasing at hair. It was one of those perfect winter days when even a jersey was superfluous.

That was one of the reasons he had chosen to live here. That and the sea. If he had never in his adult life felt perfectly in sync with another human being, he knew that he was a part of this place. He was at home with the otters that crept up the beach at night, comfortable with the dolphins that leapt just beyond the wave line, and totally at ease with the birds that gathered and whooped into the wind.

He would never have said as much to a soul. It sounded too whimsical. And yet he knew that he was as much a part of this place as the rocks that crouched out there, battered by waves and tides. He could never leave.

Once he had though. Once he had lived in other places and gazed on other forms of life.

He had first seen Francesca in the interrogation room, escorted by a leaden-faced guard. Her hair had been wet and long, trailing over a grubby t-shirt. She must have managed, somehow, to get her head under the tap in her tiny cell basin. He had been impressed by the feat.

She had been in jeans, grimy from three days in a cell. The family couldn't have come yet, he remembered thinking. They always straggled in, wherever they lived, within days of their darling's arrest, with great parcels of clothing and food. The clothing, at least, usually reached them.

He had thought her hair dark when she had first sat before them, her mouth truculent, her eyes fierce and fearful. As the hours crept on, it had dried to the reddish-blonde he remembered. It was a strange colour, as he recalled it, glowing burnished and brilliant when she was strong, dimming to a dull bronze when she was not.

Those first couple of days they had interrogated her, it had glowed and burnt with her righteous fury. She had faced them down, chin jutting, refusing to speak. She had smiled at them, a great, glorious smile filled with the moral triumph she had thought to win.

There was a poignancy to it that still brought the bitter laughter to his throat. She had not yet learnt that every person who left that place had something to justify, some compromise of conscience to live with.

She had not seemed able to quiet her vividness. She had tried for ennui, attempted the sneer at what she thought to brand as their puerile antics. But her outrage had burst, in gaudy display, from eyes and hair and hands.

As her days had swum by, languid and slippery as fishes, she had turned inward. He had seen it before and had been content to wait. She had begun to watch herself and her responses too carefully. With that had come the self-doubt, followed by the confusion. That was what he waited to work with, the loss of clarity over right and wrong, over what could safely be offered and what should not.

That was the way he had worked – with time, rather than against it. His interrogation partner had been more impatient. The man had despised his partner's crudity, his need to shove and shout. He had despised the envy his partner felt at their privilege and his anger at their militant intent to turn his world upside down.

Funny, there had been some terrible story or scandal about him just a year or two ago. He was sure it had been the same man. He supposed he had finally been unable to continue swallowing all the bitterness that had been rising from his gut for all those years. As he recalled it, he had wiped out his family before blasting his belly apart with a police revolver. Something terribly symbolic in all of that, if he had the stomach for such symbolism.

But then, they had held time on their side. Time had worked for them. It wasn't even that they had thought to dig crucial nuggets of information from her. She had been a nothing, a nobody in the struggle. That was something he had needed to persuade his partner of, time and again. His partner had lacked the sophistication to understand the milieu, or to comprehend who was whom and what. To him, everyone who spoke against what he believed in had been a danger to them all.

In the end, perhaps he had been right. In the end, perhaps it had been the gathering in of the nothings and nobodies that had given an added weight to the government's need to capitulate ... but he had no appetite for the grinding back into the past that his countrymen indulged in so readily.

In any case, they had finally swooped on all the little nothings, all the clockwork soldiers in the war against conscription – because they had been a danger, frankly. Alone they were nothing, and generally they knew nothing. But all that toytown posturing had been starting to have an impact.

Their detention had been largely preventive. He, at least, had not thought to get much from people like her. But sometimes you could pick up a small piece of the puzzle that was missing. Sometimes you managed to confirm the odd leak you'd received from your spies. It was all part of the checks and balances in knowing who could be trusted. Sometimes you managed to squeeze a little statement from one of them, on some seemingly innocuous subject like their organisation's aims.

'Public knowledge, surely – these people must be stupid.' That's what they'd think anyway. And that surely it could do no harm. And yet, sometimes those innocuous little statements could be used in evidence later on. You never knew. And sometimes, having made one innocuous little statement, they could be led on to make just one more – this time possibly not quite so innocuous.

Despite their incompatibility, he and his partner had worked well together by using both their personalities, and both their methods. He had been contemptuous of his partner's coarseness – and yet he had made such good use of it.

He had sat in silence as her eyes had flinched from the malevolence of his partner's bullying, from the malice of his threats. He had sat and watched, and waited. Day upon day he had watched her shift, from bravado to doubt and then to a desperate neediness. It was the aloneness that did it, particularly to someone like her. He had watched her beginning to turn to him for protection, for the smallest touch of kindness.

It was funny, that neediness. It had happened to many of them. They had been taken forcefully from their fellows and placed in a small, square box. He had never experienced the sensory deprivation of it, but in some ways he had done the same to himself over the years. He had taken his inner self and he had closed it off from human contact. And yet he felt nothing. He felt numb.

Anyway, that had been the time for the two of them to move into true good cop bad cop style. His partner had blustered and bellowed, and then he had left. He had always muttered something about some other prisoner who needed a *warm klap*, or who would benefit mightily were he to be *opgevok*. She had never known when he would return. The threat had hung over her, had caused her to turn to him, to reach out for his protection. And all along, he had known they had a good three hours or so to themselves.

At first she had said nothing, of course. And he had shrugged, saying it didn't really matter to him. It's not that he didn't understand, or that he had no sympathy with the cause, he would say. He was an educated man after all. Did she think he hadn't dabbled in the left during his student days?

Well, why then, she would ask. How could he be involved with this? And he would speak earnestly, leaning forward to look straight into her eyes, of his belief that eventually things must change. Things must change, but that he wanted to be sure of what that change would consist of. He feared the chaos of revolution, he had said, and what it would do to the country.

'Why don't you just tell me a little about the workings of your organisation,' he had said then. Just a word or two to satisfy his partner. It wasn't as if it were a secret society. It wasn't as if it wasn't a matter for public record?

'Then why should I tell you of it?' she had asked him. And he had sighed. He had reached across and brushed the tangled hair from her forehead. She had flinched, he recalled. She had flinched, but her hands had begun to shake.

'Because I don't want you to suffer,' he had said. 'Because I want to say to my partner that that's all you know. That it would be a waste of time to get heavy with you.'

A noise had hollowed its way through the door – one of those nameless sounds of a place with echoing corridors and clanking doors. She had jumped, and he had felt the desperation coming off her. He had smelt the wildness of her desolation, her frantic primordial need for the smallest of human contacts.

'It's okay,' he had said. 'I'll protect you from him, I promise. I'll keep him away from you. But you're going to have to write something down for me. Give me something to work with, no matter how innocuous it is.'

And still she had refused. She didn't like to write things down, she had said. She couldn't know what they would use it for. Her eyes had sought his. Her eyes had caught hold of his and pleaded a case she hardly knew she was pleading.

'Look,' he had said, 'I understand about the ECC. I know what they're trying to do and, believe me, I'm not unsympathetic. Do you think that I loved being in the army?'

He had reached his hand across to her, but had withdrawn it again. 'Just something innocuous,' he had said. 'What the organisation stands for. Everyone knows that. Give me something to work with, otherwise ...'

Her eyes had closed for a moment.

'Just the aims,' she had said. 'And that's all.'

'Just the aims.' And as a reward he had stood behind her, placing his two hands upon her shoulders, kneading the knots he found there.

Those student types – they had come in with a sneer and a belief in their own superiority. How he had loved to outwit them. How very much he had enjoyed playing their game, dropping small titbits of leftist lore to confuse them, and showing them who was the cleverer, after all.

Perhaps she had been different. Perhaps his manipulation of her ... Perhaps that was why he still saw her eyes, eyes that pleaded and shrank from him, in the middle of the night. But it was too late now. It was far too late to think these things.

She had known nothing, of course. She had known nothing of any deep and secret significance. But when clarity returned, she must have understood how he had controlled her, and how out of her depth she had been.

And perhaps she must always have been left with the question, on her own dark nights. Had she known more, how much more would she have told?

FRANCESCA

Francesca stepped upon the sand. It felt damp and gritty with fear and regret. This was the third day they had come. Each day they drove through the clump of houses perched upon a shore made desolate by the whine of wind and by the scrabble of dune cover that could never quite stop the rain of sand across the road.

They had stopped in the parking lot that edged the cove. Daniel liked it here. Perhaps it made him feel safe, enclosed by rocks and a ledge of sand. There were gulleys for paddling and the odd shivering swim. There were rock pools for watching gobies and the pink wave of sea anemones.

Each day, Francesca had ventured a bit further across the rocks, watching and flinching from the sight of men, waiting and dreading what she was waiting for. It was torture, lingering in his space. He was here. She could sense him. In the bite of the breeze she could smell him again, leaning across that old desk at her. She watched for him, and yet the bile rose within her at the thought that he might come.

She had no idea why she had driven to this small seaside village, except that she had found no peace in East London. It had held no healing power, for herself or her son. But if it hadn't been there, why should she find it here?

Each day, she had wandered and waited, watching every silhouette upon the distant rocks, fishing rod in hand. And yet, this was the last man on earth she wanted to meet. Perhaps she merely wanted to see him. Maybe she needed to draw him down to size, as she had with the prison building. The instant she had seen it again, even that place of nightmares had lost the menacing bulk that she remembered.

Francesca took another step toward the rocks. Megan looked up. Suddenly she rose from where she squatted on the shoreline, making a drip castle with Daniel. Tentatively – Francesca could see the hesitation in her pause to push hair back with wrists – she approached her cousin.

'It's Saturday,' she said. 'If he's out on the beach any day at all, it's likely to be today or tomorrow.'

'I don't want to see him. I don't know what I'll say or do. Oh God ...'

'Calm down. You don't have to speak to him. Maybe you just wanted to test your bravery in tempting fate ... or something.'

'I think I'll vomit if I see him.'

'Well, maybe this was a mistake. I don't know that this is doing either of us any good. Why don't we go and have pancakes or something? We could drive around the coast and ...'

A scrum of boys was suddenly upon them, rough-housing across the sand, legs intertangling and tripping each other. Daniel gave a shriek of fear, cut off on both sides by the splashing of hard, brown feet.

Francesca turned and ran for her child, but Megan was there first, whooping him into the air in an effort at distraction. She watched them, Megan swinging him round her head, jogging Daniel into uncertain giggles. Turning, she loped him back to his drip castle. The boys had gone, tumbling across the rocks in boisterous leaps.

'You know, Frannie ...' Megan joined her cousin within licking distance of the small waves. 'You don't have to be like this. You were the victim, you know. And you did a noble thing. You don't have to act like ... like you ...'

'You don't understand.' Francesca felt the tears. At last. She had wept for so many other things. She had cried for other people, other sorrows, over movies and adverts. And yet, she had never cried over this.

'No I don't, Francesca. I don't understand.' She sounded tired. 'I have never understood what this weird attitude to your detention is all about, and what it has to do with your life now, or with Daniel even.'

'I wasn't noble, Megan. That's what it's about. I wasn't even strong. Face it. Come face to face with reality and stop burdening me with your glorified expectations.'

'Jesus Francesca, why're you attacking me now? You said yourself you never knew enough to tell them anything worthwhile.'

'But I would've, Megan. Maybe I would've. I don't know ...'

'Would've isn't "did". I don't see what the big deal is.'

'Oh God, Megan ...' she shrieked it into the wind, which whipped it up and carried it out to sea. 'Don't you see. He fucked me. My interrogator. I let him fuck me right there on the government issue desk in the interrogation room. I let him undress me. I let him put his lips ... his fingers ...'

'But then it was rape, Francesca. That's not ...'

'No, Megan, no. It wasn't rape. I ... God help me, I wanted him to.'

She was sobbing, face in aching hands. She couldn't look up to see the horror on her young cousin's face. She turned away, to the rocks and the sea. And opening her eyes to the burning sun, she saw that the man was before her.

'Oh ...' she said, in startled revulsion. 'Oh my God ... You.'

Behind her, she heard Megan take a step towards her, but the man didn't move.

'It is you,' he said. 'I thought I saw you yesterday, but I couldn't be sure. Were you looking for me?'

'Oh, my God, no. You ... I hate you more than anyone in the world.' Her sobs were clearing, her tears drying upon her face. 'I would never ... I want to vomit at the sight of you.'

He nodded and turned, sniffing the wind like a dog. He looked so very much the same, curly hair a little greyer, face just fractionally more leathery. His eyes followed the scrimmage of boys that skirmished across the rocks. He took a step, as if to follow them.

'Fuck you,' Francesca yelled at him. The lava of all the years of silent fury erupted. 'Fuck you. How dare you walk away from me. Don't you know what you've done to me? Can't you imagine what you did to my life?'

A solitary dog-walker stared as he passed, startled and possibly fearful of the rage she had loosed to batter at the wind. All the evil of the past she had released into the freshness of the present.

'I was nice to you, though.' The man had stopped and half-turned. 'I was. I looked after you. And ... you were never tortured or anything.'

'No ... To my shame, I wasn't. But you were never "nice" to me. Don't come with "nice". You tricked me. You manipulated me.'

The man turned back. He seemed detached, hunched against the wind, and perhaps her.

'That's not what you hate me for, is it?'

'No. Oh God, no, it's not.'

'I didn't rape you, Francesca.'

'No you didn't, fuck you. I wish you had. Why couldn't you at least have done that? Instead ... instead you made me hate myself. You made it impossible ever to forgive myself.'

'Was it so very terrible a thing to have done?'

She glanced at her cousin, who stood with her hands pressed to her cheeks, as though she wished to block her ears. Her eyes were wide, spilling tears unheeded upon the sand.

'Yes,' she said, quietly now. 'Yes. It was the very worst thing I could have done.'

'Perhaps we weren't quite the enemies you thought we were.'

'Yes, we were. You were one of those who held me captive. You were on the side of the oppressors. How could we ever have been less than enemies?'

'But it's all gone now. All that bullshit. Why can't it be gone?'

'No, it has not all gone now.' She shouted it at him. Glancing along the tide line, she saw that Daniel was still engrossed in his castle. Perhaps he didn't hear, or perhaps he was so innured to shouting, poor little mite, that he barely noticed. 'No, it has not gone,' she said more quietly.

'Is that your child?' he asked suddenly, and she flinched at the eyes that appraised Daniel as he rose and lurched slightly, stumbling as he headed for the water, red bucket in hand.

'Yes,' she said. 'My only child.'

He nodded. 'He looks like you. Same hair. Is there something ...'

'He has a mild form of cerebral palsy.'

He nodded again. 'Those are mine,' he said. 'Those five over there on the rocks.'

She glanced across at the five sturdy figures, mouse-brown hair cut straight across freckled faces, brown legs scuffed and scarred beneath baggies.

'I hate you,' she said, knowing that she hated him for his five perfect sons. For the unfairness of it. But that was the thing, wasn't it? It wasn't unfair at all. 'I hate you so very much.'

He nodded. 'Why did you only have the one?'

'Oh Jesus Christ ... Can't you see?'

'No, not really.'

'I did though. Fuck you. I did have another child inside me. I had your baby.'

She waited to see him flinch, but only his eyes blinked. 'I aborted him, but it was too late. He was perfect and I aborted him. I watched him fall into the toilet all waxy and white.'

The man nodded again. Megan had stopped weeping, but she held her two hands to her mouth. Her eyes though ... her eyes had lost their horror. Francesca could see no condemnation. All she could see there now was pity – and perhaps a kind of acceptance.

'I had a son born dead,' he said. 'Before that youngest one over there. He also looked like that. It's a hard thing.'

'Don't you dare compare.' She risked a glance in the direction the man pointed. Gilded by the afternoon light, the man's child flung himself into a flurry of cartwheels that stung the eyes to watch. 'You didn't kill your own child. Maybe that was your punishment, but at least you followed it with another perfect son.'

She watched the man turn aside and hunch his shoulders against the wind. As he strode toward his five flawlessly formed children, she took a step forward and added: 'And I had this broken child. I'll never forgive you, or myself, for that. He was innocent. It shouldn't have touched him.'

The man reached the boys, but stood apart, watching them almost absently. She could feel Megan beside her, but she didn't want to look at her. She felt her cousin's hand slide about her shoulders.

'You faced him,' she whispered. 'You faced him and you faced yourself. It's all gone now.'

'Maybe,' Francesca said, weeping easily now. 'But not all of it. Not yet.'

'And Francesca? I understand now. What you were always trying to tell me. I'm sorry, I ...'

'It doesn't matter any more. I just wanted it to stop fucking up all three of our lives.'

The two women stood upon the shore, small foaming waves splashing about their feet, soaking the legs of their jeans. Tears flowed down both their faces as they watched the man stand to one side of his sons. His elbows, crooked up past his hunched back, had been brilliantined by the sun. From this distance, they seemed almost like wings. Face thrust forward, hands in pockets, he could almost have been a bird – a cormorant drying its wings upon the shore.

He turned then and, without a word to his milling boys, walked back along the sand to where they still stood.

'Francesca,' he said. 'Don't say no. Just listen.'

'Go away now,' she said. 'I don't want to see you anymore.'

'No,' he said. 'No, not yet.'

'What do you want?'

'I want to take your son fishing.'

'Are you quite out of ...?'

'No, I'm not. I want to take him fishing, like I used to take my younger brother when he was little. He wasn't that strong. He was never as strong as me. But I taught him ...'

'Never. Are you mad? That is my child. My only child. And you are the man I hate most in the world.'

'I know. Let me, Francesca.'

'I don't want you to do anything for me. I don't want to feel ...'

'Maybe it's not for you, Francesca.'

They were silent then, she facing this man she hardly knew. And yet she remembered his chest, hard and brown and hairless. She remembered how she had thought she might slip into insanity if she didn't feel a touch upon her skin, a hand upon her hair. She remembered the pain of not being touched, and then the agony of his flesh upon hers.

'Let him, Francesca.' Megan was nodding. 'I think you should. He owes you that. And maybe it'll be good for Daniel.'

'I can't, Megan. I couldn't possibly. I can never forgive ...'

'Yes, but maybe you need to. Maybe you won't forgive yourself till you allow him the chance to forgive himself.'

'I haven't the ...'

'Yes, you do. It takes greatness to do that. It takes strength. And that, I know more than anyone, is what you have.'

'It's academic anyway. Daniel would never go with him. He won't leave me.'

'Could I try?' the man asked. 'If he won't, then I'll leave. I won't bother you again.'

'I know my son. He'll never go off with a stranger.'

But he did. Strange child that he was, one could never predict whom he would take to, and whom he would ignore. Perhaps it was the calm of the man, the slightly removed quiet of him. But when he had loped off to fetch his tackle, when he had brought it over to show Daniel the rods and bait, Daniel had watched, absorbed. And when the man pointed across the rocks to where they would fish, when he reached down quietly for Daniel's hand, the child had walked off without a word or a glance.

'No,' Francesca yelled. 'No. I've changed my mind. I don't want him to go. Don't take ...'

The man paused, but Megan held her back. 'Listen,' Megan said. 'Not out of sight, okay? Francesca needs to be able to see you.'

The man ducked his head and the two figures turned and trudged away.

MEGAN & FRANCESCA

They sat on the sand as the shadows crept across the land to engulf the small cove. They sat in silence, sifting the sand through their fingers as the wind caught at their hair and their t-shirts.

Francesca didn't speak, except to mutter now and again that she must have been mad. How could she have been so crazy? He was all she had, and she'd entrusted him ...

It was driving Megan crazy. The longer the man and the boy stayed away, the more she allowed her own fears to run riot across the cove. Those waves, that could knock a child into the churning sea; these rocks, that could split a small skull ... And he wasn't that strong.

Megan stole a glance at Francesca. This was her fault. She had persuaded Francesca to let Daniel go. What if something did happen? Megan allowed the sense of loss to rise in her throat so that she could just taste it. She suppressed it again just before it could choke her.

She loved that little boy, funny little ghost that he was. When she'd arrived, she had seen only the way he entrapped Francesca in a role she couldn't stomach. Francesca had needed to be so much more. The grand struggle-ista. The great campaigner. Or rather, Megan had needed Francesca to be all that. Francesca had needed to be normal. Why hadn't she seen that?

At first Megan had seen only the child's struggles. She had heard only his screams and his misery. She hadn't seen his sensitivity, or the bravery of his embattled brawl with a world that was larger than he.

'They didn't stay where we could see them, you know. You told him to and he didn't.'

'I know, Francesca. But it'll be fine. Just relax a bit. I promise, it'll be fine.'

I promise, she'd told her cousin. I promise. How could she promise such a thing, while the fear rose from her chest to smother her. But this was silly. It would be fine. Of course it would. What was he going to do? Drown the child? No matter who he'd been in the past, he wasn't going to stand by and watch a child like Daniel get hurt, was he?

He was a father. He was ... He was a human being. She would never have used those words about a man like this a year ago. But now she saw that that's what he was. And somehow it deflated him. There was something a little pathetic about a man who had spent his life so wrong-headedly.

She no longer needed him to be the devil incarnate. He had done terrible things, no doubt. Unimaginable things, perhaps. But he was a just a man. There was nothing invincible about him. It was funny what she had needed people to be, way back in the dim, distant past – all of a year ago. She had needed Francesca to be all that she herself had wished she could be. In her own arrogant way, she had thought it was all for Francesca's good. It hadn't been, though. It hadn't been for Francesca at all. It had all been for herself, every piece of it.

She still wished things for Francesca. But now she hoped they were *really* for Francesca. She wished this nightmare gone from her life. She wished her forgiveness – of the man, she supposed, but more importantly of herself. Francesca had been a young girl. So incredibly young. Funny, Francesca's had once seemed so grown-up an experience to that younger Megan. Now she would like to tell Francesca that she was crazy to have expected that trusting girl to handle so much, without cracking. She would wait a little though, before they spoke of it.

She wasn't sure what she had expected. She had feared Francesca's great secret, bracing herself for some betrayal that had destroyed a life ... or even taken one. It hadn't been as bad as that, if you looked at it rationally. The only life Francesca had destroyed was her own. Francesca's revelation had knocked the wind from her though. Francesca had been right to keep it from her. If Megan hadn't had the shit knocked out of her this past year, if she hadn't come face to face with her own fallibility, it would have repulsed her. There was something visceral about the act that had brought the revulsion rushing to her throat.

But when it fell again, it was gone. Pity had followed, and love for the tortured young girl who'd thought she should have been braver.

'Do you think he'll realise Daniel can't do what his sons ...'

'Yes, Fran-child, I do. He said his brother hadn't been strong either.'

Francesca looked up from the sand she was funnelling through her fingers. Tossing an anxious smile at her complicit cousin, she raised a hand to shade the eyes that pierced the haze at the far end of the cove. Megan hoped she understood what she had tried to convey – that Francesca no longer had to be strong for both of them. She didn't have to be the big, brave cousin all the time. Relationships cut both ways.

Watching her cousin, eyebrows fine-dusted, hair spiky with salt, Megan realised she no longer wished for her life. She wouldn't have coped any better, after all.

She imagined she could see something calmer about Francesca now. Despite the anxiety that caused her eyes to scrabble at the dense air across the beach, she appeared more ... serene seemed trite, though perhaps that's what it was. It wasn't the blank shutdown she'd evinced at home. That had been something else again, a wary watchfulness for Paul's flashpoints. This was different, she was sure of it.

So perhaps (please God, if – *when* – Daniel returned) their roadtrip was a success, after all. She'd been right to up and cart Francesca away. Funny, it had been intended only as Francesca's roadtrip. Megan had thought to be her minder. But it had ended as Megan's too.

Oh, not because she had decided anything definite about her life. She supposed she would always regard Nicholas as her tragic soul-love. And perhaps that was, as Francesca said, because it wasn't to be. He wasn't the kind of boy you could rely on, after all. Tebogo she loved in a gentler way. Perhaps that would be enough for her now. He had his own demons, of course. But then, who didn't?

No, she hadn't yet decided what she should do. But it no longer seemed to matter. Her decision could take its own sweet time. The important thing was that she had her own life. She no longer wanted either of them for theirs. They could keep their lives, thank you very much. Hers was more than enough for anyone.

'He'll be cold.'

'It doesn't matter, Francesca. Let the child be cold for once.'

'They've been gone for so long. And he didn't listen to you. I can't see him. I can't ...'

'He'll be fine.' But Megan looked worried. She looked tense and tight-faced, as though she doubted the impulse that had made her support him.

The sun sparked across the sea, in a last manic dance to escape the dark. Francesca shivered, feeling the damp rise from the cold sand. The man's five sturdy sons dashed along the shoreline, making for home and warmth. On the horizon, a ship was suddenly flooded by a burst of illumination.

'He's not very good on rocks. He could've fallen and hurt himself.'

'But he's not alone.'

'No. No, he's not.' She lifted her eyes and impressed them upon Megan's, fear turning them hard. 'He's with the man who detained and interrogated people. He's with my greatest enemy in all the world.'

'Oh God, Francesca. I'm sorry. I don't know what to do.'

'I should go look for him.'

'But we don't exactly know where they went. And what if they come back, and we're not here.'

'We'll wait ten more minutes. Then I'm going to look. You can stay here.' She felt the tears rise with the panic in her chest. Dear God, what had possessed her?

She could not sit anymore. Not for another minute. Rising, she walked to the waterline, hunching her arms about her body. It wasn't really against the cold, but more to hold herself together, to keep her chest from bursting open with the pressure of such terror.

To one side of her, the darkness had conquered everything on land and sea. To the other, the sun still tussled with the invading night, sinking at last to the horizon. It would be dark soon, pitch black. There was nothing darker than a beach at night. If she allowed it to grow any darker, she would never find them ... She stretched her eyes, making them ache with trying to see further than she was capable of.

But suddenly, out of that pale glow, she thought perhaps she could make out two figures. She couldn't be certain. And surely Daniel could never have walked so far. As she watched, they became clearer. Outlined against the dull glow, the larger of the two swung the other behind him and onto his back.

She began running, racing toward them across the sand, stumbling over driftwood, skinning her toes upon hidden rocks. She saw the small figure scramble to be free, fighting to be down.

'Mo-oom,' he yelled, and she saw him go down. He rose again. 'Mo-om.' She couldn't make out his words and she couldn't tell, from this distance, if he was fearful or perhaps in pain. She ran harder, wheezing over her painful steps to reach him.

And then he began to run toward her. Shambling and unsteady, stumbling over rocks, but with no self-consciousness at all. He just ran. And as he drew nearer, she saw that he was whooping and laughing with delight. She had never before seen him fall into such uncomplicated laughter. That was why she had failed to recognise it.

'I caught a fish, Mom. A hu-uge fish. I did it myself. I can fish. I can do it.'

She stopped in wonder before her son, too winded to reach down to him.

'I can, Mom. I can go over the rocks myself and I can fish.'

The man said not a word. Both their eyes were on the boy, on the tousled hair and glowing eyes. They both smiled – and she wondered if she caught the glint of tears in the man's eyes – as the child broke into a gabble of triumphant laughter and chatter about fishes and bait and waves and tides.

She ran her eyes down the body of her son, checking, just checking, that he was fine and unharmed. Megan reached them, a Megan torn between panting and laughter, full of relief and joy.

'Look Francesca,' she said. 'Look at your child. He's got scabby knees.'

ACKNOWLEDGEMENTS

Jennifer Cohen says her tombstone will one day read:
'Here lies Jennifer, who read Sad at the Edges six times, one more time than she read To Kill a Mockingbird.' Of course, Harper Lee probably didn't have to beg her to read each new incarnation of his novel before it was complete.

I must have very good friends because several other people offered to read one or another draft of this novel – Catherine Moye, Vanessa Bluen, Richard Beynon, Doug Band, Vicky Unwin and Harvey Tyson. Each offered suggestions that I probably sulked over before managing to overcome my peevishness enough to recognise their validity.

My first agent Vicky Unwin has managed to remain my dear friend, flitting over from England periodically to feed me champagne and oysters on British pounds. She has continued to offer advice and help at the same time as running a high-powered life of international business that no longer includes nurse-maiding people like me.

Phetole Kubjane, Bridget Hilton-Barber and Duncan Innes allowed me to steal pieces of their lives. Phetole told me wonderfully vivid stories of MK camps and military training in Russia. From Bridget, I pinched the realities of solitary confinement and a post-apartheid return to the prison that once held her. Duncan allowed me to pick away at his memories of interrogation and the methods of his jailers.

For helping me build the influences and crises that formed the attractive but feckless Nicholas, Duncan insisted that he deserved nothing less than a joint by-line. This small mention will never satisfy him, but this is all he's going to get.

Vanessa Bluen and her daughter Kelly-Jo were my Jewish consultants. From Lesley Cowling, I stole various pieces of wisdom and lore about Johannesburg. She accuses me of pilfering the phrase 'Karma City', which very nearly became the title of this book.

Deirdre Randall, whom I serendipitously met in the hairdresser, helped me with the practical realities of a child slightly affected by cerebral palsy.

Michelle Schlodder, helped me with tales from the Eastern Cape that I had forgotten. Russell Grinker has never met me, but on the strength of being the friend of a friend of a former boyfriend, answered strings of irritating e-mail queries on esoteric East London details.

My parents, Jack and Margot Richards, have sat at the other end of numerous telephones, poring over mapbooks and routes, not to mention being the sort of parents who believe their children to be the most talented on earth. Very comforting that.

Snippets of arcane medical information I gleaned from my brother, Guy Richards, who also fortuitously prevented me from dying before the book was complete – tracking down precisely what obscure third-world toxin put me in hospital for a month. And almost as serious, Brett du Toit managed to retrieve and clean up tatty bits of novel, ravaged by the Chernobyl virus – all the while fielding hysterical 2am calls from me.

Shielagh Bamber edited me with loving care for which I am grateful.

Hugh Lewin has soothed me through fears and crises and loaded me with sensible advice, most of which I've managed to heed. Wessel de Kock remained my mentor and personal News Editor for Life through this book, and various other projects, marriages and lives.

Colin McGee has relentlessly believed in this book and me – his confidence never (at least seemingly never) to flag – even when I periodically believed myself to be the worst writer in the world.

Annelise Burgess and her Special Assignment colleagues allowed themselves to be persuaded to get up at 4am so that photographer Henner Frankenfeld could take the cover pics by six, when the light was just right. As Annelise aid, it was more of a pleasure in the offering, late one night at the Xai Xai, than in the execution. Chris du Plessis lent me props from the Xai Xai and also got up at four, as did my Wits Journalism students, whom I tricked into thinking this would improve their grades.

My children, Emma and Joshua Hutton, find me embarrassing, which I probably am. But they still put up with most of my euphorias and anxieties, not to mention the many nights I was forced to research till all hours of the night in Melville or Yeoville or wherever.

Through two previous books and the start of this, I had the best reader. Encouraging, gently critical and knowledgable, Koos Viviers read each chapter as I completed it. He died before I had got very far with this book, and I missed him every day that I continued to write it.